THE

£1,000,000

BANK-NOTE

and Other New Stories

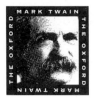

THE OXFORD MARK TWAIN

Shelley Fisher Fishkin, Editor

The Celebrated Jumping Frog of Calaveras County, and Other Sketches
Introduction: Roy Blount Jr.
Afterword: Richard Bucci

The Innocents Abroad
Introduction: Mordecai Richler
Afterword: David E. E. Sloane

Roughing It
Introduction: George Plimpton
Afterword: Henry B. Wonham

The Gilded Age
Introduction: Ward Just
Afterword: Gregg Camfield

Sketches, New and Old
Introduction: Lee Smith
Afterword: Sherwood Cummings

The Adventures of Tom Sawyer
Introduction: E. L. Doctorow
Afterword: Albert E. Stone

A Tramp Abroad
Introduction: Russell Banks
Afterword: James S. Leonard

The Prince and the Pauper
   Introduction: Judith Martin
   Afterword: Everett Emerson

Life on the Mississippi
   Introduction: Willie Morris
   Afterword: Lawrence Howe

Adventures of Huckleberry Finn
   Introduction: Toni Morrison
   Afterword: Victor A. Doyno

A Connecticut Yankee in King Arthur's Court
   Introduction: Kurt Vonnegut, Jr.
   Afterword: Louis J. Budd

Merry Tales
   Introduction: Anne Bernays
   Afterword: Forrest G. Robinson

The American Claimant
   Introduction: Bobbie Ann Mason
   Afterword: Peter Messent

The £1,000,000 Bank-Note and Other New Stories
   Introduction: Malcolm Bradbury
   Afterword: James D. Wilson

Tom Sawyer Abroad
   Introduction: Nat Hentoff
   Afterword: M. Thomas Inge

The Tragedy of Pudd'nhead Wilson and the Comedy
Those Extraordinary Twins
   Introduction: Sherley Anne Williams
   Afterword: David Lionel Smith

Personal Recollections of Joan of Arc
    Introduction: Justin Kaplan
    Afterword: Susan K. Harris

The Stolen White Elephant and Other Detective Stories
    Introduction: Walter Mosley
    Afterword: Lillian S. Robinson

How to Tell a Story and Other Essays
    Introduction: David Bradley
    Afterword: Pascal Covici, Jr.

Following the Equator and Anti-imperialist Essays
    Introduction: Gore Vidal
    Afterword: Fred Kaplan

The Man That Corrupted Hadleyburg and Other Stories and Essays
    Introduction: Cynthia Ozick
    Afterword: Jeffrey Rubin-Dorsky

The Diaries of Adam and Eve
    Introduction: Ursula K. Le Guin
    Afterword: Laura E. Skandera-Trombley

What Is Man?
    Introduction: Charles Johnson
    Afterword: Linda Wagner-Martin

The $30,000 Bequest and Other Stories
    Introduction: Frederick Busch
    Afterword: Judith Yaross Lee

Christian Science
    Introduction: Garry Wills
    Afterword: Hamlin Hill

Chapters from My Autobiography
    Introduction: Arthur Miller
    Afterword: Michael J. Kiskis

1601, and Is Shakespeare Dead?
    Introduction: Erica Jong
    Afterword: Leslie A. Fiedler

Extract from Captain Stormfield's Visit to Heaven
    Introduction: Frederik Pohl
    Afterword: James A. Miller

Speeches
    Introduction: Hal Holbrook
    Afterword: David Barrow

The £1,000,000 Bank-Note
and Other New Stories

Mark Twain

FOREWORD

SHELLEY FISHER FISHKIN

INTRODUCTION

MALCOLM BRADBURY

AFTERWORD

JAMES D. WILSON

New York   Oxford

OXFORD UNIVERSITY PRESS

1996

OXFORD UNIVERSITY PRESS

Oxford   New York

Athens, Auckland, Bangkok, Bogotá, Bombay

Buenos Aires, Calcutta, Cape Town, Dar es Salaam

Delhi, Florence, Hong Kong, Istanbul, Karachi

Kuala Lumpur, Madras, Madrid, Melbourne

Mexico City, Nairobi, Paris, Singapore

Taipei, Tokyo, Toronto

and associated companies in

Berlin, Ibadan

Copyright © 1996 by

Oxford University Press, Inc.

Introduction © 1996 by Malcolm Bradbury

Afterword © 1996 by James D. Wilson

A Note on the Illustrations © 1996 by Ray Sapirstein

Text design by Richard Hendel

Composition: David Thorne

Published by

Oxford University Press, Inc.

198 Madison Avenue, New York,

New York 10016

Oxford is a registered trademark of

Oxford University Press

Library of Congress

Cataloging-in-Publication Data

Twain, Mark, 1835–1910.

The £1,000,000 bank note and other new stories /

by Mark Twain; with an introduction by Malcolm

Bradbury and an afterword by James D. Wilson.

p. cm. — (The Oxford Mark Twain)

Includes bibliographical references.

1. Humorous stories, American. 2. Manners and

customs—Fiction. I. Title. II. Series: Twain, Mark,

1835-1910. Works. 1996.

PS1315.A1 1996

843'.4—dc20

96-16588

CIP

ISBN 0-19-510144-8 (trade ed.)

ISBN 0-19-511413-2 (lib. ed.)

ISBN 0-19-509088-8 (trade ed. set)

ISBN 0-19-511345-4 (lib. ed. set)

9 8 7 6 5 4 3 2 1

Printed in the United States of America

on acid-free paper

FRONTISPIECE

Samuel L. Clemens is photographed here in 1895,

two years after the publication of the *£1,000,000

Bank-Note and Other New Stories*. (The Mark Twain

House, Hartford, Connecticut)

CONTENTS

Editor's Note, x

Foreword SHELLEY FISHER FISHKIN, xi

Introduction MALCOLM BRADBURY, xxxi

The £1,000,000 Bank-Note and Other New Stories, follows xliv

Afterword JAMES D. WILSON, 1

For Further Reading JAMES D. WILSON, 15

A Note on the Illustrations RAY SAPIRSTEIN, 16

A Note on the Text ROBERT H. HIRST, 18

Contributors, 20

Acknowledgments, 22

EDITOR'S NOTE

The Oxford Mark Twain consists of twenty-nine volumes of facsimiles of the first American editions of Mark Twain's works, with an editor's foreword, new introductions, afterwords, notes on the texts, and essays on the illustrations in volumes with artwork. The facsimiles have been reproduced from the originals unaltered, except that blank pages in the front and back of the books have been omitted, and any seriously damaged or missing pages have been replaced by pages from other first editions (as indicated in the notes on the texts).

In the foreword, introduction, afterword, and essays on the illustrations, the titles of Mark Twain's works have been capitalized according to modern conventions, as have the names of characters (except where otherwise indicated). In the case of discrepancies between the title of a short story, essay, or sketch as it appears in the original table of contents and as it appears on its own title page, the title page has been followed. The parenthetical numbers in the introduction, afterwords, and illustration essays are page references to the facsimiles.

FOREWORD

Shelley Fisher Fishkin

Samuel Clemens entered the world and left it with Halley's Comet, little dreaming that generations hence Halley's Comet would be less famous than Mark Twain. He has been called the American Cervantes, our Homer, our Tolstoy, our Shakespeare, our Rabelais. Ernest Hemingway maintained that "all modern American literature comes from one book by Mark Twain called *Huckleberry Finn*." President Franklin Delano Roosevelt got the phrase "New Deal" from *A Connecticut Yankee in King Arthur's Court. The Gilded Age* gave an entire era its name. "The future historian of America," wrote George Bernard Shaw to Samuel Clemens, "will find your works as indispensable to him as a French historian finds the political tracts of Voltaire."[1]

There is a Mark Twain Bank in St. Louis, a Mark Twain Diner in Jackson Heights, New York, a Mark Twain Smoke Shop in Lakeland, Florida. There are Mark Twain Elementary Schools in Albuquerque, Dayton, Seattle, and Sioux Falls. Mark Twain's image peers at us from advertisements for Bass Ale (his drink of choice was Scotch), for a gas company in Tennessee, a hotel in the nation's capital, a cemetery in California.

Ubiquitous though his name and image may be, Mark Twain is in no danger of becoming a petrified icon. On the contrary: Mark Twain lives. *Huckleberry Finn* is "the most taught novel, most taught long work, and most taught piece of American literature" in American schools from junior high to the graduate level.[2] Hundreds of Twain impersonators appear in theaters, trade shows, and shopping centers in every region of the country.[3] Scholars publish hundreds of articles as well as books about Twain every year, and he is the subject of daily exchanges on the Internet. A journalist somewhere in the world finds a reason to quote Twain just about every day. Television series such as *Bonanza, Star Trek: The Next Generation,* and *Cheers* broadcast episodes that feature Mark Twain as a character. Hollywood screenwriters regularly produce movies inspired by his works, and writers of mysteries and science fiction continue to weave him into their plots.[4]

A century after the American Revolution sent shock waves throughout Europe, it took Mark Twain to explain to Europeans and to his countrymen alike what that revolution had wrought. He probed the significance of this new land and its new citizens, and identified what it was in the Old World that America abolished and rejected. The founding fathers had thought through the political dimensions of making a new society; Mark Twain took on the challenge of interpreting the social and cultural life of the United States for those outside its borders as well as for those who were living the changes he discerned.

Americans may have constructed a new society in the eighteenth century, but they articulated what they had done in voices that were largely inter-changeable with those of Englishmen until well into the nineteenth century. Mark Twain became the voice of the new land, the leading translator of what and who the "American" was — and, to a large extent, is. Frances Trollope's *Domestic Manners of the Americans,* a best-seller in England, Hector St. John de Crèvecoeur's *Letters from an American Farmer,* and Tocqueville's *Democracy in America* all tried to explain America to Europeans. But Twain did more than that: he allowed European readers to *experience* this strange "new world." And he gave his countrymen the tools to do two things they had not quite had the confidence to do before. He helped them stand before the cultural icons of the Old World unembarrassed, unashamed of America's lack of palaces and shrines, proud of its brash practicality and bold inventiveness, unafraid to reject European models of "civilization" as tainted or corrupt. And he also helped them recognize their own insularity, boorishness, arrogance, or ignorance, and laugh at it — the first step toward transcending it and becoming more "civilized," in the best European sense of the word.

Twain often strikes us as more a creature of our time than of his. He appreciated the importance and the complexity of mass tourism and public relations, fields that would come into their own in the twentieth century but were only fledgling enterprises in the nineteenth. He explored the liberating potential of humor and the dynamics of friendship, parenting, and marriage. He narrowed the gap between "popular" and "high" culture, and he meditated on the enigmas of personal and national identity. Indeed, it would be difficult to find an issue on the horizon today that Twain did not touch on somewhere in his work. Heredity versus environment? Animal rights? The boundaries of gender? The place of black voices in the cultural heritage of the United States? Twain was there.

With startling prescience and characteristic grace and wit, he zeroed in on many of the key challenges — political, social, and technological — that would face his country and the world for the next hundred years: the challenge of race relations in a society founded on both chattel slavery and ideals of equality, and the intractable problem of racism in American life; the potential of new technologies to transform our lives in ways that can be both exhilarating and terrifying — as well as unpredictable; the problem of imperialism and the difficulties entailed in getting rid of it. But he never lost sight of the most basic challenge of all: each man or woman's struggle for integrity in the face of the seductions of power, status, and material things.

Mark Twain's unerring sense of the right word and not its second cousin taught people to pay attention when he spoke, in person or in print. He said things that were smart and things that were wise, and he said them incomparably well. He defined the rhythms of our prose and the contours of our moral map. He saw our best and our worst, our extravagant promise and our stunning failures, our comic foibles and our tragic flaws. Throughout the world he is viewed as the most distinctively American of American authors — and as one of the most universal. He is assigned in classrooms in Naples, Riyadh, Belfast, and Beijing, and has been a major influence on twentieth-century writers from Argentina to Nigeria to Japan. The Oxford Mark Twain celebrates the versatility and vitality of this remarkable writer.

The Oxford Mark Twain reproduces the first American editions of Mark Twain's books published during his lifetime.[5] By encountering Twain's works in their original format — typography, layout, order of contents, and illustrations — readers today can come a few steps closer to the literary artifacts that entranced and excited readers when the books first appeared. Twain approved of and to a greater or lesser degree supervised the publication of all of this material.[6] The Mark Twain House in Hartford, Connecticut, generously loaned us its originals.[7] When more than one copy of a first American edition was available, Robert H. Hirst, general editor of the Mark Twain Project, in cooperation with Marianne Curling, curator of the Mark Twain House (and Jeffrey Kaimowitz, head of Rare Books for the Watkinson Library of Trinity College, Hartford, where the Mark Twain House collection is kept), guided our decision about which one to use.[8] As a set, the volumes also contain more than eighty essays commissioned especially for The Oxford Mark Twain, in which distinguished contributors reassess Twain's achievement as a writer and his place in the cultural conversation that he did so much to shape.

Each volume of The Oxford Mark Twain is introduced by a leading American, Canadian, or British writer who responds to Twain — often in a very personal way — as a fellow writer. Novelists, journalists, humorists, columnists, fabulists, poets, playwrights — these writers tell us what Twain taught them and what in his work continues to speak to them. Reading Twain's books, both famous and obscure, they reflect on the genesis of his art and the characteristics of his style, the themes he illuminated, and the aesthetic strategies he pioneered. Individually and collectively their contributions testify to the place Mark Twain holds in the hearts of readers of all kinds and temperaments.

Scholars whose work has shaped our view of Twain in the academy today have written afterwords to each volume, with suggestions for further reading. Their essays give us a sense of what was going on in Twain's life when he wrote the book at hand, and of how that book fits into his career. They explore how each book reflects and refracts contemporary events, and they show Twain responding to literary and social currents of the day, variously accepting, amplifying, modifying, and challenging prevailing paradigms. Sometimes they argue that works previously dismissed as quirky or eccentric departures actually address themes at the heart of Twain's work from the start. And as they bring new perspectives to Twain's composition strategies in familiar texts, several scholars see experiments in form where others saw only form-lessness, method where prior critics saw only madness. In addition to eluci-dating the work's historical and cultural context, the afterwords provide an overview of responses to each book from its first appearance to the present.

Most of Mark Twain's books involved more than Mark Twain's words: unique illustrations. The parodic visual send-ups of "high culture" that Twain himself drew for *A Tramp Abroad*, the sketch of financial manipulator Jay Gould as a greedy and sadistic "Slave Driver" in *A Connecticut Yankee in King Arthur's Court*, and the memorable drawings of Eve in *Eve's Diary* all helped Twain's books to be sold, read, discussed, and preserved. In their es-says for each volume that contains artwork, Beverly R. David and Ray Sapirstein highlight the significance of the sketches, engravings, and pho-tographs in the first American editions of Mark Twain's works, and tell us what is known about the public response to them.

The Oxford Mark Twain invites us to read some relatively neglected works by Twain in the company of some of the most engaging literary figures of our time. Roy Blount Jr., for example, riffs in a deliciously Twain-like manner on "An Item Which the Editor Himself Could Not Understand," which may well rank as one of the least-known pieces Twain ever published. Bobbie Ann Mason celebrates the "mad energy" of Twain's most obscure comic novel, *The American Claimant*, in which the humor "hurtles beyond tall tale into simon-pure absurdity."[9] Garry Wills finds that *Christian Science* "gets us very close to the heart of American culture." Lee Smith reads "Political Economy" as a sharp and funny essay on language. Walter Mosley sees "The Stolen White Elephant," a story "reduced to a series of ridiculous telegrams related by an untrustworthy narrator caught up in an adventure that is as impossible as it is ludicrous," as a stunningly compact and economical satire of a world we still recognize as our own. Anne Bernays returns to "The Private History of a Campaign That Failed" and finds "an antiwar manifesto that is also confession, dramatic monologue, a plea for understanding and absolution, and a romp that gradually turns into atrocity even as we watch." After revisiting Captain Stormfield's heaven, Frederik Pohl finds that there "is no imaginable place more pleasant to spend eternity." Indeed, Pohl writes, "one would almost be willing to die to enter it."

While less familiar works receive fresh attention in The Oxford Mark Twain, new light is cast on the best-known works as well. Judith Martin ("Miss Manners") points out that it is by reading a court etiquette book that Twain's pauper learns how to behave as a proper prince. As important as etiquette may be in the palace, Martin notes, it is even more important in the slums.

> That etiquette is a sorer point with the ruffians in the street than with the proud dignitaries of the prince's court may surprise some readers. As in our own streets, etiquette is always a more volatile subject among those who cannot count on being treated with respect than among those who have the power to command deference.

And taking a fresh look at *Adventures of Huckleberry Finn,* Toni Morrison writes,

> much of the novel's genius lies in its quiescence, the silences that pervade it and give it a porous quality that is by turns brooding and soothing. It lies in . . . the subdued images in which the repetition of a simple word, such as "lonesome," tolls like an evening bell; the moments when nothing is said, when scenes and incidents swell the heart unbearably precisely because unarticulated, and force an act of imagination almost against the will.

Engaging Mark Twain as one writer to another, several contributors to The Oxford Mark Twain offer new insights into the processes by which his books came to be. Russell Banks, for example, reads *A Tramp Abroad* as "an important revision of Twain's incomplete first draft of *Huckleberry Finn,* a second draft, if you will, which in turn made possible the third and final draft." Erica Jong suggests that *1601,* a freewheeling parody of Elizabethan manners and mores, written during the same summer Twain began *Huckleberry Finn*, served as "a warm-up for his creative process" and "primed the pump for other sorts of freedom of expression." And Justin Kaplan suggests that "one of the transcendent figures standing behind and shaping" *Joan of Arc* was Ulysses S. Grant, whose memoirs Twain had recently published, and who, like Joan, had risen unpredictably "from humble and obscure origins" to become a "military genius" endowed with "the gift of command, a natural eloquence, and an equally natural reserve."

As a number of contributors note, Twain was a man ahead of his times. *The Gilded Age* was the first "Washington novel," Ward Just tells us, because "Twain was the first to see the possibilities that had eluded so many others." Commenting on *The Tragedy of Pudd'nhead Wilson,* Sherley Anne Williams observes that "Twain's argument about the power of environment in shaping character runs directly counter to prevailing sentiment where the negro was concerned." Twain's fictional technology, wildly fanciful by the standards of his day, predicts developments we take for granted in ours. DNA cloning, fax machines, and photocopiers are all prefigured, Bobbie Ann Mason tells us, in *The American Claimant.* Cynthia Ozick points out that the "telelectrophonoscope" we meet in "From the 'London Times' of 1904" is suspiciously like what we know as "television." And Malcolm Bradbury suggests that in the "phrenophones" of "Mental Telegraphy" "the Internet was born."

Twain turns out to have been remarkably prescient about political affairs as well. Kurt Vonnegut sees in *A Connecticut Yankee* a chilling foreshadowing (or perhaps a projection from the Civil War) of "all the high-tech atrocities which followed, and which follow still." Cynthia Ozick suggests that "The Man That Corrupted Hadleyburg," along with some of the other pieces collected under that title — many of them written when Twain lived in a Vienna ruled by Karl Lueger, a demagogue Adolf Hitler would later idolize — shoot up moral flares that shed an eerie light on the insidious corruption, prejudice, and hatred that reached bitter fruition under the Third Reich. And Twain's portrait in this book of "the dissolving Austria-Hungary of the 1890s," in Ozick's view, presages not only the Sarajevo that would erupt in 1914 but also "the disintegrated components of the former Yugoslavia" and "the *fin-de-siècle* Sarajevo of our own moment."

Despite their admiration for Twain's ambitious reach and scope, contributors to The Oxford Mark Twain also recognize his limitations. Mordecai Richler, for example, thinks that "the early pages of *Innocents Abroad* suffer from being a tad broad, proffering more burlesque than inspired satire," perhaps because Twain was "trying too hard for knee-slappers." Charles Johnson notes that the Young Man in Twain's philosophical dialogue about free will and determinism (*What Is Man?*) "caves in far too soon," failing to challenge what through late-twentieth-century eyes looks like "pseudoscience" and suspect essentialism in the Old Man's arguments.

Some contributors revisit their first encounters with Twain's works, recalling what surprised or intrigued them. When David Bradley came across "Fenimore Cooper's Literary Offences" in his college library, he "did not at first realize that Twain was being his usual ironic self with all this business about the 'nineteen rules governing literary art in the domain of romantic fiction,' but by the time I figured out there was no such list outside Twain's own head, I had decided that the rules made *sense*. . . . It seemed to me they were a pretty good blueprint for writing — Negro writing included." Sherley Anne Williams remembers that part of what attracted her to *Pudd'nhead Wilson* when she first read it thirty years ago was "that Twain, writing at the end of the nineteenth century, could imagine negroes as characters, albeit white ones, who actually thought for and of themselves, whose actions were the product of their thinking rather than the spontaneous ephemera of physical instincts that stereotype assigned to blacks." Frederik Pohl recalls his first reading of *Huckleberry Finn* as "a watershed event" in his life, the first book he read as a child in which "bad people" ceased to exercise a monopoly on doing "bad things." In *Huckleberry Finn* "some seriously bad things — things like the possession and mistreatment of black slaves, like stealing and lying, even like killing other people in duels — were quite often done by people who not only thought of themselves as exemplarily moral but, by any other standards I knew how to apply, actually *were* admirable citizens." The world that

Tom and Huck lived in, Pohl writes, "was filled with complexities and contradictions," and resembled "the world I appeared to be living in myself."

Other contributors explore their more recent encounters with Twain, explaining why they have revised their initial responses to his work. For Toni Morrison, parts of *Huckleberry Finn* that she "once took to be deliberate evasions, stumbles even, or a writer's impatience with his or her material," now strike her "as otherwise: as entrances, crevices, gaps, seductive invitations flashing the possibility of meaning. Unarticulated eddies that encourage diving into the novel's undertow — the real place where writer captures reader." One such "eddy" is the imprisonment of Jim on the Phelps farm. Instead of dismissing this portion of the book as authorial bungling, as she once did, Morrison now reads it as Twain's commentary on the 1880s, a period that "saw the collapse of civil rights for blacks," a time when "the nation, as well as Tom Sawyer, was deferring Jim's freedom in agonizing play." Morrison believes that Americans in the 1880s were attempting "to bury the combustible issues Twain raised in his novel," and that those who try to kick Huck Finn out of school in the 1990s are doing the same: "The cyclical attempts to remove the novel from classrooms extend Jim's captivity on into each generation of readers."

Although imitation-Hemingway and imitation-Faulkner writing contests draw hundreds of entries annually, no one has ever tried to mount a faux-Twain competition. Why? Perhaps because Mark Twain's voice is too much a part of who we are and how we speak even today. Roy Blount Jr. suggests that it is impossible, "at least for an American writer, to parody Mark Twain. It would be like doing an impression of your father or mother: he or she is already there in your voice."

Twain's style is examined and celebrated in The Oxford Mark Twain by fellow writers who themselves have struggled with the nuances of words, the structure of sentences, the subtleties of point of view, and the trickiness of opening lines. Bobbie Ann Mason observes, for example, that "Twain loved the sound of words and he knew how to string them by sound, like different shades of one color: 'The earl's barbaric eye,' 'the Usurping Earl,' 'a double-dyed humbug.'" Twain "relied on the punch of plain words" to show writers how to move beyond the "wordy romantic rubbish" so prevalent in nineteenth-century fiction, Mason says; he "was one of the first writers in America to deflower literary language." Lee Smith believes that "American writers have benefited as much from the way Mark Twain opened up the possibilities of first-person narration as we have from his use of vernacular language." (She feels that "the ghost of Mark Twain was hovering someplace in the background" when she decided to write her novel *Oral History* from the standpoint of multiple first-person narrators.) Frederick Busch maintains that "A Dog's Tale" "boasts one of the great opening sentences" of all time: "My father was a St. Bernard, my mother was a collie, but I am a Presbyterian." And Ursula Le Guin marvels at the ingenuity of the following sentence that she encounters in *Extracts from Adam's Diary*.

. . . This made her sorry for the creatures which live in there, which she calls fish, for she continues to fasten names on to things that don't need them and don't come when they are called by them, which is a matter of no consequence to her, as she is such a numskull anyway; so she got a lot of them out and brought them in last night and put them in my bed to keep warm, but I have noticed them now and then all day, and I don't see that they are any happier there than they were before, only quieter.[10]

Le Guin responds,

Now, that is a pure Mark-Twain-tour-de-force sentence, covering an immense amount of territory in an effortless, aimless ramble that seems to be heading nowhere in particular and ends up with breathtaking accuracy at the gold mine. Any sensible child would find that funny, perhaps not following all its divagations but delighted by the swing of it, by the word "numskull," by the idea of putting fish in the bed; and as that child grew older and reread it, its reward would only grow; and if that grown-up child had to write an essay on the piece and therefore earnestly studied and pored over this sentence, she would end up in unmitigated admiration of its vocabulary, syntax, pacing, sense, and rhythm, above all the beautiful timing of the last two words; and she would, and she does, still find it funny.

The fish surface again in a passage that Gore Vidal calls to our attention, from *Following the Equator*: "'The Whites always mean well when they take human fish out of the ocean and try to make them dry and warm and happy and comfortable in a chicken coop,' which is how, through civilization, they did away with many of the original inhabitants. Lack of empathy is a principal theme in Twain's meditations on race and empire."

Indeed, empathy — and its lack — is a principal theme in virtually all of Twain's work, as contributors frequently note. Nat Hentoff quotes the following thoughts from Huck in *Tom Sawyer Abroad*:

> I see a bird setting on a dead limb of a high tree, singing with its head tilt-ed back and its mouth open, and before I thought I fired, and his song stopped and he fell straight down from the limb, all limp like a rag, and I run and picked him up and he was dead, and his body was warm in my hand, and his head rolled about this way and that, like his neck was broke, and there was a little white skin over his eyes, and one little drop of blood on the side of his head; and laws! I could n't see nothing more for the tears; and I hain't never murdered no creature since that war n't doing me no harm, and I ain't going to.[11]

"The Humane Society," Hentoff writes, "has yet to say anything as powerful — and lasting."

Readers of The Oxford Mark Twain will have the pleasure of revisiting Twain's Mississippi landmarks alongside Willie Morris, whose own lower Mississippi Valley boyhood gives him a special sense of connection to Twain. Morris knows firsthand the mosquitoes described in *Life on the Mississippi* — so colossal that "two of them could whip a dog" and "four of them could hold a man down"; in Morris's own hometown they were so large during the flood season that "local wags said they wore wristwatches." Morris's Yazoo City and Twain's Hannibal shared a "rough-hewn democracy . . . complicated by all the visible textures of caste and class, . . . harmless boyhood fun and mischief right along with . . . rank hypocrisies, churchgoing sanctimonies, racial hatred, entrenched and unrepentant greed."

For the West of Mark Twain's *Roughing It*, readers will have George Plimpton as their guide. "What a group these newspapermen were!" Plimpton writes about Twain and his friends Dan De Quille and Joe Goodman in Virginia City, Nevada. "Their roisterous carryings-on bring to mind the kind of frat-house enthusiasm one associates with college humor magazines like the *Harvard Lampoon*." Malcolm Bradbury examines Twain as "a living example of what made the American so different from the European." And Hal Holbrook, who has interpreted Mark Twain on stage for some forty years, describes how Twain "played" during the civil rights movement, during the Vietnam War, during the Gulf War, and in Prague on the eve of the demise of Communism.

Why do we continue to read Mark Twain? What draws us to him? His wit? His compassion? His humor? His bravura? His humility? His understanding of who and what we are in those parts of our being that we rarely open to view? Our sense that he knows we can do better than we do? Our sense that he knows we can't? E. L. Doctorow tells us that children are attracted to *Tom Sawyer* because in this book "the young reader confirms his own hope that no matter how troubled his relations with his elders may be, beneath all their disapproval is their underlying love for him, constant and steadfast." Readers in general, Arthur Miller writes, value Twain's "insights into America's always uncertain moral life and its shifting but everlasting hypocrisies"; we appreciate the fact that he "is not using his alienation from the public illusions of his hour in order to reject the country implicitly as though he could live without it, but manifestly in order to correct it." Perhaps we keep reading Mark Twain because, in Miller's words, he "wrote much more like a father than a son. He doesn't seem to be sitting in class taunting the teacher but standing at the head of it challenging his students to acknowledge their own humanity, that is, their immemorial attraction to the untrue."

Mark Twain entered the public eye at a time when many of his countrymen considered "American culture" an oxymoron; he died four years before a world conflagration that would lead many to question whether the contradiction in terms was not "European civilization" instead. In between he worked in journalism, printing, steamboating, mining, lecturing, publishing, and editing, in virtually every region of the country. He tried his hand at humorous sketches, social satire, historical novels, children's books, poetry, drama, science fiction, mysteries, romance, philosophy, travelogue, memoir, polemic, and several genres no one had ever seen before or has ever seen since. He invented a self-pasting scrapbook, a history game, a vest strap, and a gizmo for keeping bed sheets tucked in; he invested in machines and processes designed to revolutionize typesetting and engraving, and in a food supplement called "Plasmon." Along the way he cheerfully impersonated himself and prior versions of himself for doting publics on five continents while playing out a charming rags-to-riches story followed by a devastating riches-to-rags story followed by yet another great American comeback. He had a long-running real-life engagement in a sumptuous comedy of manners, and then in a real-life tragedy not of his own design: during the last fourteen years of his life almost everyone he ever loved was taken from him by disease and death.

Mark Twain has indelibly shaped our views of who and what the United States is as a nation and of who and what we might become. He understood the nostalgia for a "simpler" past that increased as that past receded — and he saw through the nostalgia to a past that was just as complex as the present. He recognized better than we did ourselves our potential for greatness and our potential for disaster. His fictions brilliantly illuminated the world in which he lived, changing it — and us — in the process. He knew that our feet often danced to tunes that had somehow remained beyond our hearing; with perfect pitch he played them back to us.

My mother read *Tom Sawyer* to me as a bedtime story when I was eleven. I thought Huck and Tom could be a lot of fun, but I dismissed Becky Thatcher as a bore. When I was twelve I invested a nickel at a local garage sale in a book that contained short pieces by Mark Twain. That was where I met Twain's Eve. Now, *that's* more like it, I decided, pleased to meet a female character I could identify *with* instead of against. Eve had spunk. Even if she got a lot wrong, you had to give her credit for trying. "The Man That Corrupted

Hadleyburg" left me giddy with satisfaction: none of my adolescent reveries of getting even with my enemies were half as neat as the plot of the man who got back at that town. "How I Edited an Agricultural Paper" set me off in uncontrollable giggles.

People sometimes told me that I looked like Huck Finn. "It's the freckles," they'd explain—not explaining anything at all. I didn't read *Huckleberry Finn* until junior year in high school in my English class. It was the fall of 1965. I was living in a small town in Connecticut. I expected a sequel to *Tom Sawyer*. So when the teacher handed out the books and announced our assignment, my jaw dropped: "Write a paper on how Mark Twain used irony to attack racism in *Huckleberry Finn*."

The year before, the bodies of three young men who had gone to Mississippi to help blacks register to vote—James Chaney, Andrew Goodman, and Michael Schwerner—had been found in a shallow grave; a group of white segregationists (the county sheriff among them) had been arrested in connection with the murders. America's inner cities were simmering with pent-up rage that began to explode in the summer of 1965, when riots in Watts left thirty-four people dead. None of this made any sense to me. I was confused, angry, certain that there was something missing from the news stories I read each day: the why. Then I met Pap Finn. And the Phelpses.

Pap Finn, Huck tells us, "had been drunk over in town" and "was just all mud." He erupts into a drunken tirade about "a free nigger . . . from Ohio—a mulatter, most as white as a white man," with "the whitest shirt on you ever see, too, and the shiniest hat; and there ain't a man in town that's got as fine clothes as what he had."

> . . . they said he was a p'fessor in a college, and could talk all kinds of languages, and knowed everything. And that ain't the wust. They said he could *vote*, when he was at home. Well, that let me out. Thinks I, what is the country a-coming to? It was 'lection day, and I was just about to go and vote, myself, if I warn't too drunk to get there; but when they told me there was a State in this country where they'd let that nigger vote, I drawed out. I says I'll never vote agin. Them's the very words I said. . . . And to see the

cool way of that nigger — why, he wouldn't a give me the road if I hadn't shoved him out o' the way.[12]

Later on in the novel, when the runaway slave Jim gives up his freedom to nurse a wounded Tom Sawyer, a white doctor testifies to the stunning altruism of his actions. The Phelpses and their neighbors, all fine, upstanding, well-meaning, churchgoing folk,

> agreed that Jim had acted very well, and was deserving to have some notice took of it, and reward. So every one of them promised, right out and hearty, that they wouldn't curse him no more.
>
> Then they come out and locked him up. I hoped they was going to say he could have one or two of the chains took off, because they was rotten heavy, or could have meat and greens with his bread and water, but they didn't think of it.[13]

Why did the behavior of these people tell me more about why Watts burned than anything I had read in the daily paper? And why did a drunk Pap Finn railing against a black college professor from Ohio whose vote was as good as his own tell me more about white anxiety over black political power than anything I had seen on the evening news?

Mark Twain knew that there was nothing, absolutely *nothing*, a black man could do — including selflessly sacrificing his freedom, the only thing of value he had — that would make white society see beyond the color of his skin. And Mark Twain knew that depicting racists with chilling accuracy would expose the viciousness of their world view like nothing else could. It was an insight echoed some eighty years after Mark Twain penned Pap Finn's rantings about the black professor, when Malcolm X famously asked, "Do you know what white racists call black Ph.D.'s?" and answered, " '*Nigger!*' "[14]

Mark Twain taught me things I needed to know. He taught me to understand the raw racism that lay behind what I saw on the evening news. He taught me that the most well-meaning people can be hurtful and myopic. He taught me to recognize the supreme irony of a country founded in freedom that continued to deny freedom to so many of its citizens. Every time I hear of another effort to kick Huck Finn out of school somewhere, I recall everything that Mark Twain taught *this* high school junior, and I find myself jumping into the fray.[15] I remember the black high school student who called CNN during the phone-in portion of a 1985 debate between Dr. John Wallace, a black educator spearheading efforts to ban the book, and myself. She accused Dr. Wallace of insulting her and all black high school students by suggesting they weren't smart enough to understand Mark Twain's irony. And I recall the black cameraman on the *CBS Morning News* who came up to me after he finished shooting another debate between Dr. Wallace and myself. He said he had never read the book by Mark Twain that we had been arguing about — but now he really wanted to. One thing that puzzled him, though, was why a white woman was defending it and a black man was attacking it, because as far as he could see from what we'd been saying, the book made whites look pretty bad.

As I came to understand *Huckleberry Finn* and *Pudd'nhead Wilson* as commentaries on the era now known as the nadir of American race relations, those books pointed me toward the world recorded in nineteenth-century black newspapers and periodicals and in fiction by Mark Twain's black contemporaries. My investigation of the role black voices and traditions played in shaping Mark Twain's art helped make me aware of their role in shaping all of American culture.[16] My research underlined for me the importance of changing the stories we tell about who we are to reflect the realities of what we've been.[17]

Ever since our encounter in high school English, Mark Twain has shown me the potential of American literature and American history to illuminate each other. Rarely have I found a contradiction or complexity we grapple with as a nation that Mark Twain had not puzzled over as well. He insisted on taking America seriously. And he insisted on *not* taking America seriously: "I think that there is but a single specialty with us, only one thing that can be called by the wide name 'American,'" he once wrote. "That is the national devotion to ice-water."[18]

Mark Twain threw back at us our dreams and our denial of those dreams, our greed, our goodness, our ambition, and our laziness, all rattling around together in that vast echo chamber of our talk — that sharp, spunky American talk that Mark Twain figured out how to write down without robbing it of its energy and immediacy. Talk shaped by voices that the official arbiters of "culture" deemed of no importance — voices of children, voices of slaves, voices of servants, voices of ordinary people. Mark Twain listened. And he made us listen. To the stories he told us, and to the truths they conveyed. He still has a lot to say that we need to hear.

Mark Twain lives — in our libraries, classrooms, homes, theaters, movie houses, streets, and most of all in our speech. His optimism energizes us, his despair sobers us, and his willingness to keep wrestling with the hilarious and horrendous complexities of it all keeps us coming back for more. As the twenty-first century approaches, may he continue to goad us, chasten us, delight us, berate us, and cause us to erupt in unrestrained laughter in unexpected places.

NOTES

1. Ernest Hemingway, *Green Hills of Africa* (New York: Charles Scribner's Sons, 1935), 22. George Bernard Shaw to Samuel L. Clemens, July 3, 1907, quoted in Albert Bigelow Paine, *Mark Twain: A Biography* (New York: Harper and Brothers, 1912), 3:1398.

2. Allen Carey-Webb, "Racism and *Huckleberry Finn*: Censorship, Dialogue and Change," *English Journal* 82, no. 7 (November 1993):22.

3. See Louis J. Budd, "Impersonators," in J. R. LeMaster and James D. Wilson, eds., *The Mark Twain Encyclopedia* (New York: Garland Publishing Company, 1993), 389–91.

4. See Shelley Fisher Fishkin, "Ripples and Reverberations," part 3 of *Lighting Out for the Territory: Reflections on Mark Twain and American Culture* (New York: Oxford University Press, 1996).

5. There are two exceptions. Twain published chapters from his autobiography in the *North American Review* in 1906 and 1907, but this material was not published in book form in Twain's lifetime; our volume reproduces the material as it appeared in the *North American Review*. The other exception is our final volume, *Mark Twain's Speeches*, which appeared two months after Twain's death in 1910.

An unauthorized handful of copies of *1601* was privately printed by an Alexander Gunn of Cleveland at the instigation of Twain's friend John Hay in 1880. The first American edition authorized by Mark Twain, however, was printed at the United States Military Academy at West Point in 1882; that is the edition reproduced here.

It should further be noted that four volumes — *The Stolen White Elephant and Other Detective Stories*, *Following the Equator and Anti-imperialist Essays*, *The Diaries of Adam and Eve*, and *1601, and Is Shakespeare Dead?* — bind together material originally published separately. In each case the first American edition of the material is the version that has been reproduced, always in its entirety. Because Twain constantly recycled and repackaged previously published works in his collections of short pieces, a certain amount of duplication is unavoidable. We have selected volumes with an eye toward keeping this duplication to a minimum.

Even the twenty-nine-volume Oxford Mark Twain has had to leave much out. No edition of Twain can ever claim to be "complete," for the man was too prolix, and the file drawers of both ephemera and as yet unpublished texts are deep.

6. With the possible exception of *Mark Twain's Speeches*. Some scholars suspect Twain knew about this book and may have helped shape it, although no hard evidence to that effect has yet surfaced. Twain's involvement in the production process varied greatly from book to book. For a fuller sense of authorial intention, scholars will continue to rely on the superb definitive editions of Twain's works produced by the Mark Twain Project at the University of California at Berkeley as they become available. Dense with annotation documenting textual emendation and related issues, these editions add immeasurably to our understanding of Mark Twain and the genesis of his works.

7. Except for a few titles that were not in its collection. The American Antiquarian Society in Worcester, Massachusetts, provided the first edition of *King Leopold's Soliloquy*; the Elmer Holmes Bobst Library of New York University furnished the 1906–7 volumes of the *North American Review* in which *Chapters from My Autobiography* first appeared; the Harry Ransom Humanities Research Center at the University of Texas at Austin made their copy of the West Point edition of *1601* available; and the Mark Twain Project provided the first edition of *Extract from Captain Stormfield's Visit to Heaven*.

8. The specific copy photographed for Oxford's facsimile edition is indicated in a note on the text at the end of each volume.

9. All quotations from contemporary writers in this essay are taken from their introductions to the volumes of The Oxford Mark Twain, and the quotations from Mark Twain's works are taken from the texts reproduced in The Oxford Mark Twain.

10. *The Diaries of Adam and Eve*, The Oxford Mark Twain [hereafter OMT] (New York: Oxford University Press, 1996), p. 33.

11. *Tom Sawyer Abroad*, OMT, p. 74.

12. *Adventures of Huckleberry Finn*, OMT, p. 49–50.

13. Ibid., p. 358.

14. Malcolm X, *The Autobiography of Malcolm X*, with the assistance of Alex Haley (New York: Grove Press, 1965), p. 284.

15. I do not mean to minimize the challenge of teaching this difficult novel, a challenge for which all teachers may not feel themselves prepared. Elsewhere I have developed some concrete strategies for approaching the book in the classroom, including teaching it in the context of the history of American race relations and alongside books by black writers. See Shelley Fisher Fishkin, "Teaching *Huckleberry Finn*," in James S. Leonard, ed., *Making Mark Twain Work in the Classroom* (Durham: Duke University Press, forthcoming). See also Shelley Fisher Fishkin, *Was Huck Black? Mark Twain and African-American Voices* (New York: Oxford University Press, 1993), pp. 106–8, and a curriculum kit in preparation at the Mark Twain House in Hartford, containing teaching suggestions from myself, David Bradley, Jocelyn Chadwick-Joshua, James Miller, and David E. E. Sloane.

16. See Fishkin, *Was Huck Black?* See also Fishkin, "Interrogating 'Whiteness,' Complicating 'Blackness': Remapping American Culture," in Henry Wonham, ed., *Criticism and the Color Line: Desegregating American Literary Studies* (New Brunswick: Rutgers UP, 1996, pp. 251–90 and in shortened form in *American Quarterly* 47, no. 3 (September 1995):428–66.

17. I explore the roots of my interest in Mark Twain and race at greater length in an essay entitled "Changing the Story," in Jeffrey Rubin-Dorsky and Shelley Fisher Fishkin, eds., *People of the Book: Thirty Scholars Reflect on Their Jewish Identity* (Madison: U of Wisconsin Press, 1996), pp. 47–63.

18. "What Paul Bourget Thinks of Us," *How to Tell a Story and Other Essays*, OMT, p. 197.

INTRODUCTION

Malcolm Bradbury

The £1,000,000 *Bank-Note and Other New Stories* is surely the most delightful of Mark Twain's later books, which are famous for their mixed quality and their somber mood. And the title tale, a bouncy story of money, love and luck set in London, is amongst Twain's warmest and most effective humorous narratives. It's all the more amazing, then, that the tale and the volume as a whole have generally avoided the ministrations of the critics, a good many of whom have never even granted it a mention. What makes this even stranger is that the book, which appeared from Charles L. Webster and Company, New York, in 1893 (the year of the Chicago World Columbian Exposition, at which Frederick Jackson Turner announced his famous "frontier thesis" just as the frontier line officially closed, and also a year of financial panic), came out right on the famous tragic cusp in Twain's life. In fact when he published this story about a great gift of money he himself was just coming to the lowest point in his fortunes — though reading the story we can scarcely sense this.

At the start of the 1890s, Twain was the greatest popular American writer, and his fame was on the world scale. But the former itinerant printer and scourge of the American Gilded Age had acquired, in the mood of the times, some striking capitalist ambitions of his own. Schemes, speculation and investment had long been the central themes of many of his novels and stories. And he had invested in a good many schemes himself: a steam pulley, a steam generator, a watch company, an insurance house. He had also ventured into the difficult waters of modern popular publishing as chief investor and senior partner in the Webster company, which brought out General Grant's memoirs as well as many of his own books (including this one).

But not all was going well. Though there was little doubt that the principal asset of the Webster list was Twain himself, it seemed to have acquired a corner in war and high piety. The *£1,000,000 Bank-Note* therefore came out alongside such titles as Matt Crim's novel *Elizabeth: Christian Scientist* ("The story deals with the career of a refined and deeply religious girl, who leaves her home in the Georgia mountains with the object of converting the world to Christian Science"), the selected poems of Walt Whitman, a volume on tenting on the plains, and various reforming and progressive works by Henry George. But as the 1890s began, the house was running into growing trouble. Twain had commissioned an autobiography from his friend the old evangelist Henry Ward Beecher — but he promptly died, taking his $5,000 advance off to heaven with him. An expensive life of the sitting pope, Leo XIII, for which Twain foresaw the most enormous sales, had proved far less infallible than he expected. He'd also invested in a highly ambitious ten-volume *Library of American Literature*. Twain had come to see himself as a great modern publisher, opening up the writing marketplace of his day. But the problem was not just that his capitalistic instincts were less acute than he imagined. Publishing had also diverted him from what, after all, he did best — which was writing books, not printing them.

Even worse, though, was the unhappy adventure of the Paige typesetting machine. Twain, the former printer turned famed writer, had become wildly excited by the economic prospects and technological splendors of this grand new invention; it promised, he thought, to do nothing less than create the next Gutenberg revolution. James Paige's elaborate printing machine — which its inventor kept constantly dismantling and reconstructing — was to Twain's adoring eyes a marvel, a mechanical brain. He called it an "inspired bugger" which would make all the earlier wonders of human invention — the cotton gin, the Babbage calculator, the Arkwright spinning frame, the locomotive — seem like "mere toys, simplicities," and would even send Thomas Alva Edison into spasms of envy. Paige was, he pronounced, "the Shakespeare of mechanical invention" — and there's no doubt he was a plausible publicist, a living Colonel Sellers (of *The Gilded Age* and *The American Claimant*), in behalf of his own machine.

New invention was all the rage in America, and at the Chicago fair of 1893 the great Hall of Machines seemed the very symbol of the American future (as the historian Henry Adams remarked, observing the wonders that packed its white plaster of paris halls, it made one realize America would claim the twentieth century, and led him to speculate whether the new American would be able to run his machine and his woman too). Twain was a natural devotee of all such things; as he says in this present book, "our day is indifferent to old ideas, and even considers that their age makes their value questionable, but jumps at a new idea with enthusiasm and high hope — a hope which is high because it has not been accustomed to being disappointed." The Paige machine became Twain's great emblem; in fact it has been rightly said that it seemed to serve as the ultimate model or paradigm of his entire mechanistic view of experience and human nature. He began wildly pouring the profits of his writing, his lecturing, his publishing, his wife's inheritance, into the project, spending up to $3,000 a month on the invention. He dreamt of it, fantasized about it, envisioning a world sale of 100,000 for this wonderful machine, which could set 12,000 ems an hour, needed only one instead of four or five operators, and didn't join a union. Unfortunately it did not work either, or not at the crucial moments. Whenever rich investors visited to inspect the marvel, its pieces were usually to be found lying all over the floor.

Twain's anxious confidence in the project is plainly displayed in *A Connecticut Yankee in King Arthur's Court* (1889), the story of the ingenious Hartford machine shop superintendent who goes back to sixth-century British Camelot, and aims to bring the wonders of technology to the stuffy knights of the Round Table. Advertising, bicycles and modern weaponry are soon available; Hank Morgan is the master of modern technical invention. Unfortunately his skill with technology finally produces not just democratic enlightenment but war and a vast, murderous mechanical holocaust, and ultimately brings about universal destruction, including his own. Twain had closely identified his book with Paige's machine. He wrote it as his involvement with Paige escalated, and proposed to inscribe the final line on the day

Paige's work was done ("I want to finish the day the machine finishes"). The book was completed, late, with what seems like an almost unwittingly grim and prophetic conclusion. The machine, alas, never was. The unhappy truth was just starting to become visible. Twain was headed not toward what he anticipated, like so many in the early 1890s — that is, becoming a great technological entrepreneur and a millionaire capitalist — but toward a very public bankruptcy. Supported by his friends in commerce, the big trusts and government, he remained outwardly confident and buoyant. After all, he was the great writer of his day, sought and admired by everyone. But he was already beginning to sense the scale of his risk and the danger of disaster. His calls were not always returned; promising investors seemed always about to plunge with a massive capital injection, but then suddenly noticed that there were rival linotype machines which appeared to be performing better.

By 1891 the storm clouds were already gathering. Twain soon saw he had only one route through the trouble; he had better write his way out of it. He was now in his fifties, and suffering various bodily pains and family woes. He had always been the child of fortune, the golden boy, but it seemed fortune was no longer smiling. He was living high off the hog, and surrounded by claimants. He had imaginatively united writing and business, joined the speculator in money and the speculator in fiction, and the two were now confounding him. He turned to a solution he had seized on before; in June 1891 he set off for Europe. He intended to close down his house, reduce his expenses, and turn his attention from being an entrepreneur to reclaiming his role as the world's greatest humorous writer.

Europe had generally been lucky ground for Twain. In fact his literary fortunes, and fortune, had been founded on it. In 1867, at the age of thirty-one, as a little-known Western humorist, he had gone off on "The Grand Holy Land Pleasure Excursion": a remarkable cruise on the *Quaker City*, one of the new steamships that were serving the no less new spirit of modern mass tourism, which boomed once the Civil War was over. The *Quaker City* cruise was a mixture of tourist romp to the ever more accessible wonders of Europe and solemn pilgrimage to the Holy Land. Two noted figures who would play a significant part in Twain's latter-day adventures, Henry Ward Beecher and

General William Sherman, were supposed to accompany and dignify the cruise. But Beecher proved just as unreliable on this occasion as he did when Twain needed him later, and Sherman had to go and fight Indians instead. In their absence, Twain — who had signed on as a travel correspondent for a California newspaper — became the cruise celebrity, as well as its recorder. As for the account he gave of it all, it was to set down for literary eternity the classic encounter between the innocent American tourist and the vaunted, and maybe overvaunted, world of Europe.

Twain's comic vision captured the age of the new tourist to perfection. It was the triumph of the *Quaker City* voyage, he said, to invent a pleasure cruise that offered absolutely no pleasure, was in fact a "funeral excursion without a corpse." There was that rare thing, a temperance ship's captain, and prayer meetings were regularly held on board. To the wonders of these new American pilgrims were added the wonders of old Europe itself. Everywhere there were dirt and disease, touts and tricksters, suspect beggars and false guides, bands of gesticulating foreigners with lies in their mouths and fraud in their hearts. There were so many sites and galleries, and an apparently unending supply of "Old Masters." The New World innocents responded appropriately, as they often still do. "We examined modern and ancient statuary with a critical eye in Florence, Rome, or any where we found it, and praised it if we saw fit, and if we didn't we said we preferred the wooden Indians in front of the cigar stores of America." Where others, like Nathaniel Hawthorne, had gazed at the art and history of Europe with an educated but anxious American awe, Twain developed and expressed a new culture, of irreverent, deconstructive comic innocence. So the newspaper record of the five-month voyage became a sensation, and the book that collected the record, *The Innocents Abroad, or The New Pilgrim's Progress* (1869), was an extraordinary popular publishing success. Its literary aim, Twain explained, was "to suggest to the reader how *he* would be likely to see Europe and the East if he looked at them with his own eyes instead of the eyes of those who had travelled in those countries before him." The comic tone carried all before it; nothing, nowhere, no one was spared. Twain had invented a wonderfully new and original voice, an impertinently vernacular tone that had the energy of a vital culture behind it. William Dean Howells saw the point when he wrote his review: "There is an amount of pure human nature in the book that rarely gets into literature." Sold through subscription circuits, supported by a marvelously successful lecture tour, it was the work that established his reputation, his voice, his basic spirit as a writer.

This founding transaction between Twain's novel American innocence and the older world of Europe would go on to provide him staple material over the long curve of his writing life. We all know very well that Twain was a Western writer, and that the heartland material of his writing, and the power of his distinctive voice, lay in the Mississippi Valley of his pre–Civil War boyhood. However, no less important in the shaping of his vivid American imagination were his complicated and ambiguous encounters with the vast social and moral transformations of post–Civil War America, the complex phenomena of the era to which he himself attached the name "the Gilded Age." It was, it seemed to him, a time of national redemption and greatness, an age of "lightning-shod Mercuries." But it was no less an age of moral flux and bewilderment. By way of resort from the crude energies of the Gilded Age, Twain, like many fellow Americans, looked elsewhere, in nostalgia or romantic expectation, sometimes for reassurance, sometimes to engage in an unresolved criticism of his own contemporary society. The Mississippi Valley was one such alternative world, which he peopled gloriously with its own rich culture. But there was another one, Europe. Twain perceived himself as a republican critic of its monarchical ways and medieval flavors, but what lay on the other side of the Atlantic never for a moment ceased to fascinate him. After all, it had left its imprint all over the Mississippi Valley itself (as the "Castles and Culture" chapter of *Life on the Mississippi* tells us), fed the aristocratic romanticism and squirearchy that helped lead the South into false chivalry and the Civil War, but equally created the Shakespearean plays and the playful childhood fantasies that colored the culture of the river.

Hence Twain's literary imagination was filled not just with mid-American tall tales and the poetry of Southwestern voices but with European tales and fables: of medieval jousts and kingly courts, of princes and paupers exchanged in the cradle, of American heirs to English fortunes (perhaps he was one himself). A good many of his novels and short stories were actually burlesque versions of British or European romances: *The Prince and the Pauper*, *A Connecticut Yankee*, *The American Claimant*, and so on. One of his favourite ways of finding a new plot or resurrecting his older and familiar popular characters — Huck Finn, Tom Sawyer, Colonel Sellers — was to take them off for innocent adventures in Europe or give them fantasies about European ranks and titles. What's more, he had become a regular traveler to Europe himself. The onetime innocent abroad was abroad often. Over his lifetime he crossed the Atlantic about twenty-five times; by his death he had spent more than ten years in Europe. There had been the two happy visits to England on lecture tours in 1872 and 1873, when, just as America had hailed Charles Dickens, so the British hailed him. Dangerous thoughts even crossed his mind: "I would rather live in England than America — which is treason," he noted. Five years later, again wanting "to breathe the free air of Europe," he went on a walking tour in Germany, which he enjoyed no less. That led to his delightful volume of burlesque travels, *A Tramp Abroad* (1880) — a far less innocent account this time, much more knowing and benign. For a time he fell out of love with Europe as the republican and entrepreneurial excitements of modern America claimed him. After all, he himself seemed a living example of what made the American so different from the European, with his demotic irreverence, his democratic openness to change and invention, his eternal restless energy. The contrast often went into the imaginative transactions of his writing — and into the trip of 1891, which, as things turned out, marked the start of a decade in which he would spend something like seven years of his fast-changing life in Europe.

For Twain the nineties were a disastrous decade, when his view of himself as the child of fortune, his vision of life as a progress, his faith in invention and technology, were all transformed. He was not alone in his crisis; for his close contemporaries William Dean Howells and Henry James, the decade that led up to the century's turn was marked by doubts, disasters, changes in literary direction and a waning of their optimistic American confidence. It was plain to all that the American nineteenth century was closing in turbulence: in the unorganized growth of cities and their transformation by rapid immigration and labor problems, the rise of social protest and political violence, the dangerous, unchecked domination of trusts and corporations and the philosophies of Social Darwinism. Always responsive to changes in the cultural weather, Twain was no less buffeted by the shifting mood in ideology and opinion, and the rise in social and political pessimism; as the decade went on, this displayed itself in the deeply changing temper and implication of his writing. But of the three writers, it was Twain who was to take the most severe personal battering and experience the most profound and destructive change of vision.

Like other American writers after him, including Stephen Crane and Scott Fitzgerald, Twain sailed east, in 1891, on a modern steamship, under the happy illusion that moving across the ocean to Europe automatically produced a vast drop in your expenses, however high off the hog you actually lived. The Clemenses started off well enough in Germany, renting a cheap apartment in Berlin, which in an essay in this book he calls "the German Chicago," as in its way it was: it was a new capital city for a nation even newer than his own. But cheap lodgings hardly suited the best-known American writer, who was soon dining with the kaiser and meeting Mommsen, and whose greatly admired work was just about to appear in a German collected edition. He moved to a large suite in a hotel on the Unter den Linden, writing little but socializing much. So the trip went on, with Mark Twain moving all over Europe, relishing his fame and exploiting his fascination with travel. Planning what he was known to be good at, another travel book, Twain hired a boat to sail down the Rhône from Châtillon to Arles. (Henry James had made and recorded his own Little Tour of France along the great French river somewhat earlier, but he used coach and steam train; Twain naturally preferred a raft.) But like a fair bit of Twain's writing now, this work, *The Innocents Adrift*, was never properly completed. It was to join the growing pile of his unpublished papers, until an edited version at last appeared posthumously.

Meantime, although he began working hard on various articles and books, expenses mounted. There were visits to the famous spas; both he and his wife were now regularly ill, and their daughter Jean suffered a serious ailment which eventually proved to be epilepsy. They moved on to Italy, and settled in the huge and well-staffed Villa Viviani at Settignano, "affording the most charming view to be found on this planet." He describes the villa in his "Whisper to the Reader," the preface he added to the most important book he wrote there, *Pudd'nhead Wilson*, where he stakes his claim to a European literary ancestry. The book was written, he gleefully explains, in a villa "three miles back of Florence, on the hills," with "the busts of Cerretani senators and other grandees of this line looking approvingly down upon me as they used to look down upon Dante, and mutely asking me to adopt them into my family, which I do with pleasure, for my remotest ancestors are but spring chickens compared with these robed and stately antiques, and it will be a great and satisfying lift for me, that six hundred years will." Despite various illnesses, the months at Settignano (September 1892 to June 1893) happily proved a productive episode for Twain. He not only wrote, in *Pudd'nhead Wilson*, what is undoubtedly his best late novel — his most profound reflection on the conditions of slavery, the pains of black life, and the complex frontier culture of the Mississippi River, which was now drifting away in time and which he now saw from a European distance — but a massive amount of other work, producing eighteen hundred pages in five months. Eighteen ninety-three was a very good writing year; it also saw the publication of this present book, which took shape after he had completed the title story (an idea for which had been in his notebook since 1879) in Florence in 1892.

But problems at home could not be neglected. Twain frequently went back and forth across the Atlantic to deal with his difficulties. Back in the States he found not just the Columbian year, when America seemed to take a great technical stride forward into the urban and industrial future, but a growing financial panic as railroads collapsed and share prices tumbled. And there were new and more terrible problems both with the publishing house and the ever delayed typesetting machine. Twain now began to see what was coming: "Get me out of business!" he cried. For a spell it seemed that the Standard Oil tycoon Henry Rogers had ridden to the rescue, but the slide could not be stopped. In 1894 bankruptcy came at last. Twain found himself more than $100,000 in debt — not least to his own wife — and set out on a world lecture tour to recoup what he could of his fortunes. Then, in 1896, when he was re-covering at a rented house in Guildford, England, he heard that his beloved daughter Susy, just about to come and join them, had died of meningitis, at the age of twenty-four. The despair her death generated seeped into his spir-it and into nearly all his subsequent works. He wrote furiously, traveled wide-ly. In Vienna he started the first of the pessimistic and tragic "Mysterious Stranger" stories. Never finished, but published posthumously in several ver-sions, these stories show the fundamental change in his vision. Life was a nightmare, a diabolic dream; the path from buoyant comedy now led onward into pessimistic darkness and the human doom: "nothing left but You, a remnant, a tradition, belated fag-end of a foolish dream, a dream so inge-niously dreamed that it seemed real all the time." *The £1,000,000 Bank-Note and Other New Stories* is interesting, among other reasons, because it belongs so exactly to the moment before the final turn into darkness, when Twain's comedy still has a great deal to do with hope, joy and success.

Like a good many of Twain's shorter tales, "The £1,000,000 Bank-Note" is unreservedly about the mystery, magic and wonder of money, and its effects on those who either come under or learn how to manipulate its spell. This story of a mining-broker's clerk from San Francisco, who goes adrift on a boat and ends up in London with only a single dollar in his pocket, is a classic Twainian tale of economic manipulation, rags to riches, ultimate and splen-did financial success. As a result of a bet between two rich brothers, our narrator — Twain, surely mischievously, grants him the splendid name of America's greatest contemporary historian; he's called Henry Adams — is given the chance of surviving in the world's financial capital for an entire month with a million-pound bank note — the only one of its kind, and too big to be transactable. What follows is a dreamy fantasy about the ambiguous space that lies between destitution and wealth. Adams is paradoxically placed, being poor and rich at the same time: "Could I afford it? No; I had nothing in the world but a million pounds" (18). But poverty isn't Twain's real theme; the story evolves into a comic drama — not so different from *The American Claimant* (1892), with which it was later reprinted — about the great encounter between American ingenuity and the stuffy rules of British society. Without spending a penny, our cunning confidence man of a narrator is soon out of his ragged clothing and scoring a dramatic social ascent. His line of credit extends endlessly — just like romantic good luck. Eating-house owners gladly feed him, court tailors willingly dress him, all on the strength of his unchangeable note. Adams is yet another of Twain's clever, independent Yankees, his extravagant speculators and American claimants, playing their boyish tricks on the world to win success.

Twain is soon milking this benign story with his burlesque humor and his sharp observation of British life and customs. The London gossip columns fill with news of the "vest-pocket million-pounder," and this gives Adams a chance of social acclaim. His newspaper fame rises "until I reached the highest altitude possible, and there I remained, taking precedence of all dukes not royal, and of all ecclesiastics except the primate of all England. But mind, this was not fame; as yet I had achieved only notoriety" (24). Almost effortlessly, fame comes our hero's way, when he at last wins the high accolade of a caricature in *Punch*. The American minister invites him to dinner, and proves a family acquaintance. Our American upstart is soon behaving like a typical Twain hero, causing chaos at the distinguished dinner table by upsetting the rules of precedence that govern British life. The comedy of democracy and rank unfolds, in the manner of *A Connecticut Yankee*: "the matter of precedence could n't be settled, and so there was no dinner. . . . The Duke of Shoreditch wanted to take precedence . . . holding that he outranked a minister who represented merely a nation and not a monarch; but I stood for my rights, and refused to yield" (30–31). And when the duke tries "to play birth and antiquity," Adams claims a prior descent from his own namesake, Adam himself (31).

To develop and resolve the story, Twain brings in two of his familiar plot devices. Adams promptly falls in love at the dinnerless dinner with the most beautiful girl in the room, Portia Langham, an English rose who just as quickly falls in love with him, his story and his financial acumen: "We talked salary; never anything but salary and love; sometimes love, sometimes salary, sometimes love and salary together" (39). He also meets his double, in the shape of an old American friend who has suffered the opposite fortune: having come to London to interest the "capitalists" in an American mine, he has failed and is facing ruin. Adams salvages his friend's fortunes by lending the support of his name and his fame, and when the mine is sold he has soon earned a million dollars on his own account. When, at the end of his trial month, he reports to the brothers on his adventures with the note, all is set for the romantic conclusion of a joyful comedy. Portia, who accompanies him, proves to be . . . well, you can guess. In a glow of comic good humor, salary and love, love and salary, win the day. In the world of "The £1,000,000 Bank-Note," speculation and capitalism, along with love and ingenuity, still work fine, in life and fiction; American smartness and benevolent British capital make a happy marriage. It would take a counter-story, "The Man That Corrupted Hadleyburg," where money and speculation are used to expose the moral hypocrisy of an entire community, to explore — in a later and far darker time — the alternative conclusion.

If "The £1,000,000 Bank-Note" euphorically captures Twain's still romantic dream of financial and emotional success, and no less his pleasant reengagement with Europe, the other pieces he put into the volume, most of them recently written for magazine publication, generally show the encounter with an age of mental change and with a shifting European world. One piece, "About All Kinds of Ships," mixing burlesque and reportage, tells the story of the ever transforming transatlantic passage as it has changed over his own lifetime, from the days of the *Quaker City* to the shuttling age of the new transatlantic steamers, vast cosmopolitan floating hotels far quieter than a city and speeding between Old World and New ("this monstrous mass of steel is driven five hundred miles through the water in twenty-four hours"). His lively account of Berlin, "The German Chicago," is based on the very appropriate observation that this imperial European city is in many respects newer than any in America. There are two interesting literary burlesques, one of an eighteenth-century medical dictionary, the other of an extraordinary trophy from the lost shelves of Southern fiction, *The Enemy Conquered*, an egregious novella which justly earns the kind of treatment Twain had already, and unkindly, dealt out to James Fenimore Cooper's "literary offences." Since, like all writers, Twain resented paying tax on his royalties, especially to a foreign monarch, we have his "Petition to the Queen of England" disputing the matter. But the other most brilliant piece after "Bank-Note" is undoubtedly "Playing Courier," a tour de force chapter of confusions that occur when the narrator offers to act as courier to a traveling party in Geneva; the result is a farce where pratfall is endlessly added to pratfall with all the zany splendor of early silent cinema.

On the decidedly serious side is "Mental Telegraphy," originally written in 1878, as he says in his forenote, to go into his earlier volume of European travels, *A Tramp Abroad*. He had removed it, thinking readers would find it a joke, although "I was in earnest," but now the nineties interest in paranormal or "psychic" phenomena, which Twain increasingly shared, had encouraged him to update and print it. What he was in earnest about were the strange coincidences that amounted to telepathy, or mental telegraphy. The piece consists mostly of anecdotal examples: cases where he and an acquaintance sit down to write to each other at the same time ("as if," he says, using a favorite metaphor, the one from which *Pudd'nhead Wilson* actually began, "you two were harnessed together like the Siamese twins, and must duplicate each other's movements"), or share common thoughts or ideas, or write virtually identical books. But some interesting preoccupations derived from Twain's experiences in the nineties intrude into, or maybe are prefigured by, this earlier text. How striking it is that the same new machine is simultaneously invented by different people in different parts of the world (this was just what had happened with the Paige machine). How odd that his relatives should be able to predict his preoccupation with inheriting an English estate (Twain, reflecting on old family connections, had dreamily imagined becoming the earl of Durham). How strange that life should resemble a waking dream. And the piece ends, perhaps inevitably, with the expectation of a new popular invention. Surely what we need next are phrenophones — machines which can shoot thoughts from brain to brain, replacing the telegraph. You could say that in the pages of this volume the Internet was born.

From this book it was onward to *Pudd'nhead Wilson*, famously a bricolage of a book, which started from the story "Those Extraordinary Twins," a farce about Siamese twins with very different characters who want to go in opposite directions, have quite different tastes (one is temperance, one a drunk) and fight on different sides in the Civil War. But then another plot began to overlap with it, the story of two babies exchanged in the cradle, one of them a slave and the other free. Twain had been reading Sir Francis Galton's important study *Finger Prints* (1892), the book which changed criminology (and detective fiction), and he aimed to bring this in too. And so "the tale kept spreading along and spreading along, and other people got to intruding themselves and taking up more and more room with their talk and their affairs." The mother story became the history of the black slave Roxana and her son Tom Driscoll, and the tale, very fortunately for us, "changed itself from a farce to a tragedy while I was going along with it," as Twain explained the novel's odd evolution in his whimsically frank afternote: "The reader already knows how the expert works; he knows now how the other kind do it." As had happened before, with *Huckleberry Finn*, during the process of composition something had deepened, something had changed. Comic farce and romance had grown anxious and generated something else, a charged sense of moral and human complexity. The resulting book is remarkable for several reasons: for its compelling and felt portrait of Roxana; for its overwhelming spirit of irony; for its engaging application of popular science and the tactics of the detective story to a plot of tragic inevitability; for its judgment on the profound contradictions of Southern and Mississippi River life in the age of slavery; but above all for its sense that all of us are in some fashion slaves — to culture, to heredity, to our genetic formation, to the eternal human flaw. As a result, there can be no doubt that *Pudd'nhead Wilson* is the one great tragic prize from these ever more troubled European years, when writing became an escape, a drudgery, a way to try and understand. But *The £1,000,000 Bank-Note* is one of the chief comic pleasures these years also yielded. It still deserves our serious interest.

THE

£1,000,000

BANK-NOTE

and Other New Stories

THE £1000000 BANK NOTE

MARK TWAIN

THE £1,OOO,OOO BANK-NOTE

"GIVE ME THE CHANGE, PLEASE."

THE

£1,000,000 BANK-NOTE

AND

OTHER NEW STORIES

BY

MARK TWAIN

NEW YORK
CHARLES L. WEBSTER & COMPANY
1893

CONTENTS

THE £1,000,000 BANK-NOTE, - - - - 9

MENTAL TELEGRAPHY, - - - - 45

A CURE FOR THE BLUES, - - - - 77

THE ENEMY CONQUERED; OR, LOVE TRIUMPHANT, 106

ABOUT ALL KINDS OF SHIPS, - - - - 154

PLAYING COURIER, - - - - - 184

THE GERMAN CHICAGO, - - - - - 210

A PETITION TO THE QUEEN OF ENGLAND, - 233

A MAJESTIC LITERARY FOSSIL, - - - 241

THE £1,000,000 BANK-NOTE.

WHEN I was twenty-seven years old, I was a mining-broker's clerk in San Francisco, and an expert in all the details of stock traffic. I was alone in the world, and had nothing to depend upon but my wits and a clean reputation; but these were setting my feet in the road to eventual fortune, and I was content with the prospect.

My time was my own after the afternoon board, Saturdays, and I was accustomed to put it in on a little sail-boat on the bay. One day I ventured too far, and was carried out to sea. Just at nightfall, when hope was about gone, I was picked up by a small brig which was bound for London. It was a long and stormy voyage, and they made me work my passage without pay, as a common sailor. When I stepped ashore in London my clothes were ragged and shabby, and I had only a dollar in my pocket. This money fed and sheltered me twenty-four hours. During the next twenty-four I went without food and shelter.

9

About ten o'clock on the following morning, seedy
and hungry, I was dragging myself along Portland
Place, when a child that was passing, towed by a
nursemaid, tossed a luscious big pear—minus one
bite — into the gutter. I stopped, of course, and
fastened my desiring eye on that muddy treasure.
My mouth watered for it, my stomach craved it, my
whole being begged for it. But every time I made
a move to get it some passing eye detected my
purpose, and of course I straightened up, then, and
looked indifferent, and pretended that I had n't
been thinking about the pear at all. This same
thing kept happening and happening, and I could
n't get the pear. I was just getting desperate enough
to brave all the shame, and to seize it, when a window behind me was raised, and a gentleman spoke
out of it, saying:

" Step in here, please."

I was admitted by a gorgeous flunkey, and shown
into a sumptuous room where a couple of elderly
gentlemen were sitting. They sent away the servant, and made me sit down. They had just finished
their breakfast, and the sight of the remains of it
almost overpowered me. I could hardly keep my
wits together in the presence of that food, but as I
was not asked to sample it, I had to bear my trouble
as best I could.

Now, something had been happening there a little before, which I did not know anything about until a good many days afterward, but I will tell you about it now. Those two old brothers had been having a pretty hot argument a couple of days before, and had ended by agreeing to decide it by a bet, which is the English way of settling everything.

You will remember that the Bank of England once issued two notes of a million pounds each, to be used for a special purpose connected with some public transaction with a foreign country. For some reason or other only one of these had been used and canceled; the other still lay in the vaults of the Bank. Well, the brothers, chatting along, happened to get to wondering what might be the fate of a perfectly honest and intelligent stranger who should be turned adrift in London without a friend, and with no money but that million-pound bank-note, and no way to account for his being in possession of it. Brother A said he would starve to death; Brother B said he would n't. Brother A said he could n't offer it at a bank or anywhere else, because he would be arrested on the spot. So they went on disputing till Brother B said he would bet twenty thousand pounds that the man would live thirty days, *any way*, on that million, and keep out of jail, too. Brother A took him up. Brother B went down to the Bank and bought that note. Just like an Englishman, you see; pluck to the backbone. Then he dictated a letter, which one of his clerks wrote out in a beautiful round hand, and then the two brothers sat at the window a whole day watching for the right man to give it to.

They saw many honest faces go by that were not intelligent enough; many that were intelligent, but not honest enough; many that were both, but the possessors were not poor enough, or, if poor enough, were not strangers. There was always a defect, until I came along; but they agreed that I filled the bill all around; so they elected me unanimously, and there I was, now, waiting to know why I was called in. They began to ask me questions about myself, and pretty soon they had my story. Finally they told me I would answer their purpose. I said I was sincerely glad, and asked what it was. Then one of them handed me an envelope, and said I would find the explanation inside. I was going to open it, but he said no; take it to my lodgings, and look it over carefully, and not be hasty or rash. I was puzzled, and wanted to discuss the matter a little further, but they did n't; so I took my leave, feeling hurt and insulted to be made the butt of what was apparently some kind of a practical joke, and yet

obliged to put up with it, not being in circumstances
to resent affronts from rich and strong folk.

I would have picked up the pear, now, and eaten
it before all the world, but it was gone; so I had
lost that by this unlucky business, and the thought
of it did not soften my feeling toward those men.
As soon as I was out of sight of that house I opened
my envelope, and saw that it contained money! My
opinion of those people changed, I can tell you! I
lost not a moment, but shoved note and money into
my vest-pocket, and broke for the nearest cheap
eating-house. Well, how I did eat! When at last
I could n't hold any more, I took out my money
and unfolded it, took one glimpse and nearly fainted.
Five millions of dollars! Why, it made my head
swim.

I must have sat there stunned and blinking at the
note as much as a minute before I came rightly to
myself again. The first thing I noticed, then, was
the landlord. His eye was on the note, and he was
petrified. He was worshiping, with all his body
and soul, but he looked as if he could n't stir hand
or foot. I took my cue in a moment, and did the
only rational thing there was to do. I reached the
note toward him, and said carelessly:

" Give me the change, please."

Then he was restored to his normal condition,

and made a thousand apologies for not being able to break the bill, and I could n't get him to touch it. He wanted to look at it, and keep on looking at it; he could n't seem to get enough of it to quench the thirst of his eye, but he shrank from touching it as if it had been something too sacred for poor common clay to handle. I said:

"I am sorry if it is an inconvenience, but I must insist. Please change it; I have n't anything else."

But he said that was n't any matter; he was quite willing to let the trifle stand over till another time. I said I might not be in his neighborhood again for a good while; but he said it was of no consequence, he could wait, and, moreover, I could have anything I wanted, any time I chose, and let the account run as long as I pleased. He said he hoped he was n't afraid to trust as rich a gentleman as I was, merely because I was of a merry disposition, and chose to play larks on the public in the matter of dress. By this time another customer was entering, and the landlord hinted to me to put the monster out of sight; then he bowed me all the way to the door, and I started straight for that house and those brothers, to correct the mistake which had been made before the police should hunt me up, and help me do it. I was pretty nervous, in fact pretty badly frightened, though, of course, I was no way in fault;

but I knew men well enough to know that when
they find they 've given a tramp a million-pound
bill when they thought it was a one-pounder, they
are in a frantic rage against *him* instead of quarrel-
ing with their own near-sightedness, as they ought.
As I approached the house my excitement began
to abate, for all was quiet there, which made me
feel pretty sure the blunder was not discovered yet.
I rang. The same servant appeared. I asked for
those gentlemen.

"They are gone." This in the lofty, cold way of
that fellow's tribe.

"Gone ? Gone where ?"

"On a journey."

"But whereabouts ?"

"To the Continent, I think."

"The Continent ?"

"Yes, sir."

"Which way—by what route ?"

"I can't say, sir."

"When will they be back ?"

"In a month, they said."

"A month! Oh, this is awful! Give me *some*
sort of idea of how to get a word to them. It 's of
the last importance."

"I can't, indeed. I 've no idea where they 've
gone, sir."

"Then I must see some member of the family."

"Family 's away too; been abroad months—in Egypt and India, I think."

"Man, there 's been an immense mistake made. They 'll be back before night. Will you tell them I 've been here, and that I will keep coming till it 's all made right, and they need n't be afraid?"

"I 'll tell them, if they come back, but I am not expecting them. They said you would be here in an hour to make inquiries, but I must tell you it 's all right, they 'll be here on time and expect you."

So I had to give it up and go away. What a riddle it all was! I was like to lose my mind. They would be here " on time." What could that mean? Oh, the letter would explain, maybe. I had forgotten the letter; I got it out and read it. This is what it said:

You are an intelligent and honest man, as one may see by your face. We conceive you to be poor and a stranger. Inclosed you will find a sum of money. It is lent to you for thirty days, without interest. Report at this house at the end of that time. I have a bet on you. If I win it you shall have any situation that is in my gift—any, that is, that you shall be able to prove yourself familiar with and competent to fill.

No signature, no address, no date.

Well, here was a coil to be in! You are posted on what had preceded all this, but I was not. It

was just a deep, dark puzzle to me. I had n't the
least idea what the game was, nor whether harm
was meant me or a kindness. I went into a park,
and sat down to try to think it out, and to consider
what I had best do.

At the end of an hour, my reasonings had crystal-
lized into this verdict.

Maybe those men mean me well, maybe they
mean me ill; no way to decide that — let it go.
They 've got a game, or a scheme, or an experiment, of some kind on hand; no way to determine
what it is—let it go. There 's a bet on me; no way
to find out what it is—let it go. That disposes of
the indeterminable quantities; the remainder of the
matter is tangible, solid, and may be classed and
labeled with certainty. If I ask the Bank of England to place this bill to the credit of the man it be-
longs to, they 'll do it, for they know him, although
I don't; but they will ask me how I came in possession of it, and if I tell the truth, they 'll put me in
the asylum, naturally, and a lie will land me in jail.
The same result would follow if I tried to bank the
bill anywhere or to borrow money on it. I have
got to carry this immense burden around until those
men come back, whether I want to or not. It is
useless to me, as useless as a handful of ashes, and
yet I must take care of it, and watch over it, while

I beg my living.   I could n't *give* it away, if I should
try, for neither honest citizen nor highwayman would
accept it or meddle with it for anything.   Those
brothers are safe.   Even if I lose their bill, or burn
it, they are still safe, because they can stop payment,
and the Bank will make them whole; but meantime,
I 've got to do a month's suffering without wages or
profit—unless I help win that bet, whatever it may
be, and get that situation that I am promised.   I
should like to get that; men of their sort have situations in their gift that are worth having.

I got to thinking a good deal about that situation.
My hopes began to rise high.   Without doubt the
salary would be large.   It would begin in a month;
after that I should be all right.   Pretty soon I was
feeling first rate.   By this time I was tramping the
streets again.   The sight of a tailor-shop gave me
a sharp longing to shed my rags, and to clothe myself decently once more.   Could I afford it?   No; I
had nothing in the world but a million pounds.   So
I forced myself to go on by.   But soon I was drifting back again.   The temptation persecuted me
cruelly.   I must have passed that shop back and
forth six times during that manful struggle.   At last
I gave in; I had to.   I asked if they had a misfit
suit that had been thrown on their hands.   The fellow I spoke to nodded his head toward another fel-

low, and gave me no answer. I went to the indicated fellow, and he indicated another fellow with *his* head, and no words. I went to him, and he said:

"'Tend to you presently."

I waited till he was done with what he was at, then he took me into a back room, and overhauled a pile of rejected suits, and selected the rattiest one for me. I put it on. It did n't fit, and was n't in any way attractive, but it was new, and I was anxious to have it; so I did n't find any fault, but said with some diffidence:

"It would be an accommodation to me if you could wait some days for the money. I have n't any small change about me."

The fellow worked up a most sarcastic expression of countenance, and said:

"Oh, you have n't? Well, of course, I did n't expect it. I 'd only expect gentlemen like you to carry large change."

I was nettled, and said:

"My friend, you should n't judge a stranger always by the clothes he wears. I am quite able to pay for this suit; I simply did n't wish to put you to the trouble of changing a large note."

He modified his style a little at that, and said, though still with something of an air:

"I did n't mean any particular harm, but as long

as rebukes are going, I might say it was n't quite your affair to jump to the conclusion that we could n't change any note that you might happen to be carrying around.   On the contrary, we *can*."

I handed the note to him, and said:

" Oh, very well; I apologize."

He received it with a smile, one of those large smiles which goes all around over, and has folds in it, and wrinkles, and spirals, and looks like the place where you have thrown a brick in a pond; and then in the act of his taking a glimpse of the bill this smile froze solid, and turned yellow, and looked like those wavy, wormy spreads of lava which you find hardened on little levels on the side of Vesuvius.   I never before saw a smile caught like that, and perpetuated.   The man stood there holding the bill, and looking like that, and the pro-prietor hustled up to see what was the matter, and said briskly:

"Well, what 's up ? what 's the trouble ? what 's wanting ? "

I said: "There is n't any trouble.   I 'm waiting for my change."

" Come, come; get him his change, Tod; get him his change."

Tod retorted: " Get him his change!   It 's easy to say, sir; but look at the bill yourself."

The proprietor took a look, gave a low, eloquent whistle, then made a dive for the pile of rejected clothing, and began to snatch it this way and that, talking all the time excitedly, and as if to himself:

"Sell an eccentric millionaire such an unspeakable suit as that! Tod's a fool—a born fool. Always doing something like this. Drives every millionaire away from this place, because he can't tell a millionaire from a tramp, and never could. Ah, here's the thing I'm after. Please get those things off, sir, and throw them in the fire. Do me the favor to put on this shirt and this suit; it's just the thing, the very thing—plain, rich, modest, and just ducally nobby; made to order for a foreign prince—you may know him, sir, his Serene Highness the Hospodar of Halifax; had to leave it with us and take a mourning-suit because his mother was going to die—which she did n't. But that's all right; we can't always have things the way we—that is, the way they—there! trousers all right, they fit you to a charm, sir; now the waistcoat; aha, right again! now the coat —lord! look at that, now! Perfect—the whole thing! I never saw such a triumph in all my experience."

I expressed my satisfaction.

"Quite right, sir, quite right; it'll do for a make-shift, I'm bound to say. But wait till you see what we'll get up for you on your own measure. Come,

Tod, book and pen; get at it.   Length of leg, 32 ”
—and so on.   Before I could get in a word he had
measured me, and was giving orders for dress-suits,
morning suits, shirts, and all sorts of things.   When
I got a chance I said:

" But, my dear sir, I *can't* give these orders, unless
you can wait indefinitely, or change the bill."

" Indefinitely!   It 's a weak word, sir, a weak
word.   Eternally—*that's* the word, sir.   Tod, rush
these things through, and send them to the gentleman's address without any waste of time.   Let the
minor customers wait.   Set down the gentleman's
address and—"

" I'm changing my quarters.   I will drop in and
leave the new address."

" Quite right, sir, quite right.   One moment—let
me show you out, sir.   There—good day, sir, good
day."

Well, don't you see what was bound to happen ?
I drifted naturally into buying whatever I wanted,
and asking for change.   Within a week I was sump-
tuously equipped with all needful comforts and luxuries, and was housed in an expensive private hotel
in Hanover Square.   I took my dinners there, but
for breakfast I stuck by Harris's humble feeding-
house, where I had got my first meal on my million-
pound bill.   I was the making of Harris.   The fact

had gone all abroad that the foreign crank who carried million-pound bills in his vest-pocket was the
patron saint of the place. That was enough. From
being a poor, struggling, little hand-to-mouth enterprise, it had become celebrated, and overcrowded
with customers. Harris was so grateful that he
forced loans upon me, and would not be denied;
and so, pauper as I was, I had money to spend, and
was living like the rich and the great. I judged that
there was going to be a crash by and by, but I was
in, now, and must swim across or drown. You see
there was just that element of impending disaster to
give a serious side, a sober side, yes, a tragic side,
to a state of things which would otherwise have
been purely ridiculous. In the night, in the dark,
the tragedy part was always to the front, and always
warning, always threatening; and so I moaned and
tossed, and sleep was hard to find. But in the cheerful daylight the tragedy element faded out and disappeared, and I walked on air, and was happy to
giddiness, to intoxication, you may say.

And it was natural; for I had become one of the
notorieties of the metropolis of the world, and it
turned my head, not just a little, but a good deal.
You could not take up a newspaper, English,
Scotch, or Irish, without finding in it one or more
references to the "vest-pocket million-pounder"

and his latest doings and sayings. At first, in these mentions, I was at the bottom of the personal-gossip column; next, I was listed above the knights, next above the baronets, next above the barons, and so on, and so on, climbing steadily, as my notoriety augmented, until I reached the highest altitude possible, and there I remained, taking precedence of all dukes not royal, and of all ecclesiastics except the primate of all England. But mind, this was not fame; as yet I had achieved only notoriety. Then came the climaxing stroke—the accolade, so to speak —which in a single instance transmuted the perishable dross of notoriety into the enduring gold of fame: "Punch" caricatured me! Yes, I was a made man, now; my place was established. I might be joked about still, but reverently, not hilariously, not rudely; I could be smiled at, but not laughed at. The time for that had gone by. "Punch" pictured me all a-flutter with rags, dickering with a beef-eater for the Tower of London. Well, you can imagine how it was with a young fellow who had never been taken notice of before, and now all of a sudden could n't say a thing that was n't taken up and repeated everywhere; could n't stir abroad without constantly overhearing the remark flying from lip to lip, "There he goes; that's him!" could n't take his breakfast without a crowd to look on; could n't ap-

pear in an opera-box without concentrating there
the fire of a thousand lorgnettes. Why, I just swam
in glory all day long—that is the amount of it.

You know, I even kept my old suit of rags, and
every now and then appeared in them, so as to have
the old pleasure of buying trifles, and being insulted,
and then shooting the scoffer dead with the million-
pound bill. But I could n't keep that up. The
illustrated papers made the outfit so familiar that
when I went out in it I was at once recognized and
followed by a crowd, and if I attempted a purchase
the man would offer me his whole shop on credit
before I could pull my note on him.

About the tenth day of my fame I went to fulfill
my duty to my flag by paying my respects to the
American minister. He received me with the enthusiasm proper in my case, upbraided me for being
so tardy in my duty, and said that there was only
one way to get his forgiveness, and that was to take
the seat at his dinner-party that night made vacant
by the illness of one of his guests. I said I would,
and we got to talking. It turned out that he and
my father had been schoolmates in boyhood, Yale
students together later, and always warm friends up
to my father's death. So then he required me to
put in at his house all the odd time I might have to
spare, and I was very willing, of course.

In fact I was more than willing; I was glad. When
the crash should come, he might somehow be able
to save me from total destruction; I did n't know
how, but he might think of a way, maybe. I could
n't venture to unbosom myself to him at this late
date, a thing which I would have been quick to do
in the beginning of this awful career of mine in London. No, I could n't venture it now; I was in too
deep; that is, too deep for me to be risking revela-
tions to so new a friend, though not clear beyond
my depth, as *I* looked at it. Because, you see, with
all my borrowing, I was carefully keeping within
my means—I mean within my salary. Of course I
could n't *know* what my salary was going to be, but
I had a good enough basis for an estimate in the
fact that, if I won the bet, I was to have *choice* of
any situation in that rich old gentleman's gift provided I was competent—and I should certainly prove
competent; I had n't any doubt about that. And
as to the bet, I was n't worrying about that; I had
always been lucky. Now my estimate of the salary
was six hundred to a thousand a year; say, six hundred for the first year, and so on up year by year,
till I struck the upper figure by proved merit. At
present I was only in debt for my first year's salary.
Everybody had been trying to lend me money, but
I had fought off the most of them on one pretext or

another; so this indebtedness represented only £300 borrowed money, the other £300 represented my keep and my purchases. I believed my second year's salary would carry me through the rest of the month if I went on being cautious and economical, and I intended to look sharply out for that. My month ended, my employer back from his journey, I should be all right once more, for I should at once divide the two years' salary among my creditors by assignment, and get right down to my work.

It was a lovely dinner-party of fourteen. The Duke and Duchess of Shoreditch, and their daughter the Lady Anne - Grace - Eleanor - Celeste - and - so-forth-and-so-forth-de-Bohun, the Earl and Countess of Newgate, Viscount Cheapside, Lord and Lady Blatherskite, some untitled people of both sexes, the minister and his wife and daughter, and his daughter's visiting friend, an English girl of twenty-two, named Portia Langham, whom I fell in love with in two minutes, and she with me—I could see it without glasses. There was still another guest, an American—but I am a little ahead of my story. While the people were still in the drawing-room, whetting up for dinner, and coldly inspecting the late comers, the servant announced:

" Mr. Lloyd Hastings."

The moment the usual civilities were over, Hastings caught sight of me, and came straight with cordially outstretched hand ; then stopped short when about to shake, and said with an embarrassed look:

" I beg your pardon, sir, I thought I knew you."

" Why, you do know me, old fellow."

" No ! Are *you* the — the — "

" Vest-pocket monster ? I am, indeed. Don't be afraid to call me by my nickname ; I 'm used to it."

" Well, well, well, this is a surprise. Once or twice I 've seen your own name coupled with the nickname, but it never occurred to me that *you* could be the Henry Adams referred to. Why, it is n't six months since you were clerking away for Blake Hopkins in Frisco on a salary, and sitting up nights on an extra allowance, helping me arrange and verify the Gould and Curry Extension papers and statistics. The idea of your being in London, and a vast millionaire, and a colossal celebrity ! Why, it 's the Arabian Nights come again. Man, I can't take it in at all; can't realize it; give me time to settle the whirl in my head."

" The fact is, Lloyd, you are no worse off than I am. I can't realize it myself."

" Dear me, it *is* stunning, now is n't it ? Why, it 's just three months to-day since we went to the Miners' restaurant—"

" No; the What Cheer."

" Right, it *was* the What Cheer; went there at
two in the morning, and had a chop and coffee after
a hard six hours' grind over those Extension papers,
and I tried to persuade you to come to London with
me, and offered to get leave of absence for you and
pay all your expenses, and give you something over
if I succeeded in making the sale; and you would
not listen to me, said I would n't succeed, and you
could n't afford to lose the run of business and be
no end of time getting the hang of things again
when you got back home.   And yet here you are.
How odd it all is!   How did you happen to come,
and whatever *did* give you this incredible start?"

" Oh, just an accident.   It 's a long story—a
romance, a body may say.   I 'll tell you all about
it, but not now."

" When?"

" The end of this month."

" That 's more than a fortnight yet.   It 's too much
of a strain on a person's curiosity.   Make it a week."

" I can't.   You 'll know why, by and by.   But
how 's the trade getting along?"

His cheerfulness vanished like a breath, and he
said with a sigh:

" You were a true prophet, Hal, a true prophet.   I
wish I had n't come.   I don't want to talk about it."

"But you must. You must come and stop with me to-night, when we leave here, and tell me all about it."

"Oh, may I? Are you in earnest?" and the water showed in his eyes.

"Yes; I want to hear the whole story, every word."

"I'm so grateful! Just to find a human interest once more, in some voice and in some eye, in me and affairs of mine, after what I've been through here—lord! I could go down on my knees for it!"

He gripped my hand hard, and braced up, and was all right and lively after that for the dinner— which did n't come off. No; the usual thing happened, the thing that is always happening under that vicious and aggravating English system—the matter of precedence could n't be settled, and so there was no dinner. Englishmen always eat dinner before they go out to dinner, because *they* know the risks they are running; but nobody ever warns the stranger, and so he walks placidly into the trap. Of course nobody was hurt this time, because we had all been to dinner, none of us being novices except Hastings, and he having been informed by the minister at the time that he invited him that in deference to the English custom he had not provided any dinner. Everybody took a lady and processioned down to the dining-room, because it is usual to go through

the motions; but there the dispute began. The
Duke of Shoreditch wanted to take precedence, and
sit at the head of the table, holding that he outranked a minister who represented merely a nation and
not a monarch; but I stood for my rights, and refused to yield. In the gossip column I ranked all
dukes not royal, and said so, and claimed precedence of this one. It could n't be settled, of
course, struggle as we might and did, he finally (and
injudiciously) trying to play birth and antiquity,
and I " seeing " his Conqueror and " raising " him
with Adam, whose direct posterity I was, as shown
by my name, while *he* was of a collateral branch, as
shown by *his*, and by his recent Norman origin;
so we all processioned back to the drawing-room
again and had a perpendicular lunch—plate of sar-
dines and a strawberry, and you group yourself and
stand up and eat it. Here the religion of precedence
is not so strenuous; the two persons of highest rank
chuck up a shilling, the one that wins has first go at
his strawberry, and the loser gets the shilling. The
next two chuck up, then the next two, and so on.
After refreshment, tables were brought, and we all
played cribbage, sixpence a game. The English
never play any game for amusement. If they can't
make something or lose something,—they don't
care which,—they won't play.

We had a lovely time; certainly two of us had,
Miss Langham and I. I was so bewitched with her
that I could n't count my hands if they went above
a double sequence; and when I struck home I never
discovered it, and started up the outside row again,
and would have lost the game every time, only the
girl did the same, she being in just my condition,
you see; and consequently neither of us ever got
out, or cared to wonder why we did n't; we only
just knew we were happy, and did n't wish to know
anything else, and did n't want to be interrupted.
And I *told* her—I did indeed—told her I loved her;
and she—well, she blushed till her hair turned red,
but she liked it ; she *said* she did. Oh, there was
never such an evening ! Every time I pegged I
put on a postscript; every time she pegged she acknowledged receipt of it, counting the hands the
same. Why, I could n't even say " Two for his
heels " without adding, " *My*, how sweet you do
look ! " and she would say, " Fifteen two, fifteen
four, fifteen six, and a pair are eight, and eight are
sixteen—*do* you think so ? "—peeping out aslant
from under her lashes, you know, so sweet and cunning. Oh, it was just *too*-too !

Well, I was perfectly honest and square with her;
told her I had n't a cent in the world but just the
million-pound note she 'd heard so much talk about,

and *it* did n't belong to me; and that started her curiosity, and then I talked low, and told her the whole history right from the start, and it nearly killed her, laughing. What in the nation she could find to laugh about, *I* could n't see, but there it was; every half minute some new detail would fetch her, and I would have to stop as much as a minute and a half to give her a chance to settle down again. Why, she laughed herself lame, she did indeed; I never saw anything like it. I mean I never saw a painful story—a story of a person's troubles and worries and fears—produce just *that* kind of effect before. So I loved her all the more, seeing she could be so cheerful when there was n't anything to be cheerful about; for I might soon need that kind of wife, you know, the way things looked. Of course I told her we should have to wait a couple of years, till I could catch up on my salary; but she did n't mind that, only she hoped I would be as careful as possible in the matter of expenses, and not let them run the least risk of trenching on our third year's pay. Then she began to get a little worried, and wondered if we were making any mistake, and starting the salary on a higher figure for the first year than I would get. This was good sense, and it made me feel a little less confident than I had been feeling before; but it

gave me a good business idea, and I brought it
frankly out.

"Portia, dear, would you mind going with me
that day, when I confront those old gentlemen?"

She shrank a little, but said:

"N-o; if my being with you would help hearten
you. But—would it be quite proper, do you think?"

"No, I don't know that it would; in fact I'm
afraid it would n't: but you see, there 's so *much* dependent upon it that—"

"Then I 'll go anyway, proper or improper," she
said, with a beautiful and generous enthusiasm.
"Oh, I shall be so happy to think I 'm helping."

"Helping, dear? Why, you 'll be doing it all.
You 're so beautiful and so lovely and so winning,
that with you there I can pile our salary up till I
break those good old fellows, and they 'll never
have the heart to struggle."

Sho! you should have seen the rich blood mount,
and her happy eyes shine!

"You wicked flatterer! There is n't a word of
truth in what you say, but still I 'll go with you.
Maybe it will teach you not to expect other people
to look with your eyes."

Were my doubts dissipated? Was my confidence
restored? You may judge by this fact: privately I
raised my salary to twelve hundred the first year on

the spot.   But I did n't tell her; I saved it for a surprise.

All the way home I was in the clouds, Hastings talking, I not hearing a word.   When he and I entered
my parlor, he brought me to myself with his fervent
appreciations of my manifold comforts and luxuries.

" Let me just stand here a little and look my fill !
Dear me, it 's a palace; it 's just a palace! And in it
everything a body *could* desire, including cozy coal
fire and supper standing ready.   Henry, it does n't
merely make me realize how rich you are; it makes
me realize, to the bone, to the marrow, how poor I
am—how poor I am, and how miserable, how de-
feated, routed, annihilated ! "

Plague take it ! this language gave me the cold
shudders.   It scared me broad awake, and made me
comprehend that I was standing on a half-inch
crust, with a crater underneath.   *I* did n't know I
had been dreaming—that is, I had n't been allowing myself to know it for a while back; but *now*—
oh, dear ! Deep in debt, not a cent in the world, a
lovely girl's happiness or woe in my hands, and
nothing in front of me but a salary which might
never—oh, *would* never—materialize ! Oh, oh, oh,
I am ruined past hope; nothing can save me !

"Henry, the mere unconsidered drippings of your
daily income would—"

"Oh, my daily income! Here, down with this hot Scotch, and cheer up your soul. Here 's with you! Or, no—you 're hungry; sit down and—"

"Not a bite for me; I 'm past it. I can't eat, these days; but I 'll drink with you till I drop. Come!"

"Barrel for barrel, I 'm with you! Ready? Here we go! Now, then, Lloyd, unreel your story while I brew."

"Unreel it? What, again?"

"Again? What do you mean by that?"

"Why, I mean do you want to hear it *over* again?"

"Do I want to hear it *over* again? This *is* a puzzler. Wait; don't take any more of that liquid. You don't need it."

"Look here, Henry, you alarm me. Did n't I tell you the whole story on the way here?"

"You?"

"Yes, I."

"I 'll be hanged if I heard a word of it."

"Henry, this is a serious thing. It troubles me. What did you take up yonder at the minister's?"

Then it all flashed on me, and I owned up, like a man.

"I took the dearest girl in this world—prisoner!"

So then he came with a rush, and we shook, and

shook, and shook till our hands ached; and he did
n't blame me for not having heard a word of a story
which had lasted while we walked three miles. He
just sat down then, like the patient, good fellow he
was, and told it all over again. Synopsized, it
amounted to this: He had come to England with
what he thought was a grand opportunity; he had
an " option " to sell the Gould and Curry Extension
for the " locators " of it, and keep all he could get
over a million dollars. He had worked hard, had
pulled every wire he knew of, had left no honest ex-
pedient untried, had spent nearly all the money he
had in the world, had not been able to get a solitary
capitalist to listen to him, and his option would run
out at the end of the month. In a word, he was
ruined. Then he jumped up and cried out:

"Henry, you can save me! You can save me, and
you 're the only man in the universe that can. Will
you do it? *Won't* you do it?"

"Tell me how. Speak out, my boy."

"Give me a million and my passage home for my
'option'! Don't, *don't* refuse!"

I was in a kind of agony. I was right on the
point of coming out with the words, "Lloyd, I 'm a
pauper myself — absolutely penniless, and in *debt!*"
But a white-hot idea came flaming through my head,
and I gripped my jaws together, and calmed myself

down till I was as cold as a capitalist. Then I said, in a commercial and self-possessed way :

"I will save you, Lloyd —"

"Then I 'm already saved ! God be merciful to you forever ! If ever I—"

"Let me finish, Lloyd. I will save you, but not in that way; for that would not be fair to you, after your hard work, and the risks you 've run. I don't need to buy mines; I can keep my capital moving, in a commercial centre like London without that; it 's what I 'm at, all the time; but here is what I 'll do. I know all about that mine, of course; I know its immense value, and can swear to it if anybody wishes it. You shall sell out inside of the fortnight for three millions cash, using my name freely, and we 'll divide, share and share alike."

Do you know, he would have danced the furniture to kindling-wood in his insane joy, and broken everything on the place, if I had n't tripped him up and tied him.

Then he lay there, perfectly happy, saying :

"I may use your name ! Your name — think of it ! Man, they 'll flock in droves, these rich Londoners; they 'll *fight* for that stock ! I 'm a made man, I 'm a made man forever, and I 'll never forget you as long as I live !"

In less than twenty-four hours London was abuzz !

I had n't anything to do, day after day, but sit at home, and say to all comers :

"Yes; I told him to refer to me. I know the man, and I know the mine. His character is above reproach, and the mine is worth far more than he asks for it."

Meantime I spent all my evenings at the minister's with Portia. I did 't say a word to her about the mine; I saved it for a surprise. We talked salary; never anything but salary and love; sometimes love, sometimes salary, sometimes love and salary together. And my! the interest the minister's wife and daughter took in our little affair, and the endless ingenuities they invented to save us from interruption, and to keep the minister in the dark and unsuspicious—well, it was just lovely of them!

When the month was up, at last, I had a million dollars to my credit in the London and County Bank, and Hastings was fixed in the same way. Dressed at my level best, I drove by the house in Portland Place, judged by the look of things that my birds were home again, went on toward the minister's and got my precious, and we started back, talking salary with all our might. She was so excited and anxious that it made her just intolerably beautiful. I said :

"Dearie, the way you 're looking it 's a crime to

strike for a salary a single penny under three thousand a year."

"Henry, Henry, you 'll ruin us !"

"Don't you be afraid. Just keep up those looks, and trust to me. It 'll all come out right."

So as it turned out, I had to keep bolstering up *her* courage all the way. She kept pleading with me, and saying :

"Oh, please remember that if we ask for too much we may get no salary at all; and then what will become of us, with no way in the world to earn our living ?"

We were ushered in by that same servant, and there they were, the two old gentlemen. Of course they were surprised to see that wonderful creature with me, but I said :

"It 's all right, gentlemen; she is my future stay and helpmate."

And I introduced them to her, and called them by name. It did n't surprise them; they knew I would know enough to consult the directory. They seated us, and were very polite to me, and very solicitous to relieve her from embarrassment, and put her as much at her ease as they could. Then I said :

"Gentlemen, I am ready to report."

"We are glad to hear it," said *my* man, "for now

we can decide the bet which my brother Abel and I made. If you have won for me, you shall have any situation in my gift. Have you the million-pound note?"

"Here it is, sir," and I handed it to him.

"I 've won!" he shouted, and slapped Abel on the back. "*Now* what do you say, brother?"

"I say he *did* survive, and I 've lost twenty thousand pounds. I never would have believed it."

"I 've a further report to make," I said, "and a pretty long one. I want you to let me come soon, and detail my whole month's history; and I promise you it 's worth hearing. Meantime, take a look at that."

"What, man! Certificate of deposit for £200,000? Is it yours?"

"Mine. I earned it by thirty days' judicious use of that little loan you let me have. And the only use I made of it was to buy trifles and offer the bill in change."

"Come, this is astonishing! It 's incredible, man!"

"Never mind, I 'll prove it. Don't take my word unsupported."

But now Portia's turn was come to be surprised. Her eyes were spread wide, and she said:

"Henry, is that really your money? Have you been fibbing to me?"

" I have indeed, dearie. But you 'll forgive me, *I* know."

She put up an arch pout, and said :

" Don't you be so sure. You are a naughty thing to deceive me so ! "

" Oh, you 'll get over it, sweetheart, you 'll get over it; it was only fun, you know. Come, let 's be going."

" But wait, wait ! The situation, you know. I want to give you the situation," said my man.

" Well," I said, " I 'm just as grateful as I can be, but really I don't want one."

" But you can have the very choicest one in my gift."

" Thanks again, with all my heart; but I don't even want *that* one."

" Henry, I 'm ashamed of you. You don't half thank the good gentleman. May I do it for you ? "

" Indeed you shall, dear, if you can improve it. Let us see you try."

She walked to my man, got up in his lap, put her arm round his neck, and kissed him right on the mouth. Then the two old gentlemen shouted with laughter, but I was dumfounded, just petrified, as you may say. Portia said :

" Papa, he has said you have n't a situation in your gift that he 'd take; and I feel just as hurt as —"

" My darling! is that your papa ?"

" Yes; he 's my steppapa, and the dearest one that ever was. You understand now, don't you, why I was able to laugh when you told me at the minister's, not knowing my relationships, what trouble and worry papa's and Uncle Abel's scheme was giving you ?"

Of course I spoke right up, now, without any fooling, and went straight to the point.

" Oh, my dearest dear sir, I want to take back what I said. You *have* got a situation open that I want."

" Name it."

" Son-in-law."

" Well, well, well ! But you know, if you have n't ever served in that capacity, you of course can't furnish recommendations of a sort to satisfy the conditions of the contract, and so—"

" Try me — oh, do, I beg of you ! Only just try me thirty or forty years, and if—"

" Oh, well, all right; it 's but a little thing to ask. take her along."

Happy, we too ? There are not words enough in the unabridged to describe it. And when London got the whole history, a day or two later, of my month's adventures with that bank-note, and how they ended, did London talk, and have a good time ? Yes.

My Portia's papa took that friendly and hospitable bill back to the Bank of England and cashed it; then the Bank canceled it and made him a present of it, and he gave it to us at our wedding, and it has always hung in its frame in the sacredest place in our home, ever since. For it gave me my Portia. But for it I could not have remained in London, would not have appeared at the minister's, never should have met her. And so I always say, " Yes, it 's a million-pounder, as you see; but it never made but one purchase in its life, and *then* got the article for only about a tenth part of its value."

MENTAL TELEGRAPHY.

A MANUSCRIPT WITH A HISTORY.

NOTE TO THE EDITOR.—By glancing over the enclosed bundle of rusty old manuscript, you will perceive that I once made a great discovery : the discovery that certain sorts of things which, from the beginning of the world, had always been regarded as merely "curious coincidences"—that is to say, accidents - were no more accidental than is the sending and receiving of a telegram an accident. I made this discovery sixteen or seventeen years ago, and gave it a name— "Mental Telegraphy." It is the same thing around the outer edges of which the Psychical Society of England began to grope (and play with) four or five years ago, and which they named "Telepathy." Within the last two or three years they have penetrated toward the heart of the matter, however, and have found out that mind can act upon mind in a quite detailed and elaborate way over vast stretches of land and water. And they have succeeded in doing, by their great credit and influence, what I could never have done—they have convinced the world that mental telegraphy is not a jest, but a fact, and that it is a thing not rare, but exceedingly common. They have done our age a service—and a very great service, I think.

In this old manuscript you will find mention of an extraordinary experience of mine in the mental telegraphic line, of date about the year 1874 or 1875—the one concerning the Great Bonanza book. It was this experience that called my attention to the matter under consideration. I began to keep a record, after that, of such experiences of mine as seemed explicable by the theory that minds telegraph thoughts to each other. In 1878 I went to Germany and began to write

45

the book called *A Tramp Abroad*. The bulk of this old batch of manuscript was written at that time and for that book. But I removed it when I came to revise the volume for the press ; for I feared that the public would treat the thing as a joke and throw it aside, whereas I was in earnest.

At home, eight or ten years ago, I tried to creep in under shelter of an authority grave enough to protect the article from ridicule—the *North American Review*. But Mr. Metcalf was too wary for me. He said that to treat these mere "coincidences" seriously was a thing which the *Review* couldn't dare to do ; that I must put either my name or my *nom de plume* to the article, and thus save the *Review* from harm. But I could n't consent to that; it would be the surest possible way to defeat my desire that the public should receive the thing seriously, and be willing to stop and give it some fair degree of attention. So I pigeonholed the MS., because I could not get it published anonymously.

Now see how the world has moved since then. These small experiences of mine, which were too formidable at that time for admission to a grave magazine—if the magazine must allow them to appear as something above and beyond "accidents" and "coincidences"—are trifling and commonplace now, since the flood of light recently cast upon mental telegraphy by the intelligent labors of the Psychical Society. But I think they are worth publishing, just to show what harmless and ordinary matters were considered dangerous and incredible eight or ten years ago.

As I have said, the bulk of this old manuscript was written in 1878 ; a later part was written from time to time two, three, and four years afterward. The "Postscript" I add to-day.

MAY, '78.—Another of those apparently trifling things has happened to me which puzzle and perplex all men every now and then, keep them thinking an hour or two, and leave their minds barren of explanation or solution at last. Here it is—and it looks inconsequential enough, I am obliged to say. A few days ago I said: "It must be that Frank Millet does n't know we are in Germany, or he would have written long before this. I have been on the point of dropping him a line at least a dozen times during the past six weeks, but I always decided to wait a day or two longer, and see if we should n't hear from him. But now I *will* write." And so I did. I directed the letter to Paris, and thought, "*Now* we shall hear from him before this letter is fifty miles from Heidelberg—it always happens so."

True enough; but *why* should it? That is the puzzling part of it. We are always talking about letters "crossing" each other, for that is one of the very commonest accidents of this life. We call it "accident," but perhaps we misname it. We have the instinct a dozen times a year that the letter we are writing is going to "cross" the other person's letter; and if the reader will rack his memory a little he will recall the fact that this presentiment had strength enough to it to make him cut his letter down to a decided briefness, because it would be a waste of time to write a letter which was going to "cross," and hence be a useless letter. I think that in my experience this instinct has generally come

to me in cases where I had put off my letter a good
while in the hope that the other person would
write.

Yes, as I was saying, I had waited five or six
weeks; then I wrote but three lines, because I felt
and seemed to know that a letter from Millet would
cross mine. And so it did. He wrote the same day that
I wrote. The letters crossed each other. His letter
went to Berlin, care of the American minister, who
sent it to me. In this letter Millet said he had been
trying for six weeks to stumble upon somebody who
knew my German address, and at last the idea had
occurred to him that a letter sent to the care of the
embassy at Berlin might possibly find me.

Maybe it was an "accident" that he finally determined to write me at the same moment that I
finally determined to write him, but I think not.

With me the most irritating thing has been to
wait a tedious time in a purely business matter,
hoping that the other party will do the writing, and
then sit down and do it myself, perfectly satisfied
that that other man is sitting down at the same
moment to write a letter which will "cross" mine.
And yet one must go on writing, just the same; because if you get up from your table and postpone,
that other man will do the same thing, exactly as if
you two were harnessed together like the Siamese

twins, and must duplicate each other's movements.

Several months before I left home a New York firm did some work about the house for me, and did not make a success of it, as it seemed to me. When the bill came, I wrote and said I wanted the work perfected before I paid. They replied that they were very busy, but that as soon as they could spare the proper man the thing should be done. I waited more than two months, enduring as patiently as possible the companionship of bells which would fire away of their own accord sometimes when nobody was touching them, and at other times would n't ring though you struck the button with a sledge-hammer. Many a time I got ready to write and then postponed it; but at last I sat down one evening and poured out my grief to the extent of a page or so, and then cut my letter suddenly short, because a strong instinct told me that the firm had begun to move in the matter. When I came down to breakfast next morning the postman had not yet taken my letter away, but the electrical man had been there, done his work, and was gone again ! He had received his orders the previous evening from his employers, and had come up by the night train.

If that was an "accident," it took about three months to get it up in good shape.

One evening last summer I arrived in Washington, registered at the Arlington Hotel, and went to my room. I read and smoked until ten o'clock; then, finding I was not yet sleepy, I thought I would take a breath of fresh air. So I went forth in the rain, and tramped through one street after another in an aimless and enjoyable way. I knew that Mr. O——, a friend of mine, was in town, and I wished I might run across him; but I did not propose to hunt for him at midnight, especially as I did not know where he was stopping. Toward twelve o'clock the streets had become so deserted that I felt lonesome; so I stepped into a cigar shop far up the Avenue, and remained there fifteen minutes, listening to some bummers discussing national politics. Suddenly the spirit of prophecy came upon me, and I said to myself, "Now I will go out at this door, turn to the left, walk ten steps, and meet Mr. O—— face to face." I did it, too! I could not see his face, because he had an umbrella before it, and it was pretty dark anyhow, but he interrupted the man he was walking and talking with, and I recognized his voice and stopped him.

That I should step out there and stumble upon Mr. O—— was nothing, but that I should know beforehand that I was going to do it was a good deal. It is a very curious thing when you come to look at it. I stood far within the cigar shop when I delivered my prophecy; I walked about five steps to the door, opened it, closed it after me, walked down a flight of three steps to the sidewalk, then turned to the left and walked four or five more, and found my man. I repeat that in itself the thing was nothing; but to know it would happen so *beforehand*, was n't that really curious?

I have criticised absent people so often, and then discovered, to my humiliation, that I was talking with their relatives, that I have grown superstitious about that sort of thing and dropped it. How like an idiot one feels after a blunder like that!

We are always mentioning people, and in that very instant they appear before us. We laugh, and say, "Speak of the devil," and so forth, and there we drop it, considering it an "accident." It is a cheap and convenient way of disposing of a grave and very puzzling mystery. The fact is it does seem to happen too often to be an accident.

Now I come to the oddest thing that ever happened to me. Two or three years ago I was lying in bed, idly musing, one morning—it was the 2d of March—when suddenly a red-hot new idea came whistling down into my camp, and exploded with such comprehensive effectiveness as to sweep the vicinity clean of rubbishy reflections, and fill the air with their dust and flying fragments. This idea, stated in simple phrase, was that the time was ripe and the market ready for a certain book; a book which ought to be written at once; a book which must command attention and be of peculiar interest —to wit, a book about the Nevada silver mines. The "Great Bonanza" was a new wonder then, and everybody was talking about it. It seemed to me that the person best qualified to write this book was Mr. William H. Wright, a journalist of Virginia, Nevada, by whose side I had scribbled many months when I was a reporter there ten or twelve years before. He might be alive still; he might be dead; I could not tell; but I would write him, anyway. I began by merely and modestly suggesting that he make such a book; but my interest grew as I went on, and I ventured to map out what I thought ought to be the plan of the work, he being an old friend, and not given to taking good intentions for ill. I even dealt with details, and suggested the order and sequence which they should follow. I was about to put the manuscript in an envelope, when the thought occurred to me that if this book should be written at my suggestion, and then no publisher happened to want it, I should feel uncomfortable; so I concluded to keep my letter back until I should have secured a publisher. I pigeonholed my document, and dropped a note to my own publisher, asking him to name a day for a business consultation. He was out of town on a far journey. My note remained unanswered, and at the end of three or four days the whole matter had passed out of my mind. On the 9th of March the postman brought three or four letters, and among them a thick one whose superscription was in a hand which seemed dimly familiar to me. I could not " place " it at first, but presently I succeeded. Then I said to a visiting relative who was present:

" Now I will do a miracle. I will tell you everything this letter contains—date, signature, and all—without breaking the seal. It is from a Mr. Wright, of Virginia, Nevada, and is dated the 2d of March— seven days ago. Mr. Wright proposes to make a book about the silver mines and the Great Bonanza, and asks what I, as a friend, think of the idea. He says his subjects are to be so and so, their order and sequence so and so, and he will close with a history of the chief feature of the book, the Great Bonanza."

I opened the letter, and showed that I had stated the date and the contents correctly. Mr. Wright's letter simply contained what my own letter, written on the same date, contained, and mine still lay in its pigeonhole, where it had been lying during the seven days since it was written.

There was no clairvoyance about this, if I rightly comprehend what clairvoyance is. I think the clairvoyant professes to actually *see* concealed writing, and read it off word for word. This was not my case. I only seemed to know, and to know absolutely, the contents of the letter in detail and due order, but I had to *word* them myself. I translated them, so to speak, out of Wright's language into my own.

Wright's letter and the one which I had written to him but never sent were in substance the same.

Necessarily this could not come by accident; such elaborate accidents cannot happen. Chance might have duplicated one or two of the details, but she would have broken down on the rest. I could not doubt—there was no tenable reason for doubting—that Mr. Wright's mind and mine had been in close and crystal-clear communication with each other across three thousand miles of mountain and desert on the morning of the 2d of March. I did not consider that both minds *originated* that succession of ideas, but that one mind originated them, and simply telegraphed them to the other. I was curious to know which brain was the telegrapher and which the receiver, so I wrote and asked for particulars. Mr. Wright's reply showed that his mind had done the originating and telegraphing and mine the receiving. Mark that significant thing, now; consider for a moment how many a splendid "original" idea has been unconsciously stolen from a man three thousand miles away! If one should question that this is so, let him look into the cyclopædia and con once more that curious thing in the history of inventions which has puzzled every one so much—that is, the frequency with which the same machine or other contrivance has been invented at the same time by several persons in different quarters of the globe. The world was without an electric telegraph for several thousand years; then Professor Henry, the American, Wheatstone in England, Morse on the sea, and a German in Munich, all invented it at the same time. The discovery of certain ways of applying steam was made in two or three countries in the same year. Is it not possible that inventors are constantly and unwittingly stealing each other's ideas whilst they stand thousands of miles asunder ?

Last spring a literary friend of mine,* who lived a hundred miles away, paid me a visit, and in the course of our talk he said he had made a discovery —conceived an entirely new idea—one which certainly had never been used in literature. He told me what it was. I handed him a manuscript, and
* W. D. Howells.

said he would find substantially the same idea in that—a manuscript which I had written a week before. The idea had been in my mind since the previous November; it had only entered his while I was putting it on paper, a week gone by. He had not yet written his; so he left it unwritten, and gracefully made over all his right and title in the idea to me.

The following statement, which I have clipped from a newspaper, is true. I had the facts from Mr. Howells's lips when the episode was new:

"A remarkable story of a literary coincidence is told of Mr. Howells's *Atlantic Monthly* serial 'Dr. Breen's Practice.' A lady of Rochester, New York, contributed to the magazine, after 'Dr. Breen's Practice' was in type, a short story which so much resembled Mr. Howells's that he felt it necessary to call upon her and explain the situation of affairs in order that no charge of plagiarism might be preferred against him. He showed her the proof-sheets of his story, and satisfied her that the similarity between her work and his was one of those strange coincidences which have from time to time occurred in the literary world."

I had read portions of Mr. Howells's story, both in MS. and in proof, before the lady offered her contribution to the magazine.

Here is another case. I clip it from a newspaper:

" The republication of Miss Alcott's novel *Moods* recalls to a writer in the Boston *Post* a singular coincidence which was brought to light before the book was first published: 'Miss Anna M. Crane, of Baltimore, published *Emily Chester,* a novel which was pronounced a very striking and strong story. A comparison of this book with *Moods* showed that the two writers, though entire strangers to each other, and living hundreds of miles apart, had both chosen the same subject for their novels, had followed almost the same line of treatment up to a certain point, where the parallel ceased, and the dénouements were entirely opposite. And even more curious, the leading characters in both books had identically the same names, so that the names in Miss Alcott's novel had to be changed. Then the book was published by Loring.' "

Four or five times within my recollection there has been a lively newspaper war in this country over poems whose authorship was claimed by two or three different people at the same time. There was a war of this kind over " Nothing to Wear," " Beautiful Snow," " Rock Me to Sleep, Mother," and also over one of Mr. Will Carleton's early ballads, I think. These were all blameless cases of unintentional and unwitting mental telegraphy, I judge.

A word more as to Mr. Wright. He had had his book in his mind some time; consequently he, and not I, had originated the idea of it. The subject was entirely foreign to my thoughts; I was wholly absorbed in other things. Yet this friend, whom I had not seen and had hardly thought of for eleven years, was able to shoot his thoughts at me across three thousand miles of country, and fill my head with them, to the exclusion of every other interest, in a single moment.   He had begun his letter after finishing his work on the morning paper—a little after three o'clock, he said.   When it was three in the morning in Nevada it was about six in Hartford, where I lay awake thinking about nothing in particular; and just about that time his ideas came pouring into my head from across the continent, and I got up and put them on paper, under the impression that they were my own original thoughts.

I have never seen any mesmeric or clairvoyant performances or spiritual manifestations which were in the least degree convincing—a fact which is not of consequence, since my opportunities have been meagre; but I am forced to believe that one human mind (still inhabiting the flesh) can communicate with another, over any sort of a distance, and without any *artificial* preparation of " sympathetic conditions " to act as a transmitting agent.   I suppose that when the sympathetic conditions happen to exist the two minds communicate with each other, and that otherwise they don't; and I suppose that if the sympathetic conditions could be kept up right along, the two minds would continue to correspond without limit as to time.

Now there is that curious thing which happens to

everybody: suddenly a succession of thoughts or sensations flocks in upon you, which startles you with the weird idea that you have ages ago experienced just this succession of thoughts or sensations in a previous existence. The previous existence is possible, no doubt, but I am persuaded that the solution of this hoary mystery lies not there, but in the fact that some far-off stranger has been telegraphing his thoughts and sensations into your consciousness, and that he stopped because some counter-current or other obstruction intruded and broke the line of communication. Perhaps they seem repetitions to you because they *are* repetitions, got at second hand from the other man. Possibly Mr. Brown, the "mind-reader," reads other people's minds, possibly he does not; but I know of a surety that I have read another man's mind, and therefore I do not see why Mr. Brown should n't do the like also.

I wrote the foregoing about three years ago, in Heidelberg, and laid the manuscript aside, purposing to add to it instances of mind-telegraphing from time to time as they should fall under my experience. Meantime the "crossing" of letters has been so frequent as to become monotonous. However, I have managed to get something useful out of this hint; for now, when I get tired of waiting upon a man whom I very much wish to hear from, I sit down and *compel* him to write, whether he wants to or not; that is to say, I sit down and write him, and then tear my letter up, satisfied that my act has forced him to write me at the same moment. I do not need to mail my letter—the writing it is the only essential thing.

Of course I have grown superstitious about this letter-crossing business—this was natural. We staid awhile in Venice after leaving Heidelberg. One day I was going down the Grand Canal in a gondola, when I heard a shout behind me, and looked around to see what the matter was; a gondola was rapidly following, and the gondolier was making signs to me to stop. I did so, and the pursuing boat ranged up alongside. There was an American lady in it— a resident of Venice. She was in a good deal of distress. She said:

" There's a New York gentleman and his wife at the Hotel Britannia who arrived a week ago, expecting to find news of their son, whom they have heard nothing about during eight months. There was no news. The lady is down sick with despair; the gentleman can't sleep or eat. Their son arrived at San Francisco eight months ago, and announced the fact in a letter to his parents the same day. That is the last trace of him. The parents have been in Europe ever since; but their trip has been spoiled, for they have occupied their time simply in drifting restlessly from place to place, and writing letters everywhere and to everybody, begging for news of their son; but the mystery remains as dense as ever. Now the gentleman wants to stop writing and go to cabling. He wants to cable San Francisco. He has never done it before, because he is afraid of—of he does n't know what—death of his son, no doubt. But he wants somebody to *advise* him to cable; wants me to do it. Now I simply can't; for if no news came, that mother yonder would die. So I have chased you up in order to get you to support me in urging him to be patient, and put the thing off a week or two longer; it may be the saving of this lady. Come along; let 's not lose any time."

So I went along, but I had a programme of my own. When I was introduced to the gentleman I said: " I have some superstitions, but they are worthy of respect. If you will cable San Francisco immediately, you will hear news of your son inside of twenty-four hours. I don't know that you will get the news from San Francisco, but you will get it from somewhere. The only necessary thing is to *cable* — that is all. The news will come within twenty-four hours. Cable Peking, if you prefer;

there is no choice in this matter. This delay is all occasioned by your not cabling long ago, when you were first moved to do it."

It seems absurd that this gentleman should have been cheered up by this nonsense, but he was; he brightened up at once, and sent his cablegram; and next day, at noon, when a long letter arrived from his lost son, the man was as grateful to me as if I had really had something to do with the hurrying up of that letter. The son had shipped from San Francisco in a sailing vessel, and his letter was written from the first port he touched at, months afterward.

This incident argues nothing, and is valueless. I insert it only to show how strong is the superstition which "letter-crossing" has bred in me. I was so sure that a cablegram sent to any place, no matter where, would defeat itself by "crossing" the incoming news, that my confidence was able to raise up a hopeless man, and make him cheery and hopeful.

But here are two or three incidents which come strictly under the head of mind-telegraphing. One Monday morning, about a year ago, the mail came in, and I picked up one of the letters and said to a friend: "Without opening this letter I will tell you what it says. It is from Mrs. ——, and she says she was in New York last Saturday, and was purposing to run up here in the afternoon train and surprise us, but at the last moment changed her mind and returned westward to her home."

I was right; my details were exactly correct. Yet we had had no suspicion that Mrs. ——— was coming to New York, or that she had even a remote intention of visiting us.

I smoke a good deal—that is to say, all the time —so, during seven years, I have tried to keep a box of matches handy, behind a picture on the mantelpiece; but I have had to take it out in trying, because George (colored), who makes the fires and lights the gas, always uses my matches, and never replaces them. Commands and persuasions have gone for nothing with him all these seven years. One day last summer, when our family had been away from home several months, I said to a member of the household:

" Now, with all this long holiday, and nothing in the way to interrupt—"

" I can finish the sentence for you," said the member of the household.

" Do it, then," said I.

" George ought to be able, by practicing, to learn to let those matches alone."

It was correctly done. That was what I was going to say. Yet until that moment George and the matches had not been in my mind for three months, and it is plain that the part of the sentence which I uttered offers not the least cue or suggestion of what I was purposing to follow it with.

My mother* is descended from the younger of two English brothers named Lambton, who settled in this country a few generations ago. The tradition goes that the elder of the two eventually fell heir to a certain estate in England (now an earldom), and died right away. This has always been the way with our family. They always die when they could make anything by not doing it. The two Lambtons left plenty of Lambtons behind them; and when at last, about fifty years ago, the English baronetcy was exalted to an earldom, the great tribe of American Lambtons began to bestir themselves—that is, those descended from the elder branch. Ever since that day one or another of these has been fretting his life uselessly away with schemes to get at his " rights." The present " rightful earl "—I mean the American one—used to write me occasionally, and try to interest me in his projected raids upon the title and estates by offering me a share in the latter portion of the spoil; but I have always managed to resist his temptations.

Well, one day last summer I was lying under a

* She was still living when this was written.

tree, thinking about nothing in particular, when an absurd idea flashed into my head, and I said to a member of the household, "Suppose I should live to be ninety-two, and dumb and blind and toothless, and just as I was gasping out what was left of me on my death-bed—"

"Wait, I will finish the sentence," said the member of the household.

"Go on," said I.

"Somebody should rush in with a document, and say, 'All the other heirs are dead, and you are the Earl of Durham!'"

That is truly what I was going to say. Yet until that moment the subject had not entered my mind or been referred to in my hearing for months before. A few years ago this thing would have astounded me, but the like could not much surprise me now, though it happened every week; for I think I *know* now that mind can communicate accurately with mind without the aid of the slow and clumsy vehicle of speech.

This age does seem to have exhausted invention nearly; still, it has one important contract on its hands yet—the invention of the *phrenophone;* that is to say, a method whereby the communicating of mind with mind may be brought under command and reduced to certainty and system. The telegraph and the telephone are going to become too slow and wordy for our needs. We must have the *thought* itself shot into our minds from a distance; then, if we need to put it into words, we can do that tedious work at our leisure. Doubtless the something which conveys our thoughts through the air from brain to brain is a finer and subtler form of electricity, and all we need do is to find out how to capture it and how to force it to do its work, as we have had to do in the case of the electric currents. Before the day of telegraphs neither one of these marvels would have seemed any easier to achieve than the other.

While I am writing this, doubtless somebody on the other side of the globe is writing it too. The question is, am I inspiring him or is he inspiring me? I cannot answer that; but that these thoughts have been passing through somebody else's mind all the time I have been setting them down I have no sort of doubt.

I will close this paper with a remark which I found some time ago in Boswell's *Johnson:*

"Voltaire's *Candide* is wonderfully similar in its plan and conduct to Johnson's *Rasselas;* insomuch that I have heard Johnson say that if they had not been published so closely one after the other that there was not time for imitation, *it would have been in vain to deny that the scheme of that which came latest was taken from the other.*"

The two men were widely separated from each other at the time, and the sea lay between.

POSTSCRIPT.

In the *Atlantic* for June, 1882, Mr. John Fiske refers to the often-quoted Darwin-and-Wallace "coincidence":

"I alluded, just now, to the 'unforeseen circumstance' which led Mr. Darwin in 1859 to break his long silence, and to write and publish the *Origin of Species*. This circumstance served, no less than the extraordinary success of his book, to show how ripe the minds of men had become for entertaining such views as those which Mr. Darwin propounded. In 1858 Mr. Wallace, who was then engaged in studying the natural history of the Malay Archipelago, sent to Mr. Darwin (as to the man most likely to understand him) a paper in which he sketched the outlines of a theory identical with that upon which Mr. Darwin had so long been at work. The same sequence of observed facts and inferences that had led Mr. Darwin to the discovery of natural selection and its consequences had led Mr. Wallace to the very threshold of the same discovery; but in Mr. Wallace's mind the theory had by no means been wrought out to the same degree of completeness to which it had been wrought in the mind of Mr. Darwin. In the preface to his charming book on Natural Selection, Mr. Wallace, with rare modesty and candor, acknowledges that whatever value his speculations may have had, they have been utterly surpassed in richness and cogency of proof by those of Mr. Darwin. This is no doubt true, and Mr. Wallace has done such good work in further illustration of the theory that he can well afford to rest content with the second place in the first announcement of it.

"The coincidence, however, between Mr. Wallace's conclusions and those of Mr. Darwin was very remarkable. But, after all, coincidences of this sort have not been uncommon in the history of scientific inquiry. Nor is it at all surprising that they should occur now and then, when we remember that a great and pregnant discovery must always be concerned with some question which many of the foremost minds in the world are busy thinking about. It was so with the discovery of the differential calculus, and again with the discovery of the planet Neptune. It was so with the interpretation of the Egyptian hieroglyphics, and with the establishment of the undulatory theory of light. It was so, to a considerable extent, with the introduction of the new chemistry, with the discovery of the mechanical equivalent of heat, and the whole doctrine of the correlation of forces. It was so with the invention of the electric telegraph and with the discovery of spectrum analysis. And it is not at all strange that it should have been so with the doctrine of the origin of species through natural selection."

He thinks these " coincidences " were apt to happen because the matters from which they sprang were matters which many of the foremost minds in the world were busy thinking about. But perhaps *one* man in each case did the telegraphing to the others. The aberrations which gave Leverrier the idea that there must be a planet of such and such mass and such and such an orbit hidden from sight out yonder in the remote abysses of space were not new; they had been noticed by astronomers for generations. Then why should it happen to occur to three people, widely separated—Leverrier, Mrs. Somerville, and Adams—to suddenly go to worrying about those aberrations all at the same time, and set themselves to work to find out what caused them, and to measure and weigh an invisible planet, and calculate its orbit, and hunt it down and catch it?— a strange project which nobody but they had ever thought of before. If one astronomer had invented that odd and happy project fifty years before, don't you think he would have telegraphed it to several others without knowing it?

But now I come to a puzzler. How is it that *inanimate* objects are able to affect the mind? They seem to do that. However, I wish to throw in a parenthesis first—just a reference to a thing everybody is familiar with—the experience of receiving a clear and particular *answer* to your telegram before your telegram has reached the sender of the answer. That is a case where your telegram has gone straight from your brain to the man it was meant for, far outstripping the wire's slow electricity, and it is an exercise of mental telegraphy which is as common as dining. To return to the influence of inanimate things. In the cases of non-professional clairvoyance examined by the Psychical Society the clairvoyant has usually been blindfolded, then some object which has been touched or worn by a person is placed in his hand; the clairvoyant immediately describes that person, and goes on and gives a history

of some event with which the text object has been
connected. If the inanimate object is able to affect
and inform the clairvoyant's mind, maybe it can do
the same when it is working in the interest of mental telegraphy. Once a lady in the West wrote me
that her son was coming to New York to remain
three weeks, and would pay me a visit if invited,
and she gave me his address. I mislaid the letter,
and forgot all about the matter till the three weeks
were about up. Then a sudden and fiery irrupton
of remorse burst up in my brain that illuminated all
the region round about, and I sat down at once and
wrote to the lady and asked for that lost address.
But, upon reflection, I judged that the stirring up
of my recollection had not been an accident, so I
added a postscript to say, never mind, I should get
a letter from her son before night. And I did get
it; for the letter was already in the town, although
not delivered yet. It had influenced me somehow.
I have had so many experiences of this sort—a dozen
of them at least—that I am nearly persuaded that
inanimate objects do not confine their activities to
helping the clairvoyant, but do every now and then
give the mental telegraphist a lift.

The case of mental telegraphy which I am coming to now comes under I don't exactly know what
head. I clipped it from one of our local papers six

or eight years ago. I know the details to be right and true, for the story was told to me in the same form by one of the two persons concerned (a clergyman of Hartford) at the time that the curious thing happened:

"A REMARKABLE COINCIDENCE.—Strange coincidences make the most interesting of stories and most curious of studies. Nobody can quite say how they come about, but everybody appreciates the fact when they do come, and it is seldom that any more complete and curious coincidence is recorded of minor importance than the following, which is absolutely true, and occurred in this city :

" At the time of the building of one of the finest residences of Hartford, which is still a very new house, a local firm supplied the wall-paper for certain rooms, contracting both to furnish and to put on the paper. It happened that they did not calculate the size of one room exactly right, and the paper of the design selected for it fell short just half a roll. They asked for delay enough to send on to the manufacturers for what was needed, and were told that there was no especial hurry. It happened that the manufacturers had none on hand, and had destroyed the blocks from which it was printed. They wrote that they had a full list of the dealers to whom they had sold that paper, and that they would write to each of these, and get from some of them a roll. It might involve a delay of a couple of weeks, but they would surely get it.

" In the course of time came a letter saying that, to their great surprise, they could not find a single roll. Such a thing was very unusual, but in this case it had so happened. Accordingly the local firm asked for further time, saying they would write to their own customers who had bought of that pattern, and would get the piece from them. But, to their surprise, this effort also failed. A long time had now elapsed, and there was no use of delaying any longer. They had contracted to paper the room, and their only course was to take off that which was insufficient and put on some other of which there was enough to go around. Accordingly at length a man was sent out to remove the paper. He got his apparatus ready, and was about to begin work, under the direction of the owner of the building, when the latter was for the moment called away. The house was large and very interesting, and so many people had rambled about it that finally admission had been refused by a sign at the door. On the occasion, however, when a gentleman had knocked and asked for leave to look about, the owner, being on the premises, had been sent for to reply to the request in person. That was the call that for the moment delayed the final preparations. The gentleman went to the door and admitted the stranger, saying he would show him about the house, but first must return for a moment to that room to finish his directions there, and he told the curious story about the paper as they went on. They entered the room together, and the first thing the stranger, who lived fifty miles away, said on looking about was, 'Why, I have that very paper on a room in my house, and I have an extra roll of it laid away, which is at your service.' In a few days the wall was papered according to the original contract. Had not the owner been at the house, the stranger would not have been admitted; had he called a day later, it would have been too late; had not the facts been almost accidentally told to him, he would probably have said nothing of the paper, and so on. The exact fitting of all the circumstances is something very remarkable, and makes one of those stories that seem hardly accidental in their nature."

Something that happened the other day brought my hoary MS. to mind, and that is how I came to dig it out from its dusty pigeonhole grave for publication. The thing that happened was a question.

A lady asked it : " Have you ever had a vision —
when awake ?" I was about to answer promptly,
when the last two words of the question began to
grow and spread and swell, and presently they
attained to vast dimensions. She did not know that
they were important; and I did not at first, but I
soon saw that they were putting me on the track of
the solution of a mystery which had perplexed me
a good deal. You will see what I mean when I get
down to it. Ever since the English Society for
Psychical Research began its searching investigations of ghost stories, haunted houses, and apparitions of the living and the dead, I have read their
pamphlets with avidity as fast as they arrived. Now
one of their commonest inquiries of a dreamer or a
vision-seer is, "Are you sure you were awake at
the time ?" If the man can't say he is sure he was
awake, a doubt falls upon his tale right there. But
if he is positive he was awake, and offers reasonable
evidence to substantiate it, the fact counts largely
for the credibility of his story. It does with the
society, and it did with me until that lady asked me
the above question the other day.

The question set me to considering, and brought
me to the conclusion that you can be asleep — at
least wholly unconscious — for a time, and not suspect that it has happened, and not have any way to

prove that it *has* happened. A memorable case was in my mind. About a year ago I was standing on the porch one day, when I saw a man coming up the walk. He was a stranger, and I hoped he would ring and carry his business into the house without stopping to argue with me; he would have to pass the front door to get to me, and I hoped he would n't take the trouble; to help, I tried to look like a stranger myself—it often works. I was looking straight at that man; he had got to within ten feet of the door and within twenty-five feet of me—and suddenly he disappeared. It was as astounding as if a church should vanish from before your face and leave nothing behind it but a vacant lot. I was unspeakably delighted. I had seen an apparition at last, with my own eyes, in broad daylight. I made up my mind to write an account of it to the society. I ran to where the spectre had been, to make sure he was playing fair, then I ran to the other end of the porch, scanning the open grounds as I went. No, everything was perfect; he could n't have escaped without my seeing him; he was an apparition, without the slightest doubt, and I would write him up before he was cold. I ran, hot with excitement, and let myself in with a latch-key. When I stepped into the hall my lungs collapsed and my heart stood still. For there sat that same apparition in a chair, all alone, and as quiet and reposeful as if he had come to stay a year! The shock kept me dumb for a moment or two, then I said, "Did you come in at that door?"

"Yes."

"Did *you* open it, or did you ring?"

"I rang, and the colored man opened it."

I said to myself: "This is astonishing. It takes George all of two minutes to answer the door-bell when he is in a hurry, and I have never seen him in a hurry. How *did* this man stand two minutes at that door, within five steps of me, and I did not see him?"

I should have gone to my grave puzzling over that riddle but for that lady's chance question last week: "Have you ever had a vision—when awake?" It stands explained now. During at least sixty seconds that day I was asleep, or at least totally unconscious, without suspecting it. In that interval the man came to my immediate vicinity, rang, stood there and waited, then entered and closed the door, and I did not see him and did not hear the door slam.

If he had slipped around the house in that interval and gone into the cellar—he had time enough— I should have written him up for the society, and magnified him, and gloated over him, and hurrahed about him, and thirty yoke of oxen could not have pulled the belief out of me that I was of the favored ones of the earth, and had seen a vision—while wide awake.

Now how are you to tell when you are awake? What are you to go by? People bite their fingers to find out. Why, you can do that in a dream.

A CURE FOR THE BLUES.

By courtesy of Mr. Cable I came into possession of a singular book eight or ten years ago. It is likely that mine is now the only copy in existence. Its title-page, unabbreviated, reads as follows:

" The Enemy Conquered; or, Love Triumphant. By G. Ragsdale McClintock,* author of ' An Address,' etc., delivered at Sunflower Hill, South Carolina, and member of the Yale Law School. New Haven: published by T. H. Pease, 83 Chapel Street, 1845."

No one can take up this book, and lay it down again unread. Whoever reads one line of it is caught, is chained; he has become the contented slave of its fascinations; and he will read and read, devour and devour, and will not let it go out of his hand till it is finished to the last line, though the house be on fire over his head. And after a first reading, he will not throw it aside, but will keep it

* The name here given is a substitute for the one actually attached to the pamphlet.

by him, with his Shakspere and his Homer, and will take it up many and many a time, when the world is dark, and his spirits are low, and be straightway cheered and refreshed. Yet this work has been allowed to lie wholly neglected, unmentioned, and apparently unregretted, for nearly half a century.

The reader must not imagine that he is to find in it wisdom, brilliancy, fertility of invention, ingenuity of construction, excellence of form, purity of style, perfection of imagery, truth to nature, clearness of statement, humanly possible situations, humanly possible people, fluent narrative, connected sequence of events—or philosophy, or logic, or sense. No; the rich, deep, beguiling charm of the book lies in the total and miraculous *absence* from it of all these qualities—a charm which is completed and perfected by the evident fact that the author, whose naïve innocence easily and surely wins our regard, and almost our worship, does not know that they are absent, does not even suspect that they are absent. When read by the light of these helps to an understanding of the situation, the book is delicious—profoundly and satisfyingly delicious.

I call it a book because the author calls it a book, I call it a work because he calls it a work; but in truth it is merely a duodecimo pamphlet of thirty-one pages. It was written for fame and money as the author very frankly—yes, and very hopefully, too, poor fellow—says in his preface. The money never came; no penny of it ever came; and how long, how pathetically long, the fame has been deferred—forty-seven years! He was young then, it would have been so much to him then; but will he care for it now?

As time is measured in America, McClintock's epoch is antiquity. In his long-vanished day the Southern author had a passion for " eloquence " ; it was his pet, his darling. He would be eloquent, or perish. And he recognized only one kind of eloquence, the lurid, the tempestuous, the volcanic. He liked words; big words, fine words, grand words, rumbling, thundering, reverberating words—with sense attaching if it could be got in without marring the sound, but not otherwise. He loved to stand up before a dazed world, and pour forth flame, and smoke, and lava, and pumice-stone, into the skies, and work his subterranean thunders, and shake himself with earthquakes, and stench himself with sulphur fumes. If he consumed his own fields and vineyards, that was a pity, yes; but he would have his eruption at any cost. Mr. McClintock's eloquence—and he is always eloquent, his crater is always spouting—is of the pattern common to his day, but he departs from the custom of the time in one respect: his brethren allowed sense to intrude when it did not mar the sound, but he does not allow it to intrude at all. For example, consider this figure, which he uses in the village " Address " referred to with such candid complacency in the title-page above quoted—" like the topmost topaz of an ancient tower." Please read it again; contemplate it; measure it; walk around it; climb up it; try to get at an approximate realization of the size of it. Is the fellow to that to be found in literature, ancient or modern, foreign or domestic, living or dead, drunk or sober? One notices how fine and grand it sounds. We know that if it was loftily uttered, it got a noble burst of applause from the villagers; yet there is n't a ray of sense in it, or meaning to it.

McClintock finished his education at Yale in 1843, and came to Hartford on a visit that same year. I have talked with men who at that time talked with him, and felt of him, and knew he was real. One needs to remember that fact, and to keep fast hold of it; it is the only way to keep McClintock's book from undermining one's faith in McClintock's actuality.

As to the book. The first four pages are devoted to an inflamed eulogy of Woman,—simply Woman in general, or perhaps as an Institution,—wherein, among other compliments to her details, he pays a unique one to her voice. He says it "fills the breast with fond alarms, echoed by every rill." It sounds well enough, but it is not true. After the eulogy he takes up his real work, and the novel begins. It begins in the woods, near the village of Sunflower Hill.

> Brightening clouds seemed to rise from the mist of the fair Chattahoochee, to spread their beauty over the thick forest, to guide the hero whose bosom beats with aspirations to conquer the enemy that would tarnish his name, and to win back the admiration of his long tried friend.

It seems a general remark, but it is not general; the hero mentioned is the to-be hero of the book; and in this abrupt fashion, and without name or description, he is shoveled into the tale. "With aspirations to conquer the enemy that would tarnish his name" is merely a phrase flung in for the sake of the sound—let it not mislead the reader. No one is trying to tarnish this person; no one has thought of it. The rest of the sentence is also merely a phrase; the man has no friend as yet, and of course has had no chance to try him, or win back his admiration, or disturb him in any other way.

The hero climbs up over "Sawney's Mountain," and down the other side, making for an old Indian "castle"—which becomes "the red man's hut" in the next sentence; and when he gets there at last, he "surveys with wonder and astonishment" the invisible structure, "which time had buried in the dust; and thought to himself his happiness was not yet complete." One does n't know why it was n't, nor how near it came to being complete, nor what was still wanting to round it up and make it so. Maybe it was the Indian; but the book does not say. At this point we have an episode:

Beside the shore of the brook sat a young man, about eighteen or twenty, who seemed to be reading some favorite book, and who had a remarkably noble countenance—eyes which betrayed more than a common mind. This of course made the youth a welcome guest, and gained him friends in whatever condition of life he might be placed. The traveler observed that he was a well built figure which showed strength and grace in every movement. He accordingly addressed him in quite a gentlemanly manner, and inquired of him the way to the village. After he had received the desired information, and was about taking his leave, the youth said, "Are you not Major Elfonzo, the great musician *— the champion of a noble cause—the modern Achilles, who gained so many victories in the Florida War?" "I bear that name," said the Major, "and those titles, trusting at the same time, that the ministers of grace will carry me triumphantly through all my laudable undertakings, and if," continued the Major, "you sir, are the patronizer of noble deeds, I should like to make you my confidant, and learn your address." The youth looked somewhat amazed, bowed low, mused for a moment, and began: "My name is Roswell. I

* Further on it will be seen that he is a country expert on the fiddle, and has a three-township fame.

have been recently admitted to the bar, and can only give a faint outline of my future success in that honorable profession; but I trust, sir, like the Eagle, I shall look down from lofty rocks upon the dwellings of man, and shall ever be ready to give you any assistance in my official capacity, and whatever this muscular arm of mine can do, whenever it shall be called from its buried greatness." The Major grasped him by the hand, and exclaimed: " O! thou exalted spirit of inspiration—thou flame of burning prosperity, may the Heaven directed blaze be the glare of thy soul, and battle down every rampart that seems to impede your progress!"

There is a strange sort of originality about McClintock; he imitates other people's styles, but nobody can imitate his, not even an idiot. Other people can be windy, but McClintock blows a gale; other people can blubber sentiment, but McClintock spews it; other people can mishandle metaphors, but only McClintock knows how to make a business of it. McClintock is always McClintock, he is always consistent, his style is always his own style. He does not make the mistake of being relevant on one page and irrelevant on another; he is irrelevant on all of them. He does not make the mistake of being lucid in one place and obscure in another; he is obscure all the time. He does not make the mistake of slipping in a name here and there that is out of character with his work; he always uses names that exactly and fantastically fit his lunatics. In the matter of undeviating consistency he stands alone in authorship. It is this that makes his style unique, and entitles it to a name of its own—McClintockian. It is this that protects it from being mistaken for anybody else's. Uncredited quotations from other writers often leave a reader in doubt as to their authorship, but McClintock is safe from that accident; an uncredited quotation from him would always be recognizable. When a boy nineteen years old, who had just been admitted to the bar, says, " I trust, sir, like the Eagle, I shall look down from lofty rocks upon the dwellings of man," we know who is speaking through that boy; we should recognize that note anywhere. There be myriads of instruments in this world's literary orchestra, and a multitudinous confusion of sounds that they make, wherein fiddles are drowned, and guitars smothered, and one sort of drum mistaken for another sort; but whensoever the brazen note of the McClintockian trombone breaks through that fog of music, that note is recognizable, and about it there can be no blur of doubt.

The novel now arrives at the point where the Major goes home to see his father. When McClintock wrote this interview, he probably believed it was pathetic.

The road which led to the town, presented many attractions. Elfonzo had bid farewell to the youth of deep feeling, and was now wending his way to the dreaming spot of his fondness. The south winds whistled through the woods, as the waters dashed against the banks, as rapid fire in the pent furnace roars. This brought him to remember while alone, that he quietly left behind the hospitality of a father's house, and gladly entered the world, with higher hopes than are often realized. But as he journeyed onward, he was mindful of the advice of his father, who had often looked sadly on the ground, when tears of cruelly deceived hope, moistened his eyes. Elfonzo had been somewhat of a dutiful son; yet fond of the amusements of life—had been in distant lands— had enjoyed the pleasure of the world, and had frequently returned to the scenes of his boyhood, almost destitute of many of the comforts of life.` In this condition, he would frequently say to his father, " Have I offended you, that you look upon me as a stranger, and frown upon me with sting-ing looks? Will you not favor me with the sound of your voice? If I have trampled upon your veneration, or have spread a humid veil of darkness around your expectations, send me back into the world, where no heart beats for me— where the foot of man has never yet trod; but give me at least one kind word—allow me to come into the presence sometimes of thy winter-worn locks." " Forbid it, Heaven, that I should be angry with thee," answered the father, " my son, and yet I send thee back to the children of the world— to the cold charity of the combat, and to a land of victory. I read another destiny in thy countenance—I learn thy in-clinations from the flame that has already kindled in my soul a strange sensation. It will seek thee, my dear Elfonzo, it will find thee—thou canst not escape that lighted torch, which shall blot out from the remembrance of men a long train of prophecies which they have foretold against thee. I once thought not so. Once, I was blind; but now the path of life is plain before me, and my sight is clear; yet Elfonzo, return to thy worldly occupation—take again in thy hand, that chord of sweet sounds—struggle with the civilized world, and with your own heart; fly swiftly to the enchanted ground —let the night-owl send forth its screams from the stubborn oak—let the sea sport upon the beach, and the stars sing together; but learn of these, Elfonzo, thy doom, and thy hiding-place. Our most innocent as well as our most lawful desires must often be denied us, that we may learn to sacrifice them to a Higher will."

Remembering such admonitions with gratitude, Elfonzo was immediately urged by the recollection of his father's family to keep moving.

McClintock has a fine gift in the matter of surprises; but as a rule they are not pleasant ones, they jar upon the feelings. His closing sentence in the last quotation is of that sort. It brings one down out of the tinted clouds in too sudden and collapsed a fashion. It incenses one against the author for a moment. It makes the reader want to take him by his winter-worn locks, and trample on his veneration, and deliver him over to the cold charity of combat, and blot him out with his own lighted torch. But the feeling does not last. The master takes again in his hand that concord of sweet sounds of his, and one is reconciled, pacified.

His steps became quicker and quicker — he hastened through the piny woods, dark as the forest was, and with joy he very soon reached the little village of repose, in whose bosom rested the boldest chivalry. His close attention to every important object—his modest questions about whatever was new to him—his reverence for wise old age, and his ardent desire to learn many of the fine arts, soon brought him into respectable notice.

One mild winter day, as he walked along the streets toward the Academy, which stood upon a small eminence, surrounded by native growth—some venerable in its appearance, others young and prosperous—all seemed inviting, and seemed to be the very place for learning as well as for genius to spend its research beneath its spreading shades. He entered its classic walls in the usual mode of southern manners.

The artfulness of this man! None knows so well as he how to pique the curiosity of the reader—and how to disappoint it. He raises the hope, here, that he is going to tell all about how one enters a classic wall in the usual mode of Southern manners; but does he? No; he smiles in his sleeve, and turns aside to other matters.

The principal of the Institution begged him to be seated, and listen to the recitations that were going on. He accordingly obeyed the request, and seemed to be much pleased. After the school was dismissed, and the young hearts regained their freedom, with the songs of the evening, laughing at the anticipated pleasures of a happy home, while others tittered at the actions of the past day, he addressed the teacher in a tone that indicated a resolution—with an undaunted mind. He said he had determined to become a student, if he could meet with his approbation, "Sir," said he, "I have spent much time in the world. I have traveled among the uncivilized inhabitants of America. I have met with friends, and combated with foes; but none of these gratify my ambition, or decide what is to be my destiny. I see the learned world have an influence with the voice of the people themselves. The despoilers of the remotest kingdoms of the earth, refer their differences to this class of persons. This the illiterate and inexperienced little dream of; and now if you will receive me as I am, with these deficiencies—with all my misguided opinions, I will give you my honor, sir, that I will never disgrace the Institution, or those who have placed you in this honorable station." The instructor, who had met with many disappointments, knew how to feel for a stranger who had been thus turned upon the charities of an unfeeling community. He looked at him earnestly, and said: " Be of good cheer—look forward, sir, to the high destination you may attain. Remember, the more elevated the mark at which you aim, the more sure, the more glorious, the more magnificent the prize." From wonder to wonder, his encouragement led the impatient listener. A strange nature bloomed before him—giant streams promised him success—gardens of hidden treasures opened to his view. All this, so vividly described, seemed to gain a new witchery from his glowing fancy.

It seems to me that this situation is new in romance. I feel sure it has not been attempted before. Military celebrities have been disguised and set at lowly occupations for dramatic effect, but I think McClintock is the first to send one of them to school. Thus, in this book, you pass from wonder to wonder, through gardens of hidden treasure, where giant streams bloom before you, and behind you, and all around, and you feel as happy, and groggy, and satisfied, with your quart of mixed metaphor aboard, as you would if it had been mixed in a sample-room, and delivered from a jug.

Now we come upon some more McClintockian

surprises—a sweetheart who is sprung upon us without any preparation, along with a name for her
which is even a little more of a surprise than she
herself is.

In 1842, he entered the class, and made rapid progress in
the English and Latin departments. Indeed, he continued
advancing with such rapidity that he was like to become the
first in his class, and made such unexpected progress, and
was so studious, that he had almost forgotten the pictured
saint of his affections. The fresh wreaths of the pine and
cypress, had waited anxiously to drop once more the dews of
Heaven upon the heads of those who had so often poured
forth the tender emotions of their souls under its boughs.
He was aware of the pleasure that he had seen there. So
one evening, as he was returning from his reading, he concluded he would pay a visit to this enchanting spot. Little
did he think of witnessing a shadow of his former happiness,
though no doubt, he wished it might be so. He continued
sauntering by the road-side, meditating on the past. The
nearer he approached the spot, the more anxious he became.
At that moment, a tall female figure flitted across his path,
with a bunch of roses in her hand; her countenance showed
uncommon vivacity, with a resolute spirit; her ivory teeth
already appeared as she smiled beautifully, promenading,—
while her ringlets of hair, dangled unconsciously around her
snowy neck. Nothing was wanting to complete her beauty.
The tinge of the rose was in full bloom upon her cheek; the
charms of sensibility and tenderness were always her associates. In Ambulinia's bosom dwelt a noble soul—one that
never faded—one that never was conquered.

Ambulinia! It can hardly be matched in fiction.
The full name is Ambulinia Valeer. Marriage will

presently round it out and perfect it.   Then it will
be Mrs. Ambulinia Valeer Elfonzo.   It takes the
chromo.

Her heart yielded to no feeling but the love of Elfonzo,
on whom she gazed with intense delight, and to whom she
felt herself more closely bound, because he sought the hand
of no other.   Elfonzo was roused from his apparent revery.
His books no longer were his inseparable companions—his
thoughts arrayed themselves to encourage him to the field
of victory.   He endeavored to speak to his supposed Ambulinia, but his speech appeared not in words.   No, his effort
was a stream of fire, that kindled his soul into a flame of admiration, and carried his senses away captive.   Ambulinia
had disappeared, to make him more mindful of his duty.   As
she walked speedily away through the piny woods, she calmly
echoed: "O! Elfonzo, thou wilt now look from thy sunbeams.   Thou shalt now walk in a new path—perhaps thy
way leads through darkness; but fear not, the stars foretell
happiness."

To McClintock that jingling jumble of fine words
meant something, no doubt, or seemed to mean
something; but it is useless for us to try to divine
what it was.   Ambulinia comes—we don't know
whence nor why; she mysteriously intimates—we
don't know what; and then she goes echoing away
—we don't know whither; and down comes the cur-
tain.   McClintock's art is subtle; McClintock's art
is deep.

Not many days afterwards, as surrounded by fragrant flowers, she sat one evening at twilight, to enjoy the cool breeze

that whispered notes of melody along the distant groves, the little birds perched on every side, as if to watch the movements of their new visitor. The bells were tolling, when Elfonzo silently stole along by the wild wood flowers, holding in his hand his favorite instrument of music—his eye continually searching for Ambulinia, who hardly seemed to perceive him, as she played carelessly with the songsters that hopped from branch to branch. Nothing could be more striking than the difference between the two. Nature seemed to have given the more tender soul to Elfonzo, and the stronger and more courageous to Ambulinia. A deep feeling spoke from the eyes of Elfonzo,—such a feeling as can only be expressed by those who are blessed as admirers, and by those who are able to return the same with sincerity of heart. He was a few years older than Ambulina: she had turned a little into her seventeenth. He had almost grown up in the Cherokee country, with the same equal proportions as one of the natives. But little intimacy had existed between them until the year forty-one—because the youth felt that the character of such a lovely girl was too exalted to inspire any other feeling than that of quiet reverence. But as lovers will not always be insulted, at all times and under all circumstances, by the frowns and cold looks of crabbed old age, which should continually reflect dignity upon those around, and treat the unfortunate as well as the fortunate with a graceful mien, he continued to use diligence and perseverance. All this lighted a spark in his heart that changed his whole character, and like the unyielding Deity that follows the storm to check its rage in the forest, he resolves for the first time to shake off his embarrassment, and return where he had before only worshiped.

At last we begin to get the major's measure. We are able to put this and that casual fact together, and build the man up before our eyes, and look at

him. And after we have got him built, we find him
worth the trouble. By the above comparison between his age and Ambulinia's, we guess the war-
worn veteran to be twenty-two; and the other facts
stand thus: he had grown up in the Cherokee country with the same equal proportions as one of the
natives—how flowing and graceful the language,
and yet how tantalizing as to meaning!—he had
been turned adrift by his father, to whom he had
been " somewhat of a dutiful son"; he wandered in
distant lands; came back frequently " to the scenes
of his boyhood, almost destitute of many of the comforts of life," in order to get into the presence of his
father's winter-worn locks, and spread a humid veil
of darkness around his expectations; but he was always promptly sent back to the cold charity of the
combat again; he learned to play the fiddle, and
made a name for himself in that line; he had dwelt
among the wild tribes; he had philosophized about
the despoilers of the kingdoms of the earth, and
found out — the cunning creature — that they refer
their differences to the learned for settlement; he
had achieved a vast fame as a military chieftain, the
Achilles of the Florida campaigns, and then had got
him a spelling-book and started to school; he had
fallen in love with Ambulinia Valeer while she was
teething, but had kept it to himself awhile, out of

the reverential awe which he felt for the child; but
now at last, like the unyielding deity who follows
the storm to check its rage in the forest, he resolves
to shake off his embarrassment, and to return where
before he had only worshiped. The major, indeed,
has made up his mind to rise up and shake his fac-
ulties together, and to see if *he* can't do that thing
himself. This is not clear. But no matter about
that: there stands the hero, compact and visible;
and he is no mean structure, considering that his
creator had never created anything before, and
hadn't anything but rags and wind to build with
this time. It seems to me that no one can contemplate this odd creature, this quaint and curious
blatherskite, without admiring McClintock, or, at
any rate, loving him and feeling grateful to him; for
McClintock made him, he gave him to us; without
McClintock we could not have had him, and would
now be poor.

But we must come to the feast again. Here is a
courtship scene, down there in the romantic glades
among the raccoons, alligators, and things, that has
merit, peculiar literary merit. See how Achilles
woos. Dwell upon the second sentence (particularly the close of it), and the beginning of the third.
Never mind the new personage, Leos, who is intruded upon us unheralded and unexplained. That

is McClintock's way; it is his habit; it is a part of
his genius; he cannot help it; he never interrupts
the rush of his narrative to make introductions:

It could not escape Ambulinia's penetrating eye, that he
sought an interview with her, which she as anxiously avoided, and assumed a more distant calmness than before, seemingly to destroy all hope. After many efforts and struggles
with his own person, with timid steps the Major approached
the damsel, with the same caution as he would have done in
a field of battle. "Lady Ambulinia," said he, trembling, "I
have long desired a moment like this. I dare not let it escape. I fear the consequences; yet I hope your indulgence
will at least hear my petition. Can you not anticipate what
I would say, and what I am about to express? Will you
not, like Minerva, who sprung from the brain of Jupiter, release me from thy winding chains or cure me—" "Say no
more, Elfonzo," answered Ambulinia, with a serious look,
raising her hand as if she intended to swear eternal hatred
against the whole world,—"another lady in my place would
have perhaps answered your question in bitter coldness. I
know not the little arts of my sex. I care but little for the
vanity of those who would chide me, and am unwilling, as
well as ashamed to be guilty of any thing that would lead
you to think 'all is not gold that glitters': so be not rash in
your resolution. It is better to repent now, than to do it in
a more solemn hour. Yes, I know what you would say. I
know you have a costly gift for me—the noblest that man
can make—your heart! you should not offer it to one so un-
worthy. Heaven, you know, has allowed my father's house
to be made a house of solitude, a home of silent obedience,
which my parents say is more to be admired than big names
and high sounding titles. Notwithstanding all this, let me
speak the emotions of an honest heart—allow me to say in
the fullness of my hopes that I anticipate better days. The

bird may stretch its wings toward the sun, which it can never reach; and flowers of the field appear to ascend in the same direction, because they cannot do otherwise : but man confides his complaints to the saints in whom he believes; for in their abodes of light they know no more sorrow. From your confession and indicative looks, I must be that person : if so, deceive not yourself."

Elfonzo replied, "Pardon me, my dear madam, for my frankness. I have loved you from my earliest days—everything grand and beautiful hath borne the image of Ambulinia: while precipices on every hand surrounded me, your guardian angel stood and beckoned me away from the deep abyss. In every trial—in every misfortune, I have met with your helping hand; yet I never dreamed or dared to cherish thy love, till a voice impaired with age encouraged the cause, and declared they who acquired thy favor, should win a victory. I saw how Leos worshiped thee. I felt my own unworthiness. I began to know jealousy, a strong guest indeed, in my bosom, yet I could see if I gained your admiration, Leos was to be my rival. I was aware that he had the influence of your parents, and the wealth of a deceased relative, which is too often mistaken for permanent and regular tranquillity; yet I have determined by your permission to beg an interest in your prayers—to ask you to animate my drooping spirits by your smiles and your winning looks; for, if you but speak, I shall be conqueror, my enemies shall stagger like Olympus shakes. And though earth and sea may tremble, and the charioteer of the sun may forget his dashing steed; yet I am assured that it is only to arm me with divine weapons, which will enable me to complete my long tried intention." "Return to yourself, Elfonzo," said Ambulinia, pleasantly, "a dream of vision has disturbed your intellect— you are above the atmosphere, dwelling in the celestial regions, nothing is there that urges or hinders, nothing that brings discord into our present litigation. I entreat you to condescend a little, and be a man, and forget it all. When

Homer describes the battle of the gods and noble men, fighting with giants and dragons, they represent under this image, our struggles with the delusions of our passions. You have exalted me, an unhappy girl, to the skies,—you have called me a saint, and portrayed in your imagination, an angel in human form. Let her remain such to you,—let her continue to be as you have supposed, and be assured that she will consider a share in your esteem, as her highest treasure. Think not that I would allure you from the path in which your conscience leads you; for you know I respect the conscience of others, as I would die for my own. Elfonzo, if I am worthy of thy love, let such conversation never again pass between us. Go, seek a nobler theme ! we will seek it in the stream of time, as the sun set in the Tigris." As she spake these words, she grasped the hand of Elfonzo, saying at the same time—" peace and prosperity attend you my hero: be up and doing." Closing her remarks with this expression, she walked slowly away, leaving Elfonzo astonished and amazed. He ventured not to follow, or detain her. Here he stood alone, gazing at the stars;—confounded as he was, here he stood.

Yes; there he stood. There seems to be no doubt about that. Nearly half of this delirious story has now been delivered to the reader. It seems a pity to reduce the other half to a cold synopsis. Pity ! it is more than a pity, it is a crime; for, to synopsize McClintock is to reduce a sky-flushing conflagration to dull embers, it is to reduce barbaric splendor to ragged poverty. McClintock never wrote a line that was not precious; he never wrote one that could be spared; he never framed one from which a word could be removed without damage. Every sentence that this master has produced may be likened to a perfect set of teeth, white, uniform, beautiful. If you pull one, the charm is gone.

Still, it is now necessary to begin to pull, and to keep it up; for lack of space requires us to synopsize.

We left Elfonzo standing there, amazed. At what, we do not know. Not at the girl's speech. No; we ourselves should have been amazed at it, of course, for none of us has ever heard anything resembling it: but Elfonzo was used to speeches made up of noise and vacancy, and could listen to them with undaunted mind like the "topmost topaz of an ancient tower"; he was used to making them himself; he—but let it go, it cannot be guessed out; we shall never know what it was that astonished him. He stood there awhile; then he said, "Alas! am I now Grief's disappointed son at last." He did not stop to examine his mind, and to try to find out what he probably meant by that, because, for one reason, "a mixture of ambition and greatness of soul moved upon his young heart," and started him for the village. He resumed his bench in school, "and reasonably progressed in his education." His heart was heavy, but he went into society, and sought surcease of sorrow in its light distractions. He made himself popular with his violin, "which seemed to have a thousand chords—more symphonious than the Muses of Apollo, and more enchanting than the ghost of the Hills." This is obscure, but let it go.

During this interval Leos did some unencouraged courting, but at last, "choked by his undertaking," he desisted.

Presently "Elfonzo again wends his way to the stately walls and new built village." He goes to the house of his beloved; she opens the door herself. To my surprise—for Ambulinia's heart had still seemed free at the time of their last interview—love beamed from the girl's eyes. One sees that Elfonzo was surprised, too; for when he caught that light, "a halloo of smothered shouts ran through every vein." A neat figure—a very neat figure, indeed! Then he kissed her. "The scene was overwhelming." They went into the parlor. The girl said it was safe, for her parents were abed, and would never know. Then we have this fine picture—flung upon the canvas with hardly an effort, as you will notice.

> Advancing toward him she gave a bright display of her rosy neck, and from her head the ambrosial locks breathed divine fragrance; her robe hung waving to his view, while she stood like a goddess confessed before him.

There is nothing of interest in the couple's inter-

view. Now at this point the girl invites Elfonzo to
a village show, where jealousy is the motive of the
play, for she wants to teach him a wholesome lesson, if he is a jealous person. But this is a sham,
and pretty shallow. McClintock merely wants a
pretext to drag in a plagiarism of his upon a scene
or two in "Othello."

The lovers went to the play. Elfonzo was one of
the fiddlers. He and Ambulinia must not be seen
together, lest trouble follow with the girl's malignant father; we are made to understand that clearly.
So the two sit together in the orchestra, in the
midst of the musicians. This does not seem to be
good art. In the first place, the girl would be in
the way, for orchestras are always packed closely
together, and there is no room to spare for people's
girls; in the next place, one cannot conceal a girl
in an orchestra without everybody taking notice of
it. There can be no doubt, it seems to me, that
this is bad art.

Leos is present. Of course one of the first things
that catches his eye is the maddening spectacle of
Ambulinia "leaning upon Elfonzo's chair." This
poor girl does not seem to understand even the
rudiments of concealment. But she is "in her
seventeenth," as the author phrases it, and that is
her justification.

Leos meditates, constructs a plan—with personal violence as a basis, of course. It was their way, down there. It is a good plain plan, without any imagination in it. He will go out and stand at the front door, and when these two come out he will "arrest Ambulinia from the hands of the insolent Elfonzo," and thus make for himself a "more prosperous field of immortality than ever was decreed by Omnipotence, or ever pencil drew or artist imagined." But dear me, while he is waiting there the couple climb out at the back window and scurry home! This is romantic enough, but there is a lack of dignity in the situation.

At this point McClintock puts in the whole of his curious play—which we skip.

Some correspondence follows now. The bitter father and the distressed lovers write the letters. Elopements are attempted. They are are idiotically planned, and they fail. Then we have several pages of romantic powwow and confusion signifying nothing. Another elopement is planned; it is to take place on Sunday, when everybody is at church. But the "hero" cannot keep the secret; he tells everybody. Another author would have found another instrument when he decided to defeat this elopement; but that is not McClintock's way. He uses the person that is nearest at hand.

The evasion failed, of course. Ambulinia, in her flight, takes refuge in a neighbor's house. Her father drags her home. The villagers gather, attracted by the racket.

Elfonzo was moved at this sight. The people followed on to see what was going to become of Ambulinia, while he, with downcast looks, kept at a distance, until he saw them enter the abode of the father, thrusting her, that was the sigh of his soul, out of his presence into a solitary apartment, when she exclaimed, " Elfonzo! Elfonzo! oh, Elfonzo! where art thou, with all thy heroes? haste, oh! haste, come thou to my relief. Ride on the wings of the wind! Turn thy force loose like a tempest, and roll on thy army like a whirlwind, over this mountain of trouble and confusion. Oh, friends! if any pity me, let your last efforts throng upon the green hills, and come to the relief of Ambulinia, who is guilty of nothing but innocent love." Elfonzo called out with a loud voice, " my God, can I stand this! arouse up, I beseech you, and put an end to this tyranny. Come, my brave boys," said he, " are you ready to go forth to your duty?" They stood around him. " Who," said he, " will call us to arms? Where are my thunderbolts of war? Speak ye, the first who will meet the foe! Who will go forth with me in this ocean of grievous temptation? If there is one who desires to go, let him come and shake hands upon the altar of devotion, and swear that he will be a hero; yes, a Hector in a cause like this, which calls aloud for a speedy remedy." " Mine be the deed," said a young lawyer, " and mine alone; Venus alone shall quit her station before I will forsake one jot or tittle of my promise to you; what is death to me? what is all this warlike army, if it is not to win a victory? I love the sleep of the lover and the mighty: nor would I give it over till the blood of my enemies should wreak with that of my own. But God forbid that our fame should soar on the blood of the slumberer." Mr. Valeer stands at his door with the frown of a demon upon his brow, with his dangerous weapon* ready to strike the first man who should enter his door. "Who will arise and go forward through blood and carnage to the rescue of my Ambulinia?" said Elfonzo. "All," exclaimed the multitude; and onward they went, with their implements of battle. Others, of a more timid nature, stood among the distant hills to see the result of the contest.

It will hardly be believed that after all this thunder and lightning not a drop of rain fell; but such is the fact. Elfonzo and his gang stood up and blackguarded Mr. Valeer with vigor all night, getting their outlay back with interest; then in the early morning the army and its general retired from the field, leaving the victory with their solitary adversary and his crowbar. This is the first time this has happened in romantic literature. The invention is original. Everything in this book is original; there is nothing hackneyed about it anywhere. Always, in other romances, when you find the author leading up to a climax, you know what is going to happen. But in this book it is different; the thing which seems inevitable and unavoidable never happens; it is circumvented by the art of the author every time.

Another elopement was attempted. It failed.

---

* It is a crowbar.

We have now arrived at the end. But it is not exciting. McClintock thinks it is; but it is n't. One day Elfonzo sent Ambulinia another note—a note proposing elopement No. 16. This time the plan is admirable; admirable, sagacious, ingenious, imaginative, deep—oh, everything, and perfectly easy. One wonders why it was never thought of before. This is the scheme. Ambulinia is to leave the breakfast-table, ostensibly to " attend to the placing of those flowers, which ought to have been done a week ago,"—artificial ones, of course; the others would n't keep so long,—and then, instead of fixing the flowers, she is to walk out to the grove, and go off with Elfonzo. The invention of this plan overstrained the author, that is plain, for he straight-way shows failing powers. The details of the plan are not many or elaborate. The author shall state them himself—this good soul, whose intentions are always better than his English:

You walk carelessly towards the academy grove, where you will find me with a lightning steed, elegantly equipped to bear you off where we shall be joined in wedlock with the fiist connubial rights.

Last scene of all, which the author, now much enfeebled, tries to smarten up and make acceptable to his spectacular heart by introducing some new properties,—silver bow, golden harp, olive branch,

—things that can all come good in an elopement, no doubt, yet are not to be compared to an umbrella for real handiness and reliability in an excursion of that kind.

And away she ran to the sacred grove, surrounded with glittering pearls, that indicated her coming. Elfonzo hails her with his silver bow and his golden harp. They meet— Ambulinia's countenance brightens — Elfonzo leads up his winged steed. "Mount," said he, "ye true hearted, ye fearless soul—the day is ours." She sprang upon the back of the young thunderbolt, a brilliant star sparkles upon her head, with one hand she grasps the reins, and with the other she holds an olive-branch. "Lend thy aid, ye strong winds," they exclaimed, "ye moon, ye sun, and all ye fair host of heaven, witness the enemy conquered." "Hold," said Elfonzo, "thy dashing steed." "Ride on," said Ambulinia, "the voice of thunder is behind us." And onward they went, with such rapidity, that they very soon arrived at Rural Retreat, where they dismounted, and were united with all the solemnities that usually attend such divine operations.

There is but one Homer, there was but one Shakspere, there is but one McClintock—and his immortal book is before you. Homer could not have written this book, Shakspere could not have written it, I could not have done it myself. There is nothing just like it in the literature of any country or of any epoch. It stands alone; it is monumental. It adds G. Ragsdale McClintock's to the sum of the republic's imperishable names.

THE

CURIOUS BOOK

COMPLETE

[The foregoing review of the great work of G. Ragsdale McClintock is liberally illuminated with sample extracts, but these cannot appease the appetite. Only the complete book, unabridged, can do that. Therefore it is here printed.—M. T.]

THE ENEMY CONQUERED; OR, LOVE TRIUMPHANT.

Sweet girl, thy smiles are full of charms,
Thy voice is sweeter still,
It fills the breast with fond alarms,
Echoed by every rill.

I BEGIN this little work with an eulogy upon woman, who
has ever been distinguished for her perseverance, her
constancy, and her devoted attention to those upon whom
she has been pleased to place her *affections*. Many have been
the themes upon which writers and public speakers have
dwelt with intense and increasing interest. Among these
delightful themes stands that of woman, the balm to all our
sighs and disappointments, and the most preëminent of all
other topics. Here the poet and orator have stood and gazed
with wonder and with admiration; they have dwelt upon her
innocence, the ornament of all her virtues. First viewing
her external charms, such as are set forth in her form and
her benevolent countenance, and then passing to the deep
hidden springs of loveliness and disinterested devotion. In
every clime, and in every age, she has been the pride of her
nation. Her watchfulness is untiring; she who guarded the
sepulchre was the first to approach it, and the last to depart
from its awful yet sublime scene. Even here, in this highly-
favored land, we look to her for the security of our institutions, and for our future greatness as a nation. But, strange
as it may appear, woman's charms and virtues are but slightly
appreciated by thousands. Those who should raise the stand-

ard of female worth, and paint her value with her virtues, in living colors, upon the banners that are fanned by the zephyrs of heaven, and hand them down to posterity as emblematical of a rich inheritance, do not properly estimate them.

Man is not sensible, at all times, of the nature and the emotions which bear that name; he does not understand, he will not comprehend; his intelligence has not expanded to that degree of glory which drinks in the vast revolution of humanity, its end, its mighty destination, and the causes which operated, and are still operating, to produce a more elevated station, and the objects which energize and enliven its consummation. This he is a stranger to; he is not aware that woman is the recipient of celestial love, and that man is dependent upon her to perfect his character; that without her, philosophically and truly speaking, the brightest of his intelligence is but the coldness of a winter moon, whose beams can produce no fruit, whose solar light is not its own, but borrowed from the great dispenser of effulgent beauty. We have no disposition in the world to flatter the fair sex, we would raise them above those dastardly principles which only exist in little souls, contracted hearts, and a distracted brain. Often does she unfold herself in all her fascinating loveliness, presenting the most captivating charms; yet we find man frequently treats such purity of purpose with indifference. Why does he do it? Why does he baffle that which is inevitably the source of his better days? Is he so much of a stranger to those excellent qualities, as not to appreciate woman, as not to have respect to her dignity? Since her art and beauty first captivated man, she has been his delight and his comfort; she has shared alike in his misfortunes and in his prosperity.

Whenever the billows of adversity and the tumultuous waves of trouble beat high, her smiles subdue their fury. Should the tear of sorrow and the mournful sigh of grief interrupt the peace of his mind, her voice removes them all, and she bends from her circle to encourage him onward.

When darkness would obscure his mind, and a thick cloud of gloom would bewilder its operations, her intelligent eye darts a ray of streaming light into his heart. Mighty and charming is that disinterested devotion which she is ever ready to exercise toward man, not waiting till the last moment of his danger, but seeks to relieve him in his early afflictions. It gushes forth from the expansive fullness of a tender and devoted heart, where the noblest, the purest, and the most elevated and refined feelings are matured, and developed in those many kind offices which invariably make her character.

In the room of sorrow and sickness, this unequaled characteristic may always be seen, in the performance of the most charitable acts; nothing that she can do to promote the happiness of him who she claims to be her protector, will be omitted; all is invigorated by the animating sunbeams which awaken the heart to songs of gayety. Leaving this point, to notice another prominent consideration, which is generally one of great moment and of vital importance. Invariably she is firm and steady in all her pursuits and aims. There is required a combination of forces and extreme opposition to drive her from her position; she takes her stand, not to be moved by the sound of Apollo's lyre, or the curved bow of pleasure.

Firm and true to what she undertakes, and that which she requires by her own aggrandizement, and regards as being within the strict rules of propriety, she will remain stable and unflinching to the last. A more genuine principle is not to be found in the most determined, resolute heart of man. For this she deserves to be held in the highest commendation, for this she deserves the purest of all other blessings, and for this she deserves the most laudable reward of all others. It is a noble characteristic, and is worthy the imitation of any age. And when we look at it in one particular aspect, it is still magnified, and grows brighter and brighter the more we reflect upon its eternal duration. What will she not do, when her word as well as her affections and *love* are pledged to her lover? Every thing that is dear to her on earth, all the hospitalities of kind and loving parents, all the sincerity and loveliness of sisters, and the benevolent devotion of brothers, who have surrounded her with every comfort; she will forsake them all, quit the harmony and sweet sound of the lute and the harp, and throw herself upon the affections of some devoted admirer, in whom she fondly hopes to find more than she has left behind, which is not often realized by many. Truth and virtue all combined! How deserving our admiration and love! Ah! cruel would it be in man, after she has thus manifested such an unshaken confidence in him, and said by her determination to abandon all the endearments and blandishments of home, to act a villainous part, and prove a traitor in the revolution of his mission, and then turn Hector over the innocent victim whom he swore to protect, in the presence of Heaven, recorded by the pen of an angel.

Striking as this trait may unfold itself in her character, and as preëminent as it may stand among the fair display of her other qualities, yet there is another, which struggles into existence, and adds an additional lustre to what she already possesses. I mean that disposition in woman which enables her, in sorrow, in grief, and in distress, to bear all with enduring patience. This she has done, and can and will do, amid the din of war and clash of arms. Scenes and occurrences which, to every appearance, are calculated to rend the heart with the profoundest emotions of trouble, do not fetter that exalted principle imbued in her very nature. It is true, her tender and feeling heart may often be moved, (as she is thus constituted,) but still she is not conquered, she has not given up to the harlequin of disappointments, her energies have not become clouded in the last moment of misfortune, but she is continually invigorated by the archetype of her affections. She may bury her face in her hands, and let the tear of anguish roll, she may promenade the delightful walks of some garden, decorated with all the flowers of nature, or she may steal out along some gently rippling stream, and there, as the silver waters uninterruptedly move forward, sheds her silent tears, they mingle with the waves, and take a last farewell of their agitated home, to seek a peaceful dwelling among the rolling floods; yet there is a voice rushing from her breast, that proclaims *victory* along the whole line and battlement of her affections.   That voice is the voice of patience and resignation; that voice is one that bears every thing calmly and dispassionately; amid the most distressing scenes, when the fates are arrayed against her peace, and apparently plotting for her destruction, still she is resigned.

Woman's affections are deep, consequently her troubles may be made to sink deep.   Although you may not be able to mark the traces of her grief and the furrowings of her anguish upon her winning countenance, yet be assured they are nevertheless preying upon her inward person, sapping the very foundation of that heart which alone was made for the weal and not the woe of man.   The deep recesses of the soul are fields for their operation.   But they are not destined simply to take the regions of the heart for their dominion, they are not satisfied merely with interrupting her better feelings; but after a while you may see the blooming cheek beginning to droop and fade, her intelligent eye no longer sparkles with the starry light of heaven, her vibrating pulse long since changed its regular motion, and her palpitating bosom beats once more for the mid-day of her glory.   Anxiety and care ultimately throw her into the arms of the haggard and grim monster death.   But, oh, how patient, under every pining influence!   Let us view the matter in bolder colors; see her when the dearest object of her affections recklessly seeks every bacchanalian pleasure, contents himself with the last rubbish of creation.   With what solicitude she awaits his return!   Sleep fails to perform its office—she weeps while the nocturnal shades of the night triumph in the stillness.   Bending over some favorite book, whilst the author throws before her mind the most beautiful imagery, she startles at every sound. The midnight silence is broken by the solemn announcement of the return of another morning. He is still absent: she listens for that voice which has so often been greeted by the melodies of her own; but, alas! stern silence is all that she receives for her vigilance.

Mark her unwearied watchfulness, as the night passes away. At last, brutalized by the accursed thing, he staggers along with rage, and shivering with cold, he makes his appearance. Not a murmur is heard from her lips. On the contrary, she meets him with a smile—she caresses him with her tender arms, with all the gentleness and softness of her sex. Here then, is seen her disposition, beautifully arrayed. Woman, thou art more to be admired than the spicy gales of Arabia, and more sought for than the gold of Golconda. We believe that Woman should associate freely with man, and we believe that it is for the preservation of her rights. She should become acquainted with the metaphysical designs of those who condescend to sing the siren song of flattery. This, we think, should be according to the unwritten law of decorum, which is stamped upon every innocent heart. The precepts of prudery are often steeped in the guilt of contamination, which blasts the expectations of better moments. Truth, and beautiful dreams — loveliness, and delicacy of character, with cherished affections of the ideal woman— gentle hopes and aspirations, are enough to uphold her in the storms of darkness, without the transferred colorings of a stained sufferer. How often have we seen it in our public prints, that woman occupies a false station in the world! and some have gone so far as to say it was an unnatural one. So long has she been regarded a weak creature, by the rabble and illiterate—they have looked upon her as an insufficient actress on the great stage of human life—a mere puppet, to fill up the drama of human existence—a thoughtless inactive being,—that she has too often come to the same conclusion herself, and has sometimes forgotten her high destination, in the meridian of her glory. We have but little sympathy or

patience for those who treat her as a mere Rosy Melindi—
who are always fishing for pretty compliments—who are satisfied by the gossamer of Romance, and who can be allured
by the verbosity of high-flown words, rich in language, but
poor and barren in sentiment. Beset, as she has been, by
the intellectual vulgar, the selfish, the designing, the cunning,
the hidden, and the artful—no wonder she has sometimes
folded her wings in despair, and forgotten her *heavenly* mission in the delirium of imagination; no wonder she searches
out some wild desert, to find a peaceful home. But this cannot always continue. A new era is moving gently onward,
old things are rapidly passing away; old superstitions, old
prejudices, and old notions are now bidding farewell to their
old associates and companions, and giving way to one whose
wings are plumed with the light of heaven, and tinged by the
dews of the morning. There is a remnant of blessedness that
clings to her in spite of all evil influence—there is enough of
the Divine Master left, to accomplish the noblest work ever
achieved under the canopy of the vaulted skies; and that
time is fast approaching, when the picture of the true woman
will shine from its frame of glory, to captivate, to win back,
to restore, and to call into being once more, *the object of her
mission.*

> Star of the brave! thy glory shed,
> O'er all the earth, thy army led—
> Bold meteor of immortal birth!
> Why come from Heaven to dwell on Earth?

Mighty and glorious are the days of youth; happy the moments of the *lover*, mingled with smiles and tears of his devoted, and long to be remembered are the achievements
which he gains with a palpitating heart and a trembling hand.
A bright and lovely dawn, the harbinger of a fair and prosperous day, had arisen over the beautiful little village of
Cumming, which is surrounded by the most romantic scenery
in the Cherokee country. Brightening clouds seemed to rise

from the mist of the fair Chattahoochee, to spread their beauty over the thick forest, to guide the hero whose bosom beats with aspirations to conquer the enemy that would tarnish his name, and to win back the admiration of his long tried friend. He endeavored to make his way through Sawney's Mountain, where many meet to catch the gales that are continually blowing for the refreshment of the stranger and the traveler. Surrounded as he was, by hills on every side, naked rocks dared the efforts of his energies. Soon the sky became overcast, the sun buried itself in the clouds, and the fair day gave place to gloomy twilight, which lay heavily on the Indian Plains. He remembered an old Indian Castle, that once stood at the foot of the Mountain. He thought if he could make his way to this, he would rest contented for a short time. The mountain air breathed fragrance—a rosy tinge rested on the glassy waters that murmured at its base. His resolution soon brought him to the remains of the red man's hut: he surveyed with wonder and astonishment, the decayed building, which time had buried in the dust, and thought to himself, his happiness was not yet complete. Beside the shore of the brook sat a young man, about eighteen or twenty, who seemed to be reading some favorite book, and who had a remarkably noble countenance—eyes which betrayed more than a common mind. This of course made the youth a welcome guest, and gained him friends in whatever condition of life he might be placed. The traveler observed that he was a well built figure which showed strength and grace in every movement. He accordingly addressed him in quite a gentlemanly manner, and inquired of him the way to the village. After he had received the desired information, and was about taking his leave, the youth said, "Are you not Major Elfonzo, the great musician—the champion of a noble cause—the modern Achilles, who gained so many victories in the Florida War?" "I bear that name," said the Major, "and those titles, trusting at the same time, that the ministers of grace will carry me triumphantly through

all my laudable undertakings, and if," continued the Major,
"you sir, are the patronizer of noble deeds, I should like to
make you my confidant, and learn your address." The youth
looked somewhat amazed, bowed low, mused for a moment,
and began: " My name is Roswell. I have been recently admitted to the bar, and can only give a faint outline of my
future success in that honorable profession; but I trust, sir,
like the Eagle, I shall look down from lofty rocks upon the
dwellings of man, and shall ever be ready to give you any
assistance in my official capacity, and whatever this muscular
arm of mine can do, whenever it shall be called from its buried
greatness." The Major grasped him by the hand, and exclaimed: " O! thou exalted spirit of inspiration—thou flame
of burning prosperity, may the Heaven directed blaze be the
glare of thy soul, and battle down every rampart that seems
to impede your progress!"

The road which led to the town, presented many attractions. Elfonzo had bid farewell to the youth of deep feeling,
and was now wending his way to the dreaming spot of his
fondness. The south winds whistled through the woods, as
the waters dashed against the banks, as rapid fire in the pent
furnace roars. This brought him to remember while alone,
that he quietly left behind the hospitality of a father's house,
and gladly entered the world, with higher hopes than are
often realized. But as he journeyed onward, he was mindful of the advice of his father, who had often looked sadly on
the ground, when tears of cruelly deceived hope, moistened
his eye. Elfonzo had been somewhat of a dutiful son; yet
fond of the amusements of life—had been in distant lands—
had enjoyed the pleasure of the world, and had frequently returned to the scenes of his boyhood, almost destitute of
many of the comforts of life. In this condition, he would
frequently say to his father, " Have I offended you, that you
look upon me as a stranger, and frown upon me with stinging looks? Will you not favor me with the sound of your
voice? If I have trampled upon your veneration, or have

spread a humid veil of darkness around your expectations, send me back into the world where no heart beats for me— where the foot of man has never yet trod; but give me at least one kind word—allow me to come into the presence sometimes of thy winter-worn locks." " Forbid it, Heaven, that I should be angry with thee," answered the father, " my son, and yet I send thee back to the children of the world— to the cold charity of the combat, and to a land of victory. I read another destiny in thy countenance—I learn thy in- clinations from the flame that has already kindled in my soul a strange sensation. It will seek thee, my dear *Elfonzo*, it will find thee—thou canst not escape that lighted torch, which shall blot out from the remembrance of men a long train of prophecies which they have foretold against thee. I once thought not so. Once, I was blind; but now the path of life is plain before me, and my sight is clear; yet Elfonzo, return to thy worldly occupation—take again in thy hand, that chord of sweet sounds—struggle with the civilized world, and with your own heart; fly swiftly to the enchanted ground —let the night-*Owl* send forth its screams from the stubborn oak—let the sea sport upon the beach, and the stars sing to- gether; but learn of these, Elfonzo, thy doom, and thy hid- ing place. Our most innocent as well as our most lawful *de- sires* must often be denied us, that we may learn to sacrifice them to a Higher will."

Remembering such admonitions with gratitude, Elfonzo was immediately urged by the recollection of his father's family to keep moving. His steps became quicker and quick- er—he hastened through the *piny* woods, dark as the forest was, and with joy he very soon reached the little village of repose, in whose bosom rested the boldest chivalry. His close attention to every important object—his modest ques- tions about whatever was new to him—his reverence for wise old age, and his ardent desire to learn many of the fine arts, soon brought him into respectable notice.

One mild winter day, as he walked along the streets tow-

ard the Academy, which stood upon a small eminence, surrounded by native growth—some venerable in its appearance,
others young and prosperous—all seemed inviting, and
seemed to be the very place for learning as well as for genius
to spend its research beneath its spreading shades. He entered its classic walls in the usual mode of southern manners.
The principal of the Institution begged him to be seated,
and listen to the recitations that were going on. He accordingly obeyed the request, and seemed to be much pleased.
After the school was dismissed, and the young hearts regained their freedom, with the songs of the evening, laughing at the anticipated pleasures of a happy home, while
others tittered at the actions of the past day, he addressed
the teacher in a tone that indicated a resolution—with an undaunted mind. He said he had determined to become a
student, if he could meet with his approbation. "Sir," said
he, "I have spent much time in the world. I have traveled
among the uncivilized inhabitants of America. I have met
with friends, and combated with foes; but none of these
gratify my ambition, or decide what is to be my destiny. I
see the learned world have an influence with the voice of the
people themselves. The despoilers of the remotest kingdoms
of the earth, refer their differences to this class of persons.
This the illiterate and inexperienced little dream of; and
now if you will receive me as I am, with these deficiencies—
with all my misguided opinions, I will give you my honor,
sir, that I will never disgrace the Institution, or those who
have placed you in this honorable station." The instructor,
who had met with many disappointments, knew how to feel
for a stranger who had been thus turned upon the charities
of an unfeeling community. He looked at him earnestly,
and said: "Be of good cheer—look forward, sir, to the high
destination you may attain. Remember, the more elevated
the mark at which you aim, the more sure, the more glorious,
the more magnificent the prize."· From wonder to wonder,
his encouragement led the impatient listener. A strange

nature bloomed before him—giant streams promised him success—gardens of hidden treasures opened to his view. All this, so vividly described, seemed to gain a new witchery from his glowing fancy.

In 1842, he entered the class, and made rapid progress in the English and Latin departments. Indeed, he continued advancing with such rapidity that he was like to become the first in his class, and made such unexpected progress, and was so studious, that he had almost forgotten the pictured saint of his affections. The fresh wreaths of the pine and cypress, had waited anxiously to drop once more the dews of Heaven upon the heads of those who had so often poured forth the tender emotions of their souls under its boughs. He was aware of the pleasure that he had seen there. So one evening, as he was returning from his reading, he concluded he would pay a visit to this enchanting spot. Little did he think of witnessing a shadow of his former happiness, though no doubt, he wished it might be so. He continued sauntering by the road-side, meditating on the past. The nearer he approached the spot, the more anxious he became. At that moment, a tall female figure flitted across his path, with a bunch of roses in her hand; her countenance showed uncommon vivacity, with a resolute spirit; her ivory teeth already appeared as she smiled beautifully, promenading,— while her ringlets of hair, dangled unconsciously around her snowy neck. Nothing was wanting to complete her beauty. The tinge of the rose was in full bloom upon her cheek; the charms of sensibility and tenderness were always her associates. In Ambulinia's bosom dwelt a noble soul—one that never faded —one that never was conquered. Her heart yielded to no feeling but the love of Elfonzo, on whom she gazed with intense delight, and to whom she felt herself more closely bound, because he sought the hand of no other. Elfonzo was roused from his apparent revery. His books no longer were his inseparable companions—his thoughts arrayed themselves to encourage him to the field of victory.

He endeavored to speak to his supposed Ambulinia, but his speech appeared not in words. No, his effort was a stream of fire, that kindled his soul into a flame of admiration, and carried his senses away captive. Ambulinia had disappeared, to make him more mindful of his duty. As she walked speedily away through the piny woods, she calmly echoed: "O! Elfonzo, thou wilt now look from thy sunbeams. Thou shalt now walk in a new path—perhaps thy way leads through darkness; but fear not, the stars foretell happiness."

Not many days afterwards, as surrounded by fragrant flowers, she sat one evening at twilight, to enjoy the cool breeze that whispered notes of melody along the distant groves, the little birds perched on every side, as if to watch the movements of their new visitor. The bells were tolling, when Elfonzo silently stole along by the wild wood flowers, holding in his hand his favorite instrument of music—his eye continually searching for Ambulinia, who hardly seemed to perceive him, as she played carelessly with the songsters that hopped from branch to branch. Nothing could be more striking than the difference between the two. Nature seemed to have given the more tender soul to Elfonzo, and the stronger and more courageous to Ambulinia. A deep feeling spoke from the eyes of Elfonzo,—such a feeling as can only be expressed by those who are blessed as admirers, and by those who are able to return the same with sincerity of heart. He was a few years older than Ambulinia: she had turned a little into her seventeenth. He had almost grown up in the Cherokee country, with the same equal proportions as one of the natives. But little intimacy had existed between them until the year forty-one—because the youth felt that the character of such a lovely girl was too exalted to inspire any other feeling than that of quiet reverence. But as lovers will not always be insulted, at all times and under all circumstances, by the frowns and cold looks of crabbed old age, which should continually reflect dignity upon those around, and treat the unfortunate as well as the fortunate with a

graceful mien, he continued to use diligence and perseverance. All this lighted a spark in his heart that changed his
whole character, and like the unyielding Deity that follows
the storm to check its rage in the forest, he resolves for the
first time to shake off his embarrassment, and return where
he had before only worshiped.

It could not escape Ambulinia's penetrating eye, that he
sought an interview with her, which she as anxiously avoided,
and assumed a more distant calmness than before, seemingly
to destroy all hope. After many efforts and struggles with
his own person, with timid steps the Major approached the
damsel, with the same caution as he would have done in a field
of battle. "Lady Ambulinia," said he, trembling, "I have
long desired a moment like this. I dare not let it escape.
I fear the consequences; yet I hope your indulgence will at
least hear my petition. Can you not anticipate what I would
say, and what I am about to express? Will you not, like
Minerva, who sprung from the brain of Jupiter, release me
from thy winding chains or cure me——" "Say no more,
Elfonzo," answered Ambulinia, with a serious look, raising
her hand as if she intended to swear eternal hatred against
the whole world,—"another lady in my place, would have
perhaps answered your question in bitter coldness. I know
not the little arts of my sex. I care but little for the vanity
of those who would chide me, and am unwilling, as well as
ashamed to be guilty of any thing that would lead you to
think 'all is not gold that glitters:' so be not rash in your
resolution. It is better to repent now, than to do it in a
more solemn hour. Yes, I know what you would say. I
know you have a costly gift for me—the noblest that man can
make—*your heart!* you should not offer it to one so un-
worthy. Heaven, you know, has allowed my father's house
to be made a house of solitude, a home of silent obedience,
which my parents say, is more to be admired than big names
and high sounding titles. Notwithstanding all this, let me
speak the emotions of an honest heart—allow me to say in

the fullness of my hopes that I anticipate better days. The
bird may stretch its wings toward the sun, which it can never
reach; and flowers of the field appear to ascend in the same
direction, because they cannot do otherwise: but man confides his complaints to the saints in whom he believes; for
in their abodes of light they know no more sorrow. From
your confession and indicative looks, I must be that person:
if so, deceive not yourself."

Elfonzo replied, "Pardon me, my dear madam, for my
frankness. I have loved you from my earliest days—every
thing grand and beautiful hath borne the image of Ambulinia: while precipices on every hand surrounded me, your
guardian angel stood and beckoned me away from the deep
abyss. In every trial—in every misfortune, I have met with
your helping hand; yet I never dreamed or dared to cherish
thy love, till a voice impaired with age encouraged the cause,
and declared they who acquired thy favor, should win a
victory. I saw how Leos worshiped thee. I felt my own unworthiness. I began to *know jealousy*, a strong guest indeed,
in my bosom, yet I could see if I gained your admiration,
Leos was to be my rival. I was aware that he had the influence of your parents, and the wealth of a deceased relative,
which is too often mistaken for permanent and regular tranquillity; yet I have determined by your permission to beg an
interest in your prayers—to ask you to animate my drooping
spirits by your smiles and your winning looks; for, if you but
speak, I shall be conqueror, my enemies shall stagger like
Olympus shakes. And though earth and sea may tremble,
and the charioteer of the sun may forget his dashing steed;
yet I am assured that it is only to arm me with divine weapons, which will enable me to complete my long tried intention." "Return to yourself, Elfonzo," said Ambulinia, pleasantly, "a dream of vision has disturbed your intellect—you
are above the atmosphere, dwelling in the celestial regions,
nothing is there that urges or hinders, nothing that brings
discord into our present litigation. I entreat you to conde-

scend a little, and be a man, and forget it all. When Homer
describes the battle of the gods and noble men, fighting with
giants and dragons, they represent under this image, our
struggles with the delusions of our passions. You have
exalted me, an unhappy girl, to the skies,—you have called
me a saint, and portrayed in your imagination, an angel in
human form. Let her remain such to you,—let her continue
to be as you have supposed, and be assured that she will
consider a share in your esteem, as her highest treasure.
Think not that I would allure you from the path in which
your conscience leads you; for you know I respect the conscience of others, as I would die for my own. Elfonzo, if I
am worthy of thy love, let such conversation never again
pass between us. Go, seek a nobler theme! we will seek it
in the stream of time, as the sun set in the Tigris." As she
spake these words, she grasped the hand of Elfonzo, saying
at the same time—"peace and prosperity attend you my
hero: be up and doing." Closing her remarks with this expression, she walked slowly away, leaving Elfonzo astonished
and amazed. He ventured not to follow, or detain her.
Here he stood alone, gazing at the stars;—confounded as he
was, here he stood. The rippling stream rolled on at his
feet. Twilight had already begun to draw her sable mantle
over the earth, and now and then, the fiery smoke would ascend from the little town which lay spread out before him.
The citizens seemed to be full of life and good humor; but
poor Elfonzo saw not a brilliant scene. No, his future life
stood before him, stripped of the hopes that once adorned
all his sanguine desires. "Alas!" said he, "am I now Grief's
disappointed son at last." Ambulinia's image rose before
his fancy. A mixture of ambition and greatness of soul,
moved upon his young heart, and encouraged him to bear
all his crosses with the patience of a Job, notwithstanding he
had to encounter with so many obstacles. He still endeavored to prosecute his studies, and reasonably progressed in
his education. Still, he was not content; there was some-

thing yet to be done, before his happiness was complete. He would visit his friends and acquaintances. They would invite him to social parties, insisting that he should partake of the amusements that were going on. This he enjoyed tolerably well. The ladies and gentlemen were generally well pleased with the Major; as he delighted all with his violin, which seemed to have a thousand chords—more symphonious than the Muses of Apollo, and more enchanting than the ghost of the Hills. He passed some days in the country. During that time Leos had made many calls upon Ambulinia, who was generally received with a great deal of courtesy by the family. They thought him to be a young man worthy of attention, though he had but little in his soul to attract the attention, or even win the affections of her whose graceful manners had almost made him a slave to every bewitching look that fell from her eyes. Leos made several attempts to tell her of his fair prospects—how much he loved her, and how much it would add to his bliss if he could but think she would be willing to share these blessings with him; but choked by his undertaking, he made himself more like an inactive drone, than he did like one who bowed at beauty's shrine.

Elfonzo again wends his way to the stately walls and new-built village. He now determines to see the end of the prophecy which had been foretold to him. The clouds burst from his sight; he believes if he can but see his Ambulinia, he can open to her view the bloody altars that have been misrepresented to stigmatize his name. He knows that her breast is transfixed with the sword of reason, and ready at all times to detect the hidden villainy of her enemies. He resolves to see her in her own home, with the consoling theme; "'I can but perish if I go.' Let the consequences be what they may," said he, "if I die, it shall be contending and struggling for my own rights."

Night had almost overtaken him when he arrived in town. Col. Elder, a noble-hearted, high-minded and independent man, met him at his door as usual, and seized him by the hand. "Well, Elfonzo," said the Col., "how does the world use you in your efforts?" "I have no objection to the world," said Elfonzo; "but the people are rather singular in some of their opinions." "Aye, well," said the Col., "you must remember that creation is made up of many mysteries: just take things by the right handle — be always sure you know which is the smooth side, before you attempt your polish — be reconciled to your fate, be it what it may, and never find fault with your condition, unless your complaining will benefit it. Perseverance is a principle that should be commendable in those who have judgment to govern it. I should never have been so successful in my hunting excursions, had I waited till the deer by some magic dream had been drawn to the muzzle of the gun, before I made an attempt to fire at the game that dared my boldness in the wild forest. The great mystery in hunting seems to be,—a good marksman, a resolute mind, a fixed determination, and my word for it, you will never return home without sounding your horn with the breath of a new victory. And so with every other undertaking. Be confident that your ammunition is of the right kind —always pull your trigger with a steady hand, and so soon as you perceive a calm, touch her off, and the spoils are yours."

This filled him with redoubled vigor, and he set out with a stronger anxiety than ever to the home of Ambulinia. A few short steps soon brought him to the door, half out of breath. He rapped gently. Ambulinia, who sat in the parlor alone, suspecting Elfonzo was near, ventured to the door, opened it, and beheld the hero, who stood in an humble attitude, bowed gracefully, and as they caught each other's looks, the light of peace beamed from the eyes of Ambulinia. Elfonzo caught the expression; a halloo of smothered shouts ran through every vein, and for the first time he dared to impress a kiss upon her cheek. The scene was overwhelming; had the temptation been less animating, he would not have ven-

tured to have acted so contrary to the desired wish of his
Ambulinia ; but who could have withstood the irresistible
temptation! What society condemns the practice, but a cold,
heartless, uncivilized people, that know nothing of the warm
attachments of refined society? Here the dead was raised
to his long cherished hopes, and the lost was found. Here
all doubt and danger were buried in the vortex of oblivion;
sectional differences no longer disunited their opinions; like
the freed bird from the cage, sportive claps its rustling wings,
wheels about to Heaven in a joyful strain, and raises its notes
to the upper sky. Ambulinia insisted upon Elfonzo to be
seated, and give her a history of his unnecessary absence;
assuring him the family had retired, consequently they would
ever remain ignorant of his visit. Advancing toward him,
she gave a bright display of her rosy neck, and from her head
the ambrosial locks breathed divine fragrance; her robe hung
waving to his view, while she stood like a goddess confessed
before him.

"It does seem to me, my dear sir," said Ambulinia, "that
you have been gone an age. Oh, the restless hours I have
spent since I last saw you, in yon beautiful grove. There is
where I trifled with your feelings for the express purpose of
trying your attachment for me. I now find you are devoted;
but ah! I trust you live not unguarded by the powers of
Heaven. Though oft did I refuse to join my hand with thine,
and as oft did I cruelly mock thy entreaties with borrowed
shapes: yes, I feared to answer thee by terms, in words sin-
cere and undissembled. O! could I pursue, and you had
leisure to hear the annals of my woes, the evening star would
shut Heaven's gates upon the impending day, before my tale
would be finished, and this night would find me soliciting
your forgiveness." "Dismiss thy fears and thy doubts,"
replied Elfonzo. "Look O! look: that angelic look of thine,
—bathe not thy visage in tears; banish those floods that are
gathering; let my confession and my presence bring thee
some relief." "Then, indeed, I will be cheerful," said Am-

bulinia, "and I think if we will go to the exhibition this evening, we certainly will see something worthy of our attention. One of the most tragical scenes is to be acted that has ever been witnessed, and one that every jealous-hearted person should learn a lesson from. It cannot fail to have a good effect, as it will be performed by those who are young and vigorous, and learned as well as enticing. You are aware, Major Elfonzo, who are to appear on the stage, and what the characters are to represent." "I am acquainted with the circumstances," replied Elfonzo, "and as I am to be one of the musicians upon that interesting occasion, I should be much gratified if you would favor me with your company during the hours of the exercises."

"What strange notions are in your mind?" inquired Ambulinia. "Now I know you have something in view, and I desire you to tell me why it is that you are so anxious that I should continue with you while the exercises are going on; though if you think I can add to your happiness and predilections, I have no particular objection to acquiesce in your request. Oh, I think I foresee, now, what you anticipate." "And will you have the goodness to tell me what you think it to be?" inquired Elfonzo. "By all means," answered Ambulinia; "a rival, sir, you would fancy in your own mind; but let me say to you, fear not! fear not! I will be one of the last persons to disgrace my sex, by thus encouraging every one who may feel disposed to visit me, who may honor me with their graceful bows and their choicest compliments. It is true, that young men too often mistake civil politeness for the finer emotions of the heart, which is tantamount to courtship; but, ah! how often are they deceived, when they come to test the weight of sunbeams, with those on whose strength hangs the future happiness of an untried life."

The people were now rushing to the Academy with impatient anxiety; the band of music was closely followed by the students; then the parents and guardians; nothing interrupted the glow of spirits which ran through every bosom,

tinged with the songs of a Virgil and the tide of a Homer.
Elfonzo and Ambulinia soon repaired to the scene, and fortunately for them both, the house was so crowded that they
took their seats together in the music department, which was
not in view of the auditory. This fortuitous circumstance
added more to the bliss of the major than a thousand such
exhibitions would have done. He forgot that he was man;
music had lost its charms for him; whenever he attempted
to carry his part, the string of the instrument would break,
the bow became stubborn, and refused to obey the loud calls
of the audience. Here, he said, was the paradise of his
home, the long sought for opportunity; he felt as though he
could send a million supplications to the throne of heaven,
for such an exalted privilege. Poor Leos, who was somewhere in the crowd, looking as attentively as if he was searching for a needle in a haystack; here he stood, wondering to
himself why Ambulinia was not there. "Where can she be?
Oh! if she was only here, how I could relish the scene! Elfonzo is certainly not in town; but what if he is? I have got
the wealth, if I have not the dignity, and I am sure that the
squire and his lady have always been particular friends of
mine, and I think with this assurance I shall be able to get
upon the blind side of the rest of the family, and make the
heaven-born Ambulinia the mistress of all I possess." Then,
again, he would drop his head, as if attempting to solve the
most difficult problem in Euclid. While he was thus conjec-
turing in his own mind, a very interesting part of the exhibition was going on, which called the attention of all present.
The curtains of the stage waved continually by the repelled
forces that were given to them, which caused Leos to behold
Ambulinia leaning upon the chair of Elfonzo. Her lofty
beauty, seen by the glimmering of the chandelier, filled his
heart with rapture, he knew not how to contain himself; to
go where they were, would expose him to ridicule; to continue where he was, with such an object before him, without
being allowed an explanation in that trying hour, would be

to the great injury of his mental as well as of his physical powers; and, in the name of high heaven, what must he do? Finally, he resolved to contain himself as well as he conveniently could, until the scene was over, and then he would plant himself at the door, to arrest Ambulinia from the hands of the insolent Elfonzo, and thus make for himself a more prosperous field of immortality than ever was decreed by Omnipotence, or ever pencil drew or artist imagined. Accordingly he made himself sentinel, immediately after the performance of the evening,—retained his position apparently in defiance of all the world, he waited, he gazed at every lady, his whole frame trembled; here he stood, until everything like human shape had disappeared from the institution, and he had done nothing; he had failed to accomplish that which he so eagerly sought for. Poor, unfortunate creature! he had not the eyes of an Argus, or he might have seen his Juno and Elfonzo, assisted by his friend Sigma, make their escape from the window, and, with the rapidity of a racehorse, hurry through the blast of the storm, to the residence of her father, without being recognized. He did not tarry long, but assured Ambulinia the endless chain of their existence was more closely connected than ever, since he had seen the virtuous, innocent, imploring, and the constant Amelia murdered by the jealous-hearted Farcillo, the accursed of the land.

The following is the tragical scene, which is only introduced to show the subject matter that enabled Elfonzo to come to such a determinate resolution, that nothing of the kind should ever dispossess him of his true character, should he be so fortunate as to succeed in his present undertaking.

Amelia was the wife of Farcillo, and a virtuous woman; Gracia, a young lady, was her particular friend and confidant. Farcillo grew jealous of Amelia, murders her, finds out that he was deceived, *and stabs himself*. Amelia appears alone, talking to herself.

A. Hail, ye solitary ruins of antiquity, ye sacred tombs and silent walks! it is your aid I invoke; it is to you, my soul, wrapt in deep meditation, pours forth its prayer. Here I wander upon the stage of mortality, since the world hath turned against me. Those whom I believed to be my friends, alas! are now my enemies, planting thorns in all my paths, poisoning all my pleasures, and turning the past to pain. What a lingering catalogue of sighs and tears lies just before me, crowding my aching bosom with the fleeting dream of humanity, which must shortly terminate. And to what purpose will all this bustle of life, these agitations and emotions of the heart have conduced, if it leave behind it nothing of utility, if it leave no traces of improvement! Can it be that I am deceived in my conclusion? No, I see that I have nothing to hope for, but everything to fear, which tends to drive me from the walks of time.

> Oh! in this dead night, if loud winds arise,
> To lash the surge and bluster in the skies,
> May the west its furious rage display,
> Toss me with storms in the watery way.

(Enter Gracia.)

G. Oh, Amelia, is it you, the object of grief, the daughter of opulence, of wisdom and philosophy, that thus complaineth? It can not be you are the child of misfortune, speaking of the monuments of former ages, which were allotted not for the reflection of the distressed, but for the fearless and bold.

A. Not the child of poverty, Gracia, or the heir of glory and peace, but of fate. Remember, I have wealth more than wit can number; I have had power more than kings could encompass; yet the world seems a desert; all nature appears an afflictive spectacle of warring passions. This blind fatality, that capriciously sports with the rules and lives of mortals, tells me that the mountains will never again send forth the water of their springs to my thirst. Oh, that I might be freed and set at liberty from wretchedness! But I fear, I fear this will never be.

G. Why, Amelia, this untimely grief? What has caused the sorrows that bespeak better and happier days, to thus lavish out such heaps of misery? You are aware that your instructive lessons embellish the mind with holy truths, by wedding its attention to none but great and noble affections.

A. This, of course, is some consolation. I will ever love my own species with feelings of a fond recollection, and while I am studying to advance the universal philanthropy, and the spotless name of my own sex, I will try to build my own upon the pleasing belief, that I have accelerated the advancement of one who whispers of departed confidence.

> And I, like some poor peasant fated to reside
> Remote from friends, in a forest wide.
> Oh, see what woman's woes and human wants require,
> Since that great day hath spread the seed of sinful fire.

G. Look up, thou poor disconsolate; you speak of quitting earthly enjoyments. Unfold thy bosom to a friend, who would be willing to sacrifice every enjoyment for the restoration of that dignity and gentleness of mind, which used to grace your walks, and which is so natural to yourself; not only that, but your paths were strewed with flowers of every hue and of every order.

> With verdant green the mountains glow,
> For thee, for thee, the lilies grow;
> Far stretched beneath the tented hills,
> A fairer flower the valley fills.

A. Oh, would to Heaven I could give you a short narrative of my former prospects for happiness, since you have acknowledged to be an unchangeable confidant—the richest of all other blessings. Oh, ye names forever glorious, ye celebrated scenes, ye renowned spot of my hymeneal moments; how replete is your chart with sublime reflections! How many profound vows, decorated with immaculate deeds, are written upon the surface of that precious spot of earth, where I yielded up my life of celibacy, bade youth with all its beauties a final adieu, took a last farewell of the laurels that had accompanied me up the hill of my juvenile career. It was then I began to descend toward the valley of disappointment and sorrow; it was then I cast my little bark upon a mysterious ocean of wedlock, with him who then smiled and caressed me, but, alas! now frowns with bitterness, and has grown jealous and cold towards me, because the ring he gave me is misplaced or lost. Oh, bear me, ye flowers of memory, softly through the eventful history of past times; and ye places that have witnessed the progression of man in the circle of so many societies, aid, oh aid my recollection, while I endeavor to trace the vicissitudes of a life devoted in endeavoring to comfort him that I claim as the object of my wishes.

> Ah! ye mysterious men, of all the world, how few
> Act just to Heaven and to your promise true!
> But He who guides the stars with a watchful eye,
> The deeds of men lay open without disguise;
> Oh, this alone will avenge the wrongs I bear,
> For all the oppressed are his peculiar care.

(*F. makes a slight noise.*)

A. Who is there—Farcillo?

G. Then I must be gone. Heaven protect you. Oh, Amelia, farewell, be of good cheer.

> May you stand, like Olympus' towers,
> Against earth and all jealous powers!
> May you, with loud shouts ascend on high,
> Swift as an eagle in the upper sky.

A. Why so cold and distant to-night, Farcillo? Come, let us each other greet, and forget all the past, and give security for the future.

F. Security! talk to me about giving security for the

future—what an insulting requisition! Have you said your prayers to-night, Madam Amelia?

A. Farcillo, we sometimes forget our duty, particularly when we expect to be caressed by others.

F. If you bethink yourself of any crime, or of any fault, that is yet concealed from the courts of Heaven and the thrones of grace, I bid you ask and solicit forgiveness for it now.

A. Oh, be kind, Farcillo, don't treat me so. What do you mean by all this?

F. Be kind, you say; you, madam, have forgot that kindness you owe to me, and bestowed it upon another; you shall suffer for your conduct when you make your peace with your God. I would not slay thy unprotected spirit. I call to Heaven to be my guard and my watch—I would not kill thy soul, in which all once seemed just, right, and perfect; but I must be brief, woman.

A. What, talk you of killing? Oh, Farcillo, Farcillo, what is the matter?

F. Aye, I do, without doubt; mark what I say, Amelia.

A. Then, O God, O Heaven, and Angels, be propitious, and have mercy upon me.

F. Amen, to that, madam, with all my heart, and with all my soul.

A. Farcillo, listen to me one moment; I hope you will not kill me.

F. Kill you, aye, that I will; attest it, ye fair host of light, record it, ye dark imps of hell!

A. Oh, I fear you—you are fatal when darkness covers your brow; yet I know not why I should fear, since I never wronged you in all my life. I stand, sir, guiltless before you.

F. You pretend to say you are guiltless! Think of thy sins, Amelia; think, oh think, hidden woman.

A. Wherein have I not been true to you? That death is unkind, cruel, and unnatural, that kills for loving.

F. Peace, and be still while I unfold to thee.

A. I will, Farcillo, and while I am thus silent, tell me the cause of such cruel coldness in an hour like this.

F. That *ring*, oh that ring I so loved, and gave thee as the ring of my heart; the allegiance you took to be faithful, when it was presented; the kisses and smiles with which you honored it. You became tired of the donor, despised it as a plague, and finally gave it to Malos, the hidden, the vile traitor.

A. No, upon my word and honor, I never did; I appeal to the Most High to bear me out in this matter. Send for Malos, and ask him.

F. Send for Malos, aye! Malos you wish to see; I thought so. I knew you could not keep his name concealed. Amelia, sweet Amelia, take heed, take heed of perjury; you are on the stage of death, to suffer for *your sins.*

A. What, not to die I hope, my Farcillo, my ever beloved.

F. Yes, madam, to die a traitor's death. Shortly your spirit shall take its exit; therefore confess freely thy sins, for to deny tends only to make me groan under the bitter cup thou hast made for me. Thou art to die with the name of traitor on thy brow!

A. Then, O Lord, have mercy upon me; give me courage, give me grace and fortitude to stand this hour of trial.

F. Amen, I say, with all my heart.

A. And, oh, Farcillo, will you have mercy, too? I never intentionally offended you in all my life; never *loved* Malos, never gave him cause to think so, as the high court of Justice will acquit me before its tribunal.

F. Oh, false, perjured woman, thou dost chill my blood, and makest me a demon like thyself. I saw the ring.

A. He found it, then, or got it clandestinely; send for him, and let him confess the truth; let his confession be sifted.

F. And you still wish to see him! I tell you, madam, he hath already confessed, and thou knowest the darkness of thy heart.

A. What, my deceived Farcillo, that I gave him the ring,

in which all my affections were concentrated? Oh, surely not.

F. Aye, he did. Ask thy conscience, and it will speak with a voice of thunder to thy soul.

A. He will not say so, he dare not, he can not.

F. No, he will not say so now, because his mouth, I trust, is hushed in death, and his body stretched to the four winds of heaven, to be torn to pieces by carnivorous birds.

A. What, is he dead, and gone to the world of spirits with that declaration in his mouth? Oh, unhappy man! Oh, insupportable hour!

F. Yes, and had all his sighs and looks and tears been lives, my great revenge could have slain them all, without the least condemnation.

A. Alas! he is ushered into eternity without testing the matter for which I am abused and sentenced and condemned to die.

F. Cursed, infernal woman! Weepest thou for him to my face? He that hath robbed me of my peace, my energy, the whole love of my life? Could I call the fabled Hydra, I would have him live and perish, survive and die, until the sun itself would grow dim with age. I would make him have the thirst of a Tantalus, and roll the wheel of an Ixion, until the stars of heaven should quit their brilliant stations.

A. Oh, invincible God, save me! Oh, unsupportable moment! Oh, heavy hour! Banish me, Farcillo — send me where no eye can ever see me, where no sound shall ever greet my ear; but, oh, slay me not, Farcillo; vent thy rage and thy spite upon this emaciated frame of mine, only spare my life.

F. Your petitions avail nothing, cruel Amelia.

A. Oh, Farcillo, perpetrate the dark deed to-morrow; let me live till then, for my past kindness to you, and it may be some kind angel will show to you that I am not only the object of innocence, but one who never loved another but your noble self.

F. Amelia, the decree has gone forth, it is to be done, and that quickly; thou art to die, madam.

A. But half an hour allow me, to see my father and my only child, to tell her the treachery and vanity of this world.

F. There is no alternative, there is no pause; my daughter shall not see its deceptive mother die; your father shall not know that his daughter fell disgraced, despised by all but her enchanting Malos.

A. Oh, Farcillo, put up thy threatening dagger into its scabbard; let it rest and be still, just while I say one prayer for thee and for my child.

F. It is too late, thy doom is fixed, thou hast not confessed to Heaven or to me, my child's protector—thou art to die. Ye powers of earth and heaven, protect and defend me in this alone. (Stabs her, while imploring for mercy.)

A. Oh, Farcillo, Farcillo, a guiltless death I die.

F. Die! die! die!

(*Gracia enters running, falls to her knees weeping, and kisses Amelia.*)

G. Oh, Farcillo, Farcillo! oh, Farcillo!

F. I am here, the genius of the age, and the avenger of my wrongs.

G. Oh, lady, speak once more; sweet Amelia, oh speak again. Gone, gone—yes, forever gone! Farcillo, oh, cold-hearted Farcillo, some evil fiend hath urged you to do this, Farcillo.

F. Say you not so again, or you shall receive the same fate. I did the glorious deed, madam—beware, then, how you talk.

G. I fear not your implements of war; I will let you know you have not the power to do me harm. If you have a heart of triple brass, it shall be reached and melted, and thy blood shall chill thy veins and grow stiff in thy arteries. Here is the ring of the virtuous and innocent murdered Amelia; I obtained it from Malos, who yet lives, in hopes that he will survive the wound given him, and says he got it clandestinely —declares Amelia to be the princess of truth and virtue, invulnerable to anything like forgetting her first devotion to thee. The world has heard of your conduct and your jealousy, and with one universal voice declare her to be the best of all in piety; that she is the star of this great universe, and a more virtuous woman never lived since the wheels of time began. Oh, had you waited till to-morrow, or until I had returned, some kind window would have been opened to her relief. But, alas! she is gone—yes, forever gone, to try the realities of an unknown world!

(*Farcillo leaning over the body of Amelia.*)

F. Malos not dead, and here is my ring! Oh, Amelia! falsely, falsely murdered! Oh, bloody deed! Oh, wretch that I am! Oh, angels forgive me! Oh, God, withhold thy vengeance! Oh, Amelia! if Heaven would make a thousand worlds like this, set with diamonds, and all of one perfect chrysolite, I would not have done this for them all, I would not have frowned and cursed as I did. Oh, she was heavenly true, nursed in the very lap of bright angels! Cursed slave that I am! Jealousy, oh! thou infernal demon! Lost, lost to every sense of honor! Oh! Amelia—heaven-born Amelia —dead, dead! Oh! oh! oh!—then let me die with thee. Farewell! farewell! ye world that deceived me! (Stabs himself.)

———

Soon after the excitement of this tragical scene was over, and the enlisted feeling for Amelia had grown more buoyant with Elfonzo and Ambulinia, he determined to visit his retired home, and make the necessary improvements to enjoy a better day; consequently he conveyed the following lines to Ambulinia:

Go tell the world that hope is glowing,
  Go bid the rocks their silence break,
Go tell the stars that love is glowing,
  Then bid the hero his lover take.

In the region where scarcely the foot of man hath ever

trod, where the woodman hath not found his way, lies a blooming grove, seen only by the sun when he mounts his lofty throne, visited only by the light of the stars, to whom are entrusted the guardianship of earth, before the sun sinks to rest in his rosy bed. High cliffs of rocks surround the romantic place, and in the small cavity of the rocky wall grows the daffodil clear and pure; and as the wind blows along the enchanting little mountain which surrounds the lonely spot, it nourishes the flowers with the dew-drops of heaven. Here is the seat of Elfonzo; darkness claims but little victory over this dominion, and in vain does she spread out her gloomy wings. Here the waters flow perpetually, and the trees lash their tops together to bid the welcome visitor a happy muse. Elfonzo during his short stay in the country, had fully persuaded himself that it was his duty to bring this solemn matter to an issue. A duty that he individually owed, as a gentleman, to the parents of Ambulinia, a duty in itself involving not only his own happiness and his own standing in society, but one that called aloud the act of the parties to make it perfect and complete. How he should communicate his intentions to get a favorable reply. he was at a loss to know; he knew not whether to address Esq. Valeer in prose or in poetry, in a jocular or an argumentative manner, or whether he should use moral suasion, legal injunction, or seize and take by reprisal; if it was to do the latter, he would have no difficulty in deciding in his own mind, but his gentlemanly honor was at stake; so he concluded to address the following letter to the father and mother of Ambulinia, as his address in person he knew would only aggravate the old gentleman, and perhaps his lady.

Cumming, Ga., January 22, 1844.

Mr. and Mrs. Valeer—

Again, I resume the pleasing task of addressing you, and once more beg an immediate answer to my many salutations. From every circumstance that has taken place, I feel in duty bound to comply with my obligations; to forfeit my word would be more than I dare do; to break my pledge, and my vows that have been witnessed, sealed, and delivered in the presence of an unseen Deity, would be disgraceful on my part, as well as ruinous to Ambulinia. I wish no longer to be kept in suspense about this matter. I wish to act gentlemanly in every particular. It is true, the promises I have made, are unknown to any but Ambulinia, and I think it unnecessary to here enumerate them, as they who promise the most, generally perform the least. Can you for a moment doubt my sincerity, or my character? My only wish is, sir, that you may calmly and dispassionately look at the situation of the case, and if your better judgment should dictate otherwise, my obligations may induce me to pluck the flower that you so diametrically opposed. We have sworn by the saints—by the gods of battle, and by that faith whereby just men are made perfect, to be united. I hope, my dear sir, you will find it convenient as well as agreeable, to give me a favorable answer, with the signature of Mrs. Valeer, as well as yourself.

With very great esteem,
your humble servant,
J. I. ELFONZO.

The moon and stars had grown pale, when Ambulinia had retired to rest. A crowd of unpleasant thoughts passed through her bosom. Solitude dwelt in her chamber—no sound from the neighboring world penetrated its stillness; it appeared a temple of silence, of repose, and of mystery. At that moment she heard a still voice calling her father. In an instant, like the flash of lightning, a thought ran through her mind, that it must be the bearer of Elfonzo's communication. "It is not a dream!" she said, "no, I cannot read dreams. Oh! I would to Heaven I was near that glowing eloquence—that poetical language,—it charms the mind in an inexpressible manner, and warms the coldest heart." While consoling herself with this strain, her father rushed into her room almost frantic with rage, exclaiming: "O, Ambulinia! Ambulinia!! undutiful, ungrateful daughter! What does this mean? Why does this letter bear such heartrending intelligence? Will you quit a father's house

with this debased wretch, without a place to lay his distracted
head; going up and down the country, with every novel object that may chance to wander through this region.   He is
a pretty man to make love known to his superiors, and you,
Ambulinia, have done but little credit to yourself by honor-
ing his visits.   O wretchedness! can it be, that my hopes of
happiness are forever blasted!   Will you not listen to a father's entreaties, and pay some regard to a mother's tears.   I
know, and I do pray that God will give me fortitude to bear
with this sea of troubles, and rescue my daughter, my Ambulinia, as a brand from the eternal burning."   "Forgive me,
father, Oh! forgive thy child," replied Ambulinia.   "My
heart is ready to break, when I see you in this grieved state
of agitation.   Oh! think not so meanly of me, as that I
mourn for my own danger.   Father, I am only woman.
Mother, I am only the templement of thy youthful years; but
will suffer courageously whatever punishment you think
proper to inflict upon me, if you will but allow me to comply
with my most sacred promises—if you will but give me my
personal right, and my personal liberty.   Oh father! if your
generosity will but give me these, I ask nothing more.
When Elfonzo offered me his heart, I gave him my hand,
never to forsake him, and now may the mighty God banish
me, before I leave him in adversity.   What a heart must I
have to rejoice in prosperity with him whose offers I have ac-
cepted, and then, when poverty comes, haggard as it may be,
—for me to trifle with the oracles of Heaven, and change
with every fluctuation that may interrupt our happiness,—
like the politician who runs the political gauntlet for office
one day, and the next day, because the horizon is darkened
a little, he is seen running for his life, for fear he might perish in its ruins.   Where is the philosophy; where is the consistency; where is the charity; in conduct like this?   Be
happy then, my beloved father, and forget me; let the sorrow of parting break down the wall of separation and make
us equal in our feeling; let me now say how ardently I love

you; let me kiss that age-worn cheek, and should my tears bedew thy face, I will wipe them away. Oh, I never can forget you; no, never, never!"

"Weep not," said the father, "Ambulinia. I will forbid Elfonzo my house, and desire that you may keep retired a few days. I will let him know, that my friendship for my family is not linked together by cankered chains; and if he ever enters upon my premises again, I will send him to his long home." "Oh, father! let me entreat you to be calm upon this occasion, and though Elfonzo may be the sport of the clouds and winds; yet I feel assured, that no fate will send him to the silent tomb, until the God of the Universe calls him hence with a triumphant voice."

Here the father turned away, exclaiming: "I will answer his letter in a very few words, and you, madam, will have the goodness to stay at home with your mother: and remember, I am determined to protect you from the consuming fire that looks so fair to your view."

CUMMING, January 22, 1844.

SIR—In regard to your request, I am as I ever have been, utterly opposed to your marrying into my family; and if you have any regard for yourself, or any gentlemanly feeling, I hope you will mention it to me no more; but seek some other one who is not so far superior to you in standing.

W. W. VALEER.

When Elfonzo read the above letter, he became so much depressed in spirits, that many of his friends thought it advisable to use other means to bring about the happy union. "Strange," said he, "that the contents of this diminutive letter should cause me to have such depressed feelings; but there is a nobler theme than this. I know not why my *military title* is not as great as that of *Squire Valeer*. For my life I cannot see that my ancestors are inferior to those who are so bitterly opposed to my marriage with Ambulinia. I know I have seen huge mountains before me, yet, when I think that I know gentlemen will insult me upon this delicate matter, should I become angry at fools and babblers, who pride themselves in their impudence and ignorance. No. My equals! I know not where to find them. My inferiors! I think it beneath me; and my superiors! I think it presumption: therefore, if this youthful heart is protected by any of the divine rights, I never will betray my trust."

He was aware that Ambulinia had a confidence, that was indeed, as firm and as resolute, as she was beautiful and interesting. He hastened to the cottage of Louisa, who received him in her usual mode of pleasantness, and informed him that Ambulinia had just that moment left. "Is it possible?" said Elfonzo. "Oh murdered hour! Why did she not remain and be the guardian of my secrets? But hasten and tell me, how she has stood this trying scene, and what are her future determinations." "You know," said Louisa, "Maj. Elfonzo, that you have Ambulinia's first love, which is of no small consequence. She came here about twilight, and shed many precious tears in consequence of her own fate with yours. We walked silently, in yon little valley you see, where we spent a momentary repose. She seemed to be quite as determined as ever, and before we left that beautiful spot she offered up a prayer to Heaven for thee." "I will see her then," replied Elfonzo, "though legions of enemies may oppose. She is mine by foreordination—she is mine by prophecy—she is mine by her own free will, and I will rescue her from the hands of her oppressors. Will you not, Miss Louisa, assist me in my capture?" "I will certainly, by the aid of Divine Providence," answered Louisa', "endeavor to break those slavish chains that bind the richest of prizes; though allow me, Major, to entreat you to use no harsh means on this important occasion; take a decided stand, and write freely to Ambulinia upon this subject, and I will see that no intervening cause hinders its passage to her. God alone will save a mourning people. Now is the day, and now is the hour to obey a command of such valuable worth." The Major felt himself grow stronger after this short interview with Louisa. He felt as if he could whip his weight in wild-cats—he knew he was master of his own feelings, and could now write a letter that would bring this litigation to *an issue.*

CUMMING, January 24, 1844.

DEAR AMBULINIA—

We have now reached the most trying moment of our lives; we are pledged not to forsake our trust; we have waited for a favorable hour to come, thinking your friends would settle the matter agreeably among themselves, and finally be reconciled to our marriage; but as I have waited in vain, and looked in vain, I have determined in my own mind to make a proposition to you, though you may think it not in accordance with your station, or compatible with your rank; yet, "sub hoc signo vinces." You know I cannot resume my visits, in consequence of the utter hostility that your father has to me; therefore the consummation of our union will have to be sought for in a more sublime sphere, at the residence of a respectable friend of this village. You cannot have any scruples upon this mode of proceeding, if you will but remember it emanates from one who loves you better than his own life—who is more than anxious to bid you welcome to a new and a happy home. Your warmest associates say come; the talented, the learned, the wise and the experienced say come;—all these with their friends say, come. Viewing these, with many other inducements, I flatter myself that you will come to the embraces of your Elfonzo; for now is the time of your acceptance and the day of your liberation. You cannot be ignorant, Ambulinia, that thou art the desire of my heart; its thoughts are too noble, and too pure, to conceal themselves from you. I shall wait for your answer to this impatiently, expecting that you will set the time to make your departure, and to be in readiness at a moment's warning to share the joys of a more preferable life. This will be handed you by Louisa, who will take a pleasure in communicating anything to you that may relieve your dejected spirits, and will assure you that I now stand ready, willing and waiting to make good my vows. I am, dear Ambulinia, yours

truly, and forever,

J. I. ELFONZO.

Louisa made it convenient to visit Mr. Valeer's, though they did not suspect her in the least, the bearer of love epistles: consequently, she was invited in the room to console Ambulinia, where they were left alone. Ambulinia was seated by a small table—her head resting on her hand—her brilliant eyes were bathed in tears. Louisa handed her the letter of Elfonzo, when another spirit animated her features— the spirit of renewed confidence that never fails to strengthen the female character in an hour of grief and sorrow like this, and as she pronounced the last accent of his name, she exclaimed, "and does he love me yet! I never will forget your generosity, Louisa. Oh, unhappy and yet blessed Louisa! may you never feel what I have felt—may you never know the pangs of love. Had I never loved, I never would have been unhappy; but I turn to Him who can save, and if His wisdom does not will my expected union, I know He will give me strength to bear my lot. Amuse yourself with this little book, and take it as an apology for my silence," said Ambulinia, "while I attempt to answer this volume of consolation." "Thank you," said Louisa, "you are excusable upon this occasion; but I pray you, Ambulinia, to be expert upon this momentous subject, that there may be nothing mistrustful upon my part." "I will," said Ambulinia, and immediately resumed her seat and addressed the following to Elfonzo:—

CUMMING, GA., January 28, 1844.

DEVOTED ELFONZO—

I hail your letter as a welcome messenger of faith, and can now say truly and firmly, that my feelings correspond with yours. Nothing shall be wanting on my part to make my obedience your fidelity. Courage and perseverance will accomplish success. Receive this as my oath, that while I grasp your hand in my own imagination, we stand united before a higher tribunal than any on earth. All the powers of my life, soul, and body, I devote to thee. Whatever dangers may threaten me, I fear not to encounter them. Perhaps I have determined upon my own destruction, by leaving the house of the best of parents; be it so, I

flee to you; I share your destiny, faithful to the end. The day
that I have concluded upon for this task, is *Sabbath* next, when
the family with the citizens are generally at church. For Heav-
en's sake let not that day pass unimproved: trust not till to-morrow, it is the cheat of life—the future that never comes—the grave
of many noble births—the cavern of ruined enterprise: which like
the lightning's flash is born, and dies, and perishes, ere the voice
of him who sees, can cry, *behold! behold!!* You may trust to
what I say, no power shall tempt me to betray confidence. Suffer
me to add one word more.

> I will soothe thee, in all thy grief,
>   Beside the gloomy river;
> And though thy love may yet be brief;
>   Mine is fixed forever.

Receive the deepest emotions of my heart for thy constant
love, and may the power of inspiration be thy guide, thy portion,
and thy all. In great haste,   Yours faithfully,
AMBULINIA.

"I now take my leave of you, sweet girl," said Louisa,
"sincerely wishing you success on Sabbath next." When
Ambulinia's letter was handed to Elfonzo, he perused it without doubting its contents. Louisa charged him to make but
few confidants; but like most young men who happened to
win the heart of a beautiful girl, he was so elated with the
idea, that he felt as a commanding general on parade, who
had confidence in all, consequently gave orders to all. The
appointed Sabbath, with a delicious breeze and cloudless sky,
made its appearance. The people gathered in crowds to the
church—the streets were filled with the neighboring citizens,
all marching to the house of worship. It is entirely useless
for me to attempt to describe the feelings of Elfonzo and
Ambulinia, who were silently watching the movements of the
multitude, apparently counting them as they entered the
house of God, looking for the last one to darken the door.
The impatience and anxiety with which they waited, and the

bliss they anticipated on the eventful day, is altogether in-
describable. Those that have been so fortunate as to embark
in such a noble enterprise, know all its realities; and those
who have not had this inestimable privilege, will have to taste
its sweets, before they can tell to others its joys, its comforts,
and its Heaven-born worth.   Immediately after Ambulinia
had assisted the family off to church, she took the advantage
of that opportunity to make good her promises.   She left a
home of enjoyment to be wedded to one whose love had been
justifiable.   A few short steps brought her to the presence of
Louisa, who urged her to make good use of her time, and
not to delay a moment, but to go with her to her brother's
house, where Elfonzo would forever make her happy.   With
lively speed, and yet a graceful air, she entered the door and
found herself protected by the champion of her confidence.
The necessary arrangements were fast making to have the
two lovers united—every thing was in readiness except the
Parson; and as they are generally very sanctimonious on
such occasions, the news got to the parents of Ambulinia,
before the everlasting knot was tied, and they both came
running, with uplifted hands and injured feelings, to arrest
their daughter from an unguarded and hasty resolution.   Elfonzo desired to maintain his ground, but Ambulinia thought
it best for him to leave, to prepare for a greater contest.   He
accordingly obeyed, as it would have been a vain endeavor
for him to have battled against a man who was armed with
deadly weapons; and besides, he could not resist the request
of such a pure heart.   Ambulinia concealed herself in the
upper story of the house, fearing the rebuke of her father;
the door was locked, and no chastisement was now expected.
Esq. Valeer, whose pride was already touched, resolved to
preserve the dignity of his family.   He entered the house almost exhausted, looking wildly for Ambulinia. " Amazed and
astonished indeed I am," said he, "at a people who call
themselves civilized, to allow such behavior as this.   Ambulinia, Ambulinia!" he cried, " come to the calls of your first,

your best, and your only friend. I appeal to you, sir," turning to the gentleman of the house, " to know where Ambulinia has gone, or where is she?" " Do you mean to insult me, sir, in my own house?" inquired the confounded gentleman. "I will burst," said Mr. V., " asunder every door in your dwelling, in search of my daughter, if you do not speak quickly, and tell me where she is. I care nothing about that outcast rubbish of creation, that mean, low-lived Elfonzo, if I can but obtain Ambulinia. Are you not going to open this door?" said he. " By the Eternal that made Heaven and earth! I will go about the work instantly, if it is not done." The confused citizens gathered from all parts of the village, to know the cause of this commotion. Some rushed into the house; the door that was locked flew open, and there stood Ambulinia, weeping. " Father, be still," said she, " and I will follow thee home." But the agitated man seized her, and bore her off through the gazing multitude. " Father!" she exclaimed, " I humbly beg your pardon—I will be dutiful—I will obey thy commands. Let the sixteen years I have lived in obedience to thee, be my future security." "I don't like to be always giving credit, when the old score is not paid up, madam;" said the father. The mother followed almost in a state of derangement, crying and imploring her to think beforehand, and ask advice from experienced persons, and they would tell her it was a rash undertaking. "Oh!" said she, " Ambulinia, my daughter, did you know what I have suffered—did you know how many nights I have whiled away in agony, in pain, and in fear, you would pity the sorrows of a heartbroken mother."

" Well, mother," replied Ambulinia, " I know I have been disobedient; I am aware that what I have done might have been done much better; but oh ! what shall I do with my honor? it is so dear to me; I am pledged to Elfonzo. His high moral worth is certainly worth some attention; moreover, my vows, I have no doubt, are recorded in the book of life, and must I give these all up? must my fair hopes be forever blasted? Forbid it father, oh! forbid it mother, forbid it heaven." "I have seen so many beautiful skies overclouded," replied the mother, "so many blossoms nipped by the frost, that I am afraid to trust you to the care of those fair days, which may be interrupted by thundering and tempestuous nights. You no doubt think as I did—life's devious ways were strewed with sweet scented flowers, but ah! how long they have lingered around me and took their flight in the vivid hopes that laughs at the drooping victims it has murdered." Elfonzo was moved at this sight. The people followed on to see what was going to become of Ambulinia, while he, with downcast looks, kept at a distance, until he saw them enter the abode of the father, thrusting her, that was the sigh of his soul, out of his presence into a solitary apartment, when she exclaimed, "Elfonzo! Elfonzo! oh, Elfonzo! where art thou, with all thy heroes? haste, oh! haste, come thou to my relief. Ride on the wings of the wind! Turn thy force loose like a tempest, and roll on thy army like a whirlwind, over this mountain of trouble and confusion. Oh, friends! if any pity me, let your last efforts throng upon the green hills, and come to the relief of Ambulinia, who is guilty of nothing but innocent love." Elfonzo called out with a loud voice, "my God, can I stand this! arouse up, I beseech you, and put an end to this tyranny. Come, my brave boys," said he, "are you ready to go forth to your duty?" They stood around him. "Who," said he, "will call us to arms? Where are my thunderbolts of war? Speak ye, the first who will meet the foe! Who will go forward with me in this ocean of grievous temptation? If there is one who desires to go, let him come and shake hands upon the altar of devotion, and swear that he will be a hero; yes, a Hector in a cause like this, which calls aloud for a speedy remedy." "Mine be the deed," said a young lawyer, "and mine alone; Venus alone shall quit her station before I will forsake one jot or tittle of my promise to you; what is death to me? what is all this warlike army, if it is not to win a victory ? I love the sleep of the lover and the mighty; nor would I give it over till the blood of my enemies should wreak with that of my own. But God forbid that our fame should soar on the blood of the slumberer." Mr. Valeer stands at his door with the frown of a demon upon his brow, with his dangerous weapon ready to strike the first man who should enter his door. " Who will arise and go forward through blood and carnage to the rescue of my Ambulinia?" said Elfonzo. " All," exclaimed the multitude; and onward they went, with their implements of battle. Others, of a more timid nature, stood among the distant hills to see the result of the contest.

Elfonzo took the lead of his band. Night arose in clouds; darkness concealed the heavens; but the blazing hopes that stimulated them gleamed in every bosom. All approached the anxious spot; they rushed to the front of the house, and with one exclamation demanded Ambulinia. " Away, be- gone, and disturb my peace no more," said Mr. Valeer. " You are a set of base, insolent, and infernal rascals. Go, the northern star points your path through the dim twilight of the night; go, and vent your spite upon the lonely hills; pour forth your love, you poor, weak minded wretch, upon your idleness and upon your guitar, and your fiddle; they are fit subjects for your admiration, for let me assure you, though this sword and iron lever are cankered, yet they frown in sleep, and let one of you dare to enter my house this night and you shall have the contents and the weight of these in- struments." " Never yet did base dishonor blur my name," said Elfonzo; " mine is a cause of renown; here are my war- riors, fear and tremble, for this night, though hell itself should oppose, I will endeavor to avenge her whom thou hast banished in solitude. The voice of Ambulina shall be heard from that dark dungeon." At that moment Ambulinia ap- peared at the window above, and with a tremulous voice said, ' live, Elfonzo ! oh ! live to raise my stone of moss ! why should such language enter your heart ? why should thy voice rend the air with such agitation? I bid thee live, once more remembering these tears of mine are shed alone for thee, in this dark and gloomy vault, and should I perish under this load of trouble, join the song of thrilling accents with the raven above my grave, and lay this tattered frame beside the banks of the Chattahoochee, or the stream of Sawney's brook; sweet will be the song of death to your Ambulinia. My ghost shall visit you in the smiles of Paradise, and tell your high fame to the minds of that region, which is far more preferable than this lonely cell. My heart shall speak for thee till the latest hour; I know faint and broken are the sounds of sorrow, yet our souls, Elfonzo, shall hear the peaceful songs together. One bright name shall be ours on high, if we are not permitted to be united here; bear in mind that I still cherish my old sentiments, and the poet will mingle the names of Elfonzo and Ambulinia in the tide of other days." "Fly, Elfonzo," said the voices of his united band, "to the wounded heart of your beloved. All enemies shall fall beneath thy sword. Fly through the clefts, and the dim spark shall sleep in death." Elfonzo rushes forward and strikes his shield against the door, which was barricaded, to prevent any intercourse. His brave sons throng around him. The people pour along the streets, both male and female, to prevent or witness the melancholy scene.

"To arms, to arms!" cried Elfonzo, "here is a victory to be won, a prize to be gained, that is more to me than the whole world beside." "It cannot be done to-night," said Mr. Valeer. "I bear the clang of death; my strength and armor shall prevail. My Ambulinia shall rest in this hall until the break of another day, and if we fall, we fall together. If we die, we die clinging to our tattered rights, and our blood alone shall tell the mournful tale of a murdered daughter and a ruined father." Sure enough, he kept watch all night, and was successful in defending his house and family. The bright morning gleamed upon the hills, night vanished away, the major and his associates felt somewhat ashamed, that they had not been as fortunate as they expected to have been; however, they still leaned upon their arms in dispersed groups; some were walking the streets, others were talking in the major's behalf. Many of the citizens suspended business, as the town presented nothing but consternation. A novelty that might end in the destruction of some worthy and respectable citizens. Mr. Valeer ventured in the streets, though not without being well armed. Some of his friends congratulated him on the decided stand he had taken, and hoped he would settle the matter amicably with Elfonzo, without any serious injury. " Me," he replied, " what, me, condescend to fellowship with a coward, and a low-live, lazy, undermining villain? no, gentlemen, this cannot be; I had rather be borne off, like the bubble upon the dark blue ocean, with Ambulinia by my side, than to have him in the ascending or descending line of relationship. Gentlemen," continued he, " if Elfonzo is so much of a distinguished character, and is so learned in the fine arts, why do you not patronize such men? why not introduce him into your families, as a gentleman of taste and of unequaled magnanimity? why are you so very anxious that he should become a relative of mine? Oh, gentlemen, I fear you yet are tainted with the curiosity of our first parents, who were beguiled by the poisonous kiss of an old ugly serpent, and who, for one *apple*, *damned* all mankind. I wish to divest myself, as far as possible, of that untutored custom. I have long since learned that the perfection of wisdom, and the end of true philosophy is to proportion our wants to our possessions, our ambition to our capacities; we will then be a happy and a virtuous people." Ambulinia was sent off to prepare for a long and tedious journey. Her new acquaintances had been instructed by her father how to treat her, and in what manner, and to keep the anticipated visit entirely secret. Elfonzo was watching the movements of everybody; some friends had told him of the plot that was laid to carry off Ambulinia. At night, he rallied some two or three of his forces, and went silently along to the stately mansion; a faint and glimmering light showed through the windows; lightly he steps to the door, there were many voices rallying fresh in fancy's eye; he tapped the shutter, it was opened instantly and he beheld once more seated beside several ladies, the hope of all his toils; he rushed toward her, she rose from her seat, rejoicing: he made one mighty grasp, when Ambulinia exclaimed, "huzza for Major Elfonzo! I will defend myself and you too, with this conquering instrument I hold in my hand; huzza, I say, I now invoke time's broad wing to shed around us some dewdrops of verdant spring."

But the hour had not come for this joyous reunion; her friends struggled with Elfonzo for some time, and finally succeeded in arresting her from his hands. He dared not injure them, because they were matrons whose courage needed no spur; she was snatched from the arms of Elfonzo, with so much eagerness, and yet with such expressive signification, that he calmly withdrew from this lovely enterprise, with an ardent hope that he should he lulled to repose by the zephyrs which whispered peace to his soul. Several long days and nights passed unmolested, all seemed to have grounded their arms of rebellion, and no callidity appeared to be going on with any of the parties. Other arrangements were made by Ambulinia; she feigned herself to be entirely the votary of a mother's care, and said, by her graceful smiles, that manhood might claim his stern dominion in some other region, where such boisterous love was not so prevalent. This gave the parents a confidence that yielded some hours of sober joy; they believed that Ambulinia would now cease to love Elfonzo, and that her stolen affections would now expire with her misguided opinions. They therefore declined the idea of sending her to a distant land. But oh! they dreamed not of the rapture that dazzled the fancy of Ambulinia, who would say, when alone, youth should not fly away on his rosy pinions, and leave her to grapple in the conflict with unknown admirers.

No frowning age shall control
The constant current of my soul,
Nor a tear from pity's eye
Shall check my sympathetic sigh.

With this resolution fixed in her mind, one dark and dreary night, when the winds whistled and the tempest roared, she received intelligence that Elfonzo was then waiting, and every preparation was then ready, at the residence of Dr. Tully, and for her to make a quick escape while the family were reposing. Accordingly she gathered her books, went to the wardrobe supplied with a variety of ornamental dressing, and ventured alone in the streets to make her way to Elfonzo, who was near at hand, impatiently looking and watching her arrival. "What forms," said she, "are those rising before me? What is that dark spot on the clouds? I do wonder what frightful ghost that is, gleaming on the red tempest? Oh, be merciful and tell me what region you are from. O tell me, ye strong spirits, or ye dark and fleeting clouds, that I yet have a friend." "A friend," said a low, whispering voice. "I am thy unchanging, thy aged, and thy disappointed mother. Oh, Ambulinia, why hast thou deceived me? Why brandish in that hand of thine a javelin of pointed steel? Why suffer that lip I have kissed a thousand times, to equivocate? My daughter, let these tears sink deep into thy soul, and no longer persist in that which may be your destruction and ruin. Come, my dear child, retract your steps, and bear me company to your welcome home." Without one retorting word, or frown from her brow, she yielded to the entreaties of her mother, and with all the mildness of her former character she went along with the silver lamp of age, to the home of candor and benevolence. Her father received her cold and formal politeness—"Where has Ambulinia been, this blustering evening, Mrs. Valeer?" inquired he. "Oh, she and I have been taking a solitary walk," said the mother; "all things, I presume, are now working for the best."

Elfonzo heard this news shortly after it happened. "What," said he, "has heaven and earth turned against me? I have been disappointed times without number. Shall I despair? —must I give it over? Heaven's decrees will not fade; I will write again—I will try again; and if it traverses a gory field, I pray forgiveness at the altar of justice."

DESOLATE HILL, CUMMING, GEO., 1844.
UNCONQUERED AND BELOVED AMBULINIA—
I have only time to say to you, not to despair; thy fame shall not perish; my visions are brightening before me. The whirl-wind's rage is past, and we now shall subdue our enemies with-out doubt. On Monday morning, when your friends are at breakfast, they will not suspect your departure, or even mistrust me being in town, as it has been reported advantageously, that I have left for the west. You walk carelessly toward the academy grove, where you will find me with a lightning steed, elegantly equipped to bear you off where we shall be joined in wedlock with the first connubial rights. Fail not to do this—think not of the tedious relations of our wrongs—be invincible. You alone oc-cupy all my ambition, and I alone will make you my happy spouse, with the same unimpeached veracity. I remain, forever, your devoted friend and admirer,   J. I. ELFONZO.

The appointed day ushered in undisturbed by any clouds; nothing disturbed Ambulinia's soft beauty. With serenity and loveliness she obeys the request of Elfonzo. The moment the family seated themselves at the table—"Excuse my ab-sence for a short time," said she, "while I attend to the plac-ing of those flowers, which should have been done a week ago." And away she ran to the sacred grove, surrounded with glittering pearls, that indicated her coming. Elfonzo hails her with his silver bow and his golden harp. They meet—Ambulinia's countenance brightens—Elfonzo leads up his winged steed. "Mount," said he, "ye true hearted, ye fearless soul—the day is ours." She sprang upon the back of the young thunderbolt, a brilliant star sparkles upon her head, with one hand she grasps the reins, and with the other she holds an olive-branch. " Lend thy aid, ye strong winds," they exclaimed, "ye moon, ye sun, and all ye fair host of heaven, witness the enemy conquered." " Hold," said Elfonzo, "thy dashing steed." " Ride on," said Ambulinia, "the voice of thunder is behind us." And onward they went, with such rapidity, that they very soon arrived at Rural Retreat, where they dismounted, and were united with all the solemnities that usually attend such divine operations. They passed the day in thanksgiving and great rejoicing, and on that evening they visited their uncle, where many of their friends and acquaintances had gathered to congratulate them in the field of untainted bliss. The kind old gentleman met them in the yard: " Well," said he, " I wish I may die, Elfonzo, if you and Ambulinia haven't tied a knot with your tongue that you can't untie with your teeth. But come in, come in, never mind, all is right—the world still moves on, and no one has fallen in this great battle."

Happy now is their lot! Unmoved by misfortune, they live among the fair beauties of the South. Heaven spreads their peace and fame upon the arch of the rainbow, and smiles propitiously at their triumph, *through the tears of the storm.*

ABOUT ALL KINDS OF SHIPS.

THE MODERN STEAMER AND THE OBSOLETE STEAMER.

WE are victims of one common superstition—
the superstition that we realize the changes
that are daily taking place in the world because we
read about them and know what they are. I should
not have supposed that the modern ship could be
a surprise to me, but it is. It seems to be as much
of a surprise to me as it could have been if I had
never read anything about it. I walk about this
great vessel, the "Havel," as she plows her way
through the Atlantic, and every detail that comes
under my eye brings up the miniature counterpart
of it as it existed in the little ships I crossed the
ocean in, fourteen, seventeen, eighteen, and twenty
years ago.

In the "Havel" one can be in several respects
more comfortable than he can be in the best hotels
on the continent of Europe. For instance, she
has several bath rooms, and they are as convenient

154

and as nicely equipped as the bath rooms in a fine private house in America ; whereas in the hotels of the continent one bath room is considered sufficient, and it is generally shabby and located in some out of the way corner of the house ; moreover, you need to give notice so long beforehand that you get over wanting a bath by the time you get it. In the hotels there are a good many different kinds of noises, and they spoil sleep; in my room in the ship I hear no sounds. In the hotels they usually shut off the electric light at midnight; in the ship one may burn it in one's room all night.

In the steamer " Batavia," twenty years ago, one candle, set in the bulkhead between two staterooms, was there to light both rooms, but did not light either of them. It was extinguished at 11 at night, and so were all the saloon lamps except one or two, which were left burning to help the passenger see how to break his neck trying to get around in the dark. The passengers sat at table on long benches made of the hardest kind of wood; in the " Havel " one sits on a swivel chair with a cushioned back to it. In those old times the dinner bill of fare was always the same: a pint of some simple, homely soup or other, boiled codfish and potatoes, slab of boiled beef, stewed prunes for dessert — on Sundays "dog in a blanket," on Thursdays "plum duff." In the modern ship the menu is choice and elaborate, and is changed daily. In the old times dinner was a sad occasion; in our day a concealed orchestra enlivens it with charming music. In the old days the decks were always wet, in our day they are usually dry, for the promenade-deck is roofed over, and a sea seldom comes aboard. In a moderately disturbed sea, in the old days, a landsman could hardly keep his legs, but in such a sea in our day, the decks are as level as a table. In the old days the inside of a ship was the plainest and barrenest thing, and the most dismal and uncomfortable that ingenuity could devise; the modern ship is a marvel of rich and costly decoration and sumptuous appointment, and is equipped with every comfort and convenience that money can buy. The old ships had no place of assembly but the dining-room, the new ones have several spacious and beautiful drawing-rooms. The old ships offered the passenger no chance to smoke except in the place that was called the "fiddle." It was a repulsive den made of rough boards (full of cracks) and its office was to protect the main hatch. It was grimy and dirty; there were no seats; the only light was a lamp of the rancid-oil-and-rag kind; the place was very cold, and never dry, for the seas broke in through the cracks every little while and drenched the cavern thoroughly. In the modern ship there are three or four large smoking-rooms, and they have card tables and cushioned sofas, and are heated by steam and lighted by electricity. There are few European hotels with such smoking-rooms.

The former ships were built of wood, and had two or three water-tight compartments in the hold with doors in them which were often left open, particularly when the ship was going to hit a rock. The modern leviathan is built of steel, and the water-tight bulkheads have no doors in them; they divide the ship into nine or ten water-tight compartments and endow her with as many lives as a cat. Their complete efficiency was established by the happy results following the memorable accident to the City of Paris a year or two ago.

One curious thing which is at once noticeable in the great modern ship is the absence of hubbub, clatter, rush of feet, roaring of orders. That is all gone by. The elaborate manœuvres necessary in working the vessel into her dock are conducted without sound; one sees nothing of the processes, hears no commands. A Sabbath stillness and solemnity reign, in place of the turmoil and racket of the earlier days. The modern ship has a spacious bridge fenced chin-high with sail-cloth, and floored with wooden gratings; and this bridge, with its fenced fore-and-aft annexes, could accommodate a seated audience of a hundred and fifty men. There are three steering equipments, each competent if the others should break. From the bridge the ship is steered, and also handled. The handling is not done by shout or whistle, but by signaling with patent automatic gongs. There are three tell-tales, with plainly lettered dials—for steering, handling the engines, and for communicating orders to the invisible mates who are conducting the landing of the ship or casting off. The officer who is astern is out of sight and too far away to hear trumpet calls; but the gongs near him tell him to haul in, pay out, make fast, let go, and so on; he hears, but the passengers do not, and so the ship seems to land herself without human help.

This great bridge is thirty or forty feet above the water, but the sea climbs up there sometimes; so there is another bridge twelve or fifteen feet higher still, for use in these emergencies. The force of water is a strange thing. It slips between one's fingers like air, but upon occasion it acts like a solid body and will bend a thin iron rod. In the "Havel" it has splintered a heavy oaken rail into broom-straws instead of merely breaking it in two as would have been the seemingly natural thing for it to do. At the time of the awful Johnstown disaster, according to the testimony of several witnesses, rocks were carried some distance on the surface of the stupendous torrent; and at St. Helena, many years ago, a vast sea-wave carried a battery of cannon forty feet up a steep slope and deposited the guns there in a row. But the water has done a still stranger thing, and it is one which is credibly vouched for. A marlinspike is an implement about a foot long which tapers from its butt to the other extremity and ends in a sharp point. It is made of iron and is heavy. A wave came aboard a ship in a storm and raged aft, breast high, carrying a marlinspike point-first with it, and with such lightning-like swiftness and force as to drive it three or four inches into a sailor's body and kill him.

In all ways the ocean greyhound of to-day is imposing and impressive to one who carries in his head no ship-pictures of a recent date. In bulk she comes near to rivaling the Ark; yet this monstrous mass of steel is driven five hundred miles through the waves in twenty-four hours. I remember the brag run of a steamer which I traveled in once on the Pacific—it was two hundred and nine miles in twenty-four hours; a year or so later I was a passenger in the excursion-tub "Quaker City," and on

one occasion in a level and glassy sea, it was claimed
that she reeled off two hundred and eleven miles
between noon and noon, but it was probably a campaign lie.   That little steamer had seventy passengers, and a crew of forty men, and seemed a good
deal of a bee-hive.   But in this present ship we are
living in a sort of solitude, these soft summer days,
with sometimes a hundred passengers scattered
about the spacious distances, and sometimes nobody
in sight at all; yet, hidden somewhere in the vessel's bulk, there are (including crew,) near eleven
hundred people.

The stateliest lines in the literature of the sea are
these:

" Britannia needs no bulwark, no towers along the steep—
Her march is o'er the mountain wave, her home is on the
        deep!"

There it is.   In those old times the little ships
climbed over the waves and wallowed down into
the trough on the other side; the giant ship of our
day does not climb over the waves, but crushes her
way through them.   Her formidable weight and
mass and impetus give her mastery over any but
extraordinary storm-waves.

The ingenuity of man!   I mean in this passing
generation.   To-day I found in the chart-room a
frame of removable wooden slats on the wall, and

on the slats was painted uninforming information
like this:

Trim-Tank........................Empty
Double-Bottom No. 1..............Full
Double-Bottom No. 2..............Full
Double-Bottom No. 3..............Full
Double-Bottom No. 4 ....Full

While I was trying to think out what kind of a
game this might be and how a stranger might best
go to work to beat it, a sailor came in and pulled
out the " Empty " end of the first slat and put it
back with its reverse side to the front, marked
" Full." He made some other change, I did not
notice what. The slat-frame was soon explained.
Its function was to indicate how the ballast in the
ship was distributed. The striking thing was, that
that ballast was water. I did not know that a ship
had ever been ballasted with water. I had merely
read, some time or other, that such an experiment
was to be tried. But that is the modern way: between the experimental trial of a new thing and its
adoption, there is no wasted time, if the trial proves
its value.

On the wall, near the slat-frame, there was an
outline drawing of the ship, and this betrayed the
fact that this vessel has twenty-two considerable
lakes of water in her. These lakes are in her bottom; they are imprisoned between her real bottom

and a false bottom. They are separated from each other, thwartships, by water-tight bulkheads, and separated down the middle by a bulkhead running from the bow four-fifths of the way to the stern. It is a chain of lakes four hundred feet long and from five to seven feet deep. Fourteen of the lakes contain fresh water brought from shore, and the aggregate weight of it is four hundred tons. The rest of the lakes contain salt water — six hundred and eighteen tons. Upwards of a thousand tons of water, altogether.

Think how handy this ballast is. The ship leaves port with the lakes all full. As she lightens forward through consumption of coal, she loses trim—her head rises, her stern sinks down. Then they spill one of the sternward lakes into the sea, and the trim is restored. This can be repeated right along as occasion may require. Also, a lake at one end of the ship can be moved to the other end by pipes and steam pumps. When the sailor changed the slat-frame to-day, he was posting a transference of that kind. The seas had been increasing, and the vessel's head needed more weighting, to keep it from rising on the waves instead of plowing through them; therefore, twenty-five tons of water had been transferred to the bow from a lake situated well toward the stern.

A water compartment is kept either full or empty. The body of water must be compact, so that it cannot slosh around. A shifting ballast would not do, of course.

The modern ship is full of beautiful ingenuities, but it seems to me that this one is the king. I would rather be the originator of that idea than of any of the others. Perhaps the trim of a ship was never perfectly ordered and preserved until now. A vessel out of trim will not steer, her speed is maimed, she strains and labors in the seas. Poor creature, for six thousand years she has had no comfort until these latest days. For six thousand years she swam through the best and cheapest ballast in the world, the only perfect ballast, but she could n't tell her master and he had not the wit to find it out for himself. It is odd to reflect that there is nearly as much water inside of this ship as there is outside, and yet there is no danger.

NOAH'S ARK.

The progress made in the great art of ship building since Noah's time is quite noticeable. Also, the looseness of the navigation laws in the time of Noah is in quite striking contrast with the strictness of the navigation laws of our time. It would not be possible for Noah to do in our day what he was per-

mitted to do in his own.   Experience has taught us
the necessity of being more particular, more con-
servative, more careful of human life.   Noah would
not be allowed to sail from Bremen in our day. The
inspectors would come and examine the Ark, and
make all sorts of objections.   A person who knows
Germany can imagine the scene and the conversation without difficulty and without missing a detail.
The inspector would be in a beautiful military uniform; he would be respectful, dignified, kindly, the
perfect gentleman, but steady as the north star to
the last requirement of his duty.   He would make
Noah tell him where he was born, and how old he
was, and what religious sect he belonged to, and the
amount of his income, and the grade and position he
claimed socially, and the name and style of his occupation, and how many wives and children he had,
and how many servants, and the name, sex and
age of the whole of them; and if he had n't a passport he would be courteously required to get one
right away.   Then he would take up the matter of
the Ark:

"What is her length?"

"Six hundred feet."

"Depth?"

"Sixty-five."

"Beam?"

" Fifty or sixty."

" Built of—"

" Wood."

" What kind ? "

" Shittim and gopher."

" Interior and exterior decorations ? "

" Pitched within and without."

" Passengers ? "

" Eight."

" Sex ? "

" Half male, the others female."

" Ages ? "

" From a hundred years up."

" Up to where ? "

" Six hundred."

" Ah—going to Chicago; good idea, too. Surgeon's name ? "

" We have no surgeon."

" Must provide a surgeon. Also an undertaker— particularly the undertaker. These people must not be left without the necessities of life at their age. Crew ? "

" The same eight."

" The same eight ? "

" The same eight."

" And half of them women ? "

" Yes, sir."

" Have they ever served as seamen ? "

" No, sir."

" Have the men ? "

" No, sir."

" Have any of you ever been to sea ? "

" No, sir."

" Where were you reared ? "

" On a farm—all of us."

" This vessel requires a crew of eight hundred men, she not being a steamer. You must provide them. She must have four mates and nine cooks. Who is captain ? "

" I am, sir."

" You must get a captain. Also a chambermaid. Also sick nurses for the old people. Who designed this vessel ? "

" I did, sir."

" Is it your first attempt ? "

" Yes, sir."

" I partly suspected it. Cargo ? "

" Animals."

" Kind ? "

" All kinds."

" Wild, or tame ? "

" Mainly wild."

" Foreign, or domestic ? "

" Mainly foreign."

" Principal wild ones ? "

" Megatherium, elephant, rhinoceros, lion, tiger, wolf, snakes—all the wild things of all climes—two of each."

" Securely caged ? "

" No, not caged."

" They must have iron cages. Who feeds and waters the menagerie ? "

" We do."

" The old people ? "

" Yes, sir."

" It is dangerous—for both. The animals must be cared for by a competent force. How many animals are there ? "

" Big ones, seven thousand; big and little together, ninety-eight thousand."

" You must provide twelve hundred keepers. How is the vessel lighted ? "

" By two windows."

" Where are they ? "

" Up under the eaves."

" Two windows for a tunnel six hundred feet long and sixty-five feet deep ? You must put in the electric light—a few arc lights and fifteen hundred incandescents. What do you do in case of leaks? How many pumps have you ? "

" None, sir."

"You must provide pumps. How do you get water for the passengers and the animals?"

"We let down the buckets from the windows."

"It is inadequate. What is your motive power?"

"What is my which?"

"Motive power. What power do you use in driving the ship?"

"None."

"You must provide sails or steam. What is the nature of your steering apparatus?"

"We have n't any."

"Have n't you a rudder?"

"No, sir."

"How do you steer the vessel?"

"We don't."

"You must provide a rudder, and properly equip it. How many anchors have you?"

"None."

"You must provide six. One is not permitted to sail a vessel like this without that protection. How many life boats have you?"

"None, sir."

"Provide twenty-five. How many life preservers?"

"None."

"You will provide two thousand. How long are you expecting your voyage to last?"

"Eleven or twelve months."

"Eleven or twelve months. Pretty slow—but you will be in time for the Exposition. What is your ship sheathed with—copper?"

"Her hull is bare—not sheathed at all."

"Dear man, the wood-boring creatures of the sea would riddle her like a sieve and send her to the bottom in three months. She *cannot* be allowed to go away, in this condition; she must be sheathed. Just a word more: Have you reflected that Chicago is an inland city and not reachable with a vessel like this?"

"Shecargo? What is Shecargo? I am not going to Shecargo."

"Indeed? Then may I ask what the animals are for?"

"Just to breed others from."

"Others? Is it possible that you have n't enough?"

"For the present needs of civilization, yes; but the rest are going to be drowned in a flood, and these are to renew the supply."

"A flood?"

"Yes, sir."

"Are you sure of that?"

"Perfectly sure. It is going to rain forty days and forty nights."

"Give yourself no concern about that, dear sir, it often does that, here."

"Not this kind of rain. This is going to cover the mountain tops, and the earth will pass from sight."

"Privately—but of course not officially—I am sorry you revealed this, for it compels me to withdraw the option I gave you as to sails or steam. I must require you to use steam. Your ship cannot carry the hundredth part of an eleven-months' water-supply for the animals. You will have to have condensed water."

"But I tell you I am going to dip water from outside with buckets."

"It will not answer. Before the flood reaches the mountain tops the fresh waters will have joined the salt seas, and it will all be salt. You must put in steam and condense your water. I will now bid you good-day, sir. Did I understand you to say that this was your very first attempt at ship-building?"

"My very first, sir, I give you the honest truth. I built this Ark without having ever had the slightest training or experience or instruction in marine architecture."

"It is a remarkable work, sir, a most remarkable work. I consider that it contains more features that are new—absolutely new and unhackneyed—than are to be found in any other vessel that swims the seas."

"This compliment does me infinite honor, dear sir, infinite; and I shall cherish the memory of it while life shall last. Sir, I offer my duty, and most grateful thanks. Adieu!"

No, the German inspector would be limitlessly courteous to Noah, and would make him feel that he was among friends, but he would n't let him go to sea with that Ark.

COLUMBUS'S CRAFT.

Between Noah's time and the time of Columbus, naval architecture underwent some changes, and from being unspeakably bad was improved to a point which may be described as less unspeakably bad. I have read somewhere, some time or other, that one of Columbus's ships was a ninety-ton vessel. By comparing that ship with the ocean greyhounds of our time one is able to get down to a comprehension of how small that Spanish bark was, and how little fitted she would be to run opposition in the Atlantic passenger trade to-day. It would take seventy-four of her to match the tonnage of the "Havel" and carry the "Havel's" trip. If I remember rightly, it took her ten weeks to make the passage. With our ideas this would now be considered an objectionable gait. She probably had a captain, a mate, and a crew consisting of four seamen and a boy. The crew of a modern greyhound numbers two hundred and fifty persons.

Columbus's ship being small and very old, we know that we may draw from these two facts several absolute certainties in the way of minor details which history has left unrecorded. For instance: being small, we know that she rolled and pitched and tumbled, in any ordinary sea, and stood on her head or her tail, or lay down with her ear in the water when storm-seas ran high; also, that she was used to having billows plunge aboard and wash her decks from stem to stern; also, that the storm-racks were on the table all the way over, and that nevertheless a man's soup was oftener landed in his lap than in his stomach; also, that the dining-saloon was about ten feet by seven, dark, airless, and suffocating with oil-stench; also, that there was only about one stateroom—the size of a grave—with a tier of two or three berths in it of the dimensions and comfortableness of coffins, and that when the light was out, the darkness in there was so thick and real that you could bite into it and and chew it like gum; also, that the only promenade was on the lofty poop-deck astern (for the ship was shaped like a high-quarter shoe)—a streak sixteen feet long by three feet wide, all the rest of the vessel being littered with ropes and flooded by the seas.

We know all these things to be true, from the mere fact that we know the vessel was small. As the vessel was old, certain other truths follow, as matters of course. For instance : she was full of rats ; she was full of cockroaches ; the heavy seas made her seams open and shut like your fingers, and she leaked like a basket ; where leakage is, there also, of necessity, is bilgewater ; and where bilgewater is, only the dead can enjoy life. This is on account of the smell. In the presence of bilge-water, Limburger cheese becomes odorless and ashamed.

From these absolutely sure data we can competently picture the daily life of the great discoverer. In the early morning he paid his devotions at the shrine of the Virgin. At eight bells he appeared on the poop-deck promenade. If the weather was chilly he came up clad from plumed helmet to spurred heel in magnificent plate armor inlaid with arabesques of gold, having previously warmed it at the galley fire. If the weather was warm, he came up in the ordinary sailor toggery of the time: great slouch hat of blue velvet with a flowing brush of snowy ostrich plumes, fastened on with a flashing cluster of diamonds and emeralds; gold-embroidered doublet of green velvet with slashed sleeves exposing under-sleeves of crimson satin; deep collar and cuff-ruffles of rich limp lace; trunk hose of pink velvet, with big knee-knots of brocaded yellow ribbon; pearl-tinted silk stockings, clocked and daintily embroidered; lemon-colored buskins of unborn kid, funnel-topped, and drooping low to expose the pretty stockings; deep gauntlets of finest white heretic skin, from the factory of the Holy Inquisition, formerly part of the person of a lady of rank; rapier with sheath crusted with jewels, and hanging from a broad baldric upholstered with rubies and sapphires.

He walked the promenade thoughtfully, he noted the aspects of the sky and the course of the wind; he kept an eye out for drifting vegetation and other signs of land; he jawed the man at the wheel for pastime; he got out an imitation egg and kept himself in practice on his old trick of making it stand on its end; now and then he hove a life-line below and fished up a sailor who was drowning on the quarter-deck; the rest of his watch he gaped and yawned and stretched and said he would n't make the trip again to discover six Americas. For that was the kind of natural human person Columbus was when not posing for posterity.

At noon he took the sun and ascertained that the good ship had made three hundred yards in twenty-four hours, and this enabled him to win the pool. Anybody can win the pool when nobody but him-

self has the privilege of straightening out the ship's
run and getting it right.

The Admiral has breakfasted alone, in state:
bacon, beans, and gin; at noon he dines alone in
state: bacon, beans, and gin; at six he sups alone
in state: bacon, beans, and gin; at eleven P.M. he
takes a night-relish, alone, in state: bacon, beans,
and gin. At none of these orgies is there any music;
the ship-orchestra is modern. After his final meal
he returned thanks for his many blessings, a little
over-rating their value, perhaps, and then he laid
off his silken splendors or his gilded hardware, and
turned in, in his little coffin-bunk, and blew out his
flickering stencher and began to refresh his lungs
with inverted sighs freighted with the rich odors of
rancid oil and bilgewater. The sighs returned as
snores, and then the rats and the cockroaches
swarmed out in brigades and divisions and army
corps and had a circus all over him. Such was the
daily life of the great discoverer in his marine basket
during several historic weeks; and the difference
between his ship and his comforts and ours is visible
almost at a glance.

When he returned, the King of Spain, marveling,
said—as history records:

"This ship seems to be leaky. Did she leak badly?"

" You shall judge for yourself, sire. I pumped

the Atlantic ocean through her sixteen times on the passage."

This is General Horace Porter's account. Other authorities say fifteen.

It can be shown that the differences between that ship and the one I am writing these historical contributions in, are in several respects remarkable. Take the matter of decoration, for instance. I have been looking around again, yesterday and to-day, and have noted several details which I conceive to have been absent from Columbus's ship, or at least slurred over and not elaborated and perfected. I observe state-room doors three inches thick, of solid oak and polished. I note companionway vestibules with walls, doors and ceilings paneled in polished hard woods, some light, some dark, all dainty and delicate joiner-work, and yet every joint compact and tight; with beautiful pictures inserted, composed of blue tiles—some of the pictures containing as many as sixty tiles—and the joinings of those tiles perfect. These are daring experiments. One would have said that the first time the ship went straining and laboring through a storm-tumbled sea those tiles would gape apart and drop out. That they have not done so is evidence that the joiner's art has advanced a good deal since the days when ships were so shackly that when a giant sea gave them a wrench the doors came unbolted. I find the walls of the dining-saloon upholstered with mellow pictures wrought in tapestry, and the ceiling aglow with pictures done in oil. In other places of assembly I find great panels filled with embossed Spanish leather, the figures rich with gilding and bronze. Everywhere I find sumptuous masses of color— color, color, color—color all about, color of every shade and tint and variety; and as a result, the ship is bright and cheery to the eye, and this cheeriness invades one's spirit and contents it. To fully appreciate the force and spiritual value of this radiant and opulent dream of color, one must stand outside at night in the pitch dark and the rain, and look in through a port, and observe it in the lavish splendor of the electric lights. The old-time ships were dull, plain, graceless, gloomy, and horribly depressing. They compelled the blues; one could not escape the blues in them. The modern idea is right: to surround the passenger with conveniences, luxuries, and abundance of inspiriting color. As a result, the ship is the pleasantest place one can be in, except, perhaps, one's home.

A VANISHED SENTIMENT.

One thing is gone, to return no more forever—the romance of the sea. Soft sentimentality about the sea has retired from the activities of this life, and is but a memory of the past, already remote and much faded.   But within the recollection of men still living, it was in the breast of every individual; and the further any individual lived from salt water the more of it he kept in stock.   It was as pervasive, as universal, as the atmosphere itself.   The mere mention of the sea, the romantic sea, would make any company of people sentimental and mawkish at once.   The great majority of the songs that were sung by the young people of the back settlements had the melancholy wanderer for subject and his mouthings about the sea for refrain.   Picnic parties paddling down a creek in a canoe when the twilight shadows were gathering, always sang

> Homeward bound, homeward bound
> From a foreign shore;

and this was also a favorite in the West with the passengers on sternwheel steamboats.   There was another—

> My boat is by the shore
>   And my bark is on the sea,
> But before I go, Tom Moore,
>   Here's a double health to thee.

And this one, also—

> O, pilot, 'tis a fearful night,
> There's danger on the deep.

And this—

> A life on the ocean wave
>   And a home on the rolling deep,
> Where the scattered waters rave
>   And the winds their revels keep !

And this—

> A wet sheet and a flowing sea,
> And a wind that follows fair.

And this—

> My foot is on my gallant deck,
> Once more the rover is free !

And the " Larboard Watch "—the person referred to below is at the masthead, or somewhere up there—

> O, who can tell what joy he feels,
> As o'er the foam his vessel reels,
> And his tired eyelids slumb'ring fall,
> He rouses at the welcome call
>   Of " Larboard watch—ahoy ! "

Yes, and there was forever and always some jack-ass-voiced person braying out—

> Rocked in the cradle of the deep,
> I lay me down in peace to sleep !

Other favorites had these suggestive titles: " The Storm at Sea;" " The Bird at Sea;" " The Sailor

Boy's Dream;" "The Captive Pirate's Lament;"
"We are far from Home on the Stormy Main"—and
so on, and so on, the list is endless. Everybody on
a farm lived chiefly amid the dangers of the deep on
those days, in fancy.

But all that is gone, now. Not a vestige of it is
left. The iron-clad, with her unsentimental aspect
and frigid attention to business, banished romance
from the war-marine, and the unsentimental steamer
has banished it from the commercial marine. The
dangers and uncertainties which made sea life romantic have disappeared and carried the poetic element
along with them. In our day the passengers never
sing sea-songs on board a ship, and the band never
plays them. Pathetic songs about the wanderer in
strange lands far from home, once so popular and
contributing such fire and color to the imagination
by reason of the rarity of that kind of wanderer,
have lost their charm and fallen silent, because
everybody is a wanderer in the far lands now, and
the interest in that detail is dead. Nobody is worried about the wanderer; there are no perils of the
sea for him, there are no uncertainties. He is safer
in the ship than he would probably be at home, for
there he is always liable to have to attend some
friend's funeral and stand over the grave in the
sleet, bareheaded—and that means pneumonia for

him, if he gets his deserts; and the uncertainties of his voyage are reduced to whether he will arrive on the other side in the appointed afternoon, or have to wait till morning.

The first ship I was ever in was a sailing vessel. She was twenty-eight days going from San Francisco to the Sandwich Islands. But the main reason for this particularly slow passage was, that she got becalmed and lay in one spot fourteen days in the centre of the Pacific two thousand miles from land. I hear no sea-songs in this present vessel, but I heard the entire layout in that one. There were a dozen young people—they are pretty old now, I reckon—and they used to group themselves on the stern, in the starlight or the moonlight, every evening, and sing sea-songs till after midnight, in that hot, silent, motionless calm. They had no sense of humor, and they always sang " Homeward Bound," without reflecting that that was practically ridiculous, since they were standing still and not proceeding in any direction at all; and they often followed that song with " Are we almost there, are we almost there, said the dying girl as she drew near home ? "

It was a very pleasant company of young people, and I wonder where they are now. Gone, oh, none knows whither; and the bloom and grace and beauty of their youth, where is that ? Among them was a liar; all tried to reform him, but none could do it. And so, gradually, he was left to himself, none of us would associate with him. Many a time since, I have seen in fancy that forsaken figure, leaning forlorn against the taffrail, and have reflected that perhaps if we had tried harder, and been more patient, we might have won him from his fault and persuaded him to relinquish it. But it is hard to tell; with him the vice was extreme, and was probably incurable. I like to think—and indeed I do think—that I did the best that in me lay to lead him to higher and better ways.

There was a singular circumstance. The ship lay becalmed that entire fortnight in exactly the same spot. Then a handsome breeze came fanning over the sea, and we spread our white wings for flight. But the vessel did not budge. The sails bellied out, the gale strained at the ropes, but the vessel moved not a hair's breadth from her place. The captain was surprised. It was some hours before we found out what the cause of the detention was. It was barnacles. They collect very fast in that part of the Pacific. They had fastened themselves to the ship's bottom; then others had fastened themselves to the first bunch, others to these, and so on, down and down and down, and the last bunch had glued the column hard and fast to the bottom of the sea, which is five miles deep at that point. So the ship was simply become the handle of a walking cane five miles long—yes, and no more movable by wind and sail than a continent is. It was regarded by every one as remarkable.

Well, the next week—however, Sandy Hook is in sight.

PLAYING COURIER.

A TIME would come when we must go from
Aix-les-Bains to Geneva, and from thence,
by a series of day-long and tangled journeys, to
Bayreuth in Bavaria. I should have to have a courier of course to take care of so considerable a party
as mine.

But I procrastinated. The time slipped along,
and at last I woke up one day to the fact that we
were ready to move and had no courier. I then resolved upon what I felt was a foolhardy thing, but I
was in the humor of it. I said I would make the
first stage without help—I did it.

I brought the party from Aix to Geneva by myself—four people. The distance was two hours and
more, and there was one change of cars. There
was not an accident of any kind, except leaving a
valise and some other matters on the platform, a
thing which can hardly be called an accident, it is
so common. So I offered to conduct the party all
the way to Bayreuth.

This was a blunder, though it did not seem so at the time. There was more detail than I thought there would be: 1. Two persons whom we had left in a Genevan pension some weeks before, must be collected and brought to the hotel; 2. I must notify the people on the Grand Quay who store trunks to bring seven of our stored trunks to the hotel and carry back seven which they would find piled in the lobby; 3. I must find out what part of Europe Bayreuth was in and buy seven railway tickets for that point; 4. I must send a telegram to a friend in the Netherlands; 5. It was now 2 in the afternoon, and we must look sharp and be ready for the first night train and make sure of sleeping-car tickets; 6. I must draw money at the bank.

It seemed to me that the sleeping-car tickets must be the most important thing, so I went to the station myself to make sure; hotel messengers are not always brisk people. It was a hot day and I ought to have driven, but it seemed better economy to walk. It did not turn out so, because I lost my way and trebled the distance. I applied for the tickets, and they asked me which route I wanted to go by, and that embarrassed me and made me lose my head, there were so many people standing around, and I not knowing anything about the routes and not supposing there were going to be two; so I judged it best to go back and map out the road and come again.

I took a cab this time, but on my way up stairs at the hotel I remembered that I was out of cigars, so I thought it would be well to get some while the matter was in my mind. It was only round the corner and I did n't need the cab. I asked the cabman to wait where he was. Thinking of the telegram and trying to word it in my head, I forgot the cigars and the cab, and walked on indefinitely. I was going to have the hotel people send the telegram, but as I could not be far from the Post Office by this time, I thought I would do it myself. But it was further than I had supposed. I found the place at last and wrote the telegram and handed it in. The clerk was a severe-looking, fidgety man, and he began to fire French questions at me in such a liquid form that I could not detect the joints between his words, and this made me lose my head again. But an Englishman stepped up and said the clerk wanted to know where he was to send the telegram. I could not tell him, because it was not my telegram, and I explained that I was merely sending it for a member of my party. But nothing would pacify the clerk but the address; so I said that if he was so particular I would go back and get it.

However, I thought I would go and collect those

lacking two persons first, for it would be best to do everything systematically and in order, and one detail at a time. Then I remembered the cab was eating up my substance down at the hotel yonder; so I called another cab and told the man to go down and fetch it to the Post Office and wait till I came.

I had a long hot walk to collect those people, and when I got there they could n't come with me because they had heavy satchels and must have a cab. I went away to find one, but before I ran across any I noticed that I had reached the neighborhood of the Grand Quay—at least I thought I had—so I judged I could save time by stepping around and arranging about the trunks. I stepped around about a mile, and although I did not find the Grand Quay, I found a cigar shop, and remembered about the cigars. I said I was going to Bayreuth, and wanted enough for the journey. The man asked me which route I was going to take. I said I did not know. He said he would recommend me to go by Zurich and various other places which he named, and offered to sell me seven second-class through tickets for $22 apiece, which would be throwing off the discount which the railroads allowed him. I was already tired of riding second-class on first-class tickets, so I took him up.

By and by I found Natural & Co.'s storage office,

and told them to send seven of our trunks to the hotel and pile them up in the lobby. It seemed to me that I was not delivering the whole of the message, still it was all I could find in my head.

Next I found the bank and asked for some money, but I had left my letter of credit somewhere and was not able to draw. I remembered now that I must have left it lying on the table where I wrote my telegram: so I got a cab and drove to the Post Office and went up stairs, and they said that a letter of credit had indeed been left on the table, but that it was now in the hands of the police authorities, and it would be necessary for me to go there and prove property. They sent a boy with me, and we went out the back way and walked a couple of miles and found the place; and then I remembered about my cabs, and asked the boy to send them to me when he got back to the Post Office. It was nightfall now, and the Mayor had gone to dinner. I thought I would go to dinner myself, but the officer on duty thought differently, and I stayed. The Mayor dropped in at half past 10, but said it was too late to do anything to-night—come at 9:30 in the morning. The officer wanted to keep me all night, and said I was a suspicious-looking person, and probably did not own the letter of credit, and did n't know what a letter of credit was, but merely saw the real owner leave it lying on the table, and wanted to get it because I was probably a person that would want anything he could get, whether it was valuable or not. But the Mayor said he saw nothing suspicious about me, and that I seemed a harmless person and nothing the matter with me but a wandering mind, and not much of that. So I thanked him and he set me free, and I went home in my three cabs.

As I was dog-tired and in no condition to answer questions with discretion, I thought I would not disturb the Expedition at that time of night, as there was a vacant room I knew of at the other end of the hall; but I did not quite arrive there, as a watch had been set, the Expedition being anxious about me. I was placed in a galling situation. The Expedition sat stiff and forbidding on four chairs in a row, with shawls and things all on, satchels and guide books in lap. They had been sitting like that for four hours, and the glass going down all the time. Yes, and they were waiting—waiting for me. It seemed to me that nothing but a sudden, happily contrived, and brilliant *tour de force* could break this iron front and make a diversion in my favor; so I shied my hat into the arena and followed it with a skip and a jump, shouting blithely:

" Ha, ha, here we all are, Mr. Merryman ! "

Nothing could be deeper or stiller than the absence of applause which followed. But I kept on; there seemed no other way, though my confidence, poor enough before, had got a deadly check and was in effect gone.

I tried to be jocund out of a heavy heart, I tried to touch the other hearts there and soften the bitter resentment in those faces by throwing off bright and airy fun and making of the whole ghastly thing a joyously humorous incident, but this idea was not well conceived. It was not the right atmosphere for it. I got not one smile; not one line in those offended faces relaxed; I thawed nothing of the winter that looked out of those frosty eyes. I started one more breezy, poor effort, but the head of the Expedition cut into the centre of it and said:

" Where have you been ? "

I saw by the manner of this that the idea was to get down to cold business now. So I began my travels but was cut short again.

" Where are the two others ? We have been in frightful anxiety about them."

" Oh, they're all right. I was to fetch a cab. I will go straight off, and —— "

" Sit down ! Don't you know it is 11 o'clock ? Where did you leave them ? "

" At the pension."

"Why didn't you bring them?"

"Because we could n't carry the satchels. And so I thought ——"

"Thought! You should not try to think. One cannot think without the proper machinery. It is two miles to that pension. Did you go there without a cab?"

"I—well I did n't intend to; it only happened so."

"How did it happen so?"

"Because I was at the Post Office and I remembered that I had left a cab waiting here, and so, to stop that expense, I sent another cab to — to ——"

"To what?"

"Well, I don't remember now, but I think the new cab was to have the hotel pay the old cab, and send it away."

"What good would that do?"

"What good would it do? It would stop the expense, would n't it?"

"By putting the new cab in its place to continue the expense?"

I did n't say anything.

"Why did n't you have the new cab come back for you?"

"Oh, that is what I did. I remember now. Yes, that is what I did. Because I recollect that when I ——"

" Well, then, why did n't it come back for you ? "

" To the Post Office ? Why, it did."

" Very well, then, how did you come to walk to the pension ? "

" I—I don't quite remember how that happened. Oh, yes, I do remember now. I wrote the despatch to send to the Netherlands, and —— "

" Oh, thank goodness, you did accomplish something ! I would n't have had you fail to send— what makes you look like that ! You are trying to avoid my eye. That despatch is the most important thing that —— You have n't sent that despatch ! "

" I have n't said I did n't send it."

" You don't need to. Oh, dear, I would n't have had that telegram fail for anything. Why did n't you send it ? "

" Well, you see, with so many things to do and think of, I—they 're very particular there, and after I had written the telegram —— "

" Oh, never mind, let it go, explanations can't help the matter now—what will he think of us ? "

" Oh, that's all right, that's all right, he 'll think we gave the telegram to the hotel people, and that they —— "

" Why, certainly ! Why did n't you do that ? There was no other rational way."

" Yes, I know, but then I had it on my mind that I must be sure and get to the bank and draw some money —— "

" Well, you are entitled to some credit, after all, for thinking of that, and I don't wish to be too hard on you, though you must acknowledge yourself that you have cost us all a good deal of trouble, and some of it not necessary. How much did you draw ? "

" Well, I—I had an idea that—that —— "

" That what ? "

" That—well, it seems to me that in the circumstances—so many of us, you know, and—and —— "

" What are you mooning about? Do turn your face this way and let me—why, you have n't drawn any money ! "

" Well, the banker said —— "

" Never mind what the banker said. You must have had a reason of your own. Not a reason, exactly, but something which —— "

" Well, then, the simple fact was that I had n't my letter of credit."

" Had n't your letter of credit ? "

" Had n't my letter of credit."

" Don't repeat me like that. Where was it ? "

" At the Post Office."

" What was it doing there ? "

"Well, I forgot it and left it there."

"Upon my word, I 've seen a good many couriers, but of all the couriers that ever I——"

"I 've done the best I could."

"Well, so you have, poor thing, and I 'm wrong to abuse you so when you 've been working your-self to death while we 've been sitting here only thinking of our vexations instead of feeling grate-ful for what you were trying to do for us. It will all come out right. We can take the 7:30 train in the morning just as well. You 've bought the tickets?"

"I have—and it 's a bargain, too. Second class."

"I 'm glad of it. Everybody else travels second class, and we might just as well save that ruinous extra charge. What did you pay?"

"Twenty-two dollars apiece—through to Bay-reuth."

"Why, I did n't know you could buy through tickets anywhere but in London and Paris."

"Some people can't, maybe; but some people can—of whom I am one of which, it appears."

"It seems a rather high price."

"On the contrary, the dealer knocked off his com-mission."

"Dealer?"

"Yes—I bought them at a cigar shop."

"That reminds me. We shall have to get up pretty early, and so there should be no packing to do. Your umbrella, your rubbers, your cigars— what is the matter?"

"Hang it, I 've left the cigars at the bank."

"Just think of it! Well, your umbrella?"

"I 'll have that all right. There 's no hurry."

"What do you mean by that?"

"Oh, that 's all right; I 'll take care of——"

"Where is that umbrella?"

"It 's just the merest step—it won't take me——"

"Where is it?"

"Well, I think I left it at the cigar shop; but any way——"

"Take your feet out from under that thing. It 's just as I expected! Where are your rubbers?"

"They—well——"

"Where are your rubbers?"

"It 's got so dry now—well, everybody says there 's not going to be another drop of——"

"Where—are—your—rubbers?"

"Well, you see—well, it was this way. First, the officer said——"

"What officer?"

"Police officer; but the Mayor, he——"

"What Mayor?"

"Mayor of Geneva; but I said——"

"Wait. What is the matter with you?"

"Who, me? Nothing. They both tried to persuade me to stay, and——"

"Stay where?"

"Well—the fact is——"

"Where have you been? What's kept you out till half-past ten at night?"

"O, you see, after I lost my letter of credit, I——"

"You are beating around the bush a good deal. Now, answer the question in just one straightforward word. Where are those rubbers?"

"They—well; they're in the county jail."

I started a placating smile, but it petrified. The climate was unsuitable. Spending three or four hours in jail did not seem to the expedition humorous. Neither did it to me, at bottom.

I had to explain the whole thing, and of course it came out then that we couldn't take the early train, because that would leave my letter of credit in hock still. It did look as if we had all got to go to bed estranged and unhappy, but by good luck that was prevented. There happened to be mention of the trunks, and I was able to say I had attended to that feature.

"There, you are just as good and thoughtful and painstaking and intelligent as you can be, and it's a shame to find so much fault with you, and there

sha'n't be another word of it. You 've done beautifully, admirably, and I 'm sorry I ever said one ungrateful word to you."

This hit deeper than some of the other things and
made me uncomfortable, because I was n't feeling
as solid about that trunk errand as I wanted to.
There seemed somehow to be a defect about it
somewhere, though I could n't put my finger on
it, and did n't like to stir the matter just now, it
being late and maybe well enough to let well
enough alone.

Of course there was music in the morning, when
it was found that we could n't leave by the early
train. But I had no time to wait; I got only the
opening bars of the overture, and then started out
to get my letter of credit.

It seemed a good time to look into the trunk
business and rectify it if it needed it, and I had a
suspicion that it did. I was too late. The con-
cierge said he had shipped the trunks to Zurich the
evening before. I asked him how he could do that
without exhibiting passage tickets.

"Not necessary in Switzerland. You pay for your
trunks and send them where you please. Nothing
goes free but your hand baggage."

"How much did you pay on them?"

"A hundred and forty francs."

" Twenty-eight dollars. There 's something wrong about that trunk business, sure."

Next I met the porter. He said:

" You have not slept well, is it not. You have the worn look. If you would like a courier, a good one has arrived last night, and is not engaged for five days already, by the name of Ludi. We recommend him; dass heiss, the Grande Hotel Beau Rivage recommends him."

I declined with coldness. My spirit was not broken yet. And I did not like having my condition taken notice of in this way. I was at the county jail by 9 o'clock, hoping that the Mayor might chance to come before his regular hour; but he did n't. It was dull there. Every time I offered to touch anything, or look at anything, or do anything, or refrain from doing anything, the policeman said it was "defendu." I thought I would practise my French on him, but he would n't have that either. It seemed to make him particularly bitter to hear his own tongue.

The Mayor came at last, and then there was no trouble; for the minute he had convened the Supreme Court—which they always do whenever there is valuable property in dispute—and got everything shipshape and sentries posted, and had prayer, by the chaplain, my unsealed letter was brought and opened, and there was n't anything in it but some photographs: because, as I remembered now, I had taken out the letter of credit so as to make room for the photographs, and had put the letter in my other pocket, which I proved to everybody's satisfaction by fetching it out and showing it with a good deal of exultation. So then the court looked at each other in a vacant kind of way, and then at me, and then at each other again, and finally let me go, but said it was imprudent for me to be at large, and asked me what my profession was. I said I was a courier. They lifted up their eyes in a kind of reverent way and said, " Du lieber Gott! " and I said a word of courteous thanks for their apparent admiration and hurried off to the bank.

However, being a courier was already making me a great stickler for order and system and one thing at a time and each thing in its own proper turn; so I passed by the bank and branched off and started for the two lacking members of the expedition. A cab lazied by and I took it upon persuasion. I gained no speed by this, but it was a reposeful turnout and I liked reposefulness. The week-long jubilations over the six hundredth anniversary of the birth of Swiss liberty and the Signing of the Compact was at flood tide, and all the streets were clothed in fluttering flags.

The horse and the driver had been drunk three days and nights, and had known no stall nor bed meantime. They looked as I felt — dreamy and seedy. But we arrived in course of time. I went in and rang, and asked a housemaid to rush out the lacking members. She said something which I did not understand, and I returned to the chariot. The girl had probably told me that those people did not belong on her floor, and that it would be judicious for me to go higher, and ring from floor to floor till I found them; for in those Swiss flats there does not seem to be any way to find the right family but to be patient and guess your way along up. I calculated that I must wait fifteen minutes, there being three details inseparable from an occasion of this sort: 1, put on hats and come down and climb in; 2, return of one to get "my other glove;" 3, presently, return of the other one to fetch "my French Verbs at a Glance." I would muse during the fifteen minutes and take it easy.

A very still and blank interval ensued, and then I felt a hand on my shoulder and started. The intruder was a policeman. I glanced up and perceived that there was new scenery. There was a good deal of a crowd, and they had that pleased and interested look which such a crowd wears when they see that somebody is out of luck. The horse was asleep, and so was the driver, and some boys had hung them and me full of gaudy decorations stolen from the innumerable banner poles. It was a scandalous spectacle. The officer said:

" I 'm sorry, but we can't have you sleeping here all day."

I was wounded and said with dignity:

"I beg your pardon, I was not sleeping; I was thinking."

" Well, you can think if you want to, but you 've got to think to yourself; you disturb the whole neighborhood."

It was a poor joke, and it made the crowd laugh. I snore at night sometimes, but it is not likely that I would do such a thing in the daytime and in such a place. The officer undecorated us, and seemed sorry for our friendlessness, and really tried to be humane, but he said we must n't stop there any longer or he would have to charge us rent—it was the law, he said, and he went on to say in a sociable way that I was looking pretty mouldy, and he wished he knew——

I shut him off pretty austerely, and said I hoped one might celebrate a little, these days, especially when one was personally concerned.

" Personally ? " he asked. " How ? "

" Because 600 years ago an ancestor of mine signed the compact."

He reflected a moment, then looked me over and said:

"Ancestor! It 's my opinion you signed it yourself. For of all the old ancient relics that ever I— but never mind about that. What is it you are waiting here for so long ?"

I said:

"I 'm not waiting here so long at all. I 'm waiting fifteen minutes till they forget a glove and a book and go back and get them." Then I told him who they were that I had come for.

He was very obliging, and began to shout inquiries to the tiers of heads and shoulders projecting from the windows above us. Then a woman away up there sung out:

"Oh, they ? Why I got them a cab and they left here long ago—half-past 8, I should say."

It was annoying. I glanced at my watch, but did n't say anything. The officer said:

"It is a quarter of 12, you see. You should have inquired better. You have been asleep three-quarters of an hour, and in such a sun as this. You are baked—baked black. It is wonderful. And you will miss your train, perhaps. You interest me greatly. What is your occupation ?"

I said I was a courier. It seemed to stun him, and before he could come to we were gone.

When I arrived in the third story of the hotel I found our quarters vacant. I was not surprised. The moment a courier takes his eye off his tribe they go shopping. The nearer it is to train time the surer they are to go. I sat down to try and think out what I had best do next, but presently the hall boy found me there, and said the expedition had gone to the station half an hour before. It was the first time I had known them to do a rational thing, and it was very confusing. This is one of the things that make a courier's life so difficult and uncertain. Just as matters are going the smoothest, his people will strike a lucid interval, and down go all his arrangements to wreck and ruin.

The train was to leave at 12 noon sharp. It was now ten minutes after 12. I could be at the station in ten minutes. I saw I had no great amount of leeway, for this was the lightning express, and on the Continent the lightning expresses are pretty fastidious about getting away some time during the advertised day. My people were the only ones remaining in the waiting room; everybody else had passed through and "mounted the train," as they say in those regions. They were exhausted with nervousness and fret, but I comforted them and heartened them up, and we made our rush.

But no; we were out of luck again. The doorkeeper was not satisfied with the tickets. He examined them cautiously, deliberately, suspiciously; then glared at me awhile, and after that he called another official. The two examined the tickets and called another official. These called others, and the convention discussed and discussed, and gesticulated and carried on until I begged that they would consider how time was flying, and just pass a few resolutions and let us go. Then they said very courteously that there was a defect in the tickets, and asked me where I got them.

I judged I saw what the trouble was, now. You see, I had bought the tickets in a cigar shop, and of course the tobacco smell was on them; without doubt the thing they were up to was to work the tickets through the Custom House and to collect duty on that smell. So I resolved to be perfectly frank; it is sometimes the best way. I said:

"Gentlemen, I will not deceive you. These railway tickets——"

"Ah, pardon, monsieur! These are not railway tickets."

"Oh," I said, "is that the defect?"

"Ah, truly yes, monsieur. These are lottery tickets, yes; and it is a lottery which has been drawn two years ago."

I affected to be greatly amused; it is all one

can do in such circumstances ; it is all one can
do, and yet there is no value in it; it deceives nobody, and you can see that everybody around pities
you and is ashamed of you. One of the hardest situations in life, I think, is to be full of grief and a
sense of defeat and shabbiness that way, and yet
have to put on an outside of archness and gaiety,
while all the time you know that your own expedition, the treasures of your heart, and whose love and
reverence you are by the custom of our civilization
entitled to, are being consumed with humiliation
before strangers to see you earning and getting a
compassion, which is a stigma, a brand—a brand
which certifies you to be—oh, anything and everything which is fatal to human respect.

I said cheerily, it was all right, just one of those
little accidents that was likely to happen to anybody—I would have the right tickets in two minutes, and we would catch the train yet, and, moreover, have something to laugh about all through
the journey. I did get the tickets in time, all
stamped and complete, but then it turned out that
I could n't take them, because in taking so much
pains about the two missing members, I had skipped
the bank and had n't the money. So then the train
left, and there did n't seem to be anything to do but
go back to the hotel, which we did; but it was kind

of melancholy and not much said. I tried to start a few subjects, like scenery and transubstantiation, and those sorts of things, but they did n't seem to hit the weather right.

We had lost our good rooms, but we got some others which were pretty scattering, but would answer. I judged things would brighten now, but the Head of the Expedition said "Send up the trunks." It made me feel pretty cold. There was a doubtful something about that trunk business. I was almost sure of it. I was going to suggest——

But a wave of the hand sufficiently restrained me, and I was informed that we would now camp for three days and see if we could rest up.

I said all right, never mind ringing; I would go down and attend to the trunks myself. I got a cab and went straight to Mr. Charles Natural's place, and asked what order it was I had left there.

"To send seven trunks to the hotel."

"And were you to bring any back?"

"No."

"You are sure I did n't tell you to bring back seven that would be found piled in the lobby?"

"Absolutely sure you did n't."

"Then the whole fourteen are gone to Zurich or Jericho or somewhere, and there is going to be more debris around that hotel when the Expedition——"

I did n't finish, because my mind was getting to be in a good deal of a whirl, and when you are that way you think you have finished a sentence when you have n't, and you go mooning and dreaming away, and the first thing you know you get run over by a dray or a cow or something.

I left the cab there—I forgot it—and on my way back I thought it all out and concluded to resign, because otherwise I should be nearly sure to be discharged. But I did n't believe it would be a good idea to resign in person; I could do it by message. So I sent for Mr. Ludi and explained that there was a courier going to resign on account of incompatibility or fatigue or something, and as he had four or five vacant days, I would like to insert him into that vacancy if he thought he could fill it. When everything was arranged I got him to go up and say to the Expedition that, owing to an error made by Mr. Natural's people, we were out of trunks here, but would have plenty in Zurich, and we 'd better take the first train, freight, gravel, or construction, and move right along.

He attended to that and came down with an invitation for me to go up—yes, certainly; and, while we walked along over to the bank to get money, and collect my cigars and tobacco, and to the cigar shop to trade back the lottery tickets and get my umbrella, and to Mr. Natural's to pay that cab and send it away, and to the county jail to get my rubbers and leave p. p. c. cards for the Mayor and Supreme Court, he described the weather to me that was prevailing on the upper levels there with the Expedition, and I saw that I was doing very well where I was.

I stayed out in the woods till 4 P. M., to let the weather moderate, and then turned up at the station just in time to take the 3 o'clock express for Zurich along with the Expedition, now in the hands of Ludi, who conducted its complex affairs with little apparent effort or inconvenience.

Well, I had worked like a slave while I was in office, and done the very best I knew how; yet all that these people dwelt upon or seemed to care to remember was the defects of my administration, not its creditable features. They would skip over a thousand creditable features to remark upon and reiterate and fuss about just one fact, till it seemed to me they would wear it out; and not much of a fact, either, taken by itself—the fact that I elected myself courier in Geneva, and put in work enough to carry a circus to Jerusalem, and yet never even got my gang out of the town. I finally said I did n't wish to hear any more about the subject, it made me tired. And I told them to their faces that I would never be a courier again to save anybody's life. And if I live long enough I'll prove it. I think it's a difficult, brain racking, overworked, and thoroughly ungrateful office, and the main bulk of its wages is a sore heart and a bruised spirit.

THE GERMAN CHICAGO

I FEEL lost, in Berlin. It has no resemblance
to the city I had supposed it was. There was
once a Berlin which I would have known, from descriptions in books—the Berlin of the last century
and the beginning of the present one: a dingy city
in a marsh, with rough streets, muddy and lantern-
lighted, dividing straight rows of ugly houses all
alike, compacted into blocks as square and plain
and uniform and monotonous and serious as so many
dry-goods boxes. But that Berlin has disappeared.
It seems to have disappeared totally, and left no
sign. The bulk of the Berlin of to-day has about
it no suggestion of a former period. The site it
stands on has traditions and a history, but the city
itself has no traditions and no history. It is a new
city; the newest I have ever seen. Chicago would
seem venerable beside it; for there many old-look-
ing districts in Chicago, but not many in Berlin.
The main mass of the city looks as if it had been

built last week, the rest of it has a just perceptibly graver tone, and looks as if it might be six or even eight months old.

The next feature that strikes one is the spaciousness, the roominess of the city. There is no other city, in any country, whose streets are so generally wide. Berlin is not merely *a* city of wide streets, it is *the* city of wide streets. As a wide-street city it has never had its equal, in any age of the world. "Unter den Linden" is three streets in one; the Potsdamerstrasse is bordered on both sides by sidewalks which are themselves wider than some of the historic thoroughfares of the old European capitals; there seem to be no lanes or alleys; there are no short-cuts; here and there, where several important streets empty into a common centre, that centre's circumference is of a magnitude calculated to bring that word spaciousness into your mind again. The park in the middle of the city is so huge that it calls up that expression once more.

The next feature that strikes one is the straightness of the streets. The short ones have n't so much as a waver in them; the long ones stretch out to prodigious distances and then tilt a little to the right or left, then stretch out on another immense reach as straight as a ray of light. A result of this arrangement is, that at night Berlin is an inspiring sight to see. Gas and the electric light are employed with a wasteful liberality, and so, wherever one goes, he has always double ranks of brilliant lights stretching far down into the night on every hand, with here and there a wide and splendid constellation of them spread out over an intervening " Platz;" and between the interminable double procession of street lamps one has the swarming and darting cab lamps, a lively and pretty addition to the fine spectacle, for they counterfeit the rush and confusion and sparkle of an invasion of fire-flies.

There is one other noticeable feature—the absolutely level surface of the site of Berlin. Berlin—to capitulate—is newer to the eye than is any other city and also blonder of complexion and tidier; no other city has such an air of roominess, freedom from crowding; no other city has so many straight streets; and with Chicago it contests the chromo for flatness of surface and for phenomenal swiftness of growth. Berlin is the European Chicago. The two cities have about the same population—say a million and a half. I cannot speak in exact terms, because I only know what Chicago's population was week before last; but at that time it was about a million and a half. Fifteen years ago Berlin and Chicago were large cities, of course, but neither of them was the giant it now is.

But now the parallels fail. Only parts of Chicago are stately and beautiful, whereas all of Berlin is stately and substantial, and it is not merely in parts but uniformly beautiful. There are buildings in Chicago that are architecturally finer than any in Berlin, I think, but what I have just said above is still true. These two flat cities would lead the world for phenomenal good health if London were out of the way. As it is, London leads, by a point or two. Berlin's death rate is only nineteen in the thousand. Fourteen years ago the rate was a third higher.

Berlin is a surprise in a great many ways—in a multitude of ways, to speak strongly and be exact. It seems to be the most governed city in the world, but one must admit that it also seems to be the best governed. Method and system are observable on every hand—in great things, in little things, in all details, of whatsoever size. And it is not method and system on paper, and there an end—it is method and system in practice. It has a rule for everything, and puts the rule in force; puts it in force against the poor and powerful alike, without favor or prejudice. It deals with great matters and minute particulars with equal faithfulness, and with a plodding and pains - taking diligence and persistency which compel admiration—and sometimes regret. There are several taxes, and they are collected quarterly. Collected is the word; they are not merely levied, they are collected—every time. This makes light taxes. It is in cities and countries where a considerable part of the community shirk payment that taxes have to be lifted to a burdensome rate. Here the police keep coming, calmly and patiently until you pay your tax. They charge you five or ten cents per visit, after the first call. By experiment you will find that they will presently collect that money.

In one respect the million and a half of Berlin's population are like a family: the head of this large family knows the names of its several members, and where the said members are located, and when and where they were born, and what they do for a living, and what their religious brand is. Whoever comes to Berlin must furnish these particulars to the police immediately; moreover, if he knows how long he is going to stay, he must say so. If he take a house he will be taxed on the rent and taxed also on his income. He will not be asked what his income is, and so he may save some lies for home consumption. The police will estimate his income from the house-rent he pays, and tax him on that basis.

Duties on imported articles are collected wi·h inflexible fidelity, be the sum large or little; but the methods are gentle, prompt, and full of the spirit of accommodation. The postman attends to the whole matter for you, in cases where the article comes by mail, and you have no trouble and suffer no inconvenience. The other day a friend of mine was informed that there was a package in the post-office for him, containing a lady's silk belt with gold clasp, and a gold chain to hang a bunch of keys on. In his first agitation he was going to try to bribe the postman to chalk it through, but acted upon his sober second thought and allowed the matter to take its proper and regular course. In a little while the postman brought the package and made these several collections: duty on the silk belt, 7½ cents; duty on the gold chain, 10 cents; charge for fetching the package, 5 cents. These devastating imposts are exacted for the protection of German home industries.

The calm, quiet, courteous, cussed persistence of the police is the most admirable thing I have encountered on this side. They undertook to persuade me to send and get a passport for a Swiss maid whom we had brought with us, and at the end of six weeks of patient, tranquil, angelic daily effort they succeeded. I was not intending to give them trouble, but I was lazy and I thought they would get tired. Meanwhile they probably thought I would be the one. It turned out just so.

One is not allowed to build unstable, unsafe or unsightly houses in Berlin; the result is this comely and conspicuously stately city, with its security from conflagrations and break-downs. It is built of architectural Gibraltars. The Building Commissioners inspect while the building is going up. It has been found that this is better than to wait till it falls down. These people are full of whims.

One is not allowed to cram poor folk into cramped and dirty tenement houses. Each individual must have just so many cubic feet of room-space, and sanitary inspections are systematic and frequent.

Everything is orderly. The fire brigade march in rank, curiously uniformed, and so grave is their demeanor that they look like a Salvation Army under conviction of sin. People tell me that when a fire alarm is sounded, the firemen assemble calmly, answer to their names when the roll is called, then proceed to the fire. There they are ranked up, military fashion, and told off in detachments by the chief, who parcels out to the detachments the several parts of the work which they are to undertake in putting out that fire. This is all done with low-voiced propriety, and strangers think these people are working a funeral. As a rule the fire is confined to a single floor in these great masses of bricks and masonry, and consequently there is little or no interest at-

taching to a fire here for the rest of the occupants
of the house.

There are abundance of newspapers in Berlin, and
there was also a newsboy, but he died. At intervals
of half a mile on the thoroughfares there are booths,
and it is at these that you buy your papers. There
are plenty of theatres, but they do not advertise in
a loud way. There are no big posters of any kind,
and the display of vast type and of pictures of act-
ors and performance framed on a big scale and done
in rainbow colors is a thing unknown. If the big
show-bills existed there would be no place to exhibit them; for there are no poster-fences, and one
would not be allowed to disfigure dead walls with
them. Unsightly things are forbidden here; Berlin is a rest to the eye.

And yet the saunterer can easily find out what
is going on at the theatres. All over the city, at
short distances apart, there are neat round pillars
eighteen feet high and about as thick as a hogs-
head, and on these the little black and white
theatre bills and other notices are posted. One
generally finds a group around each pillar reading these things. There are plenty of things in
Berlin worth importing to America. It is these
that I have particularly wished to make a note
of. When Buffalo Bill was here his biggest poster

was probably not larger than the top of an ordinary trunk.

There is a multiplicity of clean and comfortable horse-cars, but whenever you think you know where a car is going to, you would better stop ashore, because that car is not going to that place at all. The car-routes are marvelously intricate, and often the drivers get lost and are not heard of for years. The signs on the cars furnish no details as to the course of the journey; they name the end of it, and then experiment around to see how much territory they can cover before they get there. The conductor will collect your fare over again, every few miles, and give you a ticket which he has n't apparently kept any record of, and you keep it till an inspector comes aboard by and by and tears a corner off it (which he does not keep,) then you throw the ticket away and get ready to buy another. Brains are of no value when you are trying to navigate Berlin in a horse car. When the ablest of Brooklyn's editors was here on a visit he took a horse car in the early morning and wore it out trying to go to a point in the centre of the city. He was on board all day and spent many dollars in fares, and then did not arrive at the place which he had started to go to. This is the most thorough way to see Berlin, but it is also the most expensive.

But there are excellent features about the car system, nevertheless. The car will not stop for you to
get on or off, except at certain places a block or two
apart where there is a sign to indicate that that is
a halting station. This system saves many bones.
There are twenty places inside the car; when these
seats are filled, no more can enter. Four or five
persons may stand on each platform—the law decrees the number—and when these standing places
are all occupied the next applicant is refused. As
there is no crowding, and as no rowdyism is allowed,
women stand on the platforms as well as men; they
often stand there when there are vacant seats inside,
for these places are comfortable, there being little
or no jolting. A native tells me that when the first
car was put on, thirty or forty years ago, the public
had such a terror of it that they did n't feel safe inside of it or outside either. They made the company keep a man at every crossing with a red flag
in his hand. Nobody would travel in the car except
convicts on the way to the gallows. This made
business in only one direction, and the car had to
go back light. To save the company, the city government transferred the convict cemetery to the
other end of the line. This made traffic in both
directions and kept the company from going under.
This sounds like some of the information which trav-

eling foreigners are furnished with in America. To my mind it has a doubtful ring about it.

The first-class cab is neat and trim, and has leather-cushion seats and a swift horse. The second-class cab is an ugly and lubberly vehicle, and is always old. It seems a strange thing that they have never built any new ones. Still, if such a thing were done everybody that had time to flock would flock to see it, and that would make a crowd, and the police do not like crowds and disorder here. If there were an earthquake in Berlin the police would take charge of it and conduct it in that sort of orderly way that would make you think it was a prayer meeting. That is what an earthquake generally ends in, but this one would be different from those others; it would be kind of soft and self-contained, like a republican praying for a mugwump.

For a course (a quarter of an hour or less), one pays twenty-five cents in a first-class cab, and fifteen cents in a second-class. The first-class will take you along faster, for the second-class horse is old—always old—as old as his cab, some authorities say—and ill-fed and weak. He has been a first-class once, but has been degraded to second-class for long and faithful service.

Still, he must take you as *far* for 15 cents as the other horse takes you for 25. If he can't do his fif-

teen-minute distance in 15 minutes, he must still do
the distance for the 15 cents. Any stranger can
check the distance off—by means of the most curious map I am acquainted with. It is issued by the
city government and can be bought in any shop for
a trifle. In it every street is sectioned off like a
string of long beads of different colors. Each long
bead represents a minute's travel, and when you have
covered fifteen of the beads you have got your money's
worth. This map of Berlin is a gay-colored maze, and
looks like pictures of the circulation of the blood.

The streets are very clean. They are kept so—
not by prayer and talk and the other New York
methods, but by daily and hourly work with scrap-
ers and brooms; and when an asphalted street has
been tidily scraped after a rain or a light snowfall,
they scatter clean sand over it. This saves some of
the horses from falling down. In fact this is a city
government which seems to stop at no expense
where the public convenience, comfort and health
are concerned—except in one detail. That is the
naming of the streets and the numbering of the
houses. Sometimes the name of a street will change
in the middle of a block. You will not find it out
till you get to the next corner and discover the new
name on the wall, and of course you don't know
just when the change happened.

The names are plainly marked on the corners—on all the corners—there are no exceptions. But the numbering of the houses—there has never been anything like it since original chaos. It is not possible that it was done by this wise city government. At first one thinks it was done by an idiot; but there is too much variety about it for that; an idiot could not think of so many different ways of making confusion and propagating blasphemy. The numbers run up one side the street and down the other. That is endurable, but the rest is n't. They often use one number for three or four houses—and sometimes they put the number on only one of the houses and let you guess at the others. Sometimes they put a number on a house—4, for instance—then put 4*a*, 4*b*, 4*c* on the succeeding houses, and one becomes old and decrepit before he finally arrives at 5. A result of this systemless system is, that when you are at No. 1 in a street, you have n't any idea how far it may be to No. 150; it may be only six or eight blocks, it may be a couple of miles. Frederick street is long, and is one of the great thoroughfares. The other day a man put up his money behind the assertion that there were more refreshment-places in that street than numbers on the houses—and he won. There were 254 numbers and 257 refreshment-places. Yet as I have said, it is a long street.

But the worst feature of all this complex business is, that in Berlin the numbers do not travel in any one direction; no, they travel along until they get to 50 or 60, perhaps, then suddenly you find yourself up in the hundreds—140, maybe; the next will be 139—then you perceive by that sign that the numbers are now traveling toward you from the opposite direction. They will keep that sort of insanity up as long as you travel that street; every now and then the numbers will turn and run the other way. As a rule there is an arrow under the number, to show by the direction of its flight which way the numbers are proceeding. There are a good many suicides in Berlin; I have seen six reported in a single day. There is always a deal of learned and laborious arguing and ciphering going on as to the cause of this state of things. If they will set to work and number their houses in a rational way perhaps they will find out what was the matter.

More than a month ago Berlin began to prepare to celebrate Professor Virchow's seventieth birthday. When the birthday arrived, the middle of October, it seemed to me that all the world of science arrived with it; deputation after deputation came, bringing the homage and reverence of far cities and centres of learning, and during the whole of a long day the hero of it sat and received such witness of his greatness as has seldom been vouchsafed to any man in any walk of life in any time ancient or modern. These demonstrations were continued in one form or another day after day, and were presently merged in similar demonstrations to his twin in science and achievement, Professor Helmholtz, whose seventieth birthday is separated from Virchow's, by only about three weeks; so nearly as this did these two extraordinary men come to being born together. Two such births have seldom signalized a single year in human history.

But perhaps the final and closing demonstration was peculiarly grateful to them. This was a Commers given in their honor the other night, by 1,000 students. It was held in a huge hall, very long and very lofty, which had five galleries, far above everybody's head, which were crowded with ladies—four or five hundred, I judged.

It was beautifully decorated with clustered flags and various ornamental devices, and was brilliantly lighted. On the spacious floor of this place were ranged, in files, innumerable tables, seating twenty-four persons each, extending from one end of the great hall clear to the other and with narrow aisles between the files. In the centre on one side was a high and tastefully decorated platform twenty or thirty feet long, with a long table on it behind which sat the half dozen chiefs of the givers of the Commers in the rich mediæval costumes of as many different college corps. Behind these youths a band of musicians was concealed. On the floor directly in front of this platform were half a dozen tables which were distinguished from the outlying continent of tables by being covered instead of left naked. Of these the central table was reserved for the two heroes of the occasion and twenty particularly eminent professors of the Berlin University, and the other covered tables were for the occupancy of a hundred less distinguished professors.

I was glad to be honored with a place at the table of the two heroes of the occasion, although I was not really learned enough to deserve it. Indeed there was a pleasant strangeness in being in such company; to be thus associated with twenty-three men who forget more every day than I ever knew. Yet there was nothing embarrassing about it, because loaded men and empty ones look about alike, and I knew that to that multitude there I was a professor. It required but little art to catch the ways and attitude of those men and imitate them, and I had no difficulty in looking as much like a professor as anybody there.

We arrived early; so early that only Professors Virchow and Helmholtz and a dozen guests of the special tables were ahead of us, and 300 or 400 students. But people were arriving in floods, now, and within fifteen minutes all but the special tables were occupied and the great house was crammed, the aisles included. It was said that there were 4,000 men present. It was a most animated scene, there is no doubt about that; it was a stupendous beehive. At each end of each table stood a corps student in the uniform of his corps. These quaint costumes are of brilliant colored silks and velvets, with sometimes a high plumed hat, sometimes a broad Scotch cap, with a great plume wound about it, sometimes—oftenest—a little shallow silk cap on the tip of the crown, like an inverted saucer; sometimes the pantaloons are snow-white, sometimes of other colors; the boots in all cases come up well above the knee; and in all cases also white gauntlets are worn; the sword is a rapier with a bowl-shaped guard for the hand, painted in several colors. Each corps has a uniform of its own, and all are of rich material, brilliant in color, and exceedingly picturesque; for they are survivals of the vanished costumes of the Middle Ages, and they reproduce for us the time when men were beautiful to look at. The student who stood guard at our end of the table was of grave countenance and great frame and grace of form, and he was doubtless an accurate reproduction, clothes and all, of

some ancestor of his of two or three centuries ago—
a reproduction as far as the outside, the animal man,
goes, I mean.

As I say, the place was now crowded. The nearest aisle was packed with students standing up, and
they made a fence which shut off the rest of the
house from view. As far down this fence as you
could see all these wholesome young faces were
turned in one direction, all these intent and worshiping eyes were centred upon one spot—the place
where Virchow and Helmholtz sat. The boys
seemed lost to everything, unconscious of their own
existence; they devoured these two intellectual
giants with their eyes, they feasted upon them, and
the worship that was in their hearts shone in their
faces. It seemed to me that I would rather be
flooded with a glory like that, instinct with sincerity,
innocent of self-seeking than win a hundred battles
and break a million hearts.

There was a big mug of beer in front of each of
us, and more to come when wanted. There was
also a quarto pamphlet containing the words of the
songs to be sung. After the names of the officers of
the feast were these words in large type:

"*Während des Kommerses herrscht allge-
meiner Burgfriede.*"

I was not able to translate this to my satisfaction, but a professor helped me out. This was his explanation: The students in uniform belong to different college corps; not all students belong to corps; none join the corps except those who enjoy fighting. The corps students fight duels with swords every week, one corps challenging another corps to furnish a certain number of duelists for the occasion, and it is only on this battle-field that students of different corps exchange courtesies. In common life they do not drink with each other or speak. The above line now translates itself: there is truce during the Commers, war is laid aside and fellowship takes its place.

Now the performance began. The concealed band played a piece of martial music; then there was a pause. The students on the platform rose to their feet, the middle one gave a toast to the Emperor, then all the house rose, mugs in hand. At the call "One—two—three!" all glasses were drained and then brought down with a slam on the tables in unison. The result was as good an imitation of thunder as I have ever heard. From now on, during an hour, there was singing, in mighty chorus. During each interval between songs a number of the special guests—the professors—arrived. There seemed to be some signal whereby the students on the plat-

form were made aware that a professor had arrived
at the remote door of entrance; for you would see
them suddenly rise to their feet, strike an erect military attitude, then draw their swords; the swords
of all their brethren standing guard at the innumerable tables would flash from the scabbards and be
held aloft—a handsome spectacle! Three clear bugle notes would ring out, then all these swords would
come down with a crash, twice repeated, on the
tables, and be uplifted and held aloft again;
then in the distance you would see the gay uniforms
and uplifted swords of a guard of honor clearing the
way and conducting the guest down to his place.
The songs were stirring, the immense outpour from
young life and young lungs, the crash of swords and
the thunder of the beer mugs gradually worked a
body up to what seemed the last possible summit of
excitement. It surely seemed to me that I had
reached that summit, that I had reached my limit,
and that there was no higher lift desirable for me.
When apparently the last eminent guest had long
ago taken his place, again those three bugle blasts
rang out and once more the swords leaped from their
scabbards. Who might this late comer be? Nobody was interested to inquire. Still, indolent eyes
were turned toward the distant entrance, we saw
the silken gleam and the lifted swords of a guard of

honor plowing through the remote crowds. Then we saw that end of the house rising to its feet; saw it rise abreast the advancing guard all along, like a wave. This supreme honor had been offered to no one before. Then there was an excited whisper at our table—"MOMMSEN!" and the whole house rose. Rose and shouted and stamped and clapped, and banged the beer mugs. Just simply a storm! Then the little man with his long hair and Emersonian face edged his way past us and took his seat. I could have touched him with my hand—Mommsen! —think of it!

This was one of those immense surprises that can happen only a few times in one's life. I was not dreaming of him, he was to me only a giant myth, a world-shadowing spectre, not a reality. The surprise of it all can be only comparable to a man's suddenly coming upon Mont Blanc with its awful form towering into the sky, when he did n't suspect he was in its neighborhood. I would have walked a great many miles to get a sight of him, and here he was, without trouble or tramp or cost of any kind. Here he was, clothed in a Titanic deceptive modesty which made him look like other men. Here he was, carrying the Roman world and all the Cæsars in his hospitable skull and doing it as easily as that other luminous vault, the skull of the universe, carries the Milky Way and the constellations.

One of the professors said that once upon a time an American young lady was introduced to Mommsen, and found herself badly scared and speechless. She dreaded to see his mouth unclose, for she was expecting him to choose a subject several miles above her comprehension, and did n't suppose he *could* get down to the world that other people lived in; but when his remark came, her terrors disappeared: "Well how do you do? Have you read Howells's last book? *I* think it 's his best."

The active ceremonies of the evening closed with the speeches of welcome delivered by two students and the replies made by Professors Virchow and Helmholtz.

Virchow has long been a member of the city government of Berlin. He works as hard for the city as does any other Berlin alderman, and gets the same pay—nothing. I don't know that we in America could venture to ask our most illustrious citizen to serve in a board of aldermen, and if we might venture it I am not positively sure that we could elect him. But here the municipal system is such that the best men in the city consider it an honor to serve gratis as aldermen, and the people have the good sense to prefer these men and to elect them year after year.   As a result, Berlin is a thoroughly well-governed city.   It is a free city; its affairs are not meddled with by the State; they are managed by its own citizens, and after methods of their own devising.

A PETITION TO THE QUEEN OF ENGLAND.

HARTFORD, *Nov.* 6, 1887.

MADAM: You will remember that last May Mr. Edward Bright, the clerk of the Inland Revenue Office, wrote me about a tax which he said was due from me to the Government on books of mine published in London—that is to say, an income tax on the royalties. I do not know Mr. Bright, and it is embarrassing to me to correspond with strangers; for I was raised in the country and have always lived there, the early part in Marion county Missouri before the war, and this part in Hartford county Connecticut, near Bloomfield and about 8 miles this side of Farmington, though some call it 9, which it is impossible to be, for I have walked it many and many a time in considerably under three hours, and General Hawley says he has done it in two and a quarter, which is not likely; so it has seemed best that I write your Majesty. It is true that I do not know your Majesty personally, but I have met the Lord Mayor, and if the rest of the family are like him, it is but just that it should be named royal; and likewise plain that in a family matter like this, I cannot better forward my case than to frankly carry it to the head of the family itself. I have also met the Prince of Wales once in the fall of 1873, but it was not in any familiar way, but in a quite informal way, being casual, and was of course a surprise to us both. It was in Oxford street, just where you come out of Oxford into Regent Circus, and just as he turned up one side of the circle at the head of a procession, I went down the other side on the top of an omnibus. He will remember me on account of a gray coat with flap pockets that I wore, as I was the only person on the omnibus that had on that kind of a coat; I remember him of course as easy as I would a comet. He looked quite proud and satisfied, but that is not to be wondered at, he has a good situation. And once I called on your Majesty, but you were out.

But that is no matter, it happens with everybody. However, I have wandered a little, away from what I started about. It was this way. Young Bright wrote my London publishers Chatto and Windus— their place is the one on the left as you come down Piccadilly, about a block and a half above where the minstrel show is—he wrote them that he wanted them to pay income tax on the royalties of some foreign authors, namely, " Miss De La Ramé (Ouida), Dr. Oliver Wendell Holmes, Mr. Francis Bret Harte, and Mr. Mark Twain." Well, Mr. Chatto diverted him from the others, and tried to divert him from me, but in this case he failed. So then, young Bright wrote me. And not only that, but he sent me a printed document the size of a news paper, for me to sign, all over in different places. Well, it was that kind of a document that the more you study it the more it undermines you and makes everything seem uncertain to you ; and so, while in that condition, and really not responsible for my acts, I wrote Mr. Chatto to pay the tax and charge to me. Of course my idea was, that it was for only one year, and that the tax would be only about one per cent or along there somewhere, but last night I met Professor Sloane of Princeton —you may not know him, but you have probably seen him every now and then, for he goes to England a good deal, a large man and very handsome and absorbed in thought, and if you have noticed such a man on platforms after the train is gone, that is the one, he generally gets left, like all those specialists and other scholars who know everything but how to apply it—and he said it was a back tax for *three* years, and no one per cent, but two and a half !

That gave what had seemed a little matter, a new aspect. I then began to study the printed document again, to see if I could find anything in it that might modify my case, and I had what seems to be a quite promising success. For instance, it opens thus — polite and courteous, the way those English government documents always are—I do not say that to hear myself talk, it is just the fact, and it is a credit :

" To Mr. Mark Twain : IN PURSUANCE of the Acts of Parliament for granting to Her Majesty Duties and Profits," etc.

I had not noticed that before. My idea had been that it was for the Government, and so I wrote *to* the Government; but now I saw that it was a private matter, a family matter, and that the proceeds went to yourself, not the Government. I would always rather treat with principals, and I am glad I noticed that clause. With a principal, one can always get at a fair and right understanding, whether it is about potatoes, or continents, or any of those things, or something entirely different; for the size or nature of the thing does not affect the fact ; whereas, as a rule, a subordinate is more or less troublesome to satisfy. And yet this is not against them, but the other way. They have their duties to do, and must be harnessed to rules, and not

allowed any discretion. Why if your Majesty should
equip young Bright with discretion—I mean his own
discretion—it is an even guess that he would discretion you out of house and home in 2 or 3 years. He
would not *mean* to get the family into straits, but
that would be the upshot, just the same. Now
then, with Bright out of the way, this is not going
to be any Irish question; it is going to be settled
pleasantly and satisfactorily for all of us, and when
it is finished your Majesty is going to stand with the
American people just as you have stood for fifty
years, and surely no monarch can require better
than that of an alien nation. They do not all pay
a British income tax, but the most of them will in
time, for we have shoals of new authors coming
along every year; and of the population of your
Canada, upwards of four-fifths are wealthy Americans, and more going there all the time.

Well, another thing which I noticed in the Document, was an item about " Deductions." I will
come to that presently, your Majesty. And another
thing was this: that Authors are not mentioned in
the Document at all. No, we have " Quarries,
Mines, Iron Works, Salt Springs, Alum Mines,
Water Works, Canals, Docks, Drains, Levels, Fish-
ings, Fairs, Tolls, Bridges, Ferries," and so-forth
and so-forth and so-on—well, as much as a yard or

a yard and a half of them, I should think—anyway a very large quantity or number. I read along—down, and down, and down the list, further, and further, and further, and as I approached the bottom my hopes began to rise higher and higher, because I saw that everything in England, *that* far, was taxed by name and in detail, except perhaps the family, and maybe Parliament, and yet still no mention of Authors. Apparently they were going to be overlooked. And sure enough, they were! My heart gave a great bound. But I was too soon. There was a foot note, in Mr. Bright's hand, which said: "You are taxed under Schedule D, section 14." I turned to that place, and found these three things: "Trades, Offices, Gas Works."

Of course, after a moment's reflection, hope came up again, and then certainty: Mr. Bright was in error, and clear off the track; for Authorship is not a Trade, it is an inspiration; Authorship does not keep an Office, its habitation is all out under the sky, and everywhere where the winds are blowing and the sun is shining and the creatures of God are free. Now then, since I have no Trade and keep no Office, I am not taxable under Schedule D, section 14. Your Majesty sees that; so I will go on to that other thing that I spoke of, the "deductions" —deductions from my tax which I may get allowed,

under conditions. Mr. Bright says all deductions
to be claimed by me must be restricted to the pro-
visions made in Paragraph No. 8, entitled " Wear
and Tear of Machinery, or Plant." This is curious,
and shows how far he has gotten away on his wrong
course after once he has got started wrong: for
Offices and Trades do not have Plant, they do not
have Machinery, such a thing was never heard of ;
and moreover they do not wear and tear. You see
that, your Majesty, and that it is true. Here is the
Paragraph No. 8 :

Amount claimed as a deduction for diminished value by
reason of Wear and Tear, where the Machinery or Plant be-
longs to the Person or Company carrying on the Concern, or
is let to such Person or Company so that the Lessee is bound
to maintain and deliver over the same in good condition:—

Amount £————————————

There it is—the very words.

I could answer Mr. Bright thus :

It is my pride to say that my Brain is my Plant ;
and I do not claim any deduction for diminished
value by reason of Wear and Tear, for the reason
that it does not wear and tear, but stays sound and
whole all the time. Yes, I could say to him, my
Brain is my Plant, my Skull is my Workshop, my
Hand is my Machinery, and I am the Person carry-

ing on the Concern; it is not leased to anybody, and so there is no Lessee bound to maintain and deliver over the same in good condition. There. I do not wish to any way overrate this argument and answer, dashed off just so, and not a word of it altered from the way I first wrote it, your Majesty, but indeed it does seem to pulverize that young fellow, you can see that yourself. But that is all I say; I stop there; I never pursue a person after I have got him down.

Having thus shown your Majesty that I am not taxable, but am the victim of the error of a clerk who mistakes the nature of my commerce, it only remains for me to beg that you will of your justice annul my letter that I spoke of, so that my publisher can keep back that tax-money which, in the confusion and aberration caused by the Document, I ordered him to pay. You will not miss the sum, but this is a hard year for authors; and as for lectures, I do not suppose your Majesty ever saw such a dull season.

With always great, and ever increasing respect, I beg to sign myself your Majesty's servant to command, MARK TWAIN.

HER MAJESTY THE QUEEN, LONDON.

A MAJESTIC LITERARY FOSSIL.

IF I were required to guess off-hand, and without collusion with higher minds, what is the bottom cause of the amazing material and intellectual advancement of the last fifty years, I should guess that it was the modern-born and previously non-existent disposition on the part of men to believe that a new idea can have value. With the long roll of the mighty names of history present in our minds, we are not privileged to doubt that for the past twenty or thirty centuries every conspicuous civilization in the world has produced intellects able to invent and create the things which make our day a wonder; perhaps we may be justified in inferring, then, that the reason they did not do it was that the public reverence for old ideas and hostility to new ones always stood in their way, and was a wall they could not break down or climb over. The prevailing tone of old books regarding new ideas is one of suspicion and uneasiness at times, and at other times contempt. By contrast, our day is indifferent to old ideas, and even considers that their age makes

241

their value questionable, but jumps at a new idea with enthusiasm and high hope—a hope which is high because it has not been accustomed to being disappointed. I make no guess as to just when this disposition was born to us, but it certainly is ours, was not possessed by any century before us, is our peculiar mark and badge, and is doubtless the bottom reason why we are a race of lightning-shod Mercuries, and proud of it—instead of being, like our ancestors, a race of plodding crabs, and proud of that.

So recent is this change from a three or four thousand year twilight to the flash and glare of open day that I have walked in both, and yet am not old. Nothing is to-day as it was when I was an urchin; but when I was an urchin, nothing was much different from what it had always been in this world. Take a single detail, for example—medicine. Galen could have come into my sick-room at any time during my first seven years—I mean any day when it was n't fishing weather, and there was n't any choice but school or sickness—and he could have sat down there and stood my doctor's watch without asking a question. He would have smelt around among the wilderness of cups and bottles and phials on the table and the shelves, and missed not a stench that used to glad him two thousand years before, nor discovered one that was of a later date. He would have examined me, and run across only one disappointment—I was already salivated; I would have him there; for I was always salivated, calomel was so cheap. He would get out his lancet then; but I would have him again; our family doctor did n't allow blood to accumulate in the system. However, he could take dipper and ladle, and freight me up with old familiar doses that had come down from Adam to his time and mine; and he could go out with a wheelbarrow and gather weeds and offal, and build some more, while those others were getting in their work. And if our reverend doctor came and found him there, he would be dumb with awe, and would get down and worship him. Whereas if Galen should appear among us to-day, he could not stand anybody's watch; he would inspire no awe; he would be told he was a back number, and it would surprise him to see that that fact counted against him, instead of in his favor. He would n't know our medicines; he would n't know our practice; and the first time he tried to introduce his own, we would hang him.

This introduction brings me to my literary relic. It is a *Dictionary of Medicine*, by Dr. James, of London, assisted by Mr. Boswell's Doctor Samuel Johnson, and is a hundred and fifty years old, it having been published at the time of the rebellion of '45.

If it had been sent against the Pretender's troops there probably wouldn't have been a survivor. In 1861 this deadly book was still working the cemeteries—down in Virginia. For three generations and a half it had been going quietly along, enriching the earth with its slain. Up to its last free day it was trusted and believed in, and its devastating advice taken, as was shown by notes inserted between its leaves. But our troops captured it and brought it home, and it has been out of business since. These remarks from its preface are in the true spirit of the olden time, sodden with worship of the old, disdain of the new:

If we inquire into the Improvements which have been made by the Moderns, we shall be forced to confess that we have so little Reason to value ourselves beyond the Antients, or to be tempted to contemn them, that we cannot give stronger or more convincing Proofs of our own Ignorance, as well as our Pride.

Among all the systematical Writers, I think there are very few who refuse the Preference to *Hieron, Fabricius ab Aquapendente,* as a Person of unquestion'd Learning and Judgment; and yet is he not asham'd to let his Readers know that *Celsus* among the Latins, *Paulus Aegineta* among the Greeks, and *Albucasis* among the Arabians, whom I am unwilling to place among the Moderns, tho' he liv'd but six hundred Years since, are the Triumvirate to whom he principally stands indebted, for the Assistance he had receiv'd from them in composing his excellent Book.

[In a previous paragraph are puffs of Galen, Hippocrates, and other débris of the Old Silurian Period of Medicine.]

How many Operations are there now in Use which were unknown to the Antients?

That is true. The surest way for a nation's scientific men to prove that they were proud and ignorant was to claim to have found out something fresh
in the course of a thousand years or so. Evidently
the peoples of this book's day regarded themselves
as children, and their remote ancestors as the only
grown-up people that had existed. Consider the
contrast: without offence, without over-egotism, our
own scientific men may and do regard themselves
as grown people and their grandfathers as children.
The change here presented is probably the most
sweeping that has ever come over mankind in the
history of the race. It is the utter reversal, in a
couple of generations, of an attitude which had been
maintained without challenge or interruption from
the earliest antiquity. It amounts to creating man
over again on a new plan; he was a canal-boat before, he is an ocean greyhound to-day. The change
from reptile to bird was not more tremendous, and
it took longer.

It is curious. If you read between the lines what
this author says about Brer Albucasis, you detect
that in venturing to compliment him he has to
whistle a little to keep his courage up, because Albucasis " liv'd but six hundred Years since," and

therefore came so uncomfortably near being a "modern" that one couldn't respect him without risk.

Phlebotomy, Venesection—terms to signify bleeding—are not often heard in our day, because we have ceased to believe that the best way to make a bank or a body healthy is to squander its capital; but in our author's time the physician went around with a hatful of lancets on his person all the time, and took a hack at every patient whom he found still alive. He robbed his man of pounds and pounds of blood at a single operation. The details of this sort in this book make terrific reading. Apparently even the healthy did not escape, but were bled twelve times a year, on a particular day of the month, and exhaustively purged besides. Here is a specimen of the vigorous old-time practice; it occurs in our author's adoring biography of a Doctor Aretæus, a licensed assassin of Homer's time, or thereabouts:

In a Quinsey he used Venesection, and allow'd the Blood to flow till the Patient was ready to faint away.

There is no harm in trying to cure a headache—in our day. You can't do it, but you get more or less entertainment out of trying, and that is something; besides, you live to tell about it, and that is more. A century or so ago you could have had the first of these features in rich variety, but you might fail of the other once—and once would do. I quote:

> As Dissections of Persons who have died of severe Head-achs, which have been related by Authors, are too numerous to be inserted in this Place, we shall here abridge some of the most curious and important Observations relating to this Subject, collected by the celebrated *Bonetus.*

The celebrated Bonetus's "Observation No 1" seems to me a sufficient sample, all by itself, of what people used to have to stand any time between the creation of the world and the birth of your father and mine when they had the disastrous luck to get a "Head-ach":

> A certain Merchant, about forty Years of Age, of a Melan-cholic Habit, and deeply involved in the Cares of the World, was, during the Dog-days, seiz'd with a violent pain of his Head, which some time after oblig'd him to keep his Bed.
>
> I, being call'd, order'd Venesection in the Arms, the Ap-plication of Leeches to the Vessels of his Nostrils, Forehead, and Temples, as also to those behind his Ears; I likewise prescrib'd the Application of Cupping-glasses, with Scarifica-tion, to his Back: But, notwithstanding these Precautions, he dy'd. If any Surgeon, skill'd in Arteriotomy, had been present, I should have also order'd that Operation.

I looked for "Arteriotomy" in this same Diction-ary, and found this definition, "The opening of an Artery with a View of taking away Blood." Here was a person who was being bled in the arms, forehead, nostrils, back, temples, and behind the ears, yet the celebrated Bonetus was not satisfied, but wanted to open an artery, "with a View" to inserting a pump, probably. "Notwithstanding these Precautions"—he dy'd. No art of speech could more quaintly convey this butcher's innocent surprise. Now that we know what the celebrated Bonetus did when he wanted to relieve a Head-ach, it is no trouble to infer that if he wanted to comfort a man that had a Stomach-ach he disembowelled him.

I have given one "Observation"—a single Head-ach case; but the celebrated Bonetus follows it with eleven more. Without enlarging upon the matter, I merely note this coincidence—they all "dy'd." Not one of these people got well; yet this obtuse hyena sets down every little gory detail of the several assassinations as complacently as if he imagined he was doing a useful and meritorious work in perpetuating the methods of his crimes. "Observations," indeed! They are confessions.

According to this book, "the Ashes of an Ass's hoof mix'd with Woman's milk cures chilblains." Length of time required not stated. Another item: "The constant Use of Milk is bad for the Teeth, and causes them to rot, and loosens the Gums." Yet in our day babies use it constantly without hurtful results. This author thinks you ought to wash out your mouth with wine before venturing to drink milk. Presently, when we come to notice what fiendish decoctions those people introduced into their stomachs by way of medicine, we shall wonder that they could have been afraid of milk.

It appears that they had false teeth in those days. They were made of ivory sometimes, sometimes of bone, and were thrust into the natural sockets, and lashed to each other and to the neighboring teeth with wires or with silk threads. They were not to eat with, nor to laugh with, because they dropped out when not in repose. You could smile with them, but you had to practice first, or you would overdo it. They were not for business, but just decoration. They filled the bill according to their lights.

This author says " the Flesh of Swine nourishes above all other eatables." In another place he mentions a number of things, and says " these are very easy to be digested; so is Pork." This is probably a lie. But he is pretty handy in that line; and when he has n't anything of the sort in stock himself he gives some other expert an opening. For instance, under the head of " Attractives " he introduces Paracelsus, who tells of a nameless "Specific" —quantity of it not set down—which is able to draw a hundred pounds of flesh to itself—distance not stated

—and then proceeds, "It happen'd in our own Days that an Attractive of this Kind drew a certain Man's Lungs up into his Mouth, by which he had the Misfortune to be suffocated." This is more than doubtful. In the first place, his Mouth could n't accommodate his Lungs—in fact, his Hat could n't; secondly, his Heart being more eligibly Situated, it would have got the Start of his Lungs, and being a lighter Body, it would have Sail'd in ahead and Occupied the Premises; thirdly, you will Take Notice a Man with his Heart in his Mouth has n't any Room left for his Lungs—he has got all he can Attend to; and finally, the Man must have had the Attractive in his Hat, and when he saw what was going to Happen he would have Remov'd it and Sat Down on it. Indeed he would; and then how could it Choke him to Death? I don't believe the thing ever happened at all.

Paracelsus adds this effort: "I myself saw a Plaister which attracted as much Water as was sufficient to fill a Cistern; and by these very Attractives Branches may be torn from Trees; and, which is still more surprising, a Cow may be carried up into the Air." Paracelsus is dead now; he was always straining himself that way.

They liked a touch of mystery along with their medicine in the olden time; and the medicine-man of that day, like the medicine-man of our Indian tribes, did what he could to meet the requirement:

Arcanum. A Kind of Remedy whose Manner of Preparation, or singular Efficacy, is industriously concealed, in order to enhance its Value. By the Chymists it is generally defined a thing secret, incorporeal, and immortal, which cannot be Known by Man, unless by Experience; for it is the Virtue of every thing, which operates a thousand times more than the thing itself.

To me the butt end of this explanation is not altogether clear. A little of what they knew about natural history in the early times is exposed here and there in the *Dictionary.*

The Spider. It is more common than welcome in Houses. Both the Spider and its Web are used in Medicine: The Spider is said to avert the Paroxysms of Fevers, if it be apply'd to the Pulse of the Wrist, or the Temples; but it is peculiarly recommended against a Quartan, being enclosed in the Shell of a Hazlenut.

Among approved Remedies, I find that the distill'd Water of Black Spiders is an excellent Cure for Wounds, and that this was one of the choice Secrets of Sir Walter Raleigh.

The Spider which some call the Catcher, or Wolf, being beaten into a Plaister, then sew'd up in Linen, and apply'd to the Forehead or Temples, prevents the Returns of a Tertian.

There is another Kind of Spider, which spins a white, fine, and thick Web. One of this Sort, wrapp'd in Leather, and hung about the Arm, will avert the Fit of a Quartan. Boil'd in Oil of Roses, and instilled into the Ears, it eases Pains in those Parts. *Dioscorides, Lib. 2, Cap.* 68.

Thus we find that Spiders have in all Ages been celebrated for their febrifuge Virtues; and it is worthy of Remark, that a Spider is usually given to Monkeys, and is esteem'd a sovereign Remedy for the Disorders those Animals are principally subject to.

Then follows a long account of how a dying woman, who had suffered nine hours a day with an ague during eight weeks, and who had been bled dry some dozens of times meantime without apparent benefit, was at last forced to swallow several wads of " Spiders-web," whereupon she straightway mended, and promptly got well. So the sage is full of enthusiasm over the spider-webs, and mentions only in the most casual way the discontinuance of the daily bleedings, plainly never suspecting that this had anything to do with the cure.

As concerning the venomous Nature of Spiders, *Scaliger* takes notice of a certain Species of them (which he had forgotten), whose Poison was of so great Force as to affect one *Vincentinus* thro' the Sole of his Shoe, by only treading on it.

The sage takes that in without a strain, but the following case was a trifle too bulky for him, as his comment reveals :

In Gascony, observes *Scaliger*, there is a very small Spider, which, running over a Looking-glass, will crack the same by the Force of her Poison. (*A mere Fable.*)

But he finds no fault with the following facts :

Remarkable is the Enmity recorded between this Creature and the Serpent, as also the Toad: Of the former it is reported, That, lying (as he thinks securely) under the Shadow of some Tree, the Spider lets herself down by her Thread, and, striking her Proboscis or Sting into the Head, with that Force and Efficacy, injecting likewise her venomous Juice, that, wringing himself about, he immediately grows giddy, and quickly after dies.

When the Toad is bit or stung in Fight with this Creature, the Lizard, Adder, or other that is poisonous, she finds relief from Plantain, to which she resorts. In her Combat with the Toad, the Spider useth the same Stratagem as with the Serpent, hanging by her own Thread from the Bough of some Tree, and striking her Sting into her enemy's Head, upon which the other, enraged, swells up, and sometimes bursts.

To this Effect is the Relation of *Erasmus*, which he saith he had from one of the Spectators, of a Person lying along upon the Floor of his Chamber, in the Summer-time, to sleep in a supine Posture, when a Toad, creeping out of some green Rushes, brought just before in, to adorn the Chimney, gets upon his Face, and with his Feet sits across his Lips. To force off the Toad, says the Historian, would have been accounted sudden Death to the Sleeper; and to leave her there, very cruel and dangerous; so that upon Consultation it was concluded to find out a Spider, which, together with her Web, and the Window she was fasten'd to, was brought carefully, and so contrived as to be held perpendicularly to the Man's Face; which was no sooner done, but the Spider, discovering his Enemy, let himself down, and struck in his Dart, afterwards betaking himself up again to his Web; the Toad swell'd, but as yet kept his Station: The second Wound is given quickly after by the Spider, upon which he swells yet more, but remain'd alive still.—The Spider, coming down again by his Thread, gives the third Blow; and the Toad, taking off his Feet from over the Man's Mouth, fell off dead.

To which the sage appends this grave remark, "And so much for the historical Part." Then he passes on to a consideration of "the Effects and Cure of the Poison."

One of the most interesting things about this tragedy is the double sex of the Toad, and also of the Spider.

Now the sage quotes from one Turner :

I remember, when a very young Practitioner, being sent for to a certain Woman, whose Custom was usually, when she went to the Cellar by Candle-light, to go also a Spider-hunting, setting Fire to their Webs, and burning them with the Flame of the Candle still as she pursued them. It happen'd at length, after this Whimsy had been follow'd a long time, one of them sold his Life much dearer than those Hundreds she had destroy'd ; for, lighting upon the melting Tallow of her Candle, near the Flame, and his legs being entangled therein, so that he could not extricate himself, the Flame or Heat coming on, he was made a Sacrifice to his cruel Persecutor, who delighting her Eyes with the Spectacle, still waiting for the Flame to take hold of him, he presently burst with a great Crack, and threw his Liquor, some into her Eyes, but mostly upon her Lips ; by means of which, flinging away her Candle, she cry'd out for Help, as fansying herself kill'd already with the Poison. However in the Night her Lips swell'd up excessively, and one of her Eyes was much inflam'd ; also her Tongue and Gums were somewhat affected ; and, whether from the Nausea excited by the Thoughts of the Liquor getting into her Mouth, or from the poisonous Impressions communicated by the nervous *Fibrillæ* of those Parts to those of the Ventricle, a continual Vomiting attended : To take off which, when I was call'd. I order'd a Glass of mull'd Sack, with a Scruple of Salt of

Wormwood, and some hours after a Theriacal Bolus, which she flung up again. I embrocated the Lips with the Oil of Scorpions mix'd with the Oil of Roses ; and, in Consideration of the Ophthalmy, tho' I was not certain but the Heat of the Liquor, rais'd by the Flame of the Candle before the Body of the Creature burst, might, as well as the Venom, excite the Disturbance, (altho' Mr. *Boyle's* Case of a Person blinded by this Liquor dropping from the living Spider, makes the latter sufficient ;) yet observing the great Tumefaction of the Lips, together with the other Symptoms not likely to arise from simple Heat, I was inclin'd to believe a real Poison in the Case ; and therefore not daring to let her Blood in the Arm [If a man's throat were cut in those old days, the doctor would come and bleed the other end of him], I did, however, with good Success, set Leeches to her Temples, which took off much of the Inflammation ; and her Pain was likewise abated, by instilling into her Eyes a thin Mucilage of the Seeds of Quinces and white Poppies extracted with Rose-water ; yet the Swelling on the Lips increased ; upon which, in the Night, she wore a Cataplasm prepared by boiling the Leaves of Scordium, Rue, and Elderflowers, and afterwards thicken'd with the Meal of Vetches. In the mean time, her Vomiting having left her, she had given her, between whiles, a little Draught of distill'd Water of Carduus Benedictus and Scordium, with some of the Theriaca dissolved ; and upon going off of the Symptoms, an old Woman came luckily in, who, with Assurance suitable to those People, (whose Ignorance and Poverty is their Safety and Protection,) took off the Dressings, promising to cure her in two Days time, altho' she made it as many Weeks, yet had the Reputation of the Cure ; applying only Plantain Leaves bruis'd and mixed with Cobwebs, dropping the Juice into her Eye, and giving some Spoonfuls of the same inwardly, two or three times a day.

So ends the wonderful affair. Whereupon the

sage gives Mr. Turner the following shot—strength-
ening it with italics—and passes calmly on:

*" I must remark upon this History, that the Plantain, as a
Cooler, was much more likely to cure this Disorder than warmer
Applications and Medicines."*

How strange that narrative sounds to-day, and
how grotesque, when one reflects that it was a grave
contribution to medical "science" by an old and
reputable physician! Here was all this to-do—two
weeks of it—over a woman who had scorched her
eye and her lips with candle grease. The poor
wench is as elaborately dosed, bled, embrocated,
and otherwise harried and bedeviled, as if there had
been really something the matter with her; and
when a sensible old woman comes along at last, and
treats the trivial case in a sensible way, the educated
ignoramus rails at her ignorance, serenely unconscious of his own. It is pretty suggestive of the
former snail pace of medical progress that the spider
retained his terrors during three thousand years,
and only lost them within the last thirty or forty.

Observe what imagination can do. "This same
young Woman" used to be so affected by the strong
(imaginary) smell which emanated from the burning
spiders that "the Objects about her seem'd to turn
round; she grew faint also with cold Sweats, and

sometimes a light Vomiting." There could have been Beer in that cellar as well as Spiders.

Here are some more of the effects of imagination: "*Sennertus* takes Notice of the Signs of the Bite or Sting of this Insect to be a Stupor or Numbness upon the Part, with a sense of Cold, Horror, or Swelling of the Abdomen, Paleness of the Face, involuntary Tears, Trembling, Contractions, a (****), Convulsions, cold Sweats; but these latter chiefly when the Poison has been received inwardly," whereas the modern physician holds that a few spiders taken inwardly, by a bird or a man, will do neither party any harm.

The above "Signs" are not restricted to spider bites—often they merely indicate fright. I have seen a person with a hornet in his pantaloons exhibit them all.

As to the Cure, not slighting the usual Alexipharmics taken internally, the Place bitten must be immediately washed with Salt Water, or a Sponge dipped in hot Vinegar, or fomented with a Decoction of Mallows, Origanum, and Mother of Thyme ; after which a Cataplasm must be laid on of the Leaves of Bay, Rue, Leeks, and the Meal of Barley, boiled with Vinegar, or of Garlick and Onions, contused with Goat's Dung and fat Figs. Mean time the Patient should eat Garlick and drink Wine freely.

As for me, I should prefer the spider bite. Let us close this review with a sample or two of the earthquakes which the old-time doctor used to introduce into his patient when he could find room. Under this head we have "Alexander's Golden Antidote," which is good for—well, pretty much everything. It is probably the old original first patent-medicine. It is built as follows:

Take of Afarabocca, Henbane, Carpobalsamum, each two Drams and a half; of Cloves, Opium, Myrrh, Cyperus, each two Drams; of Opobalsamum, Indian Leaf, Cinamon, Zedoary, Ginger, Coftus, Coral, Cassia, Euphorbium, Gum Tragacanth, Frankincense, Styrax Calamita, Celtic, Nard, Spignel, Hartwort, Mustard, Saxifrage, Dill, Anise, each one Dram; of Xylaloes, Rheum, Ponticum, Alipta Moschata, Castor, Spikenard, Galangals, Opoponax, Anacardium, Mastich, Brimstone, Peony, Eringo, Pulp of Dates, red and white Hermodactyls, Roses, Thyme, Acorns, Penyroyal, Gentian, the Bark of the Root of Mandrake, Germander, Valerian, Bishops Weed, Bay-Berries, long and white Pepper, Xylobalsamum, Carnabadium, Macodonian, Parsley-seeds, Lovage, the Seeds of Rue, and Sinon, of each a Dram and a half; of pure Gold, pure Silver, Pearls not perforated, the Blatta Byzantina, the Bone of the Stag's Heart, of each the Quantity of fourteen Grains of Wheat; of Sapphire, Emerald, and Jasper Stones, each one Dram; of Haslenut, two Drams; of Pellitory of Spain, Shavings of Ivory, Calamus Odoratus, each the Quantity of twenty-nine Grains of Wheat; of Honey or Sugar a sufficient Quantity.

Serve with a shovel. No; one might expect such an injunction after such formidable preparation; but it is not so. The dose recommended is "the Quantity of an Hasle-nut." Only that; it is because there is so much jewelry in it, no doubt.

Aqua Limacum. Take a great Peck of Garden-snails, and wash them in a great deal of Beer, and make your Chimney very clean, and set a Bushel of Charcoal on Fire ; and when they are thoroughly kindled, make a Hole in the Middle of the Fire, and put the Snails in, and scatter more Fire amongst them, and let them roast till they make a Noise ; then take them out, and, with a Knife and coarse Cloth, pick and wipe away all the green Froth : Then break them, Shells and all, in a Stone Mortar.   Take also a Quart of Earth-worms, and scour them with Salt, divers times over.   Then take two Handfuls of Angelica and lay them in the Bottom of the Still ; next lay two Handfuls of Celandine ; next a Quart of Rosemary-flowers ; then two Handfuls of Bears-foot and Agrimony ; then Fenugreek ; then Turmerick ; of each one Ounce: Red Dock-root, Bark of Barberry-trees, Wood-sorrel, Betony, of each two Handfuls.—Then lay the Snails and Worms on the Top of the Herbs ; and then two Hand-fuls of Goose-dung, and two Handfuls of Sheep-dung. Then put in three Gallons of Strong Ale, and place the pot where you mean to set Fire under it : Let it stand all Night, or longer ; in the Morning put in three Ounces of Cloves well beaten, and a small Quantity of Saffron, dry'd to Powder ; then six Ounces of Shavings of Hartshorn, which must be uppermost.   Fix on the Head and Refrigeratory, and distil according to Art.

There.   The book does not say whether this is all one dose, or whether you have a right to split it and take a second chance at it, in case you live.   Also, the book does not seem to specify what ailment it was for; but it is of no consequence, for of course that would come out on the inquest.

Upon looking further, I find that this formidable nostrum is "good for raising Flatulencies in the Stomach"—meaning *from* the stomach, no doubt. So it would appear that when our progenitors chanced to swallow a sigh, they emptied a sewer down their throats to expel it. It is like dislodging skippers from cheese with artillery.

When you reflect that your own father had to take such medicines as the above, and that you would be taking them to-day yourself but for the introduction of homœopathy, which forced the old-school doctor to stir around and learn something of a rational nature about his business, you may honestly feel grateful that homœopathy survived the attempts of the allopathists to destroy it, even though you may never employ any physician but an allopathist while you live.

Popular New Books ....

FROM THE LIST OF

Charles L. Webster & Co.

Fiction.

The £1,000,000 Bank-Note and Other Stories. —By
MARK TWAIN. The Bank of England once issued two notes
of a million pounds each. Two rich Englishmen—brothers—
fell into a dispute as to what would become of an honest
stranger turned adrift in London with no money but one of
these million-pound bank-notes, and no way to account for his
being in possession of it. How they found the man—a young
American—and his adventures with the note, are fully related
in the story. The book contains other stories, many of which
have never before appeared in print, and none in book form.
They include: "About Ships, from Noah's Ark to the Ves-
sels of To-day," "Playing Courier," "The German Chicago,"
"A Majestic Literary Fossil," "Letter to Queen Victoria,"
and "Mental Telegraphy." With a frontispiece by Dan Beard.
Cloth, 8vo, $1.00. Stamped leather, $1.50.

Elizabeth: Christian Scientist.—BY MATT CRIM, author of
"Adventures of a Fair Rebel," etc. The success of Miss Crim's
previous works of fiction encourages us to announce her new
novel with much confidence. The story deals with the career
of a refined and deeply religious girl, who leaves her home in
the Georgia mountains with the object of converting the world
to Christian Science. Her romantic experiences in the great
cities of the Union are vividly portrayed; and the fact that,
after all, her destiny is to be loved and wedded does not detract
from the book's interest. The true aims and spirit of Christian
Science are set forth by Miss Crim in a manner calculated to
do away with many false impressions. Cloth, 12mo, $1.00.
Paper, 50 cents.

Stories from the Rabbis.—By ABRAM S. ISAACS, PH. D., professor of German and Hebrew in the University of the City of New York. Dr. Isaacs has gathered from the Talmud and Midrash a most interesting collection of non-sectarian stories, and has re-told them in genial prose. He is thus enabled to show the Rabbis in a different character from that usually assigned them, as possessors of a cheerful humanity delightful to contemplate. The book is a capital companion for an hour's relaxation, and is also suited for reading purposes in schools and colleges. Cloth, 12mo, $1.25.

In Beaver Cove and Elsewhere.—By MATT CRIM. This volume contains all of Miss Crim's most famous short stories. These stories have received the highest praise from eminent critics, and have given Miss Crim a position among the leading lady writers of America. Illustrated by E. W. Kemble. Cloth, 8vo, $1.00. Paper, 50 cents.

"Her stories bear the stamp of genius."—*St. Paul Globe.*
"A writer who has quickly won recognition by short stories of exceptional power."—*The Independent.*
"The true Crackers are of Northern Georgia, and Matt Crim is as much their delineator as is Miss Murfree the chronicler of the mountaineers of Tennessee."—*New York Times.*

Adventures of a Fair Rebel.—By MATT CRIM. This novel is the record of a deeply passionate nature, the interest in whose story is enhanced by her devotion to a lover, also a Southerner, compelled by his convictions to take service in the Northern army. Striking descriptions of the campaign in Georgia and the siege of Atlanta are given. With a frontispiece by Dan Beard. Cloth, 8vo, $1.00. Paper, 50 cents.

"It is a love story of unusual sweetness, pathos, and candor."—*Christian Union.*
"The style is simple and straightforward, with fine touches here and there. . . . The showing forth of the best aspects on both sides of the dreadful struggle is skilfully done, avoiding false sentiment, and maintaining an almost judicial tone, which does not, however, lessen the interest of the story."—*The Nation.*

Don Finimondone: Calabrian Sketches.—By ELISABETH CAVAZZA. Though a native and resident of Portland, Me., and belonging to an old New England family, Mrs. Cavazza early became interested in Italian matters. Few American authors have so completely captured the Italian spirit as she has done in these pictures of Italian life among the lowly. ("Fiction, Fact, and Fancy Series.") Frontispiece by Dan Beard. Cloth, 12mo, 75 cents.

"Racy of the Calabrian soil."—*Cleveland Plaindealer.*
"The whole book has a pungent originality, very grateful to the jaded reader of commonplace romance."—*Christian Union.*
"Mrs. Cavazza has made a great beginning in these stories, which will bear more than one reading, and which, as the work of a New England woman, are very remarkable. They are delightful, and they are mature."—*Richard Henry Stoddard in Mail and Express.*

The Master of Silence. A Romance.—By IRVING BACHEL-
LER. Readers of Mr. Bacheller's stories and poems in the
magazines will look with interest for his first extended effort
in fiction. ("Fiction, Fact, and Fancy Series.") Cloth,
12mo, 75 cents.

"'The Master of Silence' is the first novel of Mr. Irving Bacheller,
of the newspaper syndicate, and deals in a striking way with the faculty of mind-reading."—*New York World.*
"A well-named story is already on the road to success. . . . Altogether the story is a strange character study, full of suggestion,
earnest in moral purpose, and worthy of attention."—*Cincinnati En-
quirer.*

Mr. Billy Downs and His Likes.—By RICHARD MALCOLM
JOHNSTON, author of "Dukesborough Tales." Colonel Johnston has selected a number of his most characteristic stories,
now first published in book form, for a volume of the new
"Fiction, Fact, and Fancy Series." Colonel Johnston is
easily the dean of Southern men of letters, and the announcement of a new volume from his pen calls for little comment.
Frontispiece by Dan Beard. Cloth, 12mo, 75 cents.

"A collection of five entertaining short stories from our brilliant
and very humorous Georgia friend, Richard Malcolm Johnston."—
The Independent.

Moonblight and Six Feet of Romance.—By DAN BEARD.
In "Moonblight" the artist-author has brought into play all
those resources of humor, imagination, and sarcasm for which
he is so well known, to teach under the guise of a romance
the lesson of the wrongs inflicted by capital on labor. In the
light of recent events at the Homestead mills, this book seems
to have been prophetic. Illustrated by the author. Cloth,
8vo, $1.00.

"A strange but powerful book."—*Philadelphia Bulletin.*
"He does not construct a Utopia like Bellamy; the reforms he proposes are sensible and would be profitable, if greedy capital could be
induced to consider and try them.—*Springfield Republican.*
"It is a witty, gay, poetical book, full of bright things and true
things, the seer donning a jester's garb to preach in; and one may be
sure, under the shrug and the smile, of the keen dart aimed at pride,
prejudice, self-seeking, injustice, and the praise for whatsoever is
beautiful and good."—*Hartford Courant.*

The American Claimant. — By MARK TWAIN. The most
widely known character in American fiction, Col. Mulberry
Sellers, is again introduced to readers in an original and delightful romance, replete with Mark Twain's whimsical humor.
Fully illustrated by Dan Beard. Cloth, 8vo, $1.50.

**The Prince and the Pauper. A Tale for Young People
of all Ages.**—By MARK TWAIN. New popular edition of
this "classic" of American fiction. It is a charming romance
of the life and times of Edward VI., the boy king of England,

and is considered by many to be Mark Twain's best work. Pronounced by high authorities one of the best child's stories ever written. Uniform with the cheap edition of "Huckleberry Finn." Illustrated. Cloth, 12mo, $1.00.

Adventures of Huckleberry Finn. (Tom Sawyer's Comrade.)—By MARK TWAIN. New cheap edition of the laughable adventures of Huck Finn and a runaway slave in a raft journey along the Mississippi. Contains the famous description of a Southern feud. Illustrated by E. W. Kemble. Cloth, 12mo, $1.00.

Ivan the Fool, and Other Stories.—By LEO TOLSTOI. Translated direct from the Russian by Count Norraikow, with illustrations by the celebrated Russian artist, Gribayédoff. Cloth, 12mo, $1.00.

"The stories in this volume are wonderfully simple and pure."— *Detroit Free Press.*
"As creations of fancy they take high rank."—*Boston Transcript.*
"'Ivan the Fool' is one of the most interesting and suggestive of Tolstoi's fables, and the work of translation is admirably performed." *Chicago Standard.*

Life IS Worth Living and Other Stories.—By LEO TOLSTOI. Translated direct from the Russian by Count Norraikow. This work, unlike some of his later writings, shows the great writer at his best. The stories, while entertaining in themselves, are written for a purpose, and contain abundant food for reflection. Illustrated. Cloth, 12mo, $1.00.

Merry Tales.—By MARK TWAIN. This is the opening volume of the new "Fiction, Fact, and Fancy Series." Contains some of the author's favorite sketches, including his personal reminiscences of the war as given in "The Private History of a Campaign that Failed." With portrait frontispiece. Cloth, 12mo, 75 cents.

"Very readable and amusing tales they are."—*New York Sun.*
"Thousands will welcome in permanent form these delicious bits of humor."—*Boston Traveller.*
"Some of these stories are deep with pathos; others bubble over with humor. All of them are intensely interesting and readable from the opening sentence to the closing line."—*New Orleans States.*

Poetry.

Selected Poems by Walt Whitman.—Chosen and edited by Arthur Stedman. Shortly before Mr. Whitman's death, the old poet for the first time consented to the publication of a selection from "Leaves of Grass," embracing his most popular short poems and representative passages from his longer lyrical efforts. Arranged for home and school use. With a portrait of the author. (" Fiction, Fact, and Fancy Series.") Cloth, 12mo, 75 cents.

" Mr. Stedman's choice is skilfully made."—*The Nation.*
" The volume represents all that is best in Walt Whitman."—*San Francisco Chronicle.*
" That in Walt Whitman which is virile and bardic, lyrically fresh and sweet, or epically grand and elemental, will be preserved to the edification of young men and maidens, as well as of maturer folk."—*Hartford Courant.*

Flower o' the Vine: Romantic Ballads and Sospiri di Roma.—BY WILLIAM SHARP, author of " A Fellowe and His Wife" (with Miss Howard), " Life and Letters of Joseph Severn," etc. With an introduction by Thomas A. Janvier, and a portrait of the author. As one of the most popular of the younger English poets, equal success is anticipated for this first American edition of Mr. Sharp's poems. Its welcome in the American press has been most hearty. Tastefully bound, with appropriate decorative design. Cloth, 8vo, $1.50.

" This volume of verse, by Mr. William Sharp, has a music like that of the meeting of two winds, one blown down from the Northern seas, keen and salty, the other carrying on its wings the warm fragrance of Southern fields."—*The Literary World* (Boston).
" When Mr. Sharp leaves the North with its wild stories of love and fighting and death, and carries us away with him in the ' Sospiri di Roma ' to the warmth and the splendor of the South, he equally shows the creative faculty. He is a true lover of Earth with her soothing touch and soft caress; he lies in her arms, he hears her whispered secret, and through the real discovers the spiritual."—*Philadelphia Record.*

Travel, Biography, and Essays.

Tenting on the Plains.—BY ELIZABETH B. CUSTER, author of " Boots and Saddles," " Following the Guidon," etc. New popular edition. This book was originally published in a very expensive form and sold only by subscription. Many people who have read and enjoyed " Boots and Saddles " were anxious to read Mrs. Custer's next book, but were in many cases deterred by the high price of the book. This new edition is now published to meet this demand. It contains all the illustrations of the more expensive edition, is printed from new plates, and has an attractive new cover. Cloth, 12mo, $1.00.

Subscription edition, containing a biography of General Custer, with selections from his correspondence, and a steel portrait. 8vo, $3.50 to $7.00, according to binding.

The German Emperor and His Eastern Neighbors.—BY POULTNEY BIGELOW. Mr. Bigelow was recently expelled from Russia as the author of this volume. Interesting personal notes of his old playmate's boyhood and education are given, together with a description of the Emperor's army, his course and policy since accession, and the condition of affairs on the Russian and Roumanian frontiers. With fine portrait of William II. ("Fiction, Fact, and Fancy Series.") Cloth, 12mo, 75 cents.

"An interesting contribution to evidence concerning Russia." — *Springfield Republican.*
"A much-needed correction to the avalanche of abuse heaped upon the German Emperor."—*Philadelphia Inquirer.*

Paddles and Politics Down the Danube.—By POULTNEY BIGELOW. Companion volume to "The German Emperor." A highly interesting journal of a canoe-voyage down "the Mississippi of Europe" from its source to the Black Sea, with descriptions of the resident nations, and casual discussions of the political situation. Illustrated with numerous offhand sketches made on the spot by Mr. Bigelow. ("Fiction, Fact, and Fancy Series.") Cloth, 12mo, 75 cents.

"This is the most expressive book on the Danube and the modern Danube region that has yet been published."—*Brooklyn Times.*

Writings of Christopher Columbus.—Edited with an introduction, by PAUL LEICESTER FORD. Mr. Ford has for the first time collected in one handy volume translations of those letters, etc., of Columbus which describe his experiences in the discovery and occupation of the New World. With frontispiece portrait. ("Fiction, Fact, and Fancy Series.") Cloth, 12mo, 75 cents.

"Surely the most interesting of recent contributions to Columbian literature."—*Boston Post.*

Under Summer Skies.—BY CLINTON SCOLLARD. A poet's itinerary. Professor Scollard relates, in his charming literary style, the episodes of a rambling tour through Egypt, Palestine, Italy, and the Alps. The text is interspersed with poetical interludes, suggested by passing events and scenes. Coming nearer home, visits to Arizona and the Bermudas are described in separate chapters. The volume is attractively illustrated by Margaret Landers Randolph, and is most suitable as a traveling companion or as a picture of lands beyond the reach of the reader. Cloth, 8vo, $1.00.

"These records of his wanderings are written in an engaging and unpretentious style; they abound in poetic descriptions of persons and localities, and here and there throughout the volume are delightful lyrics which lend an added grace to the prose."—*The Critic* (New York).

Autobiographia.—BY WALT WHITMAN. Edited by Arthur Stedman. The story of Whitman's life, told in his own words. These selected passages from Whitman's prose works, chosen with his approbation, are so arranged as to give a consecutive account of the old poet's career in his own picturesque language. Uniform with the new edition of Walt Whitman's "Selected Poems." ("Fiction, Fact, and Fancy Series.") Cloth, 12mo, 75 cents.

"Selections from the prose writings of Walt Whitman, that tell the story of his life in his own garrulous, homely, picturesque, off-hand, lovable way."—*Hartford Courant.*

Life of Jane Welsh Carlyle.—By MRS. ALEXANDER IRELAND. A remarkable biography of a wonderful woman, written and compiled by one in thorough sympathy with her subject, from material made public for the first time. The powerful side-light it throws upon the life and character of Thomas Carlyle will make the volume indispensable to all who venerate the genius, or are interested in the personality, of the Sage of Chelsea. Vellum, cloth (half bound), 8vo, $1.75.

"A satisfactory and even valuable memoir."—*Philadelphia Ledger.*
"We have seldom seen a more sympathetic and delightful biography."—*New York Sun.*

Essays in Miniature. — By AGNES REPPLIER, author of "Points of View," etc. A new volume of this brilliant essayist's writings, in which she discourses wittily and wisely on a number of pertinent topics. No new essayist of recent years has been received with such hearty commendation in this country or England. ("Fiction, Fact, and Fancy Series.") Cloth, 12mo, 75 cents.

"Culture and freshness are deftly mingled in these brief and often breezy papers, in which one may search in vain for a dull sentence."
—*The Book Buyer* (New York).

Books by Henry George.

A Perplexed Philosopher, being an examination of Mr. Herbert Spencer's various utterances on the land question, with some incidental references to his Synthetic Philosophy. Cloth, 12mo, $1.00. Paper, 50 cents.

"Mr. George certainly has the courage of his convictions. . . . Many who do not care for single tax theories will find enjoyment in Mr. George's dialectics, and while the fight goes on there is plenty of fur flying, with which other philosophers may line their own nests."—*The Churchman.*

Progress and Poverty.—An inquiry into the cause of industrial depressions, and of increase of want with increase of wealth: the remedy. Thirteen years of criticism and controversy have failed to shake the position of this famous work, and the steady growth of its influence is more and more justifying those who hailed it as the most important book of the century. Cloth, $1.00. Paper, 50 cents.

Social Problems.—"My endeavor has been to present the momentous social problems of our time, unincumbered by technicalities, and without that abstract reasoning which some of the principles of Political Economy require for thorough explanation."—*Extract from Author's Preface.*   Cloth, $1.00. Paper, 50 cents.

Protection or Free Trade.—An examination of the tariff question with especial regard to the interests of labor.   The most thorough and readable examination of the tariff question ever made.   The great influence this work is exerting is shown by the fact that besides its issues in other languages, no less than one million five hundred thousand copies have been issued in various forms in English alone, between its first publication in 1886 and November, 1892.   Cloth, $1.00.   Paper, 50 cents.

Works of Henry George.—A complete edition of the works of Henry George is now in preparation, comprising the four volumes already on our list, together with two or three new volumes containing the remainder of Mr. George's writings. Cloth, 12mo, $1.00 each.   Paper, 50 cents.

Miscellaneous.

Tariff Reform: The Paramount Issue.—Speeches and writings on this leading question of the day.   By WILLIAM M. SPRINGER, Chairman of the Committee on Ways and Means of the House of Representatives, Fifty-second Congress.   With portraits of the author and others.   This book is endorsed by Hon. Grover Cleveland, Hon. Adlai E. Stevenson, Hon. Calvin S. Brice, and Hon. John G. Carlisle.   Cloth, library style, $1.50.   Paper, $1.00.

The Art of Sketching.—By G. FRAIPONT.   Translated from the French by Clara Bell.   With preface by Edwin Bale, R. I.   That this little book is from the hand of a French artist will make it none the less acceptable to American students. Its references are mostly French because its author is so, and it is unnecessary, as well as undesirable, to disturb these in order to adapt them to American readers.   The treatise is mainly intended for the use of artists in Black and White.   It is short, but it is practical and good; and if Americans do not know the work of the French artists referred to, it will be a useful experience for them to search it out.   With fifty illustrations from drawings by the author.   Cloth, 12mo, $1.00.

Physical Beauty: How to Obtain and How to Preserve It.—By ANNIE JENNESS MILLER. A practical, sensible, helpful book that every woman should read, including chapters on Hygiene, Foods, Sleep, Bodily Expression, the Skin, the Eyes, the Teeth, the Hair, Dress, the Cultivation of Individuality, etc., etc. Fully illustrated, octavo, 300 pages. White Vellum, Gold and Silver Stamps, in Box, $2.00; Blue Vellum, $2.00.

" Every woman will be a more perfect woman for reading it; more perfect in soul and body."—*Philadelphia Inquirer.*

" Her arguments are sane, philosophical, and practical."—*New York World.*

" Parents may well place it in the hands of their young daughters." *Cincinnati Commercial-Gazette.*

The Speech of Monkeys.—By R. L. GARNER. Mr. Garner's articles, published in the leading periodicals and journals touching upon this subject, have been widely read and favorably commented upon by scientific men both here and abroad. "The Speech of Monkeys" embodies his researches up to the present time. It is divided into two parts, the first being a record of experiments with monkeys and other animals, and the second part a treatise on the theory of speech. The work is written so as to bring the subject within reach of the casual reader without impairing its scientific value. With portrait frontispiece. Cloth, small 8vo, $1.00.

AFTERWORD

James D. Wilson

The *£1,000,000 Bank-Note and Other New Stories* is a collage of disparate tales, personal essays, literary criticism, and travel letters with no pretense of a unifying thread. Yet despite its internal incoherence, the text is intriguing and revealing as it gathers miscellaneous, frequently inaccessible pieces that testify to the range of the author's humor and the diversity of his intellectual interests. Seen in historical, cultural, and biographical context, the book provides a surprisingly intimate glimpse of the tensions inherent in Mark Twain's evolving world view: in his attitude toward science, technology, and the arcadian world they transform; toward money and the place or role of the artist in a capitalist society; and toward faith, its desecration by superstition and ignorance, and its fragility in an essentially empirical temperament that nevertheless clings desperately to the hope of transcendence.

Released in February 1893 by Mark Twain's own publishing house, Charles L. Webster and Company, *The £1,000,000 Bank-Note and Other New Stories* shows the strain of his deteriorating financial condition in the early 1890s. The collection seems hastily put together to turn a quick profit, capitalizing on the name recognition of its internationally celebrated author and requiring little investment of time, energy, or financial resources. The book is shamelessly padded to achieve volume length: "A Cure for the Blues," for example, pillories the wretchedly written novella *The Enemy Conquered* (1845) by Samuel Watson Royston, quoting extensively — if not *ad nauseam* — to illustrate its points; then Mark Twain reprints the novella, verbatim and in its entirety (forty-seven pages), as the subsequent entry. Even the volume's title is misleading, ostensibly to lure paying customers. Only "The £1,000,000 Bank-Note," published initially in the January 1893 issue of *Century* magazine, and "Playing Courier" — originally a two-part travel letter that appeared in the *Illustrated London News* (19 and 26 December 1891), then in the *New York Sun* (8 January 1892) — can be labeled "stories" by any stretch of generic standards. Of the nine items included in the volume, only two were "new," that is, previously unpublished: "A Cure for the Blues" and "About All Kinds of Ships." Three of the others were initially articles that appeared in *Harper's*: "Mental Telegraphy," written as early as 1878 but first published in 1891; "A Petition to the Queen of England," published in December 1887; and "A Majestic Literary Fossil," which appeared in February 1890. "The German Chicago," like "Playing Courier," was one of six travel articles Mark Twain had prepared for the *New York Sun* and the S. S. McClure Syndicate.

The lack of originality in this volume of largely pedestrian sketches, however, should not be interpreted as testimony to Mark Twain's declining creative powers in the wake of his great flowering in the 1880s. Although he wrote little of consequence while living in Berlin from October 1891 to March 1892, as he was feted, even lionized, in a flurry of social engagements that left him scant time for reflection and composition, the last six months of 1892 and the first six of 1893 proved a period of considerable and fruitful literary activity. Settled in the more serene environment of Bad Nauheim, Germany, during the summer of 1892, and then from October on at the Villa Viviani in Florence, he revised *Tom Sawyer Abroad*, began writing *Personal Recollections of Joan of Arc* and *Those Extraordinary Twins*, and in late fall started transforming the latter into his next, and perhaps last, great novel, *Pudd'nhead Wilson*. Between June 1892 and June 1893, Mark Twain also wrote nine essays and five short stories, including "The Californian's Tale" and the more accomplished "Extracts from Adam's Diary," "The Esquimau Maiden's Romance," "Is He Living or Is He Dead?" and "The £1,000,000 Bank-Note" — the last three, appropriately, about money and its relationship to human values and happiness.

Indeed, money was Mark Twain's preoccupation, even monomania, in the early 1890s. Quite simply, he was going broke. The sagging fortunes of his publishing house and the prodigious drain of his fruitless investment in the Paige typesetting machine were the major culprits. The publishing house, Webster and Company, was formed in 1884 when, generally dissatisfied with previous publishers and the limited financial return on his books, Mark Twain decided to publish his own work. The firm's first release, in February 1885, was *Adventures of Huckleberry Finn*; the book sold 50,000 copies in three months and provided capital for the company's next major project, *Personal Memoirs of U.S. Grant*. This book likewise sold well and earned money, despite the enormous royalties (between $420,000 and $450,000) paid to Grant's widow. Unfortunately these initial successes were not repeated, and by 1892 the firm was struggling to stay afloat. When a bank foreclosed on a loan in April 1894, Webster and Company went under and Mark Twain, who owned a two-thirds interest, entered voluntary bankruptcy. The publishing house might have survived, however, had Mark Twain not funneled his money into the typesetting machine. His interest in the machine began in 1880 with a rather modest investment of $2,000. Over the next five years, Mark Twain sank an additional $11,000 into it. The real drain began in 1886 when inventor James Paige sold Mark Twain half ownership of the machine in exchange for an open-ended commitment to underwrite its redesign, production, and promotion. By 1887 his investment had swollen to $50,000, and he began bankrolling his partner at $3,000 a month. When he finally went bankrupt in 1894, Mark Twain had spent more than $200,000 on an elaborate and outmoded machine that never completed a single task.

The £1,000,000 Bank-Note and Other New Stories was thus assembled, and most of its contents written, during a period of impending financial collapse. Mounting medical expenses related to his wife's chronic heart condition, high living costs abroad, disappointing book sales, anxieties over waning creative activity, fears of being swindled by business associates, and the toll of his disastrous investments left Mark Twain distraught and preoccupied. Manuscript pages from the period 1892–93 show marginal notations of amounts owed creditors, household expenses, income possibilities, etc. Olivia Clemens reported that her husband often arose from his bed in the middle of the night and paced the floor in distress. Mark Twain wrote to Fred

Hall, his business partner at Webster and Company, on August 6, 1893, "I have been overwrought & unsettled in mind by apprehensions, & that is a thing that is not helpable when one is in a strange land & sees his resources melt down to a two month's supply & can't see any sure daylight beyond."[1]

Against the backdrop of Mark Twain's financial obsessions, "The £1,000,000 Bank-Note" seems, as Pascal Covici contends, "patently a dream of wish-fulfillment,"[2] a fantasy reflecting the author's desperate need for a financial windfall, or a benefactor, that would simultaneously avert bankruptcy and allow him to retain his integrity and independence. Surprisingly, given the author's anxieties, the story reflects little of the cynicism or deterministic despair characteristic of Mark Twain's other writing in this decade of personal misfortune.[3] Although Philip Foner and Maxwell Geismar see the story as a caustic satire of a social order and economic system that place a greater premium on money than on character and that willingly mistake appearance for substance,[4] "The £1,000,000 Bank-Note" is actually a fairy tale, complete with fairy godfathers and a princess. It charts the rags-to-riches ascent of Henry Adams, a virtuous and resourceful but down-and-out young mining-broker's clerk from San Francisco, who arrives in London "ragged and shabby" with a single dollar in his pocket and "nothing to depend on but [his] wits and clean reputation" (9). Exploiting stereotypes and formulas popular in the Victorian sentimental fiction Mark Twain so frequently parodies, the story echoes both O. Henry and Horatio Alger: the former in its twists of plot, coincidences, and suprise ending; the latter in its demonstration of the inevitable rewards that ensue in time from ingenuity, virtuous living, and perseverance.

The good fortune of Henry Adams in this 1893 story contrasts sharply with the fate of the Richards couple in "The Man That Corrupted Hadleyburg" (1899) or Saladin and Electra Foster in "The $30,000 Bequest" (1904), two stories based on a similar premise: the sudden acquisition of vast, unmerited, and ultimately chimerical wealth. These two bleakly naturalistic tales, however, were written after Mark Twain's total financial collapse and subsequent world lecture tour to pay off his debts, and after the death of his daughter Susy in August 1896, at age twenty-four, an emotionally and spiritually devastating blow that left Mark Twain and his wife, as he wrote to his

friend Joseph Twichell in January 1897, "chartless, adrift — derelicts; bat-
tered, water-logged, our sails a ruck of rags, our pride gone."[5] The earlier
story is morally reassuring in its demonstration of Adams' ability to resist the
temptation of easy money, to treasure instead interpersonal relationships and
such human qualities as honesty and compassion; the later stories, on the
other hand, are cynical testimonies to the malignant, corrupting influence of
wealth, or dreams of wealth, a catalytic agent that brings to the surface avari-
cious instincts sure to doom people to moral ruin and psychological disinte-
gration.[6] In all three stories, the lure of money is a moral test, engineered or
administered by a detached, godlike agent to a prototypical or representative
individual or couple. The Richardses and the Fosters fail the test, and although critics disagree whether their failure results from a moral flaw or follows inevitably from a universally programmed nature, they suffer a hellish
fate. Adams, whose name suggests the first man, passes the test, resists the
lure, retains his virtue, and thus gains his felicity. He passes the test because
the innocent Adams never covets the money: the "monster" bank note, he
says, was "useless to me, as useless as a handful of ashes" (17). Like the equally innocent Huck Finn with his "fortune," Adams remains largely unaffected
by the money to which others around him respond so avariciously.

The essay "Mental Telegraphy" serves as an excellent introduction to a
significant but frequently overlooked aspect of Mark Twain's spiritual and intellectual life: his abiding interest in occult phenomena. Although a commit-
ted rationalist and "freethinker," keenly attuned to charlatans of whatever
sort, Mark Twain dabbled throughout his adult life in various pseudosciences
popular in the nineteenth century, in an attempt to fathom, and tap into, what
he considered the very real relationship between conscious life and immater-
ial forces in the cosmos. He had an avid, if amateurish, interest in phrenology
— whose devotees included such distinguished contemporaries as Henry
Ward Beecher and Horace Mann — and in palmistry: Mark Twain studied
phrenological manuals and on several occasions sat for personal skull read-
ings, though he later ridiculed the practice in "The Secret History of
Eddypus" (written in 1901–2); and he made palmistry an avocation of his free-
thinking lawyer cum detective David Wilson in *Pudd'nhead Wilson*. He was

intrigued by claims of such paranormal mental powers as prophetic dreams, hypnotism, and telepathy, which he termed "telegraphy" to reinforce what he saw as its analogical relation to the scientifically verifiable reality of the telegraph. Fascinated by the control the mind exerts over bodily health, Mark Twain consulted a Dr. Whipple in New York, hoping to find in "mind cure" a remedy for his bronchitis; sent Susy to a mesmerist disciple of Dr. Charcot in Paris for treatment of her anemia; and investigated hypnosis as a possible cure for daughter Jean's epilepsy. This fascination also provoked his vendetta against Christian Science and its founder, Mary Baker Eddy, whom he called, in an autobiographical dictation of 22 June 1906, "the sordid and ignorant old purloiner of that gospel" of faith healing. "No one doubts — certainly not I — that the mind exercises a powerful influence over the body," Mark Twain wrote, but for that very reason he lamented the perversion of faith-healing principles in an institutionalized religion that he believed lacked scientific authenticity, played to the superstition of its adherents, and exploited them economically to build its own empire.[7]

But Mark Twain's attack on Christian Science should not obscure the fact that he shared his culture's enthusiasm for all forms of parapsychology or that he was open, even more than most, to the possibility of occult forces at work in the cosmos. While in *Personal Recollections of Joan of Arc* (1896) he exposes and denounces the cruel abuses of the established Catholic church bent on solidifying its civil power and authority, Mark Twain never calls into question the validity of Joan's visions and voices. Parapsychology and the occult became in effect his substitutes for religion, providing a vent for his profoundly spiritual inclinations and a direction for his desperate search for transcendence in a universe he increasingly came to see in naturalistic terms. He was from 1884 to 1902 a member of the English Society for Psychical Research, and as he declares in "Mental Telegraphy," from the time this organization "began its searching investigations of ghost stories, haunted houses, and apparitions of the living and the dead, I have read their pamphlets with avidity as fast as they arrived" (73). In fact, after Susy's death Mark Twain took Olivia to several séances, where they tried — poignantly but unsuccessfully — to establish contact with their deceased daughter through a spiritualist.

"Mental Telegraphy" is a pointedly humorless essay, an inductive argument grounded in personal observation and lifetime experience as testimony to the scientific validity of certain psychic phenomena. Mark Twain wrote the essay in 1878, intending it as part of *A Tramp Abroad* (1880), but he decided to omit it from that "gossipy volume . . . written by one loafer for a brother loafer to read," for fear that as a humorist his thoughts on mental telepathy would not be taken seriously by a public expecting amusing hyperbole and genial satire. He tried in the early 1880s to publish the piece anonymously in the *North American Review*, but the editors balked; without the celebrated author's name behind it, an essay based on autobiographical coincidences would have little appeal to a naturally skeptical audience. Mark Twain held "Mental Telegraphy" back until 1891, when he finally published it under his name in the December issue of *Harper's* magazine. He followed it with a sequel chronicling additional instances of psychic phenomena, "Mental Telegraphy Again," which appeared in *Harper's* in September 1895.

Mark Twain strikes the pose in the essay of one who is innately skeptical but finally overwhelmed by the sheer mass of empirically verifiable evidence that has "convinced the world that mental telegraphy is not a jest, but a fact" (45). He is "forced to believe," he confesses, "that one human mind (still inhabiting the flesh) can communicate with another, over any sort of a distance, and without any *artificial* preparation of 'sympathetic conditions' to act as a transmitting agent" (58). While he remains dubious about messages from the spirit world and the "artificial" assistance of clairvoyants, he contends that inanimate objects "give the mental telegraphist a lift" (70) as conveyors or stimulators of telepathic messages, as when an as yet undelivered letter "influences" the mind of its intended recipient. Mark Twain concludes the essay with personal testimony of a waking vision, followed by a brief speculation about its proximity to dream, thus introducing a theme that informs much of his late writing.

Mark Twain's speculations about dreams over the last fifteen years of his life assumed various forms. A number of his fragmentary "voyages of disaster" — pieces like "Which Was the Dream?," "Which Was It?," "The Enchanted Sea Wilderness," and "The Great Dark" — are variations on a single germinal idea: a tale of a wealthy, happily married family man who, Job-like, suddenly and inexplicably experiences a series of personal and family catastrophes only to awaken from his nightmarish dream and find his life unchanged. These fragments reflect Mark Twain's desperate fantasy that the misfortunes befalling him in his own life — financial ruin, Susy's death, etc. — might prove the product of a bad dream from which he is soon to awake. As the tone of the fragments grows darker, however, the protagonist discovers that the nightmare is in fact the reality and his previous happy life the fanciful illusion. More optimistic is Mark Twain's exploration of the relationship of dream to creativity. *No. 44, The Mysterious Stranger* (written from 1902 to 1908) culminates with August Feldner's discovery that all of life is a dream, the concoction of a mind with the godlike ability to create and destroy the empirical world and, more importantly, the freedom to "dream other dreams, and better!" "My Platonic Sweetheart," a late sketch published posthumously in 1912, is the most explicit statement of Mark Twain's belief in an alternative existence free of the confines of time and space. "In our dreams," he writes, "we do make the journeys we seem to make; we do see the things we seem to see; . . . they are real, not chimeras; they are living spirits, not shadows; and they are immortal and indestructible."[8]

"A Cure for the Blues" is one of Mark Twain's few attempts at literary criticism, a genre he consciously avoided, as he told Joseph Twichell in 1898: "I haven't any right to criticize books, and I don't do it except when I hate them." The lure of *The Enemy Conquered*, an obscure novella by Samuel Watson Royston (rechristened G. Ragsdale McClintock for purposes of the essay), proved irresistible, however — not because the book incurred Mark Twain's wrath but because it is so bad that it is delightful, a sure "cure for the blues": "the rich, deep, beguiling charm of the book lies in the total and miraculous *absence* from it" of all redeeming literary qualities (78). The essay may be compared to Mark Twain's more celebrated "Feinmore Cooper's Literary Offences" (1895), though its tone is less venomous and its humor less effective. In the later essay Mark Twain is taking on the "grand, awful, beautiful" style of a venerated literary figure, subjecting the doggedly persistent conventions of the romantic adventure novel of which Cooper is a master to the critical standards of a realistic aesthetic. Here he is more patronizing, for Royston poses no threat; as Mark Twain confides, it is likely that his copy of *The Enemy Conquered* "is now the only copy in existence" (77).

Mark Twain's few excursions into the realm of practical literary criticism generally offer a vigorous statement of principles consistent with his theoretical stance as a realist. In "A Cure for the Blues" he spells out his own aesthetic standard in his listing of those qualities absent in Royston's work: universal attributes of any effective writing, like "wisdom, brilliancy, fertility of invention, ingenuity of construction, excellence of form, purity of style, perfection of imagery," and the more specific demands of realistic fiction, "truth to nature, clearness of statement, humanly possible situations, humanly possible people, fluent narrative, connected sequence of events" (78). His attack on Royston's overblown style, the "kind of eloquence" that features "the lurid, the tempestuous, the volcanic," eschewing sense for the sake of the sound of "rumbling, thundering, reverberating words" (79), reflects Mark Twain's abiding preference for simple and direct language firmly grounded in reality. He had satirized verbose, inflated Victorian rhetoric in the reverend's incomprehensible responses to Scotty Briggs' queries about Buck Fanshaw's funeral in *Roughing It* (1872), in the saccharine "compositions by the young ladies" (*The Adventures of Tom Sawyer*, 1876), and in his "Comments on English Diction" (1876), where he takes Charles Dickens and Walter Scott to task for wordiness. As he writes in "Fenimore Cooper's Literary Offences," one should "eschew surplusage" and "use the right word, not its second cousin."

Another cardinal principle that governs Mark Twain's critical evaluation concerns narrative structure, or plot. Just as he lampoons the implausible plots of Cooper's romantic adventures as violations of nature, logic, and common sense, so he points out that in Royston's novella "the thing which seems inevitable and unavoidable never happens" (102). More generally, the subject of Mark Twain's ridicule in this essay is Royston's sentimental vision, which is not only patently absurd but, as he contends in his scathing attack on Walter Scott in *Life on the Mississippi* (1883), can have a disastrous influence in a social order that seriously entertains it.

The next four entries in this volume are essentially travel pieces, essays or sketches loosely based on or inspired by the author's experiences abroad and subsequent cultural reflections. It is a genre, popular in the nineteenth century, to which Mark Twain turned throughout his career: three book-length accounts of his international travels, including his first major critical success, *The Innocents Abroad* (1869), and the less cohesive *A Tramp Abroad* (1880) and *Following the Equator* (1897); early letters and lectures written for a California audience, based on his adventures in Hawaii and Central America and on his ocean voyage from San Francisco to New York in 1866 (collected by Franklin Walker and G. Ezra Dane as *Mark Twain's Travels with Mr. Brown* in 1940); miscellaneous essays and fragments written primarily in the early 1890s (collected and published posthumously by Mark Twain's literary executor Albert B. Paine as *Europe and Elsewhere* in 1923). In addition, two of Mark Twain's most enduring books, *Roughing It* (1872) and *Life on the Mississippi* (1883), are loosely based on the author's travels through the American West. A blend of autobiographical reminiscence, fiction replete with tall-tale hyperbole, essays on social and cultural conditions, and occasional philosophical speculation, the travel books uniquely defy generic classification; they do, however, provide a forum for the author's comic genius and serve as an index to his complex attitudes and world view.

Nowhere is the generic confusion more apparent than in "About All Kinds of Ships." The piece begins as an essay that recounts Mark Twain's recent transatlantic voyage on the *Havel*, a modern luxury liner "more comfortable than . . . the best hotels on the continent of Europe" (154). As Mark Twain compares the modern amenities of the *Havel* to the more primitive conditions that prevailed on his ocean voyages a generation earlier, the essay becomes a paean to the marvels of nineteenth-century science and technology. With the understated observation "The progress made in the great art of ship building since Noah's time is quite noticeable" (163), the tone and direction of the piece change abruptly, however. Mark Twain interjects a hilarious imaginary conversation between Noah and a nineteenth-century German ship inspector who, though he "would be limitlessly courteous to Noah, and would make him feel that he was among friends, . . . would n't let him go to sea with that

Ark" (171), and follows it with a comic reconstruction of Columbus's transatlantic voyage to the New World. The fictional comic interlude seems at first intended to reinforce his basic theme: that "old-time ships were dull, plain, graceless, gloomy, and horribly depressing," whereas the modern technological marvel, the luxury liner, surrounds the passenger "with conveniences, luxuries, and abundance of inspiriting color," and is "the pleasantest place one can be in, except, perhaps, one's home" (177). But the tone abruptly shifts again as Mark Twain concludes with a nostalgic coda that subverts his previous argument. "One thing is gone, to return no more forever," he notes wistfully: "the romance of the sea" (177). Here Mark Twain echoes the sentiments expressed in *Life on the Mississippi* or at the conclusion of *A Connecticut Yankee* (1889): technological progress and social evolution have brought marvelous changes and swept away many dangers and abuses — but not without cost. And that cost may be too great a price to pay. As nautical technology has improved, tamed or mastered "the dangers and uncertainties" of nature, the mystery of the sea, its charming and inspiring "poetic element," has disappeared.

The German efficiency that produced the *Havel* is also apparent in the capital city of Berlin. Mark Twain lived or visited with friends in Berlin for a good part of the eighteen months preceding the publication of this volume, and he quickly became enamored of the city's intellectual and cultural vitality, its cleanliness and efficiency. "The German Chicago" is a panegyric to the one city in Europe that "has no traditions and no history" (210). In that sense, Berlin seems more American than European. Yet despite the essay's title, the comparisons between Berlin and Chicago, as Mark Twain readily admits, are superficial. While both have a level terrain, and both had grown from provincial towns into vital metropolises in less than forty years, and hence enjoyed a palpable sense of newness, other "parallels fail." Berlin, like the *Havel*, is incomparable: a city where "everything is orderly," all "stately and substantial" and "uniformly beautiful," it is nevertheless dynamic, vital — never static. Indeed, Berlin is for Mark Twain a veritable Utopia. Yet just as the amenities of the modern, efficient luxury ocean liner come at the expense of "the romance of the sea," so there is a darker undercurrent to this Utopian modern city: "There are a good many suicides in Berlin" (223). Mark Twain buries this disturbing observation in a brief humorous tirade against the city's one quaint inefficiency, its chaotic "systemless system" of assigning street addresses. Still, the implication is unsettling: modernity and order take their toll on the human imagination and spirit.

"Playing Courier" is an amusing burlesque exploiting the common frustrations of international travel. While there are themes characteristic of Mark Twain's travel literature generally — his difficulty with the French language, for example, or the maddening bureaucracy that makes even the simplest task an onerous burden — the story is essentially a domestic farce that pokes fun at the well-intentioned but absentminded and easily distracted husband who finds life's little exasperations a bit more than he can handle. In method and tone "Playing Courier" hearkens back to the farcical adventures of the bourgeois McWilliams family: "Experience of the McWilliamses with Membranous Croup" (1875), "Mrs. McWilliams and the Lightning" (1880), and "The McWilliamses and the Burglar Alarm" (1882). Here the henpecked, absentminded husband is transferred abroad, but his endearing ineptitude remains constant. The story follows a formula that has become common in the twentieth century, from the screwball comedies of Hollywood's studio years to the contemporary television sit-com: a simple and relatively mundane conflict mounts to hyperbolic proportions until disaster seems imminent, only to be averted in the end as equilibrium is restored. The self-effacing protagonist, who narrates the tale of his own misadventures, grudgingly learns his lesson — "I elected myself courier in Geneva, and put in work enough to carry a circus to Jerusalem, and yet never even got my gang out of the town" (208) — and because the innocuous humor poses no threat, we laugh at him and smile at ourselves.

"A Petition to the Queen of England" is a slight piece that derives its humor from the American author's assumption of familiarity in addressing Queen Victoria of England in a personal appeal for restitution of taxes on his British royalties. Convinced that he is "the victim of the error of a clerk who mistakes the nature of my commerce" (240), Mark Twain labors to demonstrate that Britain's taxation laws — as deciphered from "a printed document the size of a news paper" (235) — do not apply to authors. The ingenuity of his argument to evade taxation, however, is less amusing than the naive arrogance of the folksy American supplicant who assumes, for example, that the Prince of Wales will recall their chance encounter in Oxford Street in 1873: "He will remember me on account of a gray coat with flap pockets that I wore, as I was the only person on the omnibus that had on that kind of a coat" (234). Although there is genial satire of governmental bureaucracy, which the author hopes to subvert by making this "a private matter, a family matter" (236) and petitioning the Queen directly, the letter has none of the vehemence of his attacks on British institutions and class structure in *A Connecticut Yankee.*

This volume of miscellaneous sketches concludes with a celebration of modern science couched in a stinging deconstruction of a mid-eighteenth-century dictionary of medicine that "for three generations and a half . . . had been going quietly along, enriching the earth with its slain" (244). "A Majestic Literary Fossil" parodies the reverence for antiquity, the superstition, and the crude ignorance that plagued medical science until well into Mark Twain's own century. Previously, he notes, the surest way for a man of science to demonstrate his incompetence "was to claim to have found out something fresh in the course of a thousand years"; contemporary scientists, on the contrary, "without offence, without over-egotism . . . . regard themselves as grown people and their grandfathers as children" (245). The tone of the essay resembles that of *Christian Science* (1907), where Mark Twain similarly takes a medical practice to task for its blatant disregard of both the scientific method and common sense. After allowing the quaint but horrifying medical dictionary to speak for itself, Mark Twain praises the advent of homeopathic medicine, "which forced the old-school doctor to stir around and learn something of a rational nature about his business" (260).

Most of the pieces in this volume are ephemeral, rarely read by the general public and ignored by Mark Twain scholars. Yet collectively, and juxtaposed with one another, the diverse items in *The £1,000,000 Bank-Note and Other New Stories* illuminate the wide range of Mark Twain's intellectual, spiritual, and aesthetic interests, as well as the complexity of the late Victorian mind. We find in this volume frustration and anxiety over the need for money in a capitalist society, coupled with a recognition of its irrelevance to human happiness; condemnation and parody of superstition, coupled with an enduring fascination with psychic phenomena and the occult; enthusiasm for modern science and technology, yet nostalgia for the enchanted universe it tames or decimates. These are real contradictions reconciled neither by Mark Twain nor by the age he so accurately mirrors.

NOTES

1. Cited by Albert B. Paine, *Mark Twain: A Biography*, 3 vols. (New York: Harper and Brothers, 1912), 3:967.

2. *Mark Twain's Humor: The Image of a World* (Dallas: Southern Methodist U P, 1962), 207.

3. Charles L. Crow, "The £1,000,000 Bank-Note," in *The Mark Twain Encyclopedia*, ed. J. R. LeMaster and James D. Wilson (New York: Garland, 1993), 515.

4. Philip S. Foner, *Mark Twain: Social Critic* (New York: International Publishers, 1958), 160–61; Maxwell Geismar, *Mark Twain: An American Prophet* (Boston: Houghton Mifflin, 1970), 131.

5. *Mark Twain's Letters*, ed. Albert B. Paine, 2 vols. (New York: Harper and Brothers, 1917), 2:640.

6. William R. Macnaughton, *Mark Twain's Last Years as a Writer* (Columbia: U of Missouri P, 1979), 196–98.

7. Mark Twain, *Christian Science, with Notes Containing Corrections to Date* (New York: Harper and Brothers, 1907), 34.

8. "My Platonic Sweetheart," in *The Mysterious Stranger and Other Stories* (New York: Harper and Brothers, 1922), 303.

FOR FURTHER READING

James D. Wilson

The only one of the items in this volume to receive much scholarly attention is its title story. The most substantial discussions of "The £1,000,000 Bank-Note" may be found in James D. Wilson, *A Reader's Guide to the Short Stories of Mark Twain* (Boston: G. K. Hall, 1987), 225–28, and in Ricki Morgan, "Mark Twain's Money Imagery in 'The £1,000,000 Bank-note' and 'The $30,000 Bequest,'" *Mark Twain Journal* 19:1 (1977–78), 6–10. For biographical background relevant to the period, consult Everett Emerson, *The Authentic Mark Twain: A Literary Biography of Samuel L. Clemens* (Philadelphia: U of Pennsylvania P, 1984); Justin Kaplan, *Mr. Clemens and Mark Twain* (New York: Simon and Schuster, 1966); and Maxwell Geismar, *Mark Twain: An American Prophet* (Boston: Houghton Mifflin, 1970).

Succinct scholarly overviews of various topics and themes germane to this miscellaneous collection may be found in *The Mark Twain Encyclopedia*, ed. J. R. LeMaster and James D. Wilson (New York: Garland, 1993); see especially Susan K. Harris's entries "Mental Telepathy/Extrasensory Perception" and "Dreams," Carl Dolmetsch's entry "Berlin, Germany," and Paul Witkowsky's entry "Criticism." The best treatment of Mark Twain's interest in science is Sherwood Cummings, *Mark Twain and Science: Adventures of a Mind* (Baton Rouge: Louisiana State U P, 1988). A comprehensive study of the period's fascination with the occult is Howard H. Kerr, *Mediums, Spirit-Rappers, and Roaring Radicals: Spiritualism in American Literature, 1850–1890* (Urbana: U of Illinois P, 1972); Alan Gribben focuses more specifically on Mark Twain in "'When Other Amusements Fail': Mark Twain and the Occult," in *The Haunted Dusk: American Supernatural Fiction, 1820–1920*, ed. Howard Kerr, John W. Crowley, and Charles L. Crow (Athens: U of Georgia P, 1983): 169–89.

A NOTE ON THE ILLUSTRATIONS

Ray Sapirstein

While *The £1,000,000 Bank-Note* (1893) presents only a cover design and frontispiece by way of illustration, both offer insight into the edition and its marketing. Prospective buyers who neglected to examine the volume closely may have been led to think the book was an illustrated single text rather than a collection of unillustrated short stories.

The cover, rendered anonymously — probably by Dan Beard (1850–1941), the illustrator of the frontispiece — succinctly proclaims a humorous work; the reader expects the book to live up to Twain's track record as a popular humorist. Communicating childish mischief with its ragged, primitive style and burlesque appeal, the drawing shows the hand of God waving off the wolf of starvation with the auspicious bank note. Among the ironies suggested by the image, God would seem to intervene in pecuniary matters, offering assistance in a particularly nonspiritual realm with a denomination so mighty it brings with it a cloud-parting holy aura. The implication is that a bill of such grand proportion could only issue from the Almighty himself, and deserves a comparable reverence.

The story reflects Twain's own developing financial woes, underlining the randomness with which poverty or plenty descends upon earthly existence. Money brings fame and well-wishers, poverty breeds obscurity and exclusion. Given the financial panic of 1893 and Twain's dwindling fortune, the cover illustration implies another irony. If the £1,000,000 bill appears as a godsend to stave off the wolf of starvation, perhaps Twain likewise tendered *The £1,000,000 Bank-Note* as an effort to forestall and reverse his own financial decline. The hand in the illustration thus figures as Twain's own hand, and the bank note as the book of the same name, Twain's potential deliverance from poverty.

In a more obvious manner, the floating laurel wreath that embraces the author's name communicates Twain's trademark horseplay with reversed symbols and shallow conventions. What typically would have been a banal graphic element, filling up space and framing the author's name with the suggestion of timelessness and classical antiquity, instead pokes fun at a starchy genre of book cover decoration. The wreath is askew, self-deprecatingly suggesting that Twain's reputation as a serious writer — his laurels — would float off beyond retrieval like an untethered balloon as a result of the outrageous humor in the volume.

Dan Beard's frontispiece, "Give me some change, Please," skillfully condenses the central premise of the first story, that a bill of such outrageous denomination is effectively worthless. Without great graphic detail, Beard makes quite clear what the gentleman is holding, and his adept suggestion of the landlord's body language conveys the awkwardness of the situation. Beard, most distinguished for his perceptive collaboration on *A Connecticut Yankee in King Arthur's Court,* and later a founder of the Boy Scouts of America, extracts Twain's subtle meaning with great economy. An illusion, inherently worthless paper, and the coincidence of circumstance mediate a precarious divide between affluence and poverty — a divide that seemed to grow increasingly narrow in Twain's mind.

A NOTE ON THE TEXT

Robert H. Hirst

This text of *The £1,000,000 Bank-Note and Other New Stories* is a photographic facsimile of a copy of the first American edition dated 1893 on the title page (*BAL* 3436). Two copies of the first edition were deposited with the Copyright Office on February 25, 1893. All known copies are dated 1893 on the title page, at least in part because the plates were assets of Charles L. Webster and Company, which declared bankruptcy on April 18, 1894. In 1897 the contents were collected in *The American Claimant and Other Stories and Sketches,* published by Harper and Brothers as part of a "Uniform Edition." The original volume reproduced here is in the collection of the Mark Twain House in Hartford, Connecticut (810/C625mil/1893/c. 1).

THE MARK TWAIN HOUSE

The Mark Twain House is a museum and research center dedicated to the study of Mark Twain, his works, and his times. The museum is located in the nineteen-room mansion in Hartford, Connecticut, built for and lived in by Samuel L. Clemens, his wife, and their three children, from 1874 to 1891. The Picturesque Gothic-style residence, with interior design by the firm of Louis Comfort Tiffany and Associated Artists, is one of the premier examples of domestic Victorian architecture in America. Clemens wrote *Adventures of Huckleberry Finn*, *The Adventures of Tom Sawyer*, *A Connecticut Yankee in King Arthur's Court*, *The Prince and the Pauper*, and *Life on the Mississippi* while living in Hartford.

The Mark Twain House is open year-round. In addition to tours of the house, the educational programs of the Mark Twain House include symposia, lectures, and teacher training seminars that focus on the contemporary relevance of Twain's legacy. Past programs have featured discussions of literary censorship with playwright Arthur Miller and writer William Styron; of the power of language with journalist Clarence Page, comedian Dick Gregory, and writer Gloria Naylor; and of the challenges of teaching *Adventures of Huckleberry Finn* amidst charges of racism.

CONTRIBUTORS

Malcolm Bradbury is the author of numerous novels, short stories, works of literary criticism, plays, and television series. Among his books are *Eating People Is Wrong* (1959), *Evelyn Waugh* (1962), *Stepping Westward* (1965), *The History Man* (1975), which was shortlisted for the Booker Prize, won the Royal Society of Literature/Heinemann Award, and was adapted as a television series, *Saul Bellow* (1982), *Rates of Exchange* (1983; shortlisted for the Booker Prize), *The Modern American Novel* (1984), *Doctor Criminale* (1992), *The Modern British Novel* (1993), *Present Laughter: An Anthology of Modern Comic Fiction* (1994), *Dangerous Pilgrimages: Trans-Atlantic Mythologies and the Novel* (1995), and *Class Work: An Anthology of UEA Stories* (1996). A C.B.E. and a Fellow of the Royal Society of Literature, he is professor emeritus of American Studies at the University of East Anglia in Norwich, England, where he founded Britain's best-known M.A. course in creative writing.

Shelley Fisher Fishkin, professor of American Studies and English at the University of Texas at Austin, is the author of the award-winning books *Was Huck Black? Mark Twain and African-American Voices* (1993) and *From Fact to Fiction: Journalism and Imaginative Writing in America* (1985). Her most recent book is *Lighting Out for the Territory: Reflections on Mark Twain and American Culture* (1996). She holds a Ph.D. in American Studies from Yale University, has lectured on Mark Twain in Belgium, England, France, Israel, Italy, Mexico, the Netherlands, and Turkey, as well as throughout the United States, and is president-elect of the Mark Twain Circle of America.

Robert H. Hirst is the General Editor of the Mark Twain Project at The Bancroft Library, University of California in Berkeley. Apart from that, he has no other known eccentricities.

Ray Sapirstein is a doctoral student in the American Civilization Program at the University of Texas at Austin. He curated the 1993 exhibition *Another*

Side of Huckleberry Finn: Mark Twain and Images of African Americans at the Harry Ransom Humanities Research Center at the University of Texas at Austin. He is currently completing a dissertation on the photographic illustrations in several volumes of Paul Laurence Dunbar's poetry.

James D. Wilson, professor of English at the University of Southwestern Louisiana in Lafayette, holds a B.A. from Baldwin-Wallace College in Ohio and a Ph.D. from Louisiana State University. He was a Fulbright-Hays Senior Lecturer in American Literature at the University of Milan, and the Henry Nash Smith Fellow-in-Residence at the Center for Mark Twain Studies in Elmira, New York. He has taught at Georgia State University and at Baylor University, and is former executive coordinator of the Mark Twain Circle of America. The author of *The Romantic Heroic Ideal* (1982) and *A Reader's Guide to the Short Stories of Mark Twain* (1987), and the co-editor of *The Mark Twain Encyclopedia* (1993), he is currently writing *Pilgrim Adrift: Mark Twain and Religion.*

ACKNOWLEDGMENTS

There are a number of people without whom The Oxford Mark Twain would not have happened. I am indebted to Laura Brown, senior vice president and trade publisher, Oxford University Press, for suggesting that I edit an "Oxford Mark Twain," and for being so enthusiastic when I proposed that it take the present form. Her guidance and vision have informed the entire undertaking.

Crucial as well, from the earliest to the final stages, was the help of John Boyer, executive director of the Mark Twain House, who recognized the importance of the project and gave it his wholehearted support.

My father, Milton Fisher, believed in this project from the start and helped nurture it every step of the way, as did my stepmother, Carol Plaine Fisher. Their encouragement and support made it all possible. The memory of my mother, Renée B. Fisher, sustained me throughout.

I am enormously grateful to all the contributors to The Oxford Mark Twain for the effort they put into their essays, and for having been such fine, collegial collaborators. Each came through, just as I'd hoped, with fresh insights and lively prose. It was a privilege and a pleasure to work with them, and I value the friendships that we forged in the process.

In addition to writing his fine afterword, Louis J. Budd provided invaluable advice and support, even going so far as to read each of the essays for accuracy. All of us involved in this project are greatly in his debt. Both his knowledge of Mark Twain's work and his generosity as a colleague are legendary and unsurpassed.

Elizabeth Maguire's commitment to The Oxford Mark Twain during her time as senior editor at Oxford was exemplary. When the project proved to be more ambitious and complicated than any of us had expected, Liz helped make it not only manageable, but fun. Assistant editor Elda Rotor's wonderful help in coordinating all aspects of The Oxford Mark Twain, along with literature editor T. Susan Chang's enthusiastic involvement with the project in its final stages, helped bring it all to fruition.

I am extremely grateful to Joy Johannessen for her astute and sensitive copyediting, and for having been such a pleasure to work with. And I appreciate the conscientiousness and good humor with which Kathy Kuhtz Campbell heroically supervised all aspects of the set's production. Oxford president Edward Barry, vice president and editorial director Helen McInnis, marketing director Amy Roberts, publicity director Susan Rotermund, art director David Tran, trade editorial, design and production manager Adam Bohannon, trade advertising and promotion manager Woody Gilmartin, director of manufacturing Benjamin Lee, and the entire staff at Oxford were as supportive a team as any editor could desire.

The staff of the Mark Twain House provided superb assistance as well. I would like to thank Marianne Curling, curator, Debra Petke, education director, Beverly Zell, curator of photography, Britt Gustafson, assistant director of education, Beth Ann McPherson, assistant curator, and Pam Collins, administrative assistant, for all their generous help, and for allowing us to reproduce books and photographs from the Mark Twain House collection. One could not ask for more congenial or helpful partners in publishing.

G. Thomas Tanselle, vice president of the John Simon Guggenheim Memorial Foundation, and an expert on the history of the book, offered essential advice about how to create as responsible a facsimile edition as possible. I appreciate his very knowledgeable counsel.

I am deeply indebted to Robert H. Hirst, general editor of the Mark Twain Project at The Bancroft Library in Berkeley, for bringing his outstanding knowledge of Twain editions to bear on the selection of the books photographed for the facsimiles, for giving generous assistance all along the way, and for providing his meticulous notes on the text. The set is the richer for his advice. I would also like to express my gratitude to the Mark Twain Project, not only for making texts and photographs from their collection available to us, but also for nurturing Mark Twain studies with a steady infusion of matchless, important publications.

I would like to thank Jeffrey Kaimowitz, curator of the Watkinson Library at Trinity College, Hartford (where the Mark Twain House collection is kept), along with his colleagues Peter Knapp and Alesandra M. Schmidt, for having been instrumental in Robert Hirst's search for first editions that could be safely reproduced. Victor Fischer, Harriet Elinor Smith, and especially Kenneth M. Sanderson, associate editors with the Mark Twain Project, reviewed the note on the text in each volume with cheerful vigilance. Thanks are also due to Mark Twain Project associate editor Michael Frank and administrative assistant Brenda J. Bailey for their help at various stages.

I am grateful to Helen K. Copley for granting permission to publish photographs in the Mark Twain Collection of the James S. Copley Library in La Jolla, California, and to Carol Beales and Ron Vanderhye of the Copley Library for making my research trip to their institution so productive and enjoyable.

Several contributors — David Bradley, Louis J. Budd, Beverly R. David, Robert Hirst, Fred Kaplan, James S. Leonard, Toni Morrison, Lillian S. Robinson, Jeffrey Rubin-Dorsky, Ray Sapirstein, and David L. Smith — were particularly helpful in the early stages of the project, brainstorming about the cast of writers and scholars who could make it work. Others who participated in that process were John Boyer, James Cox, Robert Crunden, Joel Dinerstein, William Goetzmann, Calvin and Maria Johnson, Jim Magnuson, Arnold Rampersad, Siva Vaidhyanathan, Steve and Louise Weinberg, and Richard Yarborough.

Kevin Bochynski, famous among Twain scholars as an "angel" who is gifted at finding methods of making their research run more smoothly, was helpful in more ways than I can count. He did an outstanding job in his official capacity as production consultant to The Oxford Mark Twain, supervising the photography of the facsimiles. I am also grateful to him for having put me in touch via e-mail with Kent Rasmussen, author of the magisterial *Mark Twain A to Z*, who was tremendously helpful as the project proceeded, sharing insights on obscure illustrators and other points, and generously being "on call" for all sorts of unforeseen contingencies.

I am indebted to Siva Vaidhyanathan of the American Studies Program of the University of Texas at Austin for having been such a superb research assistant. It would be hard to imagine The Oxford Mark Twain without the benefit of his insights and energy. A fine scholar and writer in his own right, he was crucial to making this project happen.

Georgia Barnhill, the Andrew W. Mellon Curator of Graphic Arts at the American Antiquarian Society in Worcester, Massachusetts, Tom Staley, director of the Harry Ransom Humanities Research Center at the University of Texas at Austin, and Joan Grant, director of collection services at the Elmer Holmes Bobst Library of New York University, granted us access to their collections and assisted us in the reproduction of several volumes of The Oxford Mark Twain. I would also like to thank Kenneth Craven, Sally Leach, and Richard Oram of the Harry Ransom Humanities Research Center for their help in making HRC materials available, and Jay and John Crowley, of Jay's Publishers Services in Rockland, Massachusetts, for their efforts to photograph the books carefully and attentively.

I would like to express my gratitude for the grant I was awarded by the University Research Institute of the University of Texas at Austin to defray some of the costs of researching The Oxford Mark Twain. I am also grateful to American Studies director Robert Abzug and the University of Texas for the computer that facilitated my work on this project (and to UT systems analyst Steve Alemán, who tried his best to repair the damage when it crashed). Thanks also to American Studies administrative assistant Janice Bradley and graduate coordinator Melanie Livingston for their always generous and thoughtful help.

The Oxford Mark Twain would not have happened without the unstinting, wholehearted support of my husband, Jim Fishkin, who went way beyond the proverbial call of duty more times than I'm sure he cares to remember as he shared me unselfishly with that other man in my life, Mark Twain. I am also grateful to my family — to my sons Joey and Bobby, who cheered me on all along the way, as did Fannie Fishkin, David Fishkin, Gennie Gordon, Mildred Hope Witkin, and Leonard, Gillis, and Moss

Plaine — and to honorary family member Margaret Osborne, who did the same.

My greatest debt is to the man who set all this in motion. Only a figure as rich and complicated as Mark Twain could have sustained such energy and interest on the part of so many people for so long. Never boring, never dull, Mark Twain repays our attention again and again and again. It is a privilege to be able to honor his memory with The Oxford Mark Twain.

Shelley Fisher Fishkin
Austin, Texas
April 1996